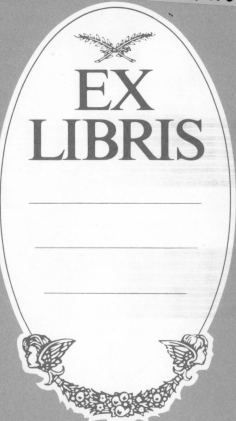

EX
LIBRIS

Romance
Treasury

Romance
Treasury

THE ROMANCE TREASURY
ASSOCIATION

NEW YORK · TORONTO · LONDON

These stories were originally published as follows:

THE HOUSE OF THE EAGLES
Copyright © 1974 by Elizabeth Ashton
First published by Mills & Boon Limited in 1974

PINK SANDS
Copyright © 1974 by Wynne May
First published by Mills & Boon Limited in 1974

RETURN TO BELLE AMBER
Copyright © 1971 by Margaret Way
First published by Mills & Boon Limited in 1971

ROMANCE TREASURY is published by
The Romance Treasury Association, Stratford, Ontario, Canada.

Editorial Board: A.W. Boon, Judith Burgess, Ruth Palmour,
Alice E. Johnson and Ilene Burgess.

Dust Jacket Art by William Biddle
Story Illustrations by William Biddle
Book design by Charles Kadin
Printed and bound by R.R. Donnelley & Sons Co.

ISBN 0-373-04083-0

Printed in U.S.A.   AO83

CONTENTS

THE HOUSE OF THE EAGLES

The House
of the Eagles

Elizabeth Ashton

Val Daventry was the most handsome man Lois had ever seen, and no one was more surprised than she when, after an argument with his glamorous girl friend, he asked Lois out.

Theirs was a short but beautiful courtship, ending with Val's departure for Germany. Lois wondered if the speculation about him could be true—that he was really a titled personage traveling incognito. But he had hinted at marriage and promised to return to the Italian hotel where Lois was working.

She would never know if he kept his word for, unjustly dismissed from her job, Lois was forced to return to England. She would just have to try to forget him!

CHAPTER ONE

LOIS LANG glanced at her wristwatch, saw that her period of duty was nearly ended, and took out the cash box, which contained the money for the visitors' foreign exchange, preparatory to putting it in the safe in the manager's room. Before the reception desk, the marble-floored vestibule stretched to glass doors leading out on to a terrace, from which a short flight of steps led down into the hotel garden. Floodlights shone on the carefully preserved grass, watered every morning, between the tall shaven trunks of the palm trees. To her right was the entrance to the lounge, doorless, with a looped-backed curtain, not in use during the spring and summer. From its lofty interior came the hum of conversation, the clink of glasses, and an occasional shrill laugh, mingled with the Italian voices from the television set. To her left, a huge mirror duplicated the vestibule, reproducing the potted plants, the wide settee behind a low table with its vase of roses, flanked by a couple of armchairs. Guests, tired of the heat and noise of the lounge, often came out there for a quiet smoke, but tonight it was deserted.

Lois carried the cash box into the manager's room, the door to which was behind her, carefully locking it in the safe, and returned behind the desk, staring irresolutely at the key board. Usually at this time she went to join the guests in the lounge, to have a drink and a chat with whoever was available, and most of them were ready to talk to the receptionist, usually seeking information of some sort, before she went up to her little room at the top of the Hotel Paradiso.

Tonight she lingered, feeling vaguely restless. She walked across the marble floor and looked at the cars parked in the drive below the terrace, of which there were several belonging to the guests, but one, a Ferrari, did not belong to the residents. So he was here again; he came every evening to escort the glamorous Nella Marshall to some place of entertainment, but although it was getting late, they had not yet gone out.

Lois leaned her forehead against the glass pane and stared unseeingly into the cool depths of the garden; an occasional car flashed past on the road that ran across the top of it, for the garden sloped slightly upward; she thought how she would like to be going somewhere that night. Though she enjoyed her work, she had little time off and no intimate friends. The guests for the most part were pleasant enough, but they came and went, and were immersed in their own affairs. She did not know any Italian families and was wary of the young men whom she encountered during her few solitary excursions. Tonight she was feeling lonely.

With a little sigh, she turned back into the vestibule, making fr the lounge, and came to a halt as angry voices broke the quiet. A man had come through from the lounge, whom she recognized as the owner of the Ferrari. Indeed, his was the sort of personality that once seen would be remembered, for he carried himself with a subtle air of distinction, which had caused speculation among the guests. He was dark-haired and bronzed by the Italian sun, and as Lois glimpsed his face, she saw that his straight black brows were knitted in a frown and he appeared to be annoyed. She noticed he was dressed elegantly in a dinner jacket and surmised that he was en route for the Casino at San Remo, where formal dress was preferred.

Milord, for so she called him to herself, turned in the entry to say to someone beyond:

"For the last time, Nella, are you coming? I'm not going to hang about all night."

A woman's light, mocking laughter came from the lounge.

"No, lover boy," the voice was shrill and slightly nasal. "I've changed my mind. Isn't that a woman's privilege? I'm stopping here tonight, why won't you stay too?"

The man made an impatient gesture. "Making me look ridiculous," he muttered. Then raising his voice: "Because I don't find this place particularly amusing."

Nella came into Lois's range of vision. She was tall and slender and very chic. Her pale gold hair gleamed under the electric light, her long dress draped her to her ankles. Round her neck she wore a diamond pendant, a perpetual source of anxiety to the management, because it was valuable and she refused to keep it in the safe. Nella Marshall was no package tourist, but spent several months every year at the Hotel Paradiso, which, she said, suited her health, but though she was a constant source of revenue to the business, the staff disliked her for her petulant ways and continual complaints.

She stared at the dark man with a provocative curl of her lips.

"But I'm finding it very amusing tonight. Umberto is from Napoli and he is full of entertaining anecdotes and is much more gallant than you're being, *amico mio*."

A flash of anger showed in the man's eyes, but he answered her blandly. "Then I won't intrude upon your tête-à-tête. Go back to his gallantries, and I'll ask the first girl I meet to take your place."

Nella shrugged her shoulders. "You won't find anything very exciting here."

Umberto from the lounge called to her, and Nella smiled.

"Be sure I shall console myself for your desertion," she said meaningfully. "And anything you pick up will be a poor substitute for me."

She went back into the lounge, but she was looking peevish, for she had been counting on an amusing evening, playing her two admirers off one against the other, a performance at which she was adept. She had not expected that this one would go off in a huff, refusing to play her game.

Lois had watched the little interlude with amusement. She was pleased that the dark stranger had called Nella's bluff. She had seen Umberto earlier in the evening and wondered at Nella's taste. Oily would have been her own description of him, but Nella's intention had been to foment jealousy between the two rivals for her favours, and now she had lost the more presentable one.

There was no doubt about his annoyance, and Lois stepped hastily aside as he strode towards the outer door. Then it must have struck him that here was the girl he was looking for, and apparently unattached, for he swung round and his eyes swept over Lois indifferently.

She was slight, of middle height, with reddish brown hair that curled about an oval face in which her eyes were set wide apart, hazel eyes that sometimes turned green. She met the stranger's gaze a little quizzically, wondering if he really meant his threat. Apparently he did, for he bowed, a trick he must have caught from his foreign associates, for she did not think he was Italian, though he addressed her in that language, which he spoke well.

"*Signorina*, owing to a misunderstanding, I find myself deserted. It is too beautiful a night to stay indoors. Will you take pity on my loneliness and come for a drive with me?"

He accompanied the invitation with a charming smile, which did not wholly disguise the anger still pulsating through him. Wearing a green mini-skirted dress that she had bought off the peg, Lois knew that she could not compare with Nella's lovely, slinky appearance; nor did she match the elegance of the black-suited figure standing before her, but she suspected that he had not even noticed how she looked.

This man had intrigued her from the first moment he had entered the hotel, several days ago, in quest of Nella Marshall. He always gave her a polite, *"buon giorno"* or *"buonna notte"*, when he passed her, but she had been of no more interest to him than a piece of furniture, like the desk behind which she was standing. She was teased by a fugitive memory, which she could not place. That aquiline profile, the deep-set eyes beneath his straight black brows, the arrogant lift of his head were vaguely familiar, but obviously they could never have met and she despaired of ever gaining his notice. Now she had it, but hardly in propitious circumstances; she was merely being asked out to spite the other woman, who had dared to stand him up.

"It's very kind of you to suggest it," she said demurely in English, while a gleam of mischief showed in her long eyes, for they both knew he was not being motivated by kindness, "but I don't think I can..."

"You're British?" he interrupted, and now he looked at her with real interest.

"English, cockney in fact. I was born within the sound of Bow Bells. Aren't you English too?"

"No, Canadian, but how come an English girl is working in a continental hotel?"

"Because it caters for English-speaking tourists, and my Italian is quite good. You might say I'm an interpreter-cum-receptionist."

"A most accomplished young lady," but his interest seemed to have waned, for he was looking towards the door. "Why don't you come? The moon is rising and a run along the coast will be very pleasant. I promise to take good care of you." He turned back towards her with his charming smile. "It's a bit hard to be turned down twice in the same evening!"

Lois hesitated, a drive along the coast sounded very

alluring, but she had made a rule never to go out with strange men. At that moment, Nella chose to make a reappearance.

"Still here, Val?" she asked insolently. "It seems the first girl you met is not being very co-operative."

The man she had addressed as Val put a proprietorial hand on Lois's shoulder.

"We were merely discussing where we would go," he returned imperturbably.

"Not the Casino in that get-up, surely?" Nella swept a contemptuous glance over Lois's dress. "I've changed my mind again, Val, I'll come with you after all."

Her Italian friend had given her some information which had made her eager to reclaim her straying swain.

"Too late," Val said firmly. "Come along, my dear," and he propelled Lois towards the entrance. "We're going for a moonlight drive," he called to Nella over his shoulder. "Doubtless Umberto will take you to the Casino, but I've lost my inclination for it."

Lois offered no resistance as he led her down the steps to his car, his hand still on her shoulder. She sensed that his anger had flared up again at Nella's cool effrontery, and she could appreciate his feelings. For herself, she was only too delighted to score off the older woman. She had had to take far too much of Nella's rudeness.

Evidently his suppressed rage found a vent in his driving, for he hurtled down the road that led from the hotel to the sea front at such a speed that Lois began to wonder if she would pay for her compliance with her life. The road was narrow and without footpaths, but he was an excellent driver and wove his way between small Fiats, dogs and pedestrians with perfect skill. She drew a breath of relief as they turned left along a broader more level road behind the town of Diano Marina. He crossed the bridge over to Torrènte San Pietro, which belied its name, by being a mere trickle of water between a mass of weeds, and turned down on to the coast road. There was a full moon, not long risen, drawing a silver path across the dark waters of the Mediterranean. The lights from the chain of towns along its coast were reflected in its lazy ripples, for this sea has no tide worth mentioning. Shops and street lamps made the roads into ribbons of light. High on its conical hill, the floodlit façade of San Giovanni Batista rose above them, crowning the village of Cervo. Then the car was rounding a headland and the lights of Laigueglia and the further city of Alassio glittered like strung jewels along the indented coast.

Lois's companion had not spoken since he had snubbed Nella.

She glanced surreptitiously from time to time at his well-cut profile silhouetted against the light from the streets, the night-dark cap of his hair, suspecting that his thoughts were still with Nella in the lounge of the hotel, and speculated about what frustrations his rage concealed.

To their left, the hills rose steeply with valleys running between them into the recesses of the Apennines. Hotels and villas were built on their lower slopes, nestling among pines and palms, dotting the hillsides with points of light. A train, emerging from a tunnel, slid past them, travelling towards distant Genoa. Out at sea the lights of a big ship, bound for Sardinia, twinkled like a galaxy of stars, until it vanished over the horizon. The car slid down the long slope into Laigueglia, through the brilliant, crowded streets, and on into Alassio. Here in a paved square, where tall palms stood sentinel over seats and flower beds, Val came to a halt.

"A drink?" he suggested.

"As you please, Mr.... ?" She looked at him interrogatively.

"Oh, call me Val, everyone does," he bade her. "And it is as *you* wish."

"Then yes, please, thank you." She noticed he had not been sufficiently interested to ask her name.

He backed the car into a parking space, jumped out and came round to open her door for her. She stood on the pavement looking about her, while he locked the car. Though not yet high season, there were plenty of tourists about, British and German predominating. They were strolling along in groups and pairs, enjoying the mild southern night. Hotels and bars with their awnings and chairs and tables spilling into the streets were on every side. Val took Lois's arm and led her towards one of the brightly lit edifices. Selecting a table, he indicated that she should be seated with a wave of his hand, then sat down opposite to her, picking up the wine list. When she had made her choice and the waiter had taken his order, for the first time he really looked at her, for Lois was certain that when he had stalked through the Hotel Paradiso, he had never seen her at all. Even when he had asked her to come out with him, he had merely noticed that she was a girl.

Slowly his gaze travelled over her, from her burnished head and wide-set greenish eyes over her neck and shoulders, to the long silken legs carelessly crossed as she sat back in her chair. She hoped fervently that her make-up was in order, and resisted an impulse to smooth her hair, meeting his intent scrutiny with negligent ease.

"Well, what's the verdict?" she asked provocatively. "Have you decided that your pick-up might be worse?"

No whit disconcerted, his eyelids crinkled into a smile.

"I was thinking I've been a bit dim not to have noticed you before. That was unpardonably remiss of me."

"Not at all. With the dazzling Miss Marshall around, I'm completely eclipsed."

Mention of the other woman brought a scowl to his face and he muttered something about spoilt beauty.

"But she is a beauty," Lois insisted, "and as such expects homage."

"A darned sight too much homage," he burst out heatedly. "I refuse to kowtow to a woman's whims..." but the arrival of the waiter with their drinks cut him short.

"Salute," he said, raising his glass. "Now tell me about yourself. How do you come to be in Italy? Have you no family, or what?"

She shrugged her shoulders. "Oh, yes, I have a family, parents and brothers, all perfectly normal, and they're comfortably settled in England. But I had a yen to travel. I'm fairly good at languages, and have had some clerical experience, so I got this job as a receptionist. It's one way of seeing a new country."

"Do you see much of Italy at the Paradiso?" he inquired.

"Well, I have time off, and I explore, a little." Her eyes became wistful; she did not have much time for exploring and little opportunity of getting to know the real country and its people. Few Italians visited the hotel, and many of the staff were also English.

"And where have your explorations led you?"

She smiled ruefully. "Not very far, I'm afraid. I've always wanted to go up into the mountains, but as yet I haven't been beyond the coast."

"Then you've missed something," he told her. "I've only been here a fortnight, but I've got around."

"You're on holiday?"

"Partly, and partly business. I've rather lingered in Liguria." (Nella, she supposed). He took out his cigarette case. "Smoke?" She shook her head. "It's a beautiful country, and the Casino at San Remo is an attraction."

"The only attraction?" she asked slyly.

He frowned. "We were going there tonight, that's why I'm dressed up. The Casino doesn't tolerate sloppy clothes."

"Miss Marshall was all dressed up too. I wonder what made her change her mind."

"She hasn't got a mind," he told her harshly. "She's governed by a succession of whims and impulses." He scowled at the tip of his cigarette. "She's decorative, I'll give her that. I suppose I liked being seen about with her, but I'm sure she thinks I'm someone else."

"A prince travelling incognito?" Lois suggested lightly.

He laughed. "I'm travelling all right, but I'm certainly not a prince. I haven't much use for the aristocracy—decadent lot, I think, clinging to outdated privileges. But let's talk of something more interesting than Nella Marshall's hen-witted notions. By the way, what's your name?"

She told him. "Lois Lang."

"Lois?" he took her up. "Not a very common name."

"It just doesn't happen to be fashionable at the moment. What else are you called? Val, of course, is an abbreviation, isn't it?"

"Yes, but never mind of what, I don't like my first name. Val Daventry, at your service. As I said, I'm here partly on pleasure, partly on business. I came into a small legacy which I didn't see why I shouldn't spend, since I've always wanted to see Europe. Next stop is Germany, and there I really have got some business appointments."

Lois thought she knew why Nella imagined he was something different from what he said he was. That patrician profile, and his proud carriage suggested a more romantic calling than that of a business man. His eyes, she discovered, were not dark, as she had first supposed, but amber-coloured, almost tawny, like those of a lion or perhaps an eagle. Again she was tantalized by an elusive memory. Somewhere she had seen eyes like his before.

He had by now completely recovered his temper and

he talked at some length about his journeyings. He had come into Italy via France and Spain, and the car he was driving was hired, but about his life in Canada he said very little. His speech varied little from standard English, only stressing certain words differently, otherwise he seemed like a countryman of her own.

"My one vice is an occasional flutter at the tables," he told her.

"I don't gamble," she said primly. "I couldn't afford to."

"Surely you could risk a few lire? Nella is reckless, but she's also lucky. It was at San Remo that I met her, and she brought me unprecedented luck."

"So she's a sort of mascot? Is that why you were so annoyed she wouldn't go to San Remo tonight?"

He coloured faintly. "I must apologize for my filthy temper. I admit I don't like being let down, but this time I can't regret it—" he looked at her with a sudden gleam in his tawny eyes, "since I've found a far more congenial companion."

She doubted the sincerity of that remark, and the gleam in his eye disconcerted her. She looked at her watch.

"It's getting late. Shouldn't we be getting back?" she asked conventionally.

"Is there any hurry? The Italians seem to stay up half the night."

"But we're not Italians, and I have to be up early," she pointed out.

"What a pity." His gaze went to the dark outline of the hills above the town. "I was going to suggest we run up into the mountains, which you have never seen, but of course if you can't forgo your beauty sleep..." He looked at her mischievously. "Couldn't you miss it for once? You may not have another opportunity for a night expedition."

Lois's wistful eyes followed the direction of his. Not

only would she enjoy such a trip, but she was reluctant
to part company with this man, who was exercising a
strange fascination over her. Tomorrow he would be
sure to make it up with Nella, and she would become,
as far as he was concerned, a robot behind the reception desk again. She looked at him a little doubtfully;
though her adventurous spirit had leaped at his suggestion, she knew it held risks.

"You don't trust me?" he asked gently. "Is that why
you're hesitating?"

She played absently with the stem of her wine glass.

"After all, we've only really met tonight."

"And you think I'm a bit of a heel to take a girl out
when I'm involved with someone else?"

"No, of course not, but..." The admission that he
was involved with Nella had pricked her.

"But...it's a lovely night and the mountains are
calling," he told her persuasively. "Nella loathes the
mountains, so you see it's a chance to visit them while
she's sulking. Besides, I'd like to show them to someone who will appreciate them. Liguria looks fine from
the Apennines."

That decided her—after all, nothing venture, nothing have, and she did not believe Val could be a menace.

"Then if you really mean it, let's go," she exclaimed
eagerly.

"Good for you," he nodded approvingly. "I'm sorry
I can't offer you a testimonial proclaiming my good
character, all I carry is my passport, but I assure you I
know how to behave myself."

And I present no temptation to do otherwise, she
thought a little sadly, as she picked up her handbag,
since I'm not beautiful nor smart like Nella.

Arrived back at the car, he took off his jacket, fold-
ing it carefully and laying it on the back seat.

"You don't mind?" he asked. "I feel a little over-
dressed for the country."

"I don't mind at all, take off anything you like," Lois said, and blushed as she realized her words were a little ambiguous. "Your shirt," she went on hastily, viewing its snowy white frills, "is also a little decorative."

"How right you are! I believe I've got a tee-shirt somewhere." He went around to the boot and rummaged in its interior, producing the garment mentioned. "But perhaps we'd better get out of town before I effect the exchange. I see that carabiniero is eyeing us suspiciously."

Beyond the confines of the town, in the shadow of a villa wall covered with bougainvillea, Val changed his shirt. Returning to the car, he put the discarded one on the back seat with his coat. Lois glanced at him surreptitiously. The thin blue shirt was short-sleeved and exposed his brown throat and arms, burned the colour of teak. His hair was ruffled by the operation, and was asserting its tendency to curl. He looked very much more approachable than he had in his formal clothes, younger and more boyish.

"I wonder if you'd put these in your bag?" he asked. "They're rather valuable and I don't want to lose them."

He was holding a pair of cuff-links.

"Willingly." She looked at them curiously as he dropped them into her palm. They were gold and seemed to be engraved with some sort of crest, but the interior car light was not strong enough to allow her to decipher it.

"I don't wonder people imagine you're a lord incognito if you wear things like that," she observed, as she put them in her handbag.

"Now don't you go getting romantic ideas," he told her. "I'm plain Mr. Daventry of Ottawa, and I've no use for titles. Those belong to my great-grandfather—perhaps they did come from England long ago."

"Did he emigrate, then?"

"I suppose so." His tone was short and she divined
that he did not want to speak of his origins. "I'm proud
to think I'm pure Canadian born and bred," he added
as if in explanation.

Lois's attention was soon diverted by the scenery, as
the car ran up a sloping valley floor with great bastions
of steep crags on either side. Val pointed out huge
gashes in a mountain side, with machinery and parked
lorries below it.

"That's where the sand comes from," he told her.
"They blast the rock and grind it before spreading it on
the beaches. This coast is naturally stony and visitors
want sand."

The road turned off from the valley and ascended in
great loops, higher and higher. Farms and villages were
shuttered and dark. Val seemed to be very well informed and pointed out objects of interest to her.

"Better than the artificiality of Alassio and Diano
Marina?" he asked, as the road led along the side of a
precipitous descent into a valley filled with misty
shadow.

"Yes, but it isn't quite real. Tonight is an excursion
into a land of fantasy. That..." she pointed to where a
ruined castle stood perched on a spur of hill with a
cluster of crumbling village houses about its walls
silvered by the moon, "... is something glimpsed in a
dream."

"It was real enough in its time. These hills have seen
a lot of warfare."

The road reached the crest of the hill and drawing
into the side, Val suggested that they should get out
and look at the view. This was magnificent. Far away
to the south was the gleam of water, edged with glittering lights; below them precipitous ravines dropped
to the valley far, far beneath them. Away to the north,
the stark, gaunt heights were black against the pale
sky. It was very still and the moonlight made the scenery weirdly impressive, accentuating the depths and

heights, delineating them in sharp black and white. Then, clear and lovely from a nearby bush, a nightingale began to sing. Lois had seen few birds in that country, and she was delighted to discover the hills still harboured a few feathered songsters.

Alone in their eyrie, she became acutely conscious of the man beside her, and when he turned to her and drew her into his arms it was all part of the dream world which seemed to enwrap them, and without resistance she gave him her lips.

It happened so naturally and spontaneously that it seemed the logical sequel of that moonlight expedition. They were man and woman alone in an enchanted realm of moon-drenched rock and boulder, fragrances from unseen herbs and the flutelike song of the nightingale. Lois could feel Val's heart beating above her own. He held her lightly but firmly, while his lips wandered over her face, touching her eyelids, her creamy throat, and settling again on her mouth. Wrapped in sensuous contentment, Val's kisses seemed part of the magic of the night.

The nightingale's notes died away, a scarf of filmy cloud veiled the moon, and a little chill breeze sprang up, stirring the sparse vegetation. Val's arms tightened and his mouth became more insistent. Lois came back to earth.

"No more," she whispered, turning her head away, and strove to free herself.

"What's the matter, sweetheart?" he murmured huskily.

"Please let me go."

Instantly he obeyed and she faced him accusingly.

"You promised to behave."

He was very near, exciting, magnetic, but she knew that he was only using her as a diversion to heal a wound to his vanity. For a few moments he had forgotten Nella Marshall, but he would remember her again.

"You're so enticing..." he murmured, in excuse.

"I am not, and I don't appreciate being used as a substitute."

"I don't understand. A substitute for what?"

"Nella Marshall."

"Oh, her!" He made a derogatory gesture with one hand. "She doesn't compare with you."

"I know she doesn't. I'm poor and plain and she's rich and beautiful."

"You're not plain, Lois, and you have an elfin charm, in fact at this moment you don't look quite human with those long, witch's eyes of yours in that little pointed face..."

She was not going to be mollified by flattery.

"Sounds like a cat," she interrupted him.

"Exactly, and cats are associated with magic. Can you see in the dark?"

"No, but I can see through you."

"Do you suppose that when I kiss a girl I'm thinking of someone else?" he asked reproachfully.

"Perhaps not at this moment, but when we get back to Diano Marina, your thoughts will all be of her again." He gave an exclamation of denial, but she went on coolly. "You've given me a very pleasant outing, please don't spoil it by becoming too importunate."

He was silent. The moon emerged from its veil, the nightingale uttered the jug-jug that was the prelude to a fresh burst of song, but the magic had fled from the night. Lois was blaming herself for succumbing to Val Daventry's kisses; he must think she was very easy game, and no doubt he had anticipated that she would ever since they had left Alassio. It was what he had brought her here for, and she had surrendered without a protest. She stole a look at him and saw he was studying her intently, but his expression was inscrutable. She turned away from him abruptly.

"Will you please take me home?"

"Certainly," he agreed, and contrarily she was piqued by his instantaneous acquiescence.

In silence they walked back to the car. The ground was uneven, broken by pieces of rock, which caused her to stumble, but he did not offer to assist her.

"Now I've offended you," she said a little sadly, "but I couldn't go...any further."

"What do you think I am?" he asked brusquely. "Who wants you to go...any further? What's a kiss in the moonlight?"

They had reached the car and he opened the door for her with a mock bow. "Enter *signorina*, and don't be scared. I respect innocence."

Lois got in, aware her colour had risen, fearing she had appeared very unsophisticated. As he had said, what was a kiss in the moonlight? Nella would have taken that and more in her stride. Yet those moments of communion had been very sweet, almost as if they were the prelude to something rich and strange...she shook herself mentally...There would be nothing more between them after tonight.

For a while he gave all his attention to his driving, for the descent was steep, the bends very sharp. They passed through stretches of woodland, sweet chestnuts, young beech and hazel. There was only one thing missing from the country; there were no lakes nor streams. It was not surprising the mountains had an arid look. Only along the valley bottom ran a sluggish river.

"It's because it dries up so quickly," Val told her in answer to her question. "I'm told that in winter there's sometimes too much water and there are floods."

Back once more in the towns, where most of the lights were extinguished, faint grey streaks above the sea proclaimed that the dawn was breaking.

Val began to question Lois about her times off duty, and she admitted that she would be free on the next afternoon until six.

"Good, then I'll come and fetch you to go swimming. You do swim?"

"Yes, but..."

"There's no but," he told her firmly. "Did you think I meant to end our acquaintanceship tonight?"

"Yes," she said simply.

He laughed. "Then you were mistaken, or can't you forgive me for being too free? I thought that was what girls expected nowadays."

"I don't, and I made myself cheap," she murmured distressfully.

"Believe me, there's nothing cheap about you," he said earnestly. "And those kisses were a very sweet experience—for me."

"But not to be repeated," she warned.

"If you say so." He looked regretful. "I promise I'll keep my distance in future."

A promise which should have reassured her, but which she found unsatisfactory.

"I suppose I'm funny," she observed, "but I've never been able to take that sort of thing for granted. It seems to me that... that demonstrations," (she had trouble in finding the right word to express her meaning) "should mean something, otherwise they're worthless."

"So you think I didn't mean anything?"

"How could you, when we've only just met?"

"Sometimes one is instantly drawn to a person. You're very—what the Latins call *simpatica*, you little copper-haired witch. Do you sit weaving spells around your clients at the hotel? I think you've woven one round me."

"Very pretty, and a load of rubbish, inspired of course by the moonlight, and the fantastic scenery we've been through. When you come to see me tomorrow, if you come, you'll find I look very plain and ordinary by daylight, and far from weaving spells, I'll be changing traveller's cheques. Could anything be more prosaic?"

"Of course I'm coming tomorrow, and you couldn't look plain and ordinary, pussy-face."

"Pussy-face?"

"You're not a cat, you're a kitten, and a kitten has one of the most charming faces of all God's creatures, triangular with big eyes and a pointed chin, and the most delightful little pink tongue."

"And big ears."

"I haven't noticed your ears, but well-bred cats have small ones."

"I've no blue blood, and kittens scratch," she smiled.

"So do most women."

"If you behave very nicely, I'll keep my claws sheathed," she promised.

"You'd better. You wouldn't like my treatment for...scratches."

"And what's that?"

"Wait and see," he threatened.

She laughed. "I'm tempted to try to find out."

"Then don't. Provoke me and it'll be a lot worse than what I did on the hill top, and I want you to come out with me tomorrow."

She reflected that Nella had annoyed him, and in consequence he seemed to be repudiating her. No, Val was definitely not a person who could be flouted with impunity.

Laughing and bantering, they continued their way until they had climbed the hill to the Paradiso.

She made him stop at the gate into the hotel grounds.

"I want to slip in unobserved," she told him. "There's a night porter on duty, but he often dozes."

Val looked at her with some concern. "Is your reputation at stake? Will you get the sack?"

"I don't think so, but up to now I've never been so late, or rather early, but I see no reason why I shouldn't if I want to."

"No reason whatever, especially as you behave so decorously." His tone was a little mocking, and she

hoped he did not despise her for being a goody-goody.
"Until tomorrow, kitten."

She slipped out of the car into the road with a casual
"Good night," half expecting he would kiss her, but he
did not. Apparently he had taken her words to heart,
and she wondered dolefully if she had not been a little
too severe. She would not have minded a farewell kiss.

The night porter was, as she had hoped, dozing, and
she reached the lift unnoticed, but on the top floor she
encountered one of the maids, a girl called Violetta.
She was one of the few who slept in the building, and
was a handsome, sulky girl, whom Lois had once had
to report for insolence.

"Buon giorno, signorina," Violetta said with a toss of
her black head. "You are early abroad."

"So are you."

"Me? I have so much to do I needs must start at
dawn." A statement which Lois knew to be untrue.
"My job is not a cushy one, like a receptionist's."

Lois made no rejoinder to that gibe and went on to
her room. Violetta's eyes followed her with a malicious
look.

As she prepared for what would only be a short rest,
Lois remembered that she had not returned Val's cuff-
links. She took them out of her bag and studied the
crest under the light. It represented an eagle with
spread wings, what heraldry calls an eagle displayed. He
had told her they belonged to his great-grandfather.
Had the former Daventry had some connection with a
noble family, or were the links merely pilfered? She
remembered that Val had seemed reluctant to speak of
his forebears.

During her short, troubled sleep, she dreamed of
crests and coronets and woke to a full recollection of
whom it was Val had reminded her. She had gone with
the friend she lived with on a coach trip to Erne Hall,
one of the stately homes of England, the seat of the
Earl of Erne and open to the public in the summertime.

Her friend Joanna had little use for such places and was bored, but Lois had been fascinated by the great building and its fine furnishings. Among the portraits was that of the fifth Earl, a fine-looking man in a satin coat and powdered wig. Lois had been so attracted by his handsome face that Joanna had made great fun of her, declaring that she had fallen in love with a creature of paint and canvas, several hundred years old. The fifth Earl had tawny eyes under straight black brows that stared out of his gilt frame, while his mouth curved in a cynical smile that was almost a sneer. Eyes that she had that night seen in a living face, the face of Val Daventry.

Was Joanna right, she wondered sleepily—she had been so impressed by his Georgian lordship that she must fancy she saw his features in another man who had attracted her, because he had similar colouring?

The likeness, if likeness there were, and it was not a figment of her excited imagination, could be only very superficial, for what possible connection could there be between Val Daventry of Canada, and the Earls of Erne?

CHAPTER TWO

NEXT morning Lois woke with a pleasurable sense of anticipation and remembered that Val had promised to call for her that afternoon to take her down to the beach for her few hours of relaxation. She lay reviewing the previous night's happenings, which had the unsubstantiality of a dream. Actually it had been a dream come true. During the days when Val had come to the hotel to call for Nella, she had been struck by his magnetic personality, his distinguished appearance which was so different from the nondescript looks of most of the hotel's visitors. Subtly she was aware that he was the type of man to whom women would always be attracted. She had made up fantasies in which some accident had occurred to gain his attention for herself, well knowing that there was no likelihood of them ever materializing. But the quarrel with Nella had precipitated her right into his arms, literally so on the hill crest.

She relived every moment of that moonlit drive and congratulated herself upon her restraint. Naturally he had expected the usual fee for taking her out and she had not been niggardly, but she had known when to stop. If he had persisted, she might have gone much further, and she was shocked at the violence of her own response. She had never been deeply stirred emotionally by a man before, and she was dimly aware that this one possessed the power to arouse in her passions which she had not known existed in the depths of her being. She must play it cool and keep her head, for she did not believe he had been more than superficially affected. He was merely seeking a holiday diversion, and such connections were never permanent.

Nella, to her advantage, had offended him and he had taken up with herself on impulse in a moment of pique. That the expedition had been more successful than either had anticipated was her great good fortune. Once he had thawed towards her they had neither of them been bored with the other's company, and he was sufficiently interested to want to see her again.

She came to her desk in a carefree, happy mood, ready to accept whatever fate, as directed by Val, held in store for her, and was dismayed when Umberto checked out. So Nella had lost her new boy-friend and would be ready to whistle Val back again, and it was probable, his anger cooled, he would be only too willing to return to her.

Nella came sauntering through the vestibule about the middle of the morning. She was wearing a smart sun-suit, which left a great deal of her exposed, and a crinoline straw hat. Significantly she was carrying a beach bag as if she intended to go down to the sea, and Lois guessed that she was expecting a penitent Val to arrive, and offer to take her wherever she wished to go.

She came to a halt in front of Lois's desk, with the polished wooden top of the counter between them, and stared at the receptionist superciliously.

"Enjoy yourself last night?" she asked. "You certainly look a bit bog-eyed this morning, which isn't surprising when you came in at dawn. Did your sex-starved instincts run away with you?"

Lois reflected that Violetta must have reported the time of her return, for no one else knew when it was and Nella had drawn her own conclusions.

"What I do during my offtime is my own affair, madam," she said calmly, glad that she had not blushed at Nella's crude inference.

"So long as it doesn't affect your work," Nella suggested nastily. Having failed to get a rise out of Lois, she decided to condescend to an explanation of the situation as she saw it.

"Owing to a misunderstanding between me and Mr. Daventry," she went on, "you got an unexpected inning, but don't kid yourself his attentions will continue. You've served his purpose, my girl, which was to make me jealous—as if I need to be jealous of a poor thing like you! He'll be arriving this morning anxious to be reconciled, and I think I shall forgive him." She pursed her small mouth and seemed to be considering. Then she nodded her head. "Yes, providing he's suitably apologetic, I certainly shall. I shouldn't mind a run into Alassio this morning. The bathing is better there."

With a final contemptuous glance at the receptionist, Nella continued her way out on to the sun terrace, where she chose a seat from which she could watch the approach to the hotel, leaving Lois considerably deflated.

After all, it was much what she had expected, she told herself drearily. She could not compete with Nella if the other girl were determined to reclaim her lover, if he were her lover, but the sunshine seemed to have become much less bright.

Visitors passed to and fro on their way to the hotel swimming pool in the grounds in various stages of undress and sunburn. Lois dealt with the arrangements for the next batch of package tourists, with her mind only half upon her work, expecting every moment to hear Val's voice on the terrace and to see him go off with Nella.

Not wanting to waste any time changing after lunch, she was dressed in a sun-top over white trousers, with a white crimplene jacket concealing her bare arms, to make her appear more seemly for work. Her towelling wrap and swimming costume were in her beach bag under the counter, but she became more and more convinced that they would not be needed.

Val did not appear to fulfil Nella's expectations, and she came down to lunch looking like a thundercloud.

Lois took her meals with the guests in the hotel dining room, but she was seated at some distance from the fuming beauty, who was accommodated at one of the best tables by the window looking out on to the swimming pool. What with mingled anxiety and anticipation, Lois could only pick at her food, while Nella's appetite seemed unimpaired, and she ordered a bottle of wine.

Lois went back to her desk, where Signora Merano, the manager's wife, should come to relieve her, but the Signora was late, which was not unusual, as Lois was rarely in a hurry to leave on the dot.

Nella returned to resume her vigil on the terrace, careful not to glance in Lois's direction as she went past. Both of them heard the car approach. From where she was standing, Lois could see the top of the steps and Nella's fleeing figure, as she ran down them, all smiles and coquettish charm; could also hear her shrill carrying voice.

"So there you are at last, darling! I've been waiting all the morning for you. Why didn't you come?"

What Val said in response to this greeting, Lois could not catch. They came up the steps with Nella clinging to his arm, and her heart gave a lurch at sight of him; but his dark head was inclined towards Nella and they passed out of view along the terrace. Lois's heart sank to zero. So that was that.

Signora Merano arrived to take over, with a brief word of apology, and Lois picked up her bag, wondering whether to wait for Val's appearance with some excuse for cancelling their outing, or if it would be more dignified to retire to her room until he was clear of the premises. She had no doubt that Nella would prevail with him; he might not even bother to acquaint her with his change of plan. She looked wistfully at the deep blue sky between the spreading fronds of the palm trees. It was an ideal day for the sea, but she had little heart for a solitary walk on the beach, after her eager anticipations.

A shadow showed beyond the glass doors, and Val came in, his eyes glittering under his knitted brows.

"For God's sake, Lois, aren't you ready?" he growled.

"Yes, but...I mean do you still...?" she was stammering.

His face cleared and he smiled. Coming up to her he drew her arm through his.

"Come and get me out of her clutches," he whispered.

Nella was still sitting on the terrace as they came out, swinging idly on a canopied hammock. She gave a little gasp of disbelief as Lois appeared on Val's arm, and sprang up to intercept them.

"Surely this isn't allowed?" she exclaimed, fixing baleful eyes on Lois. "The staff fraternizing with the guests? I shall complain to the management!"

"So far as I know there's no rule against it," Lois told her.

"And I don't happen to be staying here," Val reminded her.

Lois felt his arm tense beneath her hand. Looking up, she saw an inimical expression in his eyes as he glanced at Nella. This man was not one to forgive and forget.

Nella pouted. "No, you prefer that low dive in the Corso Roma," she said disdainfully. "It also seems you've a liking for low company."

"I'm free to choose where I stay and with whom I consort," he returned stiffly. "Good afternoon, Nella," and he walked swiftly down the steps, drawing Lois with him to his car.

"I hope she won't make trouble for you," he remarked, as he opened the door for her.

"I don't think she can," Lois told him, feeling too happy to care.

"Nasty vicious temper," Val observed, as he took

his place beside her. "The things she said to me when I told her I hadn't come to see her!"

"You've a fairly vindictive temper yourself," Lois told him as the car shot up on to the road.

"I don't like being fooled," he said shortly. "Especially by a woman. When you've had enough of me, kitten, tell me straight, I can take it, but don't try to play me off against another guy."

"As if I'd ever do that!" she exclaimed, shocked at such a suggestion.

"No, I don't think you would," he agreed. "You've got honest eyes, kitten. Now let's forget about that nasty piece of work and enjoy ourselves for the limited time that you're free."

Val's hotel might be described by Nella as a low dive, but it ran to its own private strip of beach, which was much cleaner and better cared for than the public one. Moreover it was fitted out with bathing cubicles and deck chairs. Lois appeared in a green bikini, and she saw the flash of approval in Val's eyes when he beheld her. She was already tanned, and her long straight limbs and slender body were displayed to advantage in her scanty garb. His, arrayed in black bathing trunks, was burned to the colour of teak, and save for a suspicion of dark hair on his chest, was as smooth and muscular as a Greek statue.

The water was warm and shallow, and although the Mediterranean has the reputation of being the most polluted sea in the world, it was at that point a clear and translucent blue-green.

After their swim they sat in deck chairs and let the sun soak into their bare limbs. In the bright light, Val's eyes looked lambent gold between his thick dark lashes, while hers were a shining green.

"Cats' eyes," Val said smiling, as he caught her glance. "Are they grey, green or yellow? They seem to change with the light."

"They're described on my passport as hazel," Lois told him demurely, veiling the orbs in question with her sweep of lashes. "But yours make me think of an eagle."

"I've never noticed the colour of an eagle's eyes," he returned. "Not being on familiar terms with the birds. Are you sure you don't mean an owl?"

"No, I'm quite sure I don't." She laughed. "You could never look owlish, unless perhaps when you put sunglasses on."

"I rarely use them. Eagles you know can look at the sun, but shouldn't you wear yours?"

She had not done so out of vanity, but now it occurred to her that they might effectively disguise her feelings. Most of the residents preferred the morning for their swim, so there was no one sitting near them, and Val's close proximity, his bared brown limbs were having a peculiar effect upon her; he disturbed her and her eyes might betray too much. She took her glasses out of her handbag and slipped them on her nose.

"Eclipsed," she announced, tilting back her head and looking at him challengingly from behind the tinted lenses.

"Not entirely," he said, his eyes dropping to her legs.

Deliberately she spread her towel over them.

"Tantalizing little witch," he complained, and turned his gaze seawards, seeming to lose interest in her, for his next remark was to point out the brilliant blue of the sea water.

She tried to draw him out about his home, being anxious to learn more about him, but he was not forthcoming.

"The new world is thousands of miles away," he observed lazily, "and at this moment I'm much more interested in the old. Have you ever seen anything more fascinating than the Italian hill villages? They take one right back into the Middle Ages."

He did, however, inform her that he had a kid sister, a good deal younger than himself, who was a great sportswoman, and with whom he often rode and swam.

"You remind me of her a little, kitten, you've the same eager appetite for life, but I don't think you've had much life...yet."

"I make the most of what comes my way." She was wondering if he were identifying her with the kid sister, which was a little disheartening. It was not as a sister that she wanted to appeal to him.

With an amused glint in his eyes, he said: "Not always."

She supposed he was referring to the previous night when she had checked his advances, and turned away her head.

"There's a lot more to living than erotic experiences," she said tartly.

"Oh, undoubtedly, but sex is one of the few excitements civilized existence has left to us. That's why it's so prominent among modern young people."

An observation which gave her cause for conjecture. Rubbing a finger over her bare thigh, she asked:

"Have you had a lot of girls, Val?"

"What an ambiguous sort of question!" he laughed. "I've had girl-friends, of course, but pursuing females isn't my favourite occupation."

She wanted to inquire if there were any particular friend, but in view of their short acquaintanceship, decided it was probing too intimately. He would in his own time tell her if there was a prior attachment—or would he? She glanced at his dark face and found his gaze was fixed upon her with a sensuous appraising look in his narrowed eyes, a look that belied his statement and made her heart quicken. Val Daventry was by no means indifferent to female charms, and he himself possessed a sexual attraction few women could resist. He did not need to pursue, for they would be drawn to him like bees to honey.

"I wonder you bother with an insignificant person like me," she blurted out.

"But you're not insignificant, kitten—didn't I tell you last night you had an elfin charm? Besides, I find you very restful after Nella," and he made a grimace.

"But I wouldn't bring you luck at cards?"

"That I don't know, but by your leave, I'm not going to try. You're not the sort of girl I take to casinos, and you said you don't gamble. Unless of course you very much want to go?"

"Not at all." But she was not pleased with this remark. She supposed she was not glamorous enough to take to San Remo or Monte Carlo, but was acceptable on the beach as a substitute for the kid sister, who was probably as naïve as herself.

"Talking of likenesses," she said, "you remind me of someone and I've just remembered who."

"Oh? So I'm not unique?" His expression was gently teasing.

"Well, actually it's a picture."

"I hope not a photograph of one of those ghastly singers you girls all rave about?"

"No, and I haven't raved about a pop singer since my adolescent days, I'm not that young. The man lived a long time ago. He was a belted earl."

"Kitten, kitten, you're allowing your romantic fancies to run away with you. There are no earls in our family, we're just plain farmers and business folk. I've no use for title-bearers, they're parasites feeding on the community."

She laughed. "There spoke the democratic North American, but leave us what's left of our aristocracy. It's very picturesque."

"I daresay, but you couldn't imagine me dressed up in silk and velvet and waving a rapier?"

"They don't wear robes except on state occasions, and only Servicemen carry swords, but I could imagine you in a white wig and all the etceteras. You'd look magnificent, Val."

"That'll be the day," he said, laughing.

Neither had any presentiment that a day would come when she would see him in such a garb.

She sighed. "Modern men's clothes are so dull."

"We're trying to brighten them, ma'am, but may I remind you that women are copying us by wearing trousers, and aspire to wear them figuratively as well."

"I don't imagine your wife will ever wear the trousers—figuratively," she said daringly.

"You're right, she would not," he returned. "With all due respect to Women's Lib, I intend to be master in my own house, if and when I get me a wife."

So apparently he had no one in mind for that position at the moment, which was what she had been angling to find out. Through her sunglasses she met his mocking gaze, and was aware that he knew what had been in her mind. She glanced at her watch and saw how the time had flown.

"I'm afraid I'll soon have to go back."

"Will you? What a shame, but there'll be other days. You must have something before you go, what would you like—tea, coffee, wine?"

She chose iced coffee and while he went to get it, she stared dreamily out at the sparkling sea. So he meant to see more of her before he departed, and that was a beatific prospect, for she was beginning to fall in love with him.

In the days that followed, Lois saw Val Daventry nearly every day. When she was free after dinner, he would drive up to some hill village; the road past the hotel led to their favourite one, Diano Castello. This followed the usual pattern, a sharp incline rising to a hill top, with a more shallow slope on the further side leading towards the mountains. It comprised a conglomeration of old buildings around a castle, which had been converted into a hospital, with more modern houses on its fringes. The church had a tall narrow tower and stood on the apex of the hill, with an open space before it, overlooking the countryside. The café they frequented was a little way out of the main village, with a terrace overlooking a steep declivity on two sides. There between the mountains behind and the sea in front, the whole glittering panorama of the coast was spread before them.

On the evenings they spent there, they would discuss all subjects under the sun, as young people will, and evolve theories for putting the world to rights. Val's ideas tended towards an idealized socialism, but when it came to more intimate matters, he shied away from them, so that Lois wondered if there was some secret he was fearful of revealing, or if it were merely his natural reticence. Woman-like she preferred personalities to abstract subjects, but she always followed his lead, for she was falling more and more deeply in love with him and was anxious that he should continue to enjoy her company, but of his feelings towards herself she had no clue. Sometimes she surprised a look in his eyes which gave her hope, but he never committed himself in words, and she dreaded the approach of the time when he would go, for it seemed he regarded their association as only a pleasant holiday friendship.

Nella naturally remained inimical, and never missed a chance to make some spiteful innuendo, though she never addressed Lois directly. Several times Lois saw her in the corridor talking to Violetta. The chambermaid was devoted to her, or possibly it was the lavish tips that Nella bestowed upon her for extra services.

Not that Nella could do much to injure Lois, for with the exception of Violetta, she was popular with both the guests and the staff. That she had complained to the manager was probable, for Signor Merano went out of his way to tell Lois one evening that she was the most obliging receptionist the Paradiso had ever had.

"I 'ave a great respect for ze Inglese," he said in his accented English, "and it 'as increased since I came to know you."

That was all that came of Nella's tale-bearing.

The golden days and spangled nights flew by, and inevitably the moment of parting drew nearer. Once Lois had tentatively mentioned his departure, but Val had merely shrugged his shoulders and said:

"Sufficient unto the day, let's make hay while the sun shines."

A sentiment she tried hard to support and banish the menacing shadow on the horizon of her happiness. He had never again attempted to kiss her. On that first night he had been definitely forthcoming, but he had also said that he thought that was what she would expect. Now she had told him it was not, he had slipped into this companionable, fraternal relationship, which though it might satisfy him, was very far from satisfying her. He did not seem to take much interest in sex, unless he sought amorous diversions on the nights when she was not available. That thought plunged her into a black hell of jealousy. But she was in no position to question his activities.

She decided that being in love was a far from comfortable state of being and she was finding it increasingly difficult not to betray her feelings. Thus it was that her manner towards Val became more and more guarded. Perhaps he found that off-putting, but she could not make advances unless she was sure that they would be welcome. That was the hell of it all. She suspected that he enjoyed her company because she was so undemanding, for he was tired of women who blatantly pursued him, but she was finding the role of sister more and more difficult to play. She wondered which would come first, his departure or an emotional explosion which she could no longer control.

One evening, when Lois was alone in the vestibule, totting up her accounts after the day's work, Nella approached her from the lounge. She was waiting for her escort to arrive to take her to a session at the casino, and was wearing a white dress trimmed with silver, with a white and silver stole laid across her shoulders.

Since the afternoon when Val had left her for Lois, she had pointedly ignored the receptionist, nor had she wasted any time in finding another cavalier to replace him.

To Lois's surprise, she paused by the desk, watching her lock the cash box and put it on the shelf under the counter prior to conveying it to the safe.

"Signor Merano must trust you a lot," she observed. "You handle a great deal of money. Don't you ever make mistakes?"

"I'm not infallible," Lois returned pleasantly, "but it's all part of the job, and so far I haven't made a serious error."

Nella fingered the diamond pendant about her neck.

"Nevertheless I prefer to have my valuables in my own keeping," she said nastily. "You must be exposed to considerable temptation, for I don't suppose you're paid sufficient to buy the clothes you'd like to have for all the gadding about you've been doing lately."

"I'm surprised you condescend to notice my movements, madam," Lois told her with a touch of sarcasm.

"I'm concerned for the efficiency of the hotel service," Nella said loftily. "With the receptionist in love, anything might happen. I've noticed more than once you're becoming absent-minded."

Controlling her temper with difficulty, Lois inquired why she should suppose she was in love.

Nella's eyes slid over her. "It's obvious."

Lois's skin glowed with a soft radiance, her hair had the gloss and sheen of a freshly shelled chestnut, and her eyes were all green and luminous. Nella's experience had taught her to recognise the signs, if Val Daventry did not. Lois told her coldly:

"My emotional state is my own concern, madam, and no one has complained of any laxity in my duties."

Nella laughed unpleasantly. "Not yet, perhaps, but then you're only in the initial stages. You haven't become desperate."

Lois looked at her watch. "You must excuse me, madam," she said calmly. "I'm going off duty now."

Nella leaned over the counter towards her.

"Another rendezvous with my cast-off lover?" she inquired. "Don't you find he's a little elusive about his background? Let me give you a word of warning, for you haven't much experience of men." Lois winced, knowing that statement was true, and Nella went on:

"I don't believe he's who he says he is. Umberto told me..." She broke off and looked at Lois narrowly. "But I don't want to put further romantic notions into that silly little head of yours, which is stuffed full of them already, but remember, Cinderella was only a very unlikely fairy story."

Lois sighed. Her position regarding Val was sufficiently insecure without Nella rubbing it in.

"I don't think I'm the one who is harbouring romantic notions," she returned, "and I'm quite content to accept Mr. Daventry's description of himself, which I'm sure is more reliable than anything Signor... your Italian friend told you." She could not, without looking it up, remember Umberto's surname.

"In fact you're a gullible little idiot," Nella snapped. "Never believe anything a handsome man tells you when he's on holiday. The opportunity for deception is too tempting. Bank clerks can pose as titled playboys, travelling incognito, and crooks as millionaires."

"You're not implying that Mr. Daventry is a crook or a lord?" Lois asked incredulously.

"Take your choice, but one thing sticks out a mile, he's cagey about his antecedents, surely you've noticed that?"

Lois had, but put it down to a natural reserve. Val was not the sort of man to be expansive about himself.

"When he's had enough of you, he'll move on and you'll never hear from him again," Nella announced triumphantly. "And if you've been more loving than wise you'll find yourself in a jam."

Lois reddened angrily at this unwarrantable insinuation, and she said stiffly:

"Thank you, madam, but I don't need any warning and certainly not from you."

Nella laughed shrilly. Lois caught a whiff of her exotic scent, could see the false eyelashes surrounding her hard, blue eyes, the enamel on her face. Nella was not as young as she tried to appear, but there was no denying she was an expensive work of art.

"High and mighty, aren't you, miss? But you're a nice girl," she made this assertion as though it were something to be deplored. "It's always the naïve innocents like you who end up in disaster. You don't learn your way about until it's too late."

To Lois's relief, she drew back from the counter. Her poisonous suggestions seemed to pollute the air, or was it only her scent?

"Heaven knows what he sees in you," Nella went on disparagingly. "You've got nothing, but you were there, waiting to be picked up, making sheep's eyes at him. I suppose he was flattered, but he must be getting very tired of you by now."

At which point the outer door opened and Nella's escort appeared, to Lois's great relief. Nella went to meet him gushingly, and both completely ignoring the other girl, they went out into the night.

Lois picked up the cash box and went into the inner room to put it into the safe. She knew Signor Merano trusted her implicitly, and Nella's remarks were quite unjustifiable, nor would Lois allow her private concerns to interfere with her work. She had been conscientiously punctual whatever arrangements she had made with Val, and had not even asked for any extra time off.

Love with its tensions and anxieties, the restless longing for Val's presence when he was absent, her contentment when she was with him, marred by uncertainty, the few moments of pure rapture when for a

transitory second he seemed to care, was a devastating
enough experience without Nella's jealous thrusts.

Knowing what had prompted them, Lois tried to dismiss them from her mind, but one or two of them had
gone home. She did know very little about Val Daventry and was well aware that their connection would be
severed when he moved on, but she had nothing with
which to reproach herself in her conduct towards him.

As for Nella's hints that he was other than he
seemed, they were absurd. True, on the occasion of
their first outing to Alassio, he had looked like a prince
in his dress clothes and he had worn cuff-links with an
engraved crest, but he had insisted that he had no use
for aristocrats, and during their long discussions he had
expressed democratic principles. Those, she was sure,
were perfectly genuine. The other suggestion, that he
might be a master criminal splashing his loot about,
was still more ridiculous. Nella seemed to hover between James Bond and Ruritania, but her object had
been to plant a seed of doubt in Lois's mind, not understanding that it was of no consequence to her who
he might be, since Lois was only too conscious of the
impermanence of their relationship.

Her cash box safely locked away, Lois went into the
lounge, intending to buy herself a cup of coffee at the
bar. It was after ten o'clock, and she had told Val that
she would not be free tonight, so there was no chance
of his appearance. She supposed he would have gone to
the casino, among the smart set where he considered
she would look out of place. The big room with its long
line of windows looking on to the terrace, its lofty ceiling, marble floor and bar in one corner was deserted
except for a quartet playing bridge. Lois procured her
coffee herself, being familiar with the process and unwilling to disturb the Meranos to serve her.

She sat down in one of the comfortable armchairs
and began to review the emotional aspect of her rela-
tions with Val. Nella had been completely wrong in as-

suming that they were having an affair, but she was right
when she had told Lois that she did not know her way
about. Having indicated when he had kissed her that
she despised "necking", Val had taken her at her
word, and she unhappily suspected that he had been
relieved by her attitude. He had told her that most girls
expected such attentions and was pleased that he did
not have to pay them to her, but if he had found her
sexually attractive, he would surely have shown an inclination to break down her resistance? That he had not
done, and she had no idea of how to set about interesting him in her femininity, for now she desperately
wanted him to realize that she was a woman and not
merely a playfellow.

She could not bring herself to adopt Nella's tactics—
the provocative pout, the fluttering eyelashes, the
predatory fingers, which sought every opportunity to
clutch a man's arm. They were too blatant and contrary
to her candid nature, besides which, she was sure Val
would not appreciate such overtures—from her. It was
all very depressing, and she was convinced she was too
unexciting to be able to persuade any man that she was
a worthy candidate for an affair, she just was not that
sort of girl.

Signor Merano came into the lounge and seeing that
she was unaccompanied, came to sit beside her, giving
her a genial smile.

"So you are all alone tonight, *signorina*? Where is ze
amante?"

Lois sighed; why would they all persist in regarding
Val as her lover, when he never spoke of love? She
explained that she had only just come off duty.

"*Si, si,* you are too conscientious," he said admiringly. "Many girls would have zeir man come here
while zey work, and slip in now and zen for a drink and
a word, but you, you tell 'im not to come, is it not so?
You look pale, *poverina*, such deprivation is too 'ard?
Bene, tomorrow is your 'alf day, take ze morning as

well. My wife will take your place." He chuckled. "We must make concessions to *amore, si*?"

She thanked him warmly. She had not had a whole day off since she had met Val and he had often grumbled that she was so tied, as it precluded any long expedition. Impulsively she ran to the switchboard to ring up his hotel to give him the good news. But Val, as she might have anticipated, was out. She left a message and afterwards regretted it. She was taking too much for granted, he had probably made other plans for the morning, and she could not expect him to be on call whenever she was free.

Some of Nella's unpleasant remarks returned to her. What had she got to hold the interest of a man like Val? Was it possible he was becoming tired of her company? She would rather he left before that happened, even if it did mean that she would never see him again.

If he had gone to the casino, he would meet Nella there—an unwelcome reflection, for Nella was quite capable of making some unpleasant revelations. She comforted herself by considering he was hardly likely to credit anything Nella told him knowing how she was motivated. If Nella declared that she was in love with him, he would simply laugh, but that was not a very happy thought either, for she was in love with him and it was painful to think that he might find such an idea amusing.

When finally she fell asleep, she had half decided not to accept the proffered holiday, and her dreams were a confused medley, in which Val walked off with Nella, calling over his shoulder:

"If you don't like my kisses, I can always find someone who does!"

CHAPTER THREE

THE next day produced a brilliant morning and Lois's spirits rose. She wondered how she could have been so idiotic as to think of refusing her holiday. Though she did not expect Val to turn up, it was a joy not to have to hurry to her desk. She dressed leisurely, as if for an occasion, putting on white trousers and a brightly printed sleeveless tunic. She brushed her hair until it shone like copper, put a touch of eye-shadow above her eyes, and made up her mouth. The tube said "kiss-proof" and she smiled derisively. That was an unnecessary precaution. She breakfasted with the late risers and the waiters chaffed her about being a lady of leisure. Then she went to sit on the terrace, as Val's Ferrari turned in at the gate. Her heart leaped with joyful anticipation. So he had received her message and this was his answer.

He emerged from the car and sprang up the steps, a tall, lithe figure in cream slacks and a white shirt.

"Well, this is a bonus," he greeted her. "A whole day to ourselves."

She lowered her lashes to conceal the glad light in her eyes, evoked by his presence.

"You got my message?" she asked stupidly, for of course he must have done so.

"Sure thing. I'm sorry I was out. A business conference." A shadow crossed his face. "I've got some news for you, but it can wait. No need to spoil our day."

A presage of disaster chilled her joy. "Can't you tell me now?"

"No," he answered firmly. "This is neither the time

nor the place, because…" He broke off, looking at her considering. "We shall have much to discuss." Suddenly he smiled mischievously. "Don't look so shattered, kitten, we're going to have fun first."

"Where shall we go?" she asked, trying to sound gay. If he were going to tell her he was leaving, he did not seem much concerned about it.

"Monte Carlo. I've been wanting to take you there, but it's such a long way, we need a whole day. Got your passport?"

"Oh, super; I'll run and get it." She was all eager anticipation. She had not yet found an opportunity to visit Monaco, and the very name was magic. If he had to go, they would indeed have fun first.

It was a long drive. Val took the low road along the coast; they would return, he said, by the autostrada, but it was all tunnels and there was more to see going through the towns. Under the cloudless blue sky, the coast resorts sparkled, but there was too much to absorb in detail. All Lois could recall in retrospect were a few outstanding landmarks—the long arcades in Oneglia, the Russian church in San Remo, the masses of bougainvillea covering an ancient wall in the Strada Romana at Bordighera. The rest was a welter of white buildings, impressive churches, avenues of palm trees and blue glimpses of the rock-bound coast.

The Apennines gave place to the Maritime Alps as they crossed the frontier. Cap Martin ran out into the sea bearing its burden of rich men's villas. The hills inland grew starker and stonier, looming closer over the route. Finally after passing through a maze of twisting streets, Val pulled up outside the exotic gardens at Monte Carlo.

"They're worth a visit," he told her, "and you get a fine view of the Principality from them."

The gardens were given over to cacti of every shape and form, planted on the cliff face, with paths leading up and down among their peculiar growths. Some were in flower, so the gardens did not lack for colour; some were prickly green tubes, writhing this way and that. Lois was not very interested in the plants, though she agreed that many looked definitely weird. A time was to come when she would wish that she had observed them more closely.

From a vantage point to the west, the view stretched away towards Nice, with the railway far below them, and a cemetery identifiable by its surround of cypress trees. To the east, the panorama was even more striking. Every inch of space was filled with jumbled buildings, one behind the other and since there was no more room at ground level skyscrapers were creeping up. The palace was recognizable on its spur of rock, so also the casino opposite across the harbour wherein many yachts, including the royal vessel belonging to Prince Rainier, were moored. To the north the arid grey heights raised their heads up which villas were creeping, some being built on their very crests.

Val found a place for lunch which was not excessively exorbitant, though nothing was cheap. The Hotel de Paris, he told her, charged five pounds for a cup of coffee. They wandered round the outside of the world-famous hotel, reflecting upon all the rich notables who had patronized it, and took a brief glimpse at the interior of the casino, breathtaking in its rich ornamentation.

"Since we are so near, let's take a look at Nice," Val suggested, and re-entering the car, he drove along the Moyenne Corniche, which Lois recognized from having seen it featured in many films, until they came to a bend in the road, which overlooked the honey-coloured city spread out below them, with its two miles of vast hotels strung along the Baie des Anges.

At length, wearied by so much sightseeing, Val took the new autostrada back into Italy. The great road runs behind the coast towns, with many tunnels through the mountains, and long bridges crossing ravines.

"For the privilege of driving along which we have to pay," Val remarked drily, as they stopped at one of the numerous tollgates. "It cost a fabulous sum to build and they have to reimburse themselves somehow."

The sun was beginning to sink, turning the sea to molten gold, as they reached familiar surroundings.

All day Val had been a cheerful and instructive companion, and all day Lois had been striving to push a sense of foreboding to the back of her mind, but she was conscious of a finality about the outing. It was the last one they would take together and Val meant it to be a memorable one.

He gave her dinner at his hotel in the Corso Roma, overlooking a street that was lined with orange trees. The fruit was never picked and hung in colourful balls among the dark green foliage, while here and there new blossom was in flower. Climbing roses were planted around their roots, the scented sprays curving round their trunks. They came out to take their coffee at the tables set out on the pavement, enfolded by the sensuous Italian night. People passed up and down seeking diversion, and Lois watched them idly, striving to imprint every impression, every fleeting sensation upon her memory to recall during the bleak days ahead, when Val had gone, for she had foreseen the parting that was to come.

"Why so pensive, kitten?" Val asked. "Are you tired after our long day?"

She brought her brooding gaze back to him and sighed. The lights shone down on his smooth black head, his bronzed arms and strong shoulders. She could not expect him to remember her for long, she was too plain and ordinary, and there would be other girls to act as kid sisters wherever he was going.

"You're leaving, aren't you?" she said flatly. "That's what you had to tell me."

"Yes," he confirmed quietly. "An urgent call to go to Germany. My playtime is over."

Lois had not intended to show emotion. She had been aware all along that this moment of parting must come, and had suspected all day that it was now, and had been steeling herself to meet it. But as she looked at his emotionless face, a wave of bitterness submerged her. He did not mind leaving her, she had served her turn. In Germany, if so inclined, he would pick up another girl, to be discarded in her turn when his wandering feet led him into some other country. Overwhelmed by the realization of coming loss, she said brokenly:

"Oh, Val, when you're gone, it'll be as if the sun had fallen out of the sky."

A look of almost consternation crossed his face, to be succeeded by a wondering stare.

"Kitten, can it be that you care?"

"Yes, I do." Pain made her reckless. "I've got a heart, if you haven't. We've been together every day for two weeks and now you're ready to rush off into the blue without giving me another thought. You won't miss me, I know, but I..." She gripped the edge of the table, striving to control the tears which had risen to her eyes. He leaned towards her and took one of her hands in his.

"Kitten, kitten, don't be so upset," he said gently. "I shall miss you damnably, but you've misled me. I thought you came out with me because you were lonely, and needed someone to take you about..." She made an inarticulate sound of distress. "On our first evening you said very definitely you didn't want to go any further, and I took it that all you desired was a good companion."

He looked at her interrogatively.

"That's all you wanted too," she said bitterly. "A substitute for your sister in Canada." She smiled wanly. "I tried my hardest to be sisterly, but..." Her voice died away.

"Sister!" he exclaimed contemptuously. "Kitten,

my feelings for you aren't in the least fraternal, and if we weren't in such a public place, I'd prove it to you."

She glanced up at him and saw a glow in his tawny eyes, and the lean fingers clasping hers tightened. She laughed excitedly. It seemed he was not indifferent after all.

"Then let's go somewhere private," she said daringly.

He smiled a little wryly.

"You want to be shown? God, kitten, I'd no idea you felt like this. I think we've wasted a lot of time."

A faint misgiving assailed her, to be instantly suppressed. He was going away, she would not see him again, and she wanted a warmer farewell than a mere handshake.

"We can't...part...like fishes," she said shakily.

He laughed. "I've no idea how fish make their farewells, but come." He drew her to her feet. "Let's go up to the Castello, it's been one of our favourite haunts, and it's the right place for us to say goodbye."

She allowed him to lead her to the car, with his arm encircling her waist. She was aware of him as she had never been before, and her heart was knocking against her ribs, but she had flung all caution away, all restraint. Whatever he wanted of her tonight she would give; up to now he had never seemed to desire more than her companionship, and that was galling for a girl in love.

He drove up past the hotel to the hill-top village above it, parking the car in a secluded spot, and she half dreaded, half longed for the demonstration that she had invited. But he did not touch her, beyond helping her out of the car. He locked it, and said quietly:

"Let's stroll about a bit."

He drew her arm through his, but that was all. He seemed to have something on his mind, for he was silent. She walked beside him, every nerve stretched for what he was going to say. Would it be a confession that he was bound to someone else, some girl, hitherto un-mentioned back in his home country? It was only too probable, and her impulsive words had embarrassed him.

They finally came to rest in the circular space before the church. Here a low wall separated them from a drop into the street below. The coastline was visible above the tops of the houses, a glittering panorama, lit by a thousand lights. It was very still except for an occasional car sliding down the hill. Most of the villagers were abed. From a nearby garden came the croak of bullfrogs, and a firefly shone like a jewel amidst the leaves of a nearby bush. They both sat down on the smooth top of the wall and Val lit a cigarette.

"How old are you, kitten?" he asked abruptly.

Lois was startled by the unexpected question.

"Twenty-one," she replied promptly.

"Are you really?" He sounded surprised. "But even so I can give you nearly ten years—it's a big gap."

"I like mature men," she said stubbornly.

"Thank you, mature sounds as if the grey hairs were already sprouting." He ran a hand over his black poll. "But that's because you're so young—you're very young for your years, kitten, and untouched. How did you manage to be so in a world where girls know everything before they're out of their teens?"

"I suppose you mean I'm very naïve and unsophisticated?"

"Thank God for that, I'm sick of sophisticated women."

Both of them thought of Nella, he with distaste, Lois with envy.

Val sighed. "It's something of a responsibility, and I'm well able to take care of myself," she said not very confidently.

"Are you, kitten? That I doubt." He looked away over the houses towards the sea. "You realize that my wife will have to live in Canada?"

For a moment she stared at him incredulously, then as the implication of his words reached her, a flood of joy ran through her.

"Oh, Val!" she breathed. "I'd live anywhere—with you."

"Would you, darling?" His voice was tender. "But you've only known me a fortnight."

"I think I've always known you," she said reflectively. "At least it seems like it."

He pinched her arm, and though it was too shadowed to see his face, she sensed his rueful smile.

"You haven't, you know, kitten. I've had a lot of life while you were growing up, experiences of which you might not approve."

"They're over and done with, aren't they?" she said sturdily. "They're nothing to do with me."

"Emphatically not, only your shining youth and innocence is a reproach to me."

"Bother my youth and innocence!" she flashed, impatient with this prevarication. Why could he not come to the point, if there was a point, instead of keeping her in palpitating expectancy? "They're things that will remedy with time."

"Unfortunately true, my kitten." His eyes searched her face, dimly illuminated by the light above the church. "I shall be away about a month," he went on, "and while I'm away, I want you to think very seriously about... our future."

"Val," she whispered. "Oh, Val, do you mean you're coming back?"

"Yes, of course, did you think I meant to leave you for ever?" he asked softly. "But it's too soon to make a decision yet. I shouldn't have mentioned it if I didn't have to go away and you hadn't been so upset."

This information chilled her growing elation. He did not want to commit himself. She told him so in no uncertain terms.

"You're wrong, kitten," he rebuked her. "It's you

I'm thinking about. It's so easy to be carried away in these beautiful surroundings, and you don't know me very well. I want you to wait until you're sure..."

"But I am sure," she interrupted vehemently.

"I don't think you've considered all that it entails. It would be a very big step for you. You would have to give up your friends, your family and your country."

"I haven't had much to do with my family since I went to work in London. My only real friend is there, and I'm sure I'll love your country, because it's yours."

"I could kiss you for that, but I daren't because here it's an offence to embrace in public, though there don't seem to be any policemen about. You'll write to me, of course. I'll have to write first to give you an address, as I don't know where I'm staying yet, but I can always get in touch with you? I mean you're a permanency at the Paradiso."

"Oh yes, Signor Merano asked me only the other day if I'd stay on through the winter."

"Then I'll always know where to find you. You see, you're static, while I shall be moving around."

The clock in the church tower struck a late hour; it had a tinny sound unworthy of its noble structure. Val stood up.

"I suppose we must call it a day," he sighed.

"When do you go?" Lois asked.

"Tomorrow morning, as soon as it's light."

"So early?" She was overwhelmed with dismay. His precipitate departure seemed ill-omened, as if he wanted to be away at the first possible moment.

"It's a long drive into Germany," he explained. "Up over the Brenner and across Austria. I shall be lucky if I can do it in one day."

She could not visualize the long road snaking over the mountain passes, taking him away from her into the unknown. Regardless of lurking policemen, she flung herself into his arms, clinging to him desperately.

"Don't go, Val, don't leave me!"

"But, kitten darling, I'll soon be back."

His arms closed round her trembling body and he kissed her long and closely. She surrendered to him utterly, her lips, her quivering limbs which melted into his. At long last she had gained what she had so passionately desired. Finally he put her from him, and gently disengaged himself from her clinging arms.

"That's enough, kitten," he said unsteadily, "or I shall forget myself. I have to go, darling, I'm not entirely a free agent, and I've already lingered here longer than I should have done because of you."

Desolation swept over her, an unreasonable conviction that he would never return. She had been anticipating the inevitable parting for so long that she could not assimilate his assertion that it would be only temporary.

Hysterically, she said over and over again:

"You will come back? You swear you'll come back?"

"My kitten, don't make such heavy weather of it," he chided her gently. "I'll be away a month at most, and I'll write as soon as I've an address to give you, or phone."

He drove her back to the hotel in silence. Neither could speak, their hearts were too full.

His parting kiss was tender more than passionate and he said almost gaily, "It's only *arriverderci*, sweetheart."

In her little room at the top of the hotel, Lois lay awake until the dawn broke, the dawn which would take Val out of her reach. She had discovered during the previous evening that miraculously Val did care for her, and he had hinted at a much closer relationship, but now he was gone. Her own self-betrayal had created the crisis that had led him to declare himself, but a little niggling doubt suggested that much of what he had said had been sop to placate her. His kisses had been ardent enough, he was not indifferent as she had supposed, but were they to be depended upon? When a girl offered herself, as she had done so recklessly, any full-blooded male would naturally respond. Her distress had moved him to endeavour to comfort her with promises to return, but whether they were genuine, only time would show, and she had only to wait until he wrote or phoned.

He did neither, and her doubts grew, though she tried to reassure herself by considering the many mishaps that might have occurred to account for his silence. More than once she surprised Nella hovering round the desk when the mail was delivered, but she would have no opportunity to intercept a letter as it was all taken to the manager for sorting.

The possibility that Val might have met with an accident amid the increasing holiday traffic haunted her, for she had developed all the nervous fears attendant upon the fate of a loved one. If that were so, she would never know what had occurred, for it was his next of kin in Canada who would be advised, and the idea brought home to her the tenuous nature of her connection with him. Until they were engaged she had no claim on him, and as each day passed without word from him, it became less and less likely that she ever would be.

Regarding the chances of an accident, she was unexpectedly relieved. After several anxious days, wondering how on earth she could make inquiries about Val, a young man came in one morning asking for accommodation. Lois told him regretfully that the hotel was full.

"Pity, this looks a nice place," he observed, looking about him. "Recommended to me by a fellow I met in Hamburg who'd been staying in this locality. Perhaps you know him? A dark chap, looks like a duke in disguise, but I'm darned if I can remember his name."

"Val?" she faltered. "Val Daventry?"

"Yes, that was it. Well, if you've no vacancy I'll have to try elsewhere. Good morning, miss."

He was gone before she could collect herself to ask any questions.

So Val had reached Germany and was well and uninjured, but he had not written as he had promised. There was always the possibility that his letter had gone astray, and there could be difficulties about transcontinental phone calls, also they were very expensive. If he had written he would not consider it necessary to phone. So she tried to reassure herself, fighting the growing conviction that he had not meant a word of what he had said to her at Diano Castello. She had forced the issue with her emotional outburst and perhaps at that time he had intended to return, but now he had got away, he had reconsidered the matter and decided it was better to leave well alone. She recalled how he had expressed doubts about the wisdom of a marriage between them, and though he had represented the situation from her point of view and had asked her to think it over, in reality he was voicing his own uncertainty.

She missed him sorely, and with no meeting with him to look forward to, her days assumed a dreary monotony.

Nella continued to give her constant pinpricks. On the morning after Val's departure, she had paused by the desk to say to her:

"Feeling a draught? He's gone, you know."

"Yes, I know," Lois had replied briefly. "But how did you know?"

"Oh, I met him in San Remo the night before last," Nella told her carelessly. "We had a flutter—I always bring him luck, you know—and then he told me that the time had come to move on. He confessed that he was afraid he had aroused expectations in you that he couldn't fulfil," the round eyes were malicious, "and he didn't know how to break with you. I advised him to make a few vague promises and get out fast. You'd soon forget him."

She had moved on, leaving Lois to ponder how much truth there was in her words. Val had been out when she had rung up that night, but he had mentioned a conference; however, he and his colleagues might have finished the night at San Remo, which he had not mentioned. She knew Nella had gone there that night, but she could not credit that Val would confide in her about herself, but Nella's words did nothing to restore her confidence in Val.

A little while after receiving the news that Val was in Hamburg, Lois encountered Nella going down in the lift. Miss Marshall seemed to be in a tearing rage, and all but spat at her.

"I'll get you out of this place if it kills me," she threatened shrilly. "Underhand, scheming little vixen!"

Lois had no clue as to what had produced this venom, unless Nella had contrived to intercept a message from Val, but that was so unlikely that she dismissed the thought as soon as it was born. If Val had tried to communicate with her, he had left it rather late in the day, and Nella had no access to the mail or the switchboard without being overlooked. Nevertheless the small incident had raised Lois's hopes. It was possible Nella thought Val might return and that was why she wanted to be rid of the receptionist. Lois paid scant regard to her threat, and in that she had underrated her. For one morning there was a hullabaloo. Nella Marshall's diamond pendant was missing and she insisted that it had been stolen by one of the staff. In vain Signor Merano tried to reason with her; he could vouch for all his employees, and the hotel took no responsibility for valuables that were not handed over to him for safe keeping. Nella was adamant—search the hotel staff or she would call in the police.

Signor Merano felt a police visit was bad publicity. Reluctantly he told Lois:

"*Madonna mia*, I cannot 'ave ze police 'ere. What

will ze guests zink? Zo, if ze staff leave, feeling insulted, it will be, what you say, just too bad."

Lois said she did not think he ought to give in to Nella. She doubted if she would carry out her threat, and she was enjoying the embarrassment she was causing.

He shook his head gloomily. "I dare not risk it, ze search will 'ave to be made."

So it was instigated, and carried out by himself and his wife. Signora Merano found the pendant among Lois's underwear.

"*Dio mio*, I could not my eyes believe!" the Signorina declared. "But it was zere. I would 'ave sworn by ze Madonna 'erself zat ze Signorina Lang was incapable of theft."

Lois was sure it had been planted and she had a good idea by whom. Violetta's room was on the same floor as hers, and she had a passkey, but she could produce no proof.

Signor Merano sent for her. He was shamefaced and embarrassed.

"She insists zat you go, Lois," he told her regretfully. "It is zat, or she will go to the police, and she will never come 'ere again. She is very good client, every spring she come, and if zere is a police case, it will be very difficult for you. I am sure zat you did not take it, but zey do not know you as I do. I am afraid..." actual tears shone in his dark eyes, "zere is only one way out. You will 'ave to go."

"Yes, I can see that," Lois agreed dully. She knew the whole thing had been engineered by Nella to procure her dismissal, and if the police were called in, it was obvious they would listen to her, for she had wealth and position, whereas Lois had no adequate defence, and accusations against Violetta could not be proved.

Signor Merano was well aware that he was playing a coward's part, but he naturally thought first of his hotel. One English girl was easily expendable. He salved his conscience by paying Lois's fare back to England. He said it was the least he could do.

"There's something else you can do for me," Lois told him. "If... if Signor Daventry rings up and inquires for me, will you please tell him what has happened?"

But Merano demurred. He did not wish outsiders informed of this sad occurrence. He wanted the whole sorry business forgotten.

"Then please tell him where I've gone," Lois insisted.

The hotelier looked at her commiseratingly. "You 'ave 'ad a very 'appy 'oliday affair, *si*?" he asked. "But it is over, *poverina*. Men go away and forget. Me, I speak like your *padre*. Go away and forget also. You make ze new life in your own country, *si*? Zat is best."

He patted her shoulder kindly, but Lois was not deceived. She had unwittingly brought unpleasantness into his comfortable life, for he loved the conviviality of the hotel, and he wanted to forget about her as quickly as possible. If Val learned the truth, he might insist upon vindicating her, which would precipitate the very crisis the manager was so anxious to avoid. Signor Merano, for all his expressions of sympathy, was unwilling to allow Val to contact her.

She had no choice but to go; she had not the funds to stay on in Diano Marina to see if Val returned when the month was up. Nor was she likely to be able to obtain other employment there. Signor Merano would deny her a reference if she went against his wishes, and Nella would do her best to defame her.

She had only one hope to which to cling. If Val did come back to Italy in search of her, he would get the truth out of Signor Merano and follow her. He was not the sort of man to allow himself to be put off with excuses. But would he come back?

During the flight to England, her confidence sank to

zero. Signor Merano, Nella, all of them regarded her connection with Val as a holiday interlude, and probably they were right. Two girls sitting beside her were discussing just such another episode and she could not help overhearing most of their conversation.

One, a tearful blonde, was reiterating that dear Carlo had said he would write, he had declared that he loved her, and he just could not forget her. The other, more hard-boiled, was telling her friend not to be a fool. Holiday friendships had no aftermath. Carlo would pick up another girl to console himself, and she would find another boy next year.

Lois insisted to herself that Val was different. He was not Italian for a start, and though his promise to return might have been prompted by a desire to comfort her for his inevitable departure, there had been no need to embroider it with what amounted to a proposal of marriage unless he was serious. Though his subsequent silence was disheartening, she could not wholly quench all hope, and hope had been nourished by Nella's determination to have her evicted before Val could come back, which indicated Nella thought he would appear again.

As she was certain that Signor Merano would be unwilling to disclose what had happened, or to furnish Val with the means of tracing her, Lois had confided in the head waiter, Enrico, to the extent of persuading him to promise to give Signor Daventry her home address, if he should come in search of her. This he had agreed to do.

It was fortunate for her peace of mind that she was not to know that a domestic disaster was to cause Enrico to leave the Paradiso shortly after she had gone herself.

CHAPTER FOUR

WHEN Lois left Italy, she did not go home. She shrank from the questions which she would be asked about her job and the reason for its abrupt termination. It was much easier to write a brief explanation, not the truth, but merely that she had had enough of foreign parts for the time being. She knew her parents were busy with preparations for their own holiday—in Scotland, and her sudden arrival would embarrass them. She had two elder brothers, but both were married and since their acquisition of wives had grown away from her. She felt no inclination to confide in any of them.

Instead she went to join her friend Joanna Clarke. Luckily Joanna had just parted with her flatmate and was ready and willing to have Lois to live with her again. Signor Merano had given Lois a good testimonial, ignoring the Nella episode, which showed how little he believed in it. Lois obtained a position with a travel agency and settled down to life in London. But even to Joanna, she did not mention Val.

It was bad enough waiting and hoping, watching the post, especially for any letter forwarded from her home address, without her friend sharing her anticipation which was always disappointed. Besides which, she knew Joanna was a matter-of-fact sort of girl who would pour cold water upon the frail bloom of optimism that she was cherishing. But as time went by, it began to wilt, for the date was passed when Val was due to revisit the Paradiso.

It was possible that he had found another girl in Germany to deputize for the kid sister, and she had driven all memory of Lois out of his mind. Yet some instinct insisted that Val was not fickle, and though he had dropped Nella for her, he had never pretended the other girl was more to him than a lucky mascot at the gaming tables.

She was confident that Enrico would have found an opportunity to give Val her address, if he did return, for the waiter, in common with most of her colleagues, had considered she was a victim of Nella's spite, and knew that the handsome Inglese was the cause of it. Being Italian he had a natural leaning towards romance and intrigue and had been eager to help her. It never occurred to her that he was no longer at the hotel.

Back in England, her life in Liguria had taken on a dreamlike quality. Monte Carlo, Diano Marina and Castello were remembered like a film in bright technicolor, except for the ache in her heart, there was nothing dreamlike about that, it was a painful fact, and the long-drawn-out period of waiting gave her scant comfort to assuage it, for it seemed each passing day lessened the likelihood of receiving a communication from Val.

As a diversion, which seemed like a pilgrimage, though she could not say why, except that the place had a mysterious attraction for her, she went again to Erne Hall, choosing a Sunday when Joanna was otherwise engaged. It was a glorious summer's day, almost like Italy. The coach upon which she was travelling passed through the miles of surburban London westward, until finally it reached the country. The trees were in full leaf, corn was coming into ear in the fields and the scent of new-mown hay perfumed the air. Lois felt her spirits rise. She was coming to Erne to renew her acquaintanceship with the portrait of the fifth Earl, and she had the quite unreasonable expectation that he would have some message for her.

The coach decanted its passengers at the entrance gate, where several others were parked, and Lois went with the crowd of visitors into the wide forecourt before the main building.

Erne Hall had been built on the site of an older manor house, and belonged to the period when the great houses of England had been most flourishing, the revenues from farms and cottages supporting their lords in affluence, before taxation had crippled them, and only the interest of the public in their past grandeur at the rate of fifty pence a head enabled them to be maintained at all.

From the forecourt the façade of Erne Hall was an impressive sight. A broad flight of steps led up to the great entrance door, supported by pillars, which extended upwards to a square tower adorned with stone statues. A group of statuary flanked the approach on each side. On either side of this portal, six tall windows, three above and three below, surmounted by stone balustrades and more statues, marked the main edifice, each with its paved court in front of it.

Beyond this was what might be termed the residential part of the hall. Long façades of windows, each ending in a square tower, and each approached by its own flight of shallow steps. Wings were built out from each extremity, so that the whole building formed a three-sided square.

The forecourt, which covered a wide expanse, ended in a terrace overlooking the extensive grounds. The land sloped down to a river, which emptied itself into a lake. On the further side was parkland, rising slightly upwards, bisected by a long ride, bordered by trees, in the centre of which was some sort of monument.

One wing of the building was closed to the public, for Lord Erne still lived there, but without the state that had been the prerogative of his forebears.

The river was crossed by a honey-coloured bridge overlooking the lake. There was a legend about that bridge. The fifth Earl had loved and wooed a village girl, but he would not or could not make a mesalliance.

On the night when he was celebrating his marriage to the local heiress, the girl had thrown herself off the bridge, and in the morning her drowned body was fished out of the lake. She was supposed to haunt the scene of her suicide, and there were people who swore they had seen her.

Lois went into the Great Hall with the herd of coach tourists. Pillars soared up to the roof, for it was the full height of the building. Stone galleries were built between them on the levels of the first and second floors, and were accessible from the rooms behind them. A wide staircase went up on the left, barred with a red cord for it led into the Earl's private apartments. A big door at the top of some shallow steps faced the entrance; it led into the banquet room, where, Lois knew from her former visit, the long table would be set as for a meal with its double row of carved chairs. The guide had told them that it was used by the family once a year at Christmas, when all Lord Erne's kindred foregathered to dine in state as they had done in days gone by.

Corridors went off right and left on either side of the banquet room door leading to drawing-rooms, sitting-rooms, and the library on the right. Lois detached herself from the crowd following the guide and went down the left-hand corridor. She knew the location of what she had come to see.

It hung in a little alcove, the portrait of the fifth Earl. He stood against a background of red drapery, dressed in a blue satin coat and knee-breeches, one hand caressing the head of an Irish wolfhound. It was an artificial composition, typical of its period, a hundred and fifty years ago. He wore a powdered wig, but the face it framed was one she knew. There were the slightly aquiline nose, the level black brows, the firm mouth, curved in a cynical smile that was almost a sneer, and the eyes, tawny like a lion's which seemed to look straight at her. It was not her fancy. Val Daventry and the fifth Earl might have been brothers, though the pictured face was older and more worldly. Position and power had marked it with a lordly arrogance, but the likeness was astonishing.

Lois wandered out into the grounds and down the long slope to the bridge. She had no wish to complete the tour of the rooms. Her mind was full of conjecture. Could there possibly be a link between the English Earl and the Canadian? Val's ancestors had emigrated and in spite of his denial that there were any aristocrats in his pedigree, it was credible that he had been misinformed. Younger sons went abroad to make their fortunes independent of their families. By a curious natural freak, Val had reproduced the features of a man who might be one of his forebears, and he also seemed to have inherited some of his attributes. A girl had drowned herself for love of the faithless Earl, and fidelity did not seem to be among the virtues of the Earls of Erne.

A thought struck her and she turned to the back of the brochure which she had bought at the entry, and which gave the family tree. The name Percival Daventry occurred more than once, and it was that of the fifth Earl.

She had asked if Val were an abbreviation and he had said that he used it because he did not like his first name. Had he had any idea that it stemmed from a noble family?

Lois leaned on the parapet of the bridge, looking down into the water swirling through the archways into the lake beyond. It was here that the deserted girl had stood while the Hall was lit with bright lights and echoed to the sounds of the pageantry of her lover's wedding. She could visualize it clearly—that great pile of masonry illuminated from cellars to attics, the thronging guests in velvet and satin, that black-browed man with his cynical smile sitting beside his aristocratic bride in the great banqueting room, while down here in the dark and stillness, a pale, forgotten girl found she could bear no more.

The water hypnotized her. She leaned further over the parapet. Such an easy way out, an end to all heartache and pain. Her own unhappiness over Val's desertion became intensified, as if some aura from the tragic past was enfolding her. She was not herself, she was that other girl, and the river beckoned with its promise of forgetfulness.

"Shouldn't lean so far over, miss, that water's deep."

Lois started, coming back it seemed through a maze of years to the present day. It was not dark, it was sunlit daytime, and the hall was a grey pile without light. Coming towards her across the bridge was a young girl wearing an abbreviated mini-skirt and a sleeveless blouse. Lois drew back hastily.

"You came with the coach load?" the girl asked. "They haven't finished touring the house yet."

"I know, but I got tired of trailing round in a crowd. Do you belong here?"

"Sort of—I work in the estate office. I'm Susie," the girl informed her. "Why not take a pew?" She sat down on a stone shelf that protruded below the parapet of the bridge. "Sightseeing isn't half wearing on the feet." She patted the stone bench beside her.

Lois sat down and Susie produced a packet of sandwiches.

"Always bring my lunch out here when it's fine," the girl went on. "Have one."

"No, thank you. I couldn't take your lunch."

"Go on, there's plenty here. I'm never hungry when it's so hot. That one's cucumber."

Not wanting to snub the newcomer, Lois accepted the sandwich. Susie squinted against the sunlight, looking up at the Hall.

"There'll be great goings on up there next week when Torr comes back," she announced. "They're giv-

ing a ball to celebrate his engagement. Poor old
Torr... got caught at last.''

"Who is Torr?" Lois asked without much interest.

"Why Lord Torrington, of course, I was forgetting
you're a stranger here. He's the Earl's son and heir.
Oh, he's a super guy!" Susie's eyes shone. "Not a
scrap of side. Comes into the office... 'Hi, Susie darling,' he says. 'Still pounding the old typewriter? Give
us a kiss.'" Susie giggled self-consciously. She was very
young, not much more than sixteen, Lois judged, a
slim, fair child with ingenuous blue eyes. "I'm going to
ask him if he can't sneak me in somewhere to see the
party. He will too, he's a sport."

"He's not here now?" Lois recalled she had said
"comes back".

"Oh, no, he's on the Continent, having a last fling
before the Hon. Cis—beg pardon, the Honourable Cecilia Anstruther, we all call her the Hon. Cis—gets her
hooks into him. Loves the Continent, does Torr, especially Paris and the casinos at Monte Carlo and San
Remo." Lois started. "'Course he's got to marry
money, and Miss Anstruther's well oiled, but he
doesn't love her, of that I'm sure. Poor old Torr, he's
one for the girls too, and now he'll have his wings
clipped. Rumour says Daddy wrote him a pretty strong
letter, when he was in Italy, telling him he'd got to
come home and do his duty."

Suspicion stirred in Lois as fragments of conversation
returned to her... "isn't who he says he is"... "travelling incognito"... "the opportunity for deception is
too tempting"... "elusive about his background"...
She said faintly:

"Has he ever been in Canada?"

Susie flashed her a look of surprise.

"I don't know; probably, he's been everywhere. But
it's Italy he likes best." She giggled again. "Says the
signorinas are super. He doesn't use his title when he's
abroad, he declares everyone puts up their prices if

they scent he's a lord. I bet he's led some poor souls up the garden." Her childish face became grave. "I don't suppose he's got a clue how much a broken heart can hurt."

"You've got a crush on him yourself?" Lois asked gently, for it seemed clear that Susie was infatuated with the heir of Erne.

"I'm not the only one," Susie returned. "Women are all over him. Not only is he good-looking, but he's got what it takes, though of course he'd never look at me, he thinks I'm a child."

"You are very young," Lois pointed out mechanically, for her mind was in a whirl of conjecture. Could it be possible that Val Daventry and Lord Torrington were the same person?

"I'm grown up," Susie said with an air of importance, "only he doesn't realize it, but then he's a lot older than me, nearly thirty, though he doesn't seem like it, he's always so full of fun."

A voice from the past echoed in Lois's ears.

"I can give you nearly ten years."

"I guess I'll get over it," Susie went on, her eyes on the distant hall. "I'm not like that silly girl who drowned herself, though if the guy in the picture was like Torr, she had some excuse. It seems a bit hard he's got to get tied up to that horse-faced Honourable, she's a bit grim."

"That will be a fitting revenge for all the broken hearts he's strewn behind him," Lois said caustically.

Susie looked at her wonderingly.

"You sound vicious. You can't blame him, you know, dames do throw themselves at his head."

So had she when she had sought Val's arms in Diano Castello. After all, he had made no promises, only said he would come back to see if she were still of the same mind. But he had known very well he would never come back. The summons to leave Italy could have been his father's letter, which Susie had mentioned.

"What does Lord Torrington look like?" she asked, though she suspected that she knew.

"Oh, he's a typical Daventry," Susie told her with a quaint air of patronage, as if the family were her own property. "Tall and dark with the most gorgeous eyes, yellow...no, more tawny, with the look of an eagle about him, but then Erne means eagle. I wish you could see him, then you'd know why we all fall for him."

"I wish I could," Lois agreed, for then she would know, but surely she was rushing to conclusions? Though Val had never enlarged upon his Canadian background, he could not have fabricated it—or could he? If he wished to conceal his real identity when abroad, naturally he would need to construct some sort of story to account for himself to those people with whom he became intimate. It hurt her that he had considered it was necessary to deceive herself, though the reason was obvious—not wanting to form a permanent connection he had assumed his Canadian identity as a cloak to disguise himself from the women he collected on his travels.

"There's the Harris kid again," Susie broke into her thoughts, pointing to where a small figure in blue was playing at the water's edge. "Sooner or later he's going to fall in and it's to be hoped someone will be at hand to pull him out. His mum doesn't seem to care—she's the lodgekeeper's wife, you know, not the main lodge, but one on the other side of the park. Ah, she's come to find him," as a woman's figure sped towards the child. "She ought to forbid him to play by the lake."

"I think she has, and he's disobeyed her." But Lois was indifferent to the little drama being enacted on the other side of the bridge. Mum was angry with Junior, and her scolding was followed up by a sharp slap or two.

Junior responded with a roar that was audible to the spectators on the bridge.

Mother proceeded to haul her son towards his home, and was obviously enraged by his disobedience, the more so because anger covered anxiety. They disappeared into the park.

Lois's eyes fell to the back cover of the brochure she was carrying, on which was printed the arms of Erne. Appropriately the golden shield was charged with an eagle, in correct heraldic parlance, "Or, an eagle displayed, sable."

Where had she seen that bird before? She recalled a pair of cuff-links engraved with an eagle "displayed", which Val had asked her to put in her bag for safe keeping amid the Ligurian Apennines, saying they were valuable and he did not want to lose them. She had wondered then if they were inherited or looted.

Trying to speak casually, she asked:

"When is this Lord Torrington expected home?"

Susie laughed. "No one expects Torr, he just turns up when he thinks he will. He'll have to be here for the ball next week, but I bet he doesn't show up until the last minute. It's going to be a gorgeous do." Susie's face shone with enthusiasm. "Everyone is to be in fancy dress, even the servants. That's her idea, the Hon. Cis—she's all for the stately home business and what not. Re... resuscitating the past, she calls it. I call it a lot of old hat, and I bet Torr does too. He'd prefer a modern party in casual clothes, but that wouldn't suit her ladyship, and as she can't rely upon the County to dig up its white ties and tails out of the mothballs, she's decided they must represent their ancestors. Of course it'll cost a packet, and Lord Erne isn't over-flush, but I guess now he's sure of the Anstruther pennies, he thinks he can spread a bit. The letters I've had to type to caterers and costumiers, you wouldn't believe! Of course Erne will be closed to the public for a week—did you see the notices?"

Lois had not, she had been too preoccupied with her own thoughts.

"Perhaps Lord Torrington will come as the fifth Earl?" she queried, visualizing Val in the velvet coat and

satin breeches of the period. Once she had told him
how well they would become him, never dreaming an
occasion might arise when he would be so clad, if he
were this Lord Torrington. He would look superb and
completely in character—in more ways than one.

"Oh, you've noticed that?" Susie seemed surprised.
"Well, you asked what Torr looked like, and that portrait might be him. It's typical Daventry phiz, crops up
at least once in every generation. Sure you won't have
another sandwich? I've got more than I want."

Lois declined hastily, to try to eat would choke her.
Susie gathered up the debris of her meal.

"Mustn't leave litter about," she stated, "else I'll be
barred from the grounds." She looked a little anxiously
at Lois. "Guess I've run on a bit, but you seemed so
interested. I'm not really supposed to gossip about the
family and its affairs, you see my job's confidential."
She drew herself up trying to assume an air of mature
dignity. "But you don't belong here, and I guess you'll
forget it all when you get back to London."

"Probably," Lois said mendaciously, knowing she
would not forget a word of Susie's disclosures. "And
I'm very discreet. I've held confidential posts myself.
You've a very graphic way of expressing yourself."

Susie looked gratified. "When I'm old, I'll write my
reminiscences, for the Sunday papers," she declared.
"There's always some nuts who want to know about
high life, for all we're supposed to be democrats." She
looked at Lois with sudden concern. "I say, you do
look pale. Sure you're feeling all right?"

"Oh yes, but it's very hot," Lois observed vaguely.

"And me keeping you sitting in the sun! Better get
into the shade. Would you like to come and sit in my
office? It's nice and cool there and my boss never gets
back from lunch before three."

Lois refused this kindly offer. She was normally pale,
she insisted, and did not need first aid. She wanted passionately to be alone.

Susie went off with a cheerful wave of her hand, and Lois crossed the bridge and made for the shade of the trees on the further side. The coach passengers were scheduled to partake of a light lunch in the refreshment room which had been converted from the undercroft on the opposite side of the residence to that occupied by Lord Erne. It overlooked the flower beds and the water gardens. Lois had no desire to join them; she could not in her present disturbed state endure the chatter and laughter of her fellow passengers.

The woods were deserted; a path led through a thicket to a well deep in the shade, a spot which legend said had been the bower of a royal mistress, who had also come to an unhappy end. Erne had its full quota of unfortunate ladies, Lois thought. She was mulling over all that Susie had told her about Lord Torrington, who dropped his title when he went abroad and travelled as Percival Daventry.

It seemed more than probable that he was the Val she had known, and that being so, he had been engaged to Cecilia Anstruther during the time he had squired her, and knew he must return to marry her. Having a last fling, Susie had said, and "Torr's a one for the girls." Yet that description did not ring quite true. Val had made no attempt to seduce her; even on that last night he had treated her with respectful consideration, too considerate—to spare her feelings he had said he would come back and hinted at marriage. He did not quite fit the picture of a rake and a libertine that Susie had drawn. But there must be some connection— the likeness to the fifth Earl, the similar name, the cuff-links with the Daventry badge, the fact that Lord Torrington was known to be in Italy visiting the San Remo casino at the same time, were more than coincidences. Nor had he written or phoned her after he had gone, and now she had been given a good reason for his silence.

But she was not convinced. There was only one way

in which she could make sure. She must see this Lord
Torrington unknown to him, and satisfy herself that he
was, or was not, Val. It would not be easy, since Susie
thought he would not return until the day of the ball,
and on that day Erne would be closed to visitors.

Her common sense argued that she had much better let well alone. If Val had deserted her it made no
difference who he was. She had much better put him
out of her mind and avoid Erne and its owners in future. It had been a mistake on her part to come down
today to sentimentalize over the fifth Earl and his likeness to Val Daventry. If the likeness included character, she was well rid of his descendant. She recalled
the cynical sneer on the handsome painted mouth.
She had seen that same smile on Val's lips when Nella
had provoked him. Nella! That first night when Val
had spoken to her, he had been in a furious rage because a woman had dared to stand him up. That was
what one would expect from a spoilt darling like Lord
Torrington, who believed himself invincible. He had
been quick to transfer his attentions to herself, balm
for hurt vanity, but that was all. He had taken her out
to flaunt her in Nella's face, to show the other woman
how easily he could do without her, but he had never
really been serious about herself. If she had not betrayed her own feelings to him, he would have gone
away happily without a regret. Like many men he was
moved by feminine tears, though she had not actually
wept and he had gone further than he had intended in
an attempt to comfort her. Such kindness was cruelty
when it aroused expectations which he did not intend
to fulfil.

If what she now suspected was true, there could have
been no question of a reunion. He must have known
that he could not afford to marry for love. Again her
heart revolted. Val, the man she loved, could not have
been such a heel as to deliberately talk about the disad-
vantages she would have to face if she went to Canada

with him, while he knew very well there was no question of her ever doing any such thing.

But the fact remained that he had not communicated with her, and if he were this Lord Torrington, it would explain his silence. It was possible that when he had arrived in Germany he had received even more pressing demands to return home, and had decided it would be wiser not to see her again.

In that case it was death to the faint hope that she had been cherishing, but she still could not bring herself to believe that he was this not very estimable nobleman.

The winding path wended through bushes and young trees, with occasional glimpses of the lake upon her left. It ended in a stretch of green sward, in the centre of which was the well. In the old days it must have been a pleasant sylvan spot, suitable for lovers' trysts, and once there had been a dwelling here, served by the sweet well waters, but now it had been covered in and surrounded by a heavily meshed wire fence to prevent too adventurous visitors falling in.

Looking about her, it occurred to Lois that if Val were Lord Torrington, these surroundings must be familiar to him, for here he would have spent his boyhood, and it was not surprising he had been reticent about his home life, if that home had been Erne.

It would have been fatally easy to make a slip, for Erne must be very different from the place that he alleged was where he came from. It would also explain the secret of its fascination for her. Some subtle intuition had linked it with him in her mind, even while she was wanting to deny his connection with it.

The discoveries that she had made that day had brought him back into the forefront of her thoughts with an increasing longing for his presence. The portrait had brought his features vividly before her. Lines from Shakespeare, dredged from her schooldays, recurred to her:

"Thy tongue, thy face, thy limbs, action and spirit.
Do give thee five-fold blazon."

Val bore in his person the blazon of the Daventrys of
Erne, he looked as if he might well be Lord Torrington,
and Nella had remarked it. It was only her naïve,
simple self who had been so easily deceived.

The Daventrys lived by a different code from her
own straightforward one, and beguiling unsuspecting
maidens was to them an amusing game. But still she
could not reconcile her memories of Val with such a
role.

She turned her head, half expecting to see him coming through the trees, as he might have done many
times in the past. She felt a bitter-sweet pleasure in indulging her sentimental fancies, in believing she was
treading where he had trod.

Then she remembered the kid sister, the one subject
about which he had been expansive; was she an inven-
tion too?

She referred again to the family tree in the brochure.
On the occasion of her first visit she had not glanced at
it, the lineage of the Earls of Erne having no interest
for her then. She had little dreamed how significant it
would become. She discovered that the present Earl
had had three children; Lord Torrington, his heir and a
second son who had died in boyhood, and a much
younger daughter, as the date of her birth indicated. So
the sister did exist, but it had not been in Canada where
they had ridden and swum together, but in this park,
and in that lake.

How skilfully he had deluded her with his pretence
of scorn for the aristocracy, his democratic views, but it
would have been part of the act he put on to preserve
his incognito, for a hint of his real status would have
sent his expenses soaring. Suddenly she recalled that
Val had told her Nella seemed to suspect he was other
than he was. That might have been why he became so

anxious to discard her, and Nella had suspected something, for many of her veiled remarks now became clear. She had also told Lois that Cinderella was an unlikely fairy story, meaning that Lord Torrington would not stoop to a hotel receptionist.

"Well, Cinderella had better get herself back to her kitchen, or rather the tourist office," she said aloud, for the shadows were lengthening and the coach driver would be collecting his flock, prior to their return. "And if I've any sense, I'll keep away from Erne in future. Whether Val is Lord Torrington or whether he isn't, it won't make a lot of difference to me."

But the next week-end found her back at Erne, for she was unable to keep away from it. The place had for her an irresistible fascination. Like the drowned girl she had to return, for though she had met Val in Italy, the house and grounds seemed to be permeated by his presence. It was the last day upon which the public would be admitted before the ball.

Throughout her journey she chided herself for being a fool, she had nothing to gain by haunting Erne, and moreover there was no scheduled coach tour that day and she had to make a tedious journey, changing buses. Having bought her admission ticket, she paused in the forecourt, looking at the steps which led up to the private rooms. A large notice stated, "Private. Visitors not allowed beyond this point", but tradesmen and friends must ascend those steps. Could she invent a pretext later in the week and inquire for Lord Torrington? Then she would know for certain. If he were Val, what would he do, she wondered, confronted with her unexpected presence? Awkward for him, with the Honourable Cecilia Anstruther about to be proclaimed his betrothed, but still more awkward for her.

A car drew up at the steps, and the chauffeur opened the door for its occupant to get out. He was an elderly man in shabby clothes, with an ancient deerstalker on his head, but the beetling brows and hawk's eyes, the

aquiline nose, proclaimed that he was no mean personage. Lois guessed he was the Earl. He cast a keen glance
around, saw her standing in mid-distance, said something to the chauffeur, and turned to ascend the steps.
The chauffeur moved towards her, but Lois hurried
away before he could reach her. She had been caught
gaping at her betters, and she would never have the
courage to go up those steps.

She went at once to the portrait of the fifth Earl. The
artist had used the trick that makes the eyes of a picture
appear to look straight at the observer. Today his smile
seemed more cynical than ever. The painted face betrayed the disillusionment of its subject—a man who
had drunk deep of life's pleasures and had become sati-
ated. Val might look like that in a few years' time.

Lois turned away and went out into the grounds. The
lodgekeeper's child was again playing among the reeds.
An urchin of four or five years, he was venturesome.
He was straddling a log of wood, trying to push it out
into the lake. The log rolled over and the boy went in
head first down into the weedy water. There was no
one in sight, except Lois, and she acted promptly. She
plunged in among the reeds, and found the water was
much deeper than she had expected. Before she could
reach the child, she had to swim. He was entangled
among the weeds, and she had difficulty in raising him.
She hoped he was still alive. Somehow she got him to
the bank and laying him flat applied her very rudimen-
tary knowledge of life-saving. Water poured from his
mouth and presently, to her enormous relief, he hic-
upped. Then his mother appeared on the scene and
stared in horror at the half-drowned boy.

"He'll be all right," Lois said reassuringly through
chattering teeth. "I got him out in time." There was a
chill breeze blowing and she was soaked.

"Miss... miss, I don't know how to thank you," the
woman gasped. "He's that mischievous, time and time
again I've told him..." She broke off, becoming aware

of Lois's condition. "But you're wet through!" She was stripping off her cardigan to wrap round the child. "You must come with me, and get them wet things off before you catch a chill. It's only a short way to the lodge." She picked up the child. "My name's Clara Harris," she called over her shoulder, "and I'll soon get you dry and warm."

Thankful for this offer, Lois retrieved her handbag from the bank where she had left it, and pursued her dripping way after the couple in front of her.

Arrived at the lodge, Mrs. Harris gave Lois a blanket in which to wrap herself, while her clothes were being dried, and carried her child off to bed. He—his name was Eric—was protesting loudly, for he was fast recovering from his immersion, but his parent was adamant.

"There you'll stay for the rest of the day," she said grimly. "And perhaps that'll learn you to do what you're told!"

She returned to the kitchen to make tea for the rescuer, and insisted that Lois sat in front of the electric fire in her little sitting-room, while she drank it, in spite of the warmth of the day.

"You mustn't get chilled, miss."

She brought her own cup to keep her visitor company, and after having ascertained that Lois had come with a coach load of visitors, her conversation turned to the ball, which was to be given during the following week.

"We've all been roped in to help," she told Lois, "though of course I'd be the first one to be asked, seeing as I know the layout of the Hall, my mum having worked there. 'Course, they've got a lot of waiters and whatnot coming down from London supplied by the caterers, but they'll need dish-washers and such. The Hon. Cis, she's very thorough, she says even the washers-up are to wear long dresses and mob caps, to help create what she calls atmosphere, whatever that

may be. My, it'll be a sight to be talked of for years to
come!"

"I'd give anything to see it," Lois exclaimed fervently.

"I expect you would, miss, so would many others.
It'll be a night to remember."

Lois sighed. The night when Lord Torrington became officially engaged to Cecilia Anstruther would be
a night to remember with despair, if he were indeed
Val Daventry. She only needed one glimpse to set all
her doubts at rest, either way. But how was she to see
him, without him seeing her? An idea came to her.

"Will you be needing any extra help?" she asked
tentatively.

"Shouldn't think so, miss." She suddenly perceived
Lois's drift. "You mean as you'd give a hand so as you
could see the show?"

"I wondered if it would be possible."

Mrs. Harris eyed her doubtfully. "'Tisn't the sort of
work you're used too, I'm thinking."

"I can wash dishes, Mrs. Harris, it doesn't require
much skill."

"Well, there's a right way and a wrong way of doing
everything." Suddenly she laughed. "It would be a bit
of a lark," she decided. "It could be done if I use my
loaf."

"Yes?" Lois looked at her eagerly.

Mrs. Harris sobered. "Look you, miss, I owes you a
debt I can't ever repay. Reckon you saved young Eric's
life, so if you're really set on seeing this ball, I guess I
can get you in as one of us. Mind you, all you're likely
to get is a squint through a hatch, and a lot of hard
work. 'Tisn't like being a guest, you know."

"Of course I realize that." A squint through a hatch
would show her what she wanted to know. "I don't
mind the work."

Mrs. Harris puckered her brows. "You aren't a local
girl, miss?"

"No, but I could hire a room for the night some-where," Lois suggested.

"No need to do that. You can stay here if you don't mind sharing with Eric. I've got a camp bed. Not that there'll be much of the night left by the time we're through."

Lois was profuse in her thanks. She would have to ask for the afternoon off, as the event was mid-week, and she might be late in next morning, but she would have to risk that. To see Lord Torrington had become almost an obsession with her, and the means whereby she could do so had been miraculously offered to her, at the cost of a small amount of discomfort. Almost she could have blessed Eric for falling into the lake.

Mrs. Harris cut her short. "The debt's on our side," she insisted. "There's nothing Harris and I wouldn't do for you after saving Eric. He's a scamp, but he's the light of our eyes. Reckon I'll have to get Harris to put a lock on the yard gate so he can't get out on his own. Eric'll hate it, but I'm running no more risks with that there lake."

Lois murmured that such a measure would be very wise, and her hostess reverted to the night of nights.

"You'll come here first, of course, and I'll have your dress ready for you. I'll say you're a cousin of mine and I roped you in to help. Not that you look much like kin of mine." She considered Lois's pale face, around which her hair hung in damp reddish curls, her slight figure and fine bones, which contrasted with her own comely curves. "Better open your mouth as little as you can," she advised. "You don't talk like us—not that anybody'll notice in all that crush, though we do all have to be vouched for. Private detectives hovering, I shouldn't wonder, but don't you worrit, I'll fix it."

Lois was sure she would. Mrs. Harris exuded an air of competency. Nor did she think it strange that her guest should be so anxious to view the ball. It was the most exciting event that had happened at Erne for a

very long while. Lois realized that she would have to
think up an excuse to account to Joanna for a night's
absence. She had never mentioned Val Daventry to her
and it was too late to embark upon lengthy explanations; moreover, Joanna with her shrewd common
sense would be sure to declare the whole plan was
crazy. Perhaps it was, but Lois was aware of an increasing excitement. Not only was she going to have a
"squint" at this wondrous ball, an event from which
she had learned that press photographers and reporters
were to be rigidly excluded, but she might be going to
see Val again, and she was yearning for a sight of him,
though if all the evidence that she had collected added
up correctly, he would be proved faithless. If that were
so, she would have the heartbreaking experience of
watching him plight his troth to another woman, but
that was something she was prepared to face for the
sake of knowing the truth. On the other hand, if she
discovered he was not this Lord Torrington, she would
be reassured that she had not been discarded for the
Honourable Cecilia Anstruther and she could still cherish the faint hope that he might come into her life again
with an explanation for his failure to communicate with
her.

She was determined that nothing should prevent her
from witnessing this ball when fate in the person of
young Eric had so providentially offered her the chance
to do so.

CHAPTER FIVE

Lois left London after lunch on the fateful day, having obtained her afternoon off, with a promise to work overtime to make it up, and a garbled explanation to Joanna, whose curiosity was far from satisfied. She arrived at the Harrises' cottage as the sun was beginning to sink.

She found her hostess in a state of pleasurable excitement, which had penetrated her usual phlegm. The Harrises' lives were centred in "the big house". Mrs. Harris's mother had been a housemaid there, and her husband's family had worked in the grounds as gardeners for several generations. Being simple country people, they possessed much of the old feudal attitude towards the Lord of the Manor, and the births, marriages and deaths among the Daventrys were as personal to them as those of their own kin. They considered they were part of Erne, being the Earl's people, and had not yet accepted the modern outlook towards employers.

Thus it was that Clara Harris's conversation inevitably came round to the Daventrys, whose doings were far more spectacular than her own, and when Lois arrived, she was more than usually voluble. She declared that never during all the years she had been at Erne had she seen such preparations for a single event, though in her mother's time, there had been a great to do when royalty paid the Hall a visit. The Earl intended to give Miss Anstruther a magnificent welcome into the family, since so much was expected from her. His son had arrived at midday. The gatekeeper at the main lodge had seen him pass.

"And that's a mercy," Mrs. Harris announced, while Lois's eyes went involuntarily towards the direction of the Hall, though it was not visible from the lodge, and her heart quickened its beat. The enigma was actually there, within a few furlongs of her, and he might well be Val.

"I wouldn't put it past him not to turn up," Mrs. Harris went on. "And that would be Hamlet without the Prince of Denmark, as the saying is. By the way, miss, you've got some book learning. Who was this Hamlet? I've often wondered."

"A person in the play of that name," Lois told her. "As he *is* the play, you can see it wouldn't be anything without him."

Mrs. Harris's broad face broke into a wide grin.

"As tonight's festivities wouldn't be anything without Lord Torrington. Good job he's turned up."

"He seems to be a rather irresponsible person." Lois was able to make the remark quite casually. It did not seem possible that they were actually talking about Val, nor did his careless behaviour seem in character.

"He's not all that keen on getting tied up," Mrs. Harris explained. "That sticks out a mile, in spite of the money. The Hon. Cis is a bit of a tartar, and he likes his women soft and clinging."

Lois turned her head away. She had been soft and clinging when she had said goodbye to him, but that had got her nowhere, nor was it much comfort to be told that Val did not love his future wife. He had not loved her either. He took after his ancestor, the fifth Earl, who, judging by his cynical smile, regarded women as playthings.

She said suddenly, "Will Lord Torrington's sister be there?"

"Whatever put you in mind of her?" Mrs. Harris asked, surprised. "Lady Charlotte is still in France where she's gone to learn the lingo, and she don't see eye to eye with the Hon. Cis. She's all for new-fangled ideas, and don't value her home. She wouldn't come tonight even if she were here. Pop concerts are more her line."

So that was where Val had obtained his republican ideas; he and his sister were rebels against the traditions of their environment, but in his case, he had been recalled to toe the line. That again did not fit in with Lois's knowledge of Val. She could not believe he would allow himself to be made to conform if he did not wish to do so.

Eric was sound asleep when Lois was shown into the small room that she was to share with him. Her dress was laid out on the camp bed that had been put up for her accommodation. It comprised a print dress which reached to her ankles, a white muslin fichu, white apron and mob cap. It did not take her long to slip into it, and as far as she could see in the small mirror on the dressing table, it did nothing for her. The cap concealed her hair, and the dress fitted where it touched. Mrs. Harris in a similar outfit with her rosy apple cheeks and plump figure looked much more as if she belonged to the period. It seemed a great extravagance to include even the kitchen staff in this masquerade, and knowing whose idea it was, Lois asked Mrs. Harris.

"Is the ball being given for or by Miss Anstruther?"

"Both," the good woman replied. "You see, there's no Countess now to act as hostess, and no regular housekeeper. Fifty years ago Erne had a staff of forty servants, my mother was one of them, but all that's changed. The Earl employs a Spanish couple, man and wife. Fernando's a blooming marvel, he does everything from valeting to acting as butler, and his wife Juana is the cook, but she could hardly receive the guests. The Hon. Cis will do that with Torr beside her. We'd better get going now; though we're only supposed to wash up, I daresay Fernando's got some odd jobs he'd like a hand with."

With a parting injunction to her husband to keep an

eye on Eric, he having declared he wanted nothing to do with the ball, which was nonsensical and would make a rare muck of the gardens, Lois and Mrs. Harris set forth to traverse the short distance to the Hall.

By now it was quite dark, and the grounds in front of the Hall were decorated with fairy lights. The central tower was floodlit, and the forecourt bright as day. Concealed behind some bushes, they paused to watch the cars drive up to the front steps and deposit their loads of passengers. These looked incongruous in modern transport, for they were all dressed in the clothes of the eighteenth century, men in velvet and brocade coats, women with panniers and hoops. All wore wigs or powdered hair. A red carpet covered the steps leading into the Hall, and the illuminations shone upon the costumes of the arriving guests.

"Right pretty sight, isn't it?" Mrs. Harris said admiringly. "My, clothes must have cost a mint of money in the good old days."

"Those who wore them had it," Lois pointed out. "The workers like ourselves didn't wear silk and velvet."

They made their way round to the back of the Hall, which was thronged with the caterer's staff looking uncomfortable in fancy dress. Fernando was a small dark man who was thoroughly enjoying the pomp and circumstance which had descended upon Erne. Though his country had become republican, he had a secret yearning for the former days of entertaining in great houses, and was directing the hired staff with magnificent aplomb. His wife on the other hand was a little overcome by the influx of strangers into her kitchen.

As soon as Mrs. Harris with Lois in tow appeared, Fernando intercepted them.

"It is well that you have come, Clara," he exclaimed. "And this little one is your niece?" He gave Lois a cursory glance. "Will you be so good as to put clean towels in the guest rooms? Many are staying the night, and you know where everything is. It is not everyone I can trust to wander all over the house.''

Pleased to be assigned so individual a task, and the compliment to her honesty, Mrs. Harris took Lois up the back staircase to the linen cupboard, and presented her with a pile of towels to be distributed, four for each room. Together they traversed the long corridors of the upper regions. The bedrooms in the private part were modernized with trendy furniture, but several of those in the older part had been opened for service and these retained their period appointments, fourposter beds, and massive inlaid tables and armoires.

"It 'ud give me the creeps to have to sleep in one of them," Mrs. Harris observed, indicating a vast canopied bed. She punched the mattress. "Goose feathers, you can't beat 'em for comfort."

Their task completed, Mrs. Harris laid her finger to her lips, and drew Lois on to one of the stone balconies that were built between the pillars of the Great Hall. It directly faced the stairway to the Earl's apartments, at the foot of which the hosts were welcoming their guests. Although only at first floor level the balcony seemed to be a great height above the stone paving of the Hall.

Lois laid her hands on the substantial balustrade and looked down at the picturesque throng below her. At first she saw only the gaily coloured groups of men and women, the light from the great chandeliers, which hung from the roof, spilling over their shimmering silks and satins, then her eyes went to the group directly opposite to her.

The Earl looked aristocratic and distinguished in black velvet with silver buttons. He stood between his son and his daughter-in-law to be, the ribbon of some order across his breast. Cecilia Anstruther wore pale blue, gathered up over a quilted cream underskirt. Her white wig towered above her long, patrician face, being in the style which has been reproduced in modern times under the appellation of beehive. She had a large nose and slightly prominent teeth, but art had done its best for her, and though she was a long way from being beautiful she presented a handsome appearance.

On the Earl's other side stood his son, dressed in an amber velvet coat and white satin breeches, with silk stockings and buckled shoes. His head was covered by a white wig, drawn back into a queue and tied with black ribbon. Lois caught her breath, and her heart faltered in its beat, and then began to race. She knew him, knew him well, knew every curve of those well-cut features, the deep-set eyes beneath the straight black brows, the arrogant set of his shoulders. He was looking a little bored, his mouth curved in a slightly sardonic smile, and his likeness to the fifth Earl was startling. But beyond all doubt he was the man Lois had known in Italy as Val Daventry.

So intent was her gaze that he seemed to become aware of it, for he lifted his head and his glance swept round the Hall, but he did not notice her standing in the shadows above him, and as an exceedingly pretty girl came up to him, he bowed over her outstretched hand with affected gallantry, evidently paying her some compliment, for the girl simpered and blushed. The Honourable Cecilia shot him a dagger's thrust glance. Lord Torrington was running true to form.

Until that moment, Lois's whole being had been projected towards him in a surge of love and longing, but the little incident recalled her to time and place. The man down there in the Hall was oceans away from the Val whom she had known and loved. She had only been an incident among a host of similar ones. He probably would have difficulty in recalling her name, and it was not surprising that she had waited to hear from him in vain.

The glittering scene swam before her eyes, a kaleidoscope of shifting colours, only Val's face remained in focus, but he did not look up again.

"What's the matter, miss?" Mrs. Harris asked, as she swayed against the balustrade. "Not feeling queer, are you?"

Lois was feeling very queer, but with an immense effort she pulled herself together.

"I'm all right," she said hastily. "I'm not good at heights and looking down made me feel giddy."

Mechanically she followed Mrs. Harris back along the corridors and down the back stairs. Her deductions had been perfectly correct, and she could no longer cherish a spark of hope. Val had been recalled to marry that haughty dame beside him in the Great Hall, and his playtime, as he had said, was over. The Canadian story was a complete myth manufactured to preserve his incognito when he went abroad, assumed to escape the high prices which would be charged by the hoteliers if they knew his real status, incognito too to the girls he picked up to enliven his journeyings, who had no idea that he was other than he seemed.

Lois would have been glad to be able to creep away and mourn the death of her idyll in solitude, but she had to perform the duties which were the price of her admittance.

Supper was laid in the banquet room and she was kept busy running in and out with this that and the other as the hired waiters demanded it. The vast room was hung round with portraits of departed Earls of Erne, the title was an old one. Everywhere she met those falcon eyes and the satirical smile. The Daventrys bred true to type.

The guests trooped in to eat, and the helpers were relegated to the kitchens, while the imported staff took over. There was much laughter and noise from the banquet room.

"Milord is at the top of his form," Fernando told them as he passed them on his way to the cellar. "The life of the party."

"Even the Honourable Cis can't quench him," someone remarked.

Lois overheard these observations. So Val was enjoying his engagement party, even if he did not love his intended bride. Perhaps he was highly relieved to have secured her income to maintain his home.

The washing up began, literally hundreds of plates and glasses. Erne's antiquated equipment did not run to a washing-up machine, but relied upon tubs of soapy water and willing hands. Dully Lois noticed the crest on the handles of the forks and spoons, an eagle displayed, the same as the one Val wore on his cuff-links.

There was laughter and chatter in the kitchens too. Fernando announced that they were all to drink the health of the happy pair. The Earl had provided wine for that purpose. Mrs. Harris handed Lois a brimming glass, and they all lined up to drink the toast.

"Here's to His Lordship and his estimable Lady," Fernando said. "May he be as good a master as his father is. For he's a jolly good fellow... hip, hip hooray!" Fernando was becoming a little excited, having "sampled" more than one glassful that evening. The mob of servants laughed and cheered. In the confusion, Lois turned about and poured her libation down the sink. It was asking too much of her to drink to Val after the way he had treated her.

Her feet were aching, the kitchens and sculleries were stone-paved, and the air was heavy and hot, but she welcomed the discomfort to distract her from the pain in her heart. She was so near to him, actually under his roof, but she was as far from him in spirit as if a continent divided them.

At last they seemed to have finished. The caterers and their waiters departed in their motor coach, the china and cutlery were stacked away. Lois looked round for Mrs. Harris and saw she was gossiping with some of the village girls. Fernando perceived that she was unoccupied and came up to her, carrying a silver salver upon which was a box of cigars.

"If you have finished, would you please be good enough to perform one more small errand," he said politely. "The gentlemen require these in the library, and I must go again to the cellar to fetch another bottle of the vintage port."

He thrust the salver into her hands, and went on his way. Lois knew from her past visits where the library was, but she had no wish to encounter any of the guests. She threw Mrs. Harris an agonized glance, but that worthy merely smiled encouragingly.

"Run along and then we'll go home," she called.

Seeing no help for it, Lois went down the passage towards the library. At least she was unlikely to meet Val, he would be entertaining his fiancée, and the gathering in the library appeared to be a bachelor party.

In some trepidation, she knocked on the library door, and was bidden to come in by a vibrant masculine voice.

Timidly she pushed the door ajar, and advanced a few steps inside. Most of the vast room was in shadow, only the card table being illuminated. Round it four men were seated. They were in their shirt sleeves, having discarded their coats, which had been thrown in a glowing heap on a sofa, leaving their frilled shirts exposed, with lace at throat and wrist. They had also taken off their wigs. With the dark panelling of the room behind them, their careless attitudes as they pored over their cards, they looked like an old picture of Regency rakes enjoying their gaming and their wine, which was what they were doing.

Lois's eyes were fixed upon the man opposite her, with the brown aquiline face that was so familiar to her. His long fingers were shuffling the cards, and he had loosened the lace cravat about his strong throat. He was the last person she wanted to meet face to face, would have refused this errand if she had imagined he would be in the library, but she had not expected he would be playing cards on the night of his betrothal. She wondered vaguely where Cecilia was.

The sight of him, so handsome and debonair, the dark hair ruffled on his brow, brought an unbearable ache to her heart. She was hurt by his duplicity, and growing resentment against him had helped her through this trying evening, but this unexpected encounter awoke a desperate longing for him. She wanted to run to him, beg him to tell her that it was all a mistake. That he was not the fickle Lord Torrington, and that he still loved her. Loved? He had never done that.

Instead, she stood motionless, holding the salver with the cigars upon it in front of her as if it were a votive offering to the shrine of a dead love, while the colour fled from her face, and she moistened her dry lips with the tip of her tongue. She had an oddly guilty look, for she was aware that she should not be there.

Val raised his head, and his eyes met hers.

"Kitten!" he exclaimed.

The cards dropped from his fingers and he sprang to his feet, overturning his chair, which fell behind him with a crash. One of the other men, he had his back to Lois and she could not see his face, put out a detaining hand to grasp Val's arm.

"One of your past indiscretions, Val?" he asked in a lazy, mocking voice. He flashed a glance at Lois over his shoulder, but she did not notice him, her eyes being fixed on Val. "A fetching little piece too. If she embarrasses you, I wouldn't mind having a shot at consoling her."

The other two men laughed.

"The devil you will," Val said fiercely, and flung off the detaining hand.

As he moved towards her, Lois's paralysed limbs came unstuck. She dropped the salver and cigar box and made for the door, the men's hilarious laughter ringing in her ears, as Val stumbled over someone's outthrust leg.

She fled through the labyrinth of passages intent upon escaping outside, to finding a place that was dark and cool. Val might think that she had come in search of him, as in a way she had, the ghost of a former love to haunt his betrothal feast, only she had never been his love; she was only a past indiscretion, as that mocking voice had described her. The words seemed to sear her. She never wanted to see him again, she had been too humiliated.

She gained the forecourt, where the fairy lights still shone, coloured chains of glittering points among the trees. The last cars were moving off and she dodged between them. Once she thought she heard someone call her name, but she paid no heed; she wanted to lose herself in darkness and silence.

Beyond the radius of the lights, she started down the grassy slope that led towards the river. A thin mist was rising from it. She had a strange illusion that a wraith-like figure was gliding beside her, while a thin voice wailed:

"Faithless...faithless...all men are vile!"

The wraith passed her to dissolve into the mist, the voice became the screech of an owl. The long dress, the coarse grass checked Lois's flight. She tripped and fell.

"Kitten...Lois...Are you hurt?"

She sat up to find Val was kneeling beside her, his white clothes making him look ghostly in the starlight. She had lost her cap in her precipitate flight, and she pushed the tangle of her hair out of her eyes the better to see him.

"Val," she whispered brokenly. "Oh, Val!"

Then he was holding her closely, cradling her in his arms and his lips found hers. The months of waiting were washed out in ecstasy, as the English landscape seemed to fade. They were back at Diano Castello in the velvet Italian night, and he was telling her he had come back. But he had not come back to her, he had gone from Germany to England and tonight he had become engaged to the haughty Cecilia Anstruther, who was to provide the money to preserve his heritage.

With the bitter recollection of the true state of affairs, Lois turned her head aside from his urgent mouth and pushed herself out of his arms.

Simultaneously they rose to their feet, confronting each other, two dim forms in the enfolding night, which reduced their faces to pale blurs, their expressions indistinguishable.

Their embrace had been a spontaneous action, excited by their unexpected proximity, and in her case, an eruption of pent feelings too long suppressed, but it was in the circumstances unseemly to say the least of it, though Val seemed to be entirely unrepentant, for he said a little unsteadily:

"Why do you repulse me, kitten?"

"I should have thought that was obvious," she retorted, while her shaking hand mechanically sought to rearrange her fichu which he had displaced. This man was Lord Torrington, she was reminding herself, a practised rake and deceiver, and the sooner she left him for the shelter of the cottage the better it would be for them both, but now she had found him again, she was loath to tear herself away.

"I'm afraid I'm a bit dim, I'm not with you," he said uncertainly, "unless..." a rasp of suspicion changed his voice. "What are you doing here, and why are you wearing that absurd get-up?"

Lois realized that he must consider her presence at Erne to be the height of indiscretion, although he had not hesitated to pursue her for his own gratification. Putting on a bold front, she said carelessly:

"Isn't everyone in fancy dress tonight? Including yourself? I congratulate you, Val." For the life of her she could not bring herself to address him by his title.

"You cut a fine figure as your noble kinsman, only he wasn't all that noble under his silk and velvet. That poor girl jumped off that bridge because he deserted her."

She meant to insinuate that she also had been deserted, though she had no intention of jumping off the bridge. His proximity was unnerving her, and far from feeling the anger and indignation that his conduct called for, she was wrestling with an absurd longing to throw herself back into his arms and beg him to tell her that he loved her and that the proceedings that she had witnessed that evening were only a bad dream.

"It's only a legend," he told her disdainfully, "and like most legends its accuracy is suspect. It's much more probable that he pensioned her off and she got drowned by accident."

"Oh, how can you be so cynical?" Lois had more than once identified herself with the dead girl, and Val's explanation of the story came almost as a personal affront. It flashed into her mind that Torr probably compensated his girls with cash when he had had enough of them—in other words, paid them off, and Torr and Val were one. He was speaking from personal experience, and she shrank from him in dismay.

Val said: "From his expression the gentleman we're discussing was a thorough cynic, and I bet he knew how to manage his women."

"And you think you do too?"

"I don't know what you mean by that, but what's intriguing me is what you're doing down here and why you looked so guilty when you caught sight of me."

"Did I?" She made the question a masterpiece of casual query.

"Yes, you did, and then you turned and bolted like a scared rabbit which has sighted a marauding fox, Reynard being myself. It was the last sort of reception I would have anticipated from you."

There was hurt pride and accusation in his voice, and

it evoked a swift surge of indignation in her. What had
he expected her to do? Fall into his arms when he was
officially engaged to another girl? Claim him as her
lover in front of his mocking men friends? That she
had subsequently tumbled into his embrace was a hu-
miliating reflection, and her pride would be further
abased if she allowed him to suspect that she had come
to Erne on purpose to track him down. She cried vehemently:

"I don't know what you anticipated, but I didn't
want to meet you again. If I'd have known you were in
the library, wild horses wouldn't have dragged me
there!"

Silence followed her words. From the trees on the
other side of the lake, the owl screeched again, its
weird cry loud in the stillness. Lois glanced uneasily at
her companion. Something about his attitude put her in
mind of a stricken animal. She had meant to wound,
for he had hurt her badly, but now she felt compunc-
tion, mingled with apprehension, for wounded animals
are dangerous.

At length he spoke with a lazy drawl that covered
effectively any emotion he might be feeling:

"Well, that's explicit enough, but as a matter of curiosity, is this your first visit to Erne?"

"Oh, no, I often come here."

"You do, do you?" A purr that might at any moment become a snarl. "Don't tell me it's only the Hall
you come to see."

His question was suggestive, but he could not mean
that she had come in search of him, for they both knew
he had only arrived the day before. She said lightly:

"Of course not. I've a crush on the fifth Earl. I believe I mentioned him to you in Italy, since there is a
resemblance."

"So you did, but I'd no idea then that you were so
familiar with Erne...and its denizens. How come you
never mentioned it?"

"Because I didn't think you'd be interested. I'd no idea you were connected with the place."

"Hadn't you? I think you were better informed than I was."

"How could I be? Oh, come off it, Val, you can't continue to pull wool over my eyes. I suppose because I made a fool of myself," her voice quivered, "you thought you'd let me down lightly by talking about writing and coming back."

"I did write," he said to her surprise, "but you didn't reply."

She stared at his dimly seen face disbelievingly. If there had been a letter, could Nella have managed to intercept it after all?

"And I came back," he went on, "but you'd gone without leaving any message, and nobody seemed to know where you went."

She had left a message with Enrico, which, not knowing the waiter had left, she was confident he would have delivered. She was entirely sceptical about both the letter and the supposed return. It would be easy to lie, but though she could neither prove nor disprove his assertions she did know what had transpired a few hours earlier. She had seen him that evening in the Great Hall surrounded by all the pageantry of a past age, standing between his father and his bride-to-be, receiving the congratulations of his friends. No protestations or reproaches would eliminate that scene.

Like a chameleon he changed colour according to his surroundings, but the Italian interlude could not be revived now that she knew he was the heir of Erne. Any further contact with him could only result in a liaison, and that with the Honourable Cecilia actually staying in his house was an insult, not only to herself but to the other woman. No doubt he thought a hotel receptionist was of so little account that she could be picked up and discarded according to his whim. Sadly she reproached herself for allowing him to embrace her. Her weakness had led him to believe that she could not resist him, but resist him she must; there could be no more between them.

"I had to leave the Paradiso," she said wearily, "but as that's all finished, there's no need to go into details. I'm very tired, so I'll say good night, Val."

"You're going to leave me?" he protested. "Like this?"

"Yes," she said stonily. "I've no more to say to you." Summoning all her resolution, she turned from him towards the bridge.

He overtook her in a couple of swift strides and his hand fell heavily upon her shoulder, staying her.

"You have changed," he told her, "and the only explanation I can think of for your volte-face does you no credit."

"Of course I've changed," she said fretfully. "Please let me go."

"Presently. Are you employed here?" He shot the question at her.

"No. I only came tonight because I wanted to see the ball."

"Gatecrashing?"

"Not at all. I worked for my supper."

"Indeed?" His hand tightened on her shoulder, biting into the flesh. "Why were you so anxious to see the ball?"

"Isn't my interest natural in the circumstances?" A bitter edge crept into her voice. "I wanted to see the bride-to-be."

"Cecilia?"

"Yes, Miss Anstruther. Oh, don't be so dim! Isn't a woman always interested in her successor? Wondering what the other one's got that she hasn't? Of course I know in her case it's the money. In looks I might hold my own." She gave a little brittle laugh. "Am I being presumptuous by classing myself with her?"

Val's hand dropped from her shoulder and he drew a long breath.

"So I'm right!" he exclaimed. "That's the way it is."

"Yes, that's it, and I may tell you I'm not impressed by all this fine show tonight, since it covers so much calculation and emptiness of heart. To marry for money seems to me to be horribly mercenary."

"Such high-flown sentiments are a little out of character," he remarked sarcastically. "Of course you hadn't got an eye on the main chance yourself, had you? You're incapable of being mercenary?"

His words were incomprehensible to her until it flashed into her mind that he thought she had known his identity from the start, and she had gone all out to capture him, because of his position. Nella could have enlightened her. This inaccurate supposition was so painful that she could only gasp and he went on without heeding her.

"That act at Diano Castello was merely a sideline, wasn't it? Something to fall back upon in case you failed to hit the jackpot?"

She shook her head in perplexity. "You're talking in riddles, but I've learned my lesson. I should have known better than to trust a hypocrite and a liar!"

She flung the words at him, hoping to wound, but to her surprise he accepted her description without protest.

"You should," he agreed, "but you were a bit naïve if you expected to compete with Cecilia. You couldn't hope to become a countess."

"Oh, Val!" She recoiled as if he had struck her. Throughout their meeting she had been unable to bring herself to address him by his title, he was still Val to her, but now that same title seemed to rise up between them with a new and unpleasant significance.

"How can you say that?" she faltered. "I . . . I never dreamed of such a thing, I didn't know . . ." She became incoherent.

"Methinks the lady doth protest too much," he quoted sardonically. "You strain my credulity, my dear, especially after finding you here tonight, but if you had any idea of making a last-minute appeal to a man who is resigned to doing his duty, I'm afraid your little charade has misfired. Love, you see, doesn't count when money and estates are in the balance, as I'm sure you'll be the first to admit.''

He sounded bitter, but had no cause to be so. He had pursued her when he had recognized her, his embrace had been a good simulation of love, even if it were only an upsurge of desire. She deduced that he regretted having to give her up, but if he had been honest with her, told her that he must drop her for the preservation of Erne, she could have forgiven him everything and understood. Instead he had indulged in cryptic utterances and nasty insinuations, concluding with the final thrust that she had come to Erne to endeavour to detach him from his fiancée. Possibly he was trying to justify his own conduct by blackening her motives, and she surmised that her foolish escapade had given colour to his suspicions. It was sheer bad luck that she had encountered him; she had meant to leave unrecognized.

Yet in spite of his poor opinion of her, he seemed reluctant to relinquish her; she suspected that Torr did not like having to give up his girls before he had possessed them. Possibly he *had* returned to the Paradiso in search of her, but the proposal of marriage which she had expected would have turned out to be quite a different sort of proposition.

A little breeze sprang up and moaned among the trees, stirring the mist into wraithlike forms and lifting her hair. The noise of the water gurgling through the arches of the bridge was clearly audible, reminding her of the legend the authenticity of which Val had challenged.

Involuntarily she exclaimed,

"But I would never drown myself for a man!"

He said with the insolent drawl that he assumed as a defence and which she disliked intensely: "No my pet, you're not the one-man type, but didn't it occur to you that it might be an effective threat?''

"Certainly not." She was stung. "I wouldn't descend to blackmail."

"Wouldn't you? I don't think you're over scrupulous. A cheap little dolly on the make."

She cried out with pain: "Val, how can you?"

"Oh, I can, and more. You admire the fifth Earl so much and he, I'm sure, would never let any scruple come between him and his desires. Perhaps you'd appreciate the same technique from me..." His voice thickened and roughened, and instinctively, Lois turned to run. Her action triggered off the rising passion he was holding in check. The girl's presence here that night was wholly suspect, but she was still tantalizing. Her touch-me-not air covering hidden fire had always excited him. Before she had gone a dozen steps, he lunged after her and caught her in a fierce possessive hold in which there was nothing of love, only the need to dominate and subdue.

"Women like you should be treated rough," he said between his teeth. "Come, give me your mouth..."

The rest of his sentence was lost as he buried his face in her hair. She could feel the pounding of his heart through the thin silk of his shirt and the urgency of his desire swept away her frail defences. Every pulse in her body was hammering as she submitted to the pressure of his arms, her body becoming fluid in his grasp, her lips opening under his, until from the terrace above them a woman's voice was borne to them on the breeze, a clear carrying voice with an aristocratic enunciation.

"Fernando, have you seen Lord Torrington?"

Cecilia Anstruther was looking for her errant fiancé.

Lois stiffened in Val's embrace. The man who held her had totally misrepresented himself when he had won her heart. Now she knew him for what he was, a scion of the House of Erne, following, as he himself had suggested, in the footsteps of his ancestors, who sought an unworthy satisfaction from maids in the park as a relaxation from the sterner duties their positions demanded from them.

Despair and anguish gave her additional strength. She dragged her mouth away from his and freeing one hand, clenched her fist and drove it with all her might into his face.

Instinctively he drew back his head, and for a moment his hold slackened. She twisted herself free of him and ran for the shelter of the woods beyond the bridge as if all the devils in hell were in pursuit of her.

CHAPTER SIX

A LUMINOSITY in the eastern sky proclaimed that the
dawn was not far off. Mist lay like a white shroud over
the river and lake, rising as high as the parapet of the
bridge. As Lois reached its further side, she emerged
from its whorls with their eerie suggestion of an invisible presence, on to the grass of the parkland which had
earlier been cut for hay. To her left were the trees and
bushes through which the path led to the well, to her
right the way she must take to arrive at the lodge; facing her the ground sloped slightly upward in a long
tree-lined ride, to meet the grey pre-dawn sky. About
half-way along its length was a stone column com-
memorating some battle in which a former Earl had
won renown. It was surmounted by an eagle, its wings
spread as if it were just alighting on the top of the column. The bird was outlined against the paling sky and
there was something ominous about its brooding
shape.

Realizing that she was not being followed, Lois
turned about and looked back at the hall. Its towers
were black against the increasing light, but the great
building was wrapped in darkness except for a solitary
illumination above the entrance to the private section.
The House of the Eagles and the bird on the column
complemented each other in sinister suggestion.

Val had gone back like a good dog in answer to his
mistress's call, and Lois was confused and bewildered
by the scene which had taken place between them. Her
mouth could still feel the imprint of Val's bruising
kisses, the neck of her dress was torn by his impatient

fingers, and she had nearly succumbed, her own passionate urges rising to meet his. She had forgotten that he could be nothing to her, until Cecilia's voice had recalled her to her senses, and she had managed to tear herself away. As for Val, he would have no scruples about seeking to obtain his way with her, as he had had it with so many others, she thought bitterly. She might only be a fancy, but the Daventrys expected to indulge such fancies, and had done so throughout their history. The copse along the lakeside had sheltered a royal paramour, the bridge was haunted by a lost girl's wraith, but she had no wish to join their number. Only a great and overwhelming love could offer the smallest justification for such unions, but all Val had felt for her was an upsurge of desire, intensified because circumstances had made her forbidden fruit. After her self-betrayal at Diano Castello, he thought he only had to take her in his arms and she would surrender, but she would never stoop to becoming his mistress...an absurdly old-fashioned word, but one suited to the environment of Erne, which must have witnessed so many liaisons, but she had too much self-respect to become involved in one herself.

As for his unwarrantable assumption that she had come to Erne in search of him, that was infinitely wounding. She had wanted to establish his identity, but not to encounter him, and he seemed to imagine that she had been aware of it all along. If she had been the designing character that he had insinuated, she could have made trouble for him with Cecilia by insisting that he had made promises to her out in Italy, but had he really believed she was capable of doing so? Not being entirely unsophisticated, she knew that there were women who would try to make capital out of such a situation, receiving, not the countess's coronet with which he had taunted her, but a substantial sum to ensure their silence. She shivered in the chill dawn wind, as she contemplated this mercenary world to which it was probable most of Torr's girls belonged. That he had classed her with them degraded her love and smirched it.

"Oh, Val, Val," she said aloud to the misty lake and the dark encircling woods. "All I ever wanted from you was your love, but you don't know what true love means."

That chapter of her life was finished now. She must tear his image from her heart, refuse to allow her thoughts to dwell upon what was past, and never again come to Erne.

She wished it were possible to be conveyed there and then back to her London flat and Joanna's astringent presence. Her friend had often told her that she was too soft and sentimental and easily imposed upon. Joanna had a hardboiled approach to the opposite sex, but though she had boy-friends, she had not yet secured herself a mate. Lois thought that now she would appreciate her cynical comments, but before she could return to her, she would have to go back to the Harrises' cottage to collect her own clothes. That brought her to the contemplation of her present appearance. The flimsy dress was torn and stained, her cap gone, her shoes soaked by the heavy dew. Nor could she do anything to renovate herself, she had not even a comb with which to tidy the wild disorder of her hair. She could only hope that Mrs. Harris had gone to bed, but that was extremely unlikely.

She turned in the direction of the cottage, her slippers making no sound on the sward, her long, pale dress ghostly in the faint light. Passing a clump of shrubs, she heard what sounded like a strangled shriek and some heavy body went crashing through the undergrowth. She stopped, her heart racing, wondering if the noise had been caused by a beast or a man, but whatever it was, it seemed to have gone. Quickening her steps, she hurried away. Erne Park was an eerie place to be in alone at night.

At last the lodge came in sight and she saw to her dismay that the front door was open and light from within spilled out over the flagstone path leading up to it from the garden gate. There was no help for it, she had to go on and meet her hostess's unwelcome questions.

Mrs. Harris was standing in the doorway. She had discarded her print dress and wore a man's dressing gown over her night gear. She was talking to a youth, who seemed to be in a great state of agitation.

"I tells yer I seed her plain as plain, and my heart was a-yammering. Tall as a tree she was, with her drowned hair down her back and her face as white as chalk. Give me a proper turn, it did."

"Serves you right for poaching," Mrs. Harris told him. "Let it be a lesson to you to keep out of the park at night." She caught sight of Lois standing beyond the gate. "Oh, miss, thank the Lord, there you are!"

The lad turned round, saw Lois, and with a yell of: "There she be!" he vaulted over the low garden fence and rushed away towards the village.

Mrs. Harris laughed. "Thought you were the ghost of that drowned girl," she explained. "Eh, but I was getting anxious about you and when I saw young Jack I called to him to ask if he'd seen you. I guessed his ghost was you, but come in, wherever did you get to?"

She took Lois's arm and propelled her into her neat little kitchen. Her small eyes surveyed the girl slyly. All along she had suspected there was something behind Lois's eagerness to see the ball.

Lois said faintly: "I...I couldn't find you at the end. On my way here, I...I got lost in the dark."

"Did you know?" Mrs. Harris did not believe this excuse. She looked commiseratingly at the girl's wan face. Whatever assignation she had kept that night had ended in unhappiness. This vaunted modern freedom was all very fine, but more often than not, girls would

have been better off if they had not availed themselves
of it. Her father would have thrashed her soundly if she
had dared to wander about the park in the small hours,
and she was grateful to him for the strictness that had
resulted in her marriage with a steady man.

"Sit you down," she said cheerfully, "and I'll make
you a cup of tea and then to bed with you for what's left
of the night, which isn't much."

The kitchen was bright and shining, and the warmth
from the Raeburn stove was welcome in the chill of
dawn. Lois submitted gratefully to Mrs. Harris's comforting ministrations.

"I'm afraid this dress is in a bit of a mess," she said
apologetically, "and I've lost the cap, but I'll pay..."

"No, you won't, there's nothing a wash and a stitch
or two won't put right. As for your cap, I bet you
weren't the only one who's lost theirs. There were
some flighty bits there last night."

Lois winced, suspecting that Mrs. Harris included
her with the flighty bits.

"I'm afraid I'm giving you a lot of trouble," she began hesitantly.

"Don't mention it, miss, and I reckon it's you
who've had trouble." Her eyes were full of curiosity.

Lois flushed and bowed her head, saying nothing;
what was there to say? Mrs. Harris was the last person to
whom she could describe Lord Torrington's infidelities.

Seeing that she was not going to confide in her, Mrs.
Harris stifled her disappointment and said briskly:
"Well now, off to bed with you. You won't wake Eric,
once he's off nothing short of the Last Trump 'ud wake
that child. The water's warm if you'd like a shower. We
have got one, though when the bathroom was put in,
there wasn't no room for a bath."

She showed Lois the tiny bathroom with pride, for
she had spent the earlier part of her life without such an
amenity.

"A tub in front of the kitchen fire on Saturday nights was what we had to make do with," she told her.

Showered and in her pyjamas, some of the deathly chill left Lois's limbs. Mrs. Harris came with her into the small room where her camp bed had been put up on the opposite side to where Eric lay, rosy with sleep, clutching a teddy bear.

"Bonny, isn't he?" said his mother, fondly. "I hopes you'll be comfortable, miss." She looked doubtfully at the narrow bed. "It was the best I could do."

"I'm sure I will be," Lois suppressed her own doubt. Impulsively she laid her hand on her companion's arm. "You've been an angel, Mrs. Harris, I can never thank you enough."

Mrs. Harris looked embarrassed. "I haven't done nothing." Her eyes went to her son and she said softly, "But for you he wouldn't be there." Then with a return of her usual briskness, "Best hop into bed, miss. I only hopes that idiot Jack holds his tongue. If he goes babbling all over the place as he's seen a ghost, there won't half be some talk. Only daft things like him believe the dead walk."

Lois smiled sadly. "It won't matter, because I'll be gone early tomorrow morning, and I shan't be coming here again. Good night, Mrs. Harris, and God bless you."

The wan light of early day was creeping round the thin curtains as Lois lay down on her narrow bed. The child murmured and threw out a chubby arm, sinking back into deep slumber. That was one good thing that had emerged from her visits to Erne; as his mother had said, but for Lois he would not be there. For the rest, though she vowed she would never re-enter its precincts, Erne had made an indelible impression upon her mind. She would haunt it in spirit, though her body was far away, as the spectre of that other girl was bound to it by the chains of an undying love.

But Lois did not leave Erne next day. She woke with

a sore throat and flushed face, to find it was late in the morning and Eric had been up and dressed long since. Mrs. Harris brought her a cup of tea and was concerned by her appearance. She insisted upon taking her temperature.

"You won't get up today, miss," she announced frowning at the reading. "And what's more, I'm going to get the doctor."

Lois protested weakly, but she was feeling too ill to put up much of a fight, and Mrs. Harris was adamant.

"I'm not having your death laid at my door," she declared, "and that's what it would be if you try to go back to London today. You wouldn't be able to work when you got there."

"But I'm being such a nuisance..."

"Rubbish; bit of nursing 'll be a nice change from cooking and cleaning. Now tell me who've got to be rung up and then I can do that when I've called the doctor."

Lois wrote down for her in a shaky hand the travel agents' number and that of Joanna's place of work. Exhausted by the small effort, she lay back while Mrs. Harris read what she had written.

"Isn't there anyone else as should know?" she asked insinuatingly. "Someone nearer to hand?"

Lois shook her head. "No one," she whispered, and Mrs. Harris departed upon her errand.

Lois fell into an uneasy sleep, haunted by dreams coloured by the events of the night. The eagle from the top of the column was chasing her, but its face was human, Val's face, she could hear the beat of its great wings as she struggled knee-deep through the waters of the lake while a shrouded figure beckoned to her from the bridge, and Cecilia's voice echoed through the air calling for Lord Torrington. The eagle swooped down upon her, she could feel its talons on her shoulders, and she woke with a cry. She tossed and turned, muttering about Val, Lord Torrington, the ghost and the lake, until she struggled back to full consciousness to find Mrs. Harris beside her with a hot drink and the information that the doctor was upon his way. She was looking oddly at the girl, for she had caught her murmured words.

The doctor came, and by the administration of the new antibiotics warded off the threatened pneumonia. On the second day, Lois was a great deal better, her temperature had come down and she was determined to leave as soon as possible.

Unknown to her, Mrs. Harris was wrestling with a problem of her own. Loyal as she was to the Daventrys, she was aware of the young lord's proclivities. She could not condone them, but young men would be young men, and with his looks and charm he must meet many temptations, but he should not have tampered with the affections of a nice girl like Lois Lang. The good Lord knew there were plenty of the other sort, brazen hussies, but Lois was of a different class altogether, and it was obvious that he had made her suffer. He had a lot to answer for with his casual love affairs, but perhaps this one was not so casual. If they had met upon that fateful evening, the little creature had had the courage to send milord about his business, but it had broken her heart to do so. Mrs. Harris could not make herself believe that the proposed marriage with Cecilia Anstruther was a love match, and perhaps the girl she was sheltering was Torr's true love, in which case she ought to let him know that his sweetheart was lying nigh to death literally at his gates. Beneath her brisk efficiency, Mrs. Harris concealed a romantic heart, and was thrilled to discover that she was involved in a first-class love affair.

Voicing her suppositions to her husband, she met a stern reprimand.

"Once you women scent a romance there's no holding you," he grumbled, "but don't you go interfering, Clara, it's none of your business."

Mrs. Harris thought it was. She had been involved

throughout, from the rescue of Eric, Lois's desire to go to the ball, and the girl's subsequent illness. In each of these events she saw the Hand of Fate. Naturally Lois had been peeved to discover that her lover was to wed another, but the knot was not yet tied, a reconciliation was still possible, and who but herself could bring that about?

Her favourite magazine arrived, and her horoscope for that week bore out the trend of her thoughts. Under her birth sign, she read: "A propitious time for love and romance. Don't be afraid of making an advance. Your actions will be rewarded."

That was direct guidance from the Stars, whatever her husband said.

On the third morning Lois was up and dressed. Though still feeling weak, she was determined to be on her way. Her temperature was normal, and she proposed to travel up to London that afternoon, having gone to the expense of hiring the village taxi to take her to the nearest railway station, a considerable distance away, but she knew she was not fit to wrestle with the intricate bus service.

Mrs. Harris had been as good as her word, washing and repairing the maid's dress, and it had been duly returned to the Hall. Lois was wearing the slacks and tee-shirt she had travelled down in on the night of the ball. That and a light jacket were all she had with her. She still looked pale and wan and her hair had lost its lustre. It was a grey day, and she stared disconsolately out of the window in Mrs. Harris's small sitting-room, that overlooked the bright flower beds in the tidy little garden. Eric had gone to play with friends in the village and Mrs. Harris was busy cooking, refusing Lois's offer of help.

"You sit quiet, dearie, and get your strength up," she ordered. The "miss" was now permanently dropped in favour of the endearment.

Lois was thinking of a hundred and one practical

matters; what story she would tell Joanna, her neglected office work—had they been able to cope in her
absence? What could she do to show her appreciation
of Mrs. Harris's kindness? Get some things for Eric
perhaps, or give the money to buy them. She would not
take offence at that since it was for the child. Children
had very definite uses.

The click of the gate brought her eyes down from
watching the waving trees against the skyline. A man
was coming up the flagged path to the cottage, and her
heart seemed to stop as she recognized Val. Wild conjectures rose in her mind—how did he know she was
here? What more could he possibly have to say to
her? Her heart began to beat in violent agitation, and
she put her hand over it, striving to still it. Perhaps he
was not seeking her at all, but had come with a message for Harris about some work he wanted him to do.
Hastily she drew back from the window, hoping he
had not seen her.

Mrs. Harris flew to the front door as if she were expecting this visitor. There was a murmur of voices. Lois
waited apprehensively, knowing that she could not escape without going through the passage where they
were. It was agony to know he was there, within a few
feet of her, and she must not make her presence
known. If only he would go!

Mrs. Harris threw open the door with a dramatic gesture.

"A visitor to see you, dearie."

Val stepped inside the room. Lois's apprehension
was succeeded by a swift rush of anger. It was cruel of
him to continue to pursue her, when he was committed
elsewhere, nor could she understand his motive, unless
he wished to revenge himself for the manner of their
parting. She turned from the window, ire giving a
sparkle to her eyes and colour to her pale cheeks, to
meet the familiar quizzical expression in the tawny eyes
beneath the straight black brows. That enraged her all

the more, he was not even contrite for the way he had
treated her, he even seemed amused. Moreover he
looked supremely confident, carrying himself with a
jaunty assurance, and was beautifully turned out in a
dark suit, with a flower in his buttonhole, a red carnation.

"This just isn't good enough," she began stormily.
"I don't know why..." Her voice died away and her
eyes widened in bewilderment, as the conviction came
to her that the man standing in front of her was not Val
Daventry. He was like, so very like that a stranger
would have mistaken the one for the other, but not the
eyes of a lover. He was perhaps half an inch shorter
than Val and a little stouter, but he had the same eagle
profile, tawny eyes and dark hair. There was a subtle
difference in the lines of his face. Val had sun wrinkles
at the corners of his eyes that crinkled when he smiled
and a deeper tan. This man was beginning to show lines
that were put there by dissipation, and he had a faintly
world-weary air.

"I...I'm sorry," Lois stammered, while all sorts of
conjectures thronged into her mind. "I...I don't know
who you are."

Her visitor gave her a little foreign bow, a gesture
she had seen Val perform, and doubt struck her. Was
he Val, and the slight differences she had noticed had
occurred since she had last seen him—by daylight? But
as soon as he began to speak she knew he was not. He
had a pleasant cultivated voice, but it was not Val's
voice.

"I'm Lord Torrington at your service. Your landlady
insisted that I came to see you, some rigmarole about
being ill and it was my fault, though how she worked
that out, I haven't a clue. So as I'm on my way to
Town, I thought I'd drop in to clear up the mystery,
and I must admit I was intrigued. You have been ill?"
For Lois's angry flush had been succeeded by extreme
pallor. "Sit down, my dear." He laid a compelling hand

on her shoulder, pushing her down into a chair. "Don't stand on ceremony with me."

He stepped back and regarded her curiously. "No, I've never met you before, I'm sure, so I wonder what made our good Mrs. Harris connect you with me. Ah!" Sudden recognition showed in his eyes, the eyes which were precisely similar to Val's. "But I'm wrong. Of course, you're the little girl who dropped my best Havanas all over the carpet and split up our card party."

"The past indiscretion," Lois reminded him. She put her hand to her forehead, striving to sort out her recollections. "It was you who said that, wasn't it? But it was Val who ran after me?" She blushed at the memory.

"Oh, yes, it was definitely my fire-eating cousin." His eyes twinkled mischievously. "Possibly you and he can explain the apparition that has been seen by the lakeside?"

Lois blushed again. Her mind was seething with questions; how did Val come to be at Erne? When had he linked up with Lord Torrington? And then like a shaft of sunshine through lowering clouds, came the realization that if Val were not His Lordship, he was not engaged to Cecilia Anstruther.

Lord Torrington sat down opposite to her and seemed to be enjoying the situation. He took out his cigarettes and lighted one, and his manner of doing so was exactly like Val's.

"You see, I believed all along that he was you, my lord," Lois said uncertainly.

"Please, no titles," he besought her. "Call me Torr, everyone does except Cis, and she's a square. You're not the only one who has been confused, and we've had no end of fun out of our resemblance. I insisted that we dressed precisely alike for the ball—and you can imagine the tangles which ensued." He laughed with boyish glee. "Even Cis mixed us up. I believe she made advances to him in the conservatory, and that must have embarrassed him. Cis's advances are rather like a polar bear trying to be matey." He laughed again.

"But I don't understand—how did Val get here?" she asked. So it was Val who had pursued her into the park, and his face she had slapped—would he ever forgive her for doing that? But she had no idea that he had a double. Watching Torr, whose gestures were so like the other man's, she still was not quite certain, the likeness was uncanny and she was beginning to doubt the evidence of her own senses.

"Val came to Erne because I invited him," Torr informed her. "By the way, what's your name?"

"Lois," she said mechanically, her mind on other matters. "How can Val be your cousin? He said he came from Canada."

"So he does. His great-grandfather emigrated and the family lost track of him. There was a quarrel, I believe—we're rather a violent lot, and very unforgiving, so it was never healed. He determinedly shook the dust of England from his shoes and severed all communication with the Daventrys. But he didn't change his name, and he couldn't change his face. The stock breeds true, so back comes my cousin several times removed—the exact relationship is a bit remote—bearing my face and my name, for I'm called Percival too, though I've a string of others, and in my case it's shortened to Perry, not Val, and quite unaware that Erne is his ancestral home until he turns up in London, goes to my tailor and is presented with my bill!" Torr laughed uproariously. "London's a big place, but not so big at the top. Val has an instinct for the best, so have I. He was mistaken for me so often in restaurants and theatres that he resolved to meet me. We did, in the Café Royal. There we compared notes and worked out our kinship. Of course I brought him down here. It was only right the backwoodsman should see where he sprang from, and I insisted that he must stay for the ball and see us in all our glory. Blow me if he didn't

look every inch a Daventry in that fancy rig-out.
Couldn't fail to see we were both descended from the
fifth Earl."

"Yes, I know he's like the portrait, and so are you, of
course."

Torr threw her a sharp glance. "When did you see
the picture?"

"I...I've been to Erne before. I couldn't think why
Val reminded me of it."

"Well, that's explained now."

"Yes," she said thankfully. She was remembering
that Val had told her that he had returned to the Paradiso in search of her. Then she had not known whether
to believe him and had been doubtful of his motives if
he spoke truth; now she knew he had been genuine.
With an eager light in her eyes, she asked:

"Where is Val now?"

"Oh, he's left," Torr said casually. "Got some business to finish in London and then he's going home."

Despair washed over her. Val was leaving without a
word to her. He could not forgive what she had said to
him—hadn't Lord Torrington just said they were an unforgiving race? But surely he must have realized she
thought he was Lord Torrington? A sudden icy hand
seemed to grip her heart. He *had* known she believed
he was his cousin, and his taunts had been levelled at
her supposed mercenary efforts to capture Torr. How
could he be so blind and stupid, and how was she going
to convince him of her love for himself? She would not
have a chance if he were leaving England.

"He...He's going back to Canada?" she faltered.

"So I understand." Noticing her stricken look, Torr
looked perturbed. "I say, you don't mean this...er...
charade has busted up something between you? Didn't
he explain it all when he...er...saw you in the park?"

Lois shook her head. "We were both talking at cross
purposes. I think he'd got the idea that I'd come here to
look for you, not him." Her hand went to her throat...

("Did you hope to become a countess one day?")...
"He...he wouldn't believe I'd never met you in my
life."

If he had really loved her he would have known she
was incapable of such deceit, but perhaps he had only
wanted an excuse to be rid of her, now he had discovered he belonged to the nobility. Yet Val, she was
sure, was no snob.

Lord Torrington was laughing again.

"Thought you were one of mine? Gad, that's rich!"
Then he sobered. "I say, that's a bit thick, though. Did
it lead to...ahem, a quarrel?"

Lois smiled mournfully. "I slapped his face good and
hard."

"Well done, I've always liked spirit in a woman, and
I expect he deserved it. Not that I wouldn't be honoured to lay claim to your favours."

Lois sighed. "I'm afraid I misled him. You see, I
often come here on trips, Erne has always fascinated
me." Torr raised his brows incredulously. "Oh, it does,
and...and the portrait, but Val didn't understand. He
thought I came to see a man."

"Well, that would have been more natural than to
travel all this way in a coach just to stare at a pile of
bricks," Lord Torrington suggested.

"It's lucky for you many people feel as I do," Lois
told him tartly, "or you'd lose a lot of money."

"That's true, though it always beats me what they
see in it."

"Val was very impressed with the Hall," Lois informed him. "He seems to think more of your heritage
than you do."

"It's a case of familiarity breeding contempt," he returned lightly, "though I do have a certain amount of
sentiment for the place where I was born and bred, but
I'm not crazy about it. Now, Cis makes a fetish of it."

Lois knew that this was a subtle reminder that he was
marrying for Erne's sake, but none of this was helping

her with regard to Val. With a pang it occurred to her that he might have already left the country. Lord Torrington was studying her pensive face. She had, he decided, very expressive eyes, they reflected all her moods, and were of an unusual colour. What was it Val had called her? Kitten? She was rather like a charming little cat. He said lazily:

"Accepted that you came to Erne to admire its architecture, and being a spirited female, you were incensed by my kinsman's unworthy suspicions. So you sent him packing. Now with feminine inconsistency you want him back again. What can I do to help?"

"You're very kind to offer, but if Val's all set to go back to Canada, there's not much to be done, is there?" she asked despondently.

"Nil desperandum, he won't have gone yet." Lois flashed him a hopeful glance. "As I said, I'm on my way to London. I can take you with me and together we might be able to track him down."

"Oh, would you?" Lois did not pause to consider that to go to Town in Torr's company might compromise her still further in Val's opinion. She desperately wished to intercept him before he had gone out of her reach. She had no idea what she would say to him when they did meet, but now she knew the truth, surely she could manage to remove the misapprehensions he seemed to be harbouring.

"I'll be delighted, but you've been ill, haven't you? The message received mentioned lying at death's door."

Lois laughed with faint embarrassment. "Mrs. Harris likes to be dramatic. All I had was a bit of a cold, and it's better now."

Lord Torrington's glance was slightly malicious.

"The result of an evening in the park? We can add that to Mr. Daventry's account. If you're sure you're all right, let's get going. The sooner we get after your errant lover the better."

Lois hesitated. "I don't want to be a bother."

"You won't. Reuniting estranged lovers will be a new experience for me. I'm usually the one who's trying to become disconnected." He grinned wickedly. "Got your bags packed?" He glanced at his watch. "We should be able to make the Ritz or some such in time for lunch."

"I couldn't possibly lunch with you," Lois cried, aghast.

"Why not? I refuse to embark upon any sort of campaign on an empty stomach. Makes one irritable and impatient."

Lois eyed him doubtfully. For a newly engaged man he seemed to be acting a little casually. "What about Miss Anstruther?" she asked. "Will she mind?"

He looked slightly disconcerted. "Blow me if I hadn't forgotten all about her, but Cis will understand when I've explained the circumstances to her, which I haven't time to do now. She's spending the morning with my father discussing the improvements she wishes to make. Too damn boring, talk of stresses and strains, damp-courses and other equally thrilling subjects. It isn't me she's interested in, you know, it's Erne."

"Oh, I'm sure you're wrong," Lois exclaimed, thinking how handsome and debonair he had looked while receiving, when she had believed he was Val. Not that he did not look very attractive by daylight—too attractive, she thought uneasily. She did not wish to give Val any further cause to doubt her.

Torr shrugged his shoulders. "Let's hope so," he said dubiously, "but if we're to catch that man of yours before he can book his passage back to Canada, we'd better get a move on."

That decided her. Once Val left for home, he would be beyond her reach for ever. She suppressed her lingering scruples and ran to fetch her case.

"Lord Torrington is going up to Town and has

offered me a lift," Lois hurriedly explained to her hostess. "Could you cancel the car? Here..." She thrust a couple of notes into her hand. "That'll pay for the phone call, and... er... mending the dress. Any change you can give to Eric."

Mrs. Harris looked at the money, seemed about to expostulate, when Lord Torrington sounded his horn as he drew up at the gate. Lois ran out to him, her indisposition forgotten, her eyes shining in her glowing face. As Torr ushered Lois into the front seat of the car, Mrs. Harris's eyes widened, and when Lois waved to her as the car slid away, a broad grin spread across her face.

"Bless their hearts!" she exclaimed with misplaced fervour.

CHAPTER SEVEN

GREY cloud had changed to sunshine. It was a lovely morning and Lois's spirits soared as the big car sped through the lush countryside. The harvest was beginning and unwieldy monsters of combines were at work in the fields, reaping the grain, and after a mysterious operation in their depths, spewing out the segregated grain and chaff, the straw to be collected by the baler.

Driving beside the man who was so like Val she could almost believe she was back in Italy, starting out upon one of their expeditions, although the smiling English countryside was very different from the parched Ligurian landscape. Once the confusion over Val's likeness to his kinsman had been cleared up, surely they could resume their relationship from the point where it had left off in Italy? Unfortunately that was some time ago, but his actions on the night of the ball had indicated that Val was far from indifferent to her, and surely it was to her credit that she had repulsed him because she had believed he was Lord Torrington?

Torr's so familiar profile beside her gave her the illusion that she was already in his presence. His lordship drove fast and well...like Val, but when he spoke the spell was broken, for his lazy, drawling enunciation was very different from Val's clear-cut speech, and after they had progressed some way he began to question her about her first meeting with his kinsman.

Nothing loth, she told him about her life in Italy.

"Parla italiano?" he asked.

She answered him in the same tongue, and at some length.

"You speak it very well," he complimented her. "I picked it up during my travels. Was always a bit of a dunce at school. I'm particularly fond of Italy and I know the Riviera from Genoa to Cannes, and of course," he grinned mischievously, "San Remo and Monte Carlo are my favourite haunts."

"Yes, I rather gathered that, and I fancy your likeness to Val was remarked," Lois told him a little dryly. "Several people thought he was you, travelling incognito."

"Well, I always do. Use your title and you get rooked." He chuckled appreciatively. "I wonder if he got entangled with any of my birds."

Lois did not like that suggestion. Nella, she was sure, had thought Val was his kinsman, who might well have been pointed out to her on some occasion. She had possibly seen herself as the future Countess of Erne. It explained her extreme spitefulness. She must have bitterly regretted her initial quarrel with him, but she had never anticipated that he would replace her with the receptionist.

As he had threatened, Torr insisted upon treating Lois to lunch at an expensive restaurant. He seemed disposed to linger over the meal and she had to remind him of the object of their journey. She did not like the look in his eye when he regarded her and began to wonder if she had been very foolish to accept his escort. His likeness to Val became less marked as she grew more familiar with him. The dissimilarities were more obvious, especially in his speech, though it still disconcerted her.

At last he said reluctantly:

"Well, I suppose we'd better begin the search for the lost lamb. Really, my dear, I'm beginning to envy him. I suppose you wouldn't consider accepting me as a substitute?"

"I wouldn't dream of it—besides, you're an engaged man."

He sighed. "Must you keep reminding me? I'm afraid you're one of those virtuous people who insist upon keeping to the straight and narrow. It's not only uncomfortable, but it's dull."

"Maybe but you're quite right, I've no intention of sidestepping," she assured him emphatically. "Beside, I happen to be in love with Val."

"Lucky man." He looked at her audaciously. "I wouldn't have been put off if you'd slapped my face. I've always regarded that form of assault as a subtle invitation."

"There was rather more to it than that," she said with heightened colour, "and if you're not going to help me, I'd better go back to my flat. My friend will be expecting me."

She felt very depressed. She had started out so blithely, thinking His Lordship would lead her to Val, instead of which she seemed to be becoming involved in an equivocal position with the very man Val had accused her of pursuing.

"Of course I'm going to help you," Torr declared, heaving himself out of his chair. "For a start we'll try the Regent, that's where he stayed before. He's probably gone back there."

"Why not ring up and inquire?" she suggested, thinking he might have done that in the first place instead of wasting so much time.

"That, my dear, is just what I'm going to do. No sense in taking a walk for nothing if he's not staying there. Excuse me."

He departed, striding leisurely through the grill room, and Lois noticed how all the women's eyes followed him. He was inconspicuously dressed in his dark suit, but he had an air of distinction which marked him out as a man accustomed to being treated with deference. Val had that same quality, she thought, an inheritance from a long line of ancestors born to command. But when she had first known him, Val had had no idea of his heritage. She wondered if the discovery of his noble connections had changed him. He had been apt to pour scorn upon the aristocracy, but he might have altered his ideas now he found he was part of it. She remembered uneasily he was connected with tradition and a great heritage. So Erne had come to mean something to him and perhaps now he would look higher than a mere receptionist. She never had felt very sure of him, and now her hold seemed to be becoming even more tenuous.

A mirror hanging on the wall reflected her own insignificant figure seated rather forlornly at the table with its expensive furnishings. Being used to hotel life she had felt quite at home amidst her opulent surroundings. Now she reflected that this was one of the most expensive and exclusive restaurants in London, and her casual apparel looked a little out of place. The other people lunching there were eyeing her with covert interest and the waiters betrayed an amused speculation. Torr had been welcomed by the staff as a frequent visitor. Did they all believe she was his latest pick-up? She straightened her shoulders and sat back in her chair with a slightly defiant air. They thought...let them think...it could not harm her. But if Torr succeeded in finding Val, what was he going to think? Would her explanations be adequate? She hoped so, but she could not let him fly off to Canada without making some effort to make them. A cold finger seemed to touch her heart. Suppose Torr came back with the news that they were too late and he had gone?

Lord Torrington returned smiling oddly.

"Well...is he there?" she asked tersely.

"No, Lois, I'm afraid he's not."

Her spirits fell to zero. "He's gone?" she inquired despondently.

"Yes, he's gone."

Lois turned away her head, biting her lip in desperation. She had not known until then how much she had counted on forestalling him. Now he was out of her reach, there could be no reconciliation. Perhaps he had not really wanted one, she had offended him too deeply. She well knew his stubborn pride, the pride that had made him turn from Nella when she had stood him up, the same pride which had made his great-grandfather repudiate his family.

Torr said: "He checked out this morning, but the reception clerk doesn't think he went to the airport. For one thing he was making arrangements to retain the use of his car. He did say something about going back into the country."

"The country?" She turned to stare at him. "But... but why? I mean, he hadn't any business contacts outside London, had he?"

Torr sat down, smiling mischievously. Lois was indignantly aware that her anxiety was amusing him.

"I fancy we've had a wasted journey, my dear. I expect he's gone back to Erne."

"Erne? But he'd left..." She was bewildered.

"I imagine that the business that brought him back to Town is concluded and he's seeking our rural joys again. My father gave him a standing invitation to come any time he wished."

"I can't imagine why he should want to go back to Erne."

Torr was staring at the ceiling.

"Can't you, my dear? If I were in Val's place..." He shot her an oblique glance. "Which I rather think I am at the moment, though fortunately he doesn't know it." His gaze returned to the ceiling. "I repeat, if I were in Val's place I should certainly go back to Erne, if I believed you were there, as apparently he does."

She shook her head helplessly. "He'd never go back to look for me, if that's what you mean."

"Exactly what I do mean. Don't forget I saw his face when you came in with your offering of cigars. Now he's had time to think things through, he may have arrived at the right conclusion. Shall we go and find out?"

"What? Go back to Erne? But I couldn't possibly, I've got a job—besides, where would I go?"

"To the Hall, of course. Place is big enough to accommodate an army."

"To... to stay the night? But that's quite impossible, what would your father say?"

"My father's so vague he doesn't know who's staying with him and who isn't. I'll say you've come down to see his cacti. That's the one subject he's really enthusiastic about. Do you know anything about cacti?"

"Not a thing."

"You soon will if you tell him you're interested."

"But Miss Anstruther?"

"She isn't mistress there... yet." He leaned over the table towards her, and for once he looked wholly serious. "Look, Lois, is it important to you to clear things up with Val, or isn't it?"

"Very important... but..."

Torr put a persuasive hand gently over hers.

"Let an old rake give you a word of advice. If your heart's set on an objective, go all out for it. Scruples and hesitation never won a woman, or a man either. If you want Val, go and get him."

"But I don't know if he wants me."

"Oh, he does," Torr said confidently. "He's just got some silly maggot in his brain that we've got to dislodge. That's the trouble with you proud virtuous people, instead of taking what you want, you go erecting barriers of pride, jealousy and whatnot to fog the issue. You're a very charming girl, Lois, and if you can't get round him, you aren't the woman I think you are. Well, are you coming?"

Lois stood up. "Yes," she said.

"Good for you—and by the way, talking about cacti, there's a variety that's very common in your part of Italy, with a leaf like a sword blade. Mother-in-law's tongue, some people call it. I will say one thing for Cis, her mother's dead and gone, thank goodness. What's yours like?"

"Nothing like cactus," Lois said, laughing, as they left the restaurant.

During the drive back, Lois was in a state of considerable trepidation. All very well for Lord Torrington to be so confident, but she was far from feeling so. Her mistake over Val's identity could be forgiven, it was one many people seemed to have made, but he was under a misapprehension about her relationship with Torr and to be returning with him was not the best way to dispel it. Torr himself insisted that all could be explained, but she was very uneasy about the outcome.

The evening sunlight was gilding the trees when they turned in at the big gateway at Erne, throwing long shadows across the park lands. The rooks were flying homeward to their roosting places and pigeons were circling round the main tower of the hall.

"Dratted birds, they make such a mess," Torr complained. "I'm always shooting them, but they multiply faster than I can pot them."

"It seems a shame," Lois sighed, to which he returned succinctly.

"Erne was not built to be a pigeon loft."

He brought the car to a halt before the steps leading up to the private apartments, and came round to open the door for her. Very reluctantly she stepped out into the forecourt.

"Cheer up, sweetheart," he said encouragingly. "Nobody's going to eat you, we can but do and die, and don't forget, you're passionately interested in cacti."

Side by side they walked up the long flight of shallow steps.

The private apartments contained a dining room and a sitting room on the ground floor, the latter opening out into a conservatory in which the cacti were housed. There was a modern kitchen at the back, and a small

room designated the smoking room, which was the
Earl's private sanctum.

When Lord Torrington and Lois arrived, the small
house party which had survived the ball was assembled
in the sitting room, which Lord Erne still called the
drawing room, to await the advent of dinner. Cecilia
Anstruther was wearing a décolletée dress in ivory
silk and Lord Erne a velvet smoking jacket. In addition
there was a sporting-looking couple of uncertain years,
dressed in dowdy garments, and a young pair, the female half of which, to Lois's relief, was wearing
trousers.

As Lord Torrington ushered her in, Lois found herself the focus of five pairs of curious eyes; Lord Erne
did not raise his, he was deep in a horticultural book.

"Perry," Cecilia exclaimed, "at last! Where on earth
have you been all day?"

Torr grinned. "Don't say you've missed me, darling.
I thought you were much too absorbed in pulling my
home to pieces. Dad," he turned to his father, "I've
brought Miss...er...?" He looked interrogatively at
Lois.

"Lang," she whispered.

"Oh yes, of course. Miss Lang to see you. She's dying to be shown your cacti. She's come all the way from
Italy on purpose."

Lord Erne closed his book and beamed at Lois, who
was wishing she was a hundred miles away. She feared
what Lord Torrington's impish humour would prompt
him to say next.

"I'll be delighted to show them to you after dinner,"
the Earl of Erne told Lois courteously, "but actually
they look better by daylight."

"Oh, she can see them again in the morning," Torr
announced cheerfully. "She's staying the night. I'd better tell Fernando to get a room ready for her and to
bring in her case."

Cecilia bit her lip with annoyance. "Really, Perry!"

she exclaimed. "We've got a house full already, what with a new-found cousin of yours turning up again unexpectedly..."

Lois's heart gave a leap, and she felt her colour rise. So Val was here. Torr had been right in his deductions. She glanced apprehensively towards the door.

"I thought he might," Torr interrupted his fiancée with satisfaction. He winked triumphantly at Lois. "Where's he got to?"

"He's out in the grounds," Cecilia informed him coldly. "Seems he's looking for some female he saw at the ball whom he believes is an old acquaintance. Met her in Italy or something." She gave Lois a venomous glance. "Really, this place might be a boarding house!"

Lois was sure only her breeding prevented her from making a violent outburst.

Torr rang the bell while the Earl bade Lois sit down and hastened to pour her out a drink. Lois took it mechanically and thanked him. The information that Val was looking for her had filled her with elation, he was sure to contact Mrs. Harris who would tell him about her illness, which perhaps would soften him. She wished he would appear and relieve her present embarrassment; she felt she was imposing upon Lord Erne's hospitality, and Cecilia was obviously thinking so.

Fernando entered noiselessly and looked questioningly at his master.

"Another room wanted," Lord Torrington told him. "This lady is staying the night. If necessary, open one of the State apartments."

The Spaniard's opaque eyes showed a flicker of recognition as he glanced at Lois, but he betrayed no surprise.

"Very good, my lord," he returned. "I suppose the Blue Room will be suitable?"

"Quite, if she doesn't mind sleeping in a four-poster."

"Anything will do," Lois said hastily.

"That bed's a priceless heirloom," Cecilia objected as the man withdrew after being instructed to retrieve Lois's case from the boot of Torr's car where it had reposed all day.

"Do it good to be aired," Torr returned, pouring himself a drink.

"Might one inquire where you picked...met Miss Lang?" Cecilia asked with false sweetness.

"That's a long story," her fiancé announced airily. "And as I don't want to bore you with needless repetition, I'll wait until Val gets here to tell it."

But Val was long in coming. Lois was shown to her room, a magnificent apartment with a huge bed with curtains that when drawn enclosed it like a tent. A contrast to her camp bed at the Harrises', she thought wryly, but oh, how she wished she were at the cottage. Mercifully there was a bathroom adjacent, and she washed and brushed her hair, which was all she could do as she had no dress in which to change. By now events had become too complicated for coherent reasoning, she could only let them take their course.

Upon her diffident reappearance in the drawing room, the Earl asked plaintively:

"Need we keep dinner back any longer? Our Canadian cousin appears to have lost himself."

"Certainly not," Cecilia said decisively. "I don't see why all the food should be spoilt because the riff-raff Perry has collected hasn't the manners to be punctual."

"Don't you forget yours," Torr told her with a dangerous glint in his eyes. "Certainly we won't wait any longer, but my friends aren't riff-raff, Cis."

Lois's sympathies were with the outraged woman. Torr had absented himself all day without explanation; an unknown girl had been presented to her also without explanation, she was being kept from her dinner by the vagaries of a self-invited guest, and in addition, her fiancé had reprimanded her for being rude.

Controlling her temper, she said loftily: "Of course it

is your privilege to invite whom you choose, and I apologize. I'm famished, and I'm always a little short when I'm hungry."

Her rather prominent blue eyes looked at Torr, saying as plainly as if she had spoken, "You wait until I get you alone!"

They all moved towards the door, but before they reached it, they were checked. Val Daventry appeared in its framework and stood surveying them with lowered brows. Lois's heart contracted at the sight of him actually in the flesh. His image had filled her waking thoughts ever since the ball, but it had been overlaid by that of his kinsman. She saw now how much more virile he appeared than Lord Torrington. Everything about him was a little more vivid. His hair looked denser and blacker, his eyes were brighter, his whole lithe body leaner and harder. Torr was like a slightly blurred carbon copy.

Val was obviously in a black rage, and Lois was reminded of the night when she had first spoken to him, but his anger then was like summer lightning compared with the volcanic eruption of passion which now consumed him. His brows were drawn down over smouldering eyes, his lips compressed in a savage line. Seeing Lord Torrington, he strode up to him and seized him by his coat lapels.

"You unspeakable cad!" he said in low, furious tones. "I've just come from seeing your lodgekeeper's wife. She says Lois has been staying with her until this morning, when you came to take her away, and it was only a few nights ago that your engagement was publicly announced."

He shook him violently.

"Oh!" the Hon. Cis ejaculated faintly. She turned her head to glance at Lois. "I might have known it!" Infinite contempt was expressed in her eyes, to be succeeded by a slight puzzlement.

Lois was masked from Val by the other guests, who

were looking amused. She wished the floor would open and swallow her before he saw her. In his present savage mood it did not look as though sweet reason would make any impression upon him.

Torr said: "Hold on, you old madman, you're rushing to wrong conclusions."

"Do you deny she's been staying down here so you could have access to her?"

"Yes, very definitely. Take your hands away, Val, there are ladies present."

Val released him, and made a great effort to control himself. He turned to Cecilia who was nearest to him, saying: "Forgive me, I was forgetting it isn't the done thing to assault one's host under his own roof."

"You had provocation," she returned with a bleak smile.

Val turned back to Torr. "I'll have it out with you later, when we're alone," he muttered.

The two men were eyeing each other like a pair of fighting cocks, and looked so alike, the faded matron exclaimed:

"But they're as similar as two cherries on one stem!"

Torr laughed shortly. "Oh, we come from the same stem all right. There's no doubt about that. Calm down, Val, and let's have dinner. Poor Cis is starving and I'm sure Lois must be too, it's hours since we had lunch."

"Lois?" Val inquired. His eyes raked round the room until he discovered her. She did her best to meet his look candidly, after all her only fault was to have acted indiscreetly, but her eyes fell before the blazing scorn in his. His glance went from her to Torr and his lip curled, but he said nothing. She was uncomfortably aware that the focus of his anger had shifted. He was more incensed with her than with Lord Torrington.

"She came back to look for you," Torr explained lightly.

"She didn't, she came to see my cacti," Lord Erne

contradicted him. The look he bestowed upon the two young men suggested that they were causing an unseemly disturbance in his house party. He offered his arm to Lois. "Come along, my dear. We'll go into dinner and leave them to argue if they wish to do so. If you're from Italy, have you seen the exotic gardens at Monaco?"

Gently but firmly he led her towards the dining room. How much of the foregoing altercation he had understood, Lois had no idea, but she suspected he was a good deal more aware of what went on than he betrayed. His purpose now was to pour oil on troubled waters, and he succeeded. The others followed them in silence, though the two Daventrys were still glowering, and Cecilia looked disgusted. But they were people who had been trained to conceal their feelings under a polite veneer, and the conversation throughout dinner, though strained, was general.

Lois, seated on the Earl's right hand, knew that she had been specially honoured, from the kindest of motives, and her heart went out to the gentle, courteous old man in a wave of passionate gratitude. For his sake she strove to recall all she could remember about the cactus garden at Monte Carlo, with which, it seemed, he was familiar, but she was woefully ignorant of the Latin names. Her heart ached as the recollection of that gorgeous day with Val returned to her. She wondered if he were remembering it too, and ventured to steal a look at him. She found his eyes were fixed upon her with an ominous glitter in them and hastily dropped her own. Torr was teasing Cecilia, and she hoped he was giving her the true explanation of their escapade, but she was uneasily suspicious that he was not doing so, merely exaggerating it to aggravate his fiancée.

Lord Erne was watching her with faint amusement, and she guessed that she had revealed her ignorance of his hobby. She said frankly:

"I'm afraid your son misled you, my lord. I don't

know much about cacti, but I find them fascinating, so I hope you'll tell me all about them."

She gazed at him with limpid hazel eyes.

"That will be a privilege," he said gravely. She discovered that he too had those same disturbing tawny eyes, peculiar to the Daventrys, though his were shadowed by his bushy brows. She heard Val give a strangled laugh, which he stifled in his table napkin, and she shot him an indignant glance, only to quail before the savage glint in his. It was unfair, she thought wrathfully, she was doing her best to carry off a well-nigh impossible situation; nevertheless she resolved to stick to the Earl like glue for the remainder of the evening and trust to Torr to put things right with Val.

That proved easy, for as soon as the meal was over he took her into the conservatory and she had to try to concentrate on the peculiar plants that so absorbed him. Nor was it all a pretence, for he knew how to make his subject interesting. If she had not been so conscious of Val's presence in the drawing room behind them, she would have enjoyed his discourse; as it was, she could only give him half her attention.

The interior of the room was visible from the conservatory, which was connected to it by glass doors, which had been set ajar. Val seemed to be conducting a languid flirtation with the young lady in trousers, and though Lois frequently glanced in his direction, Lord Torrington did not approach him. Instead he was devoting himself to his fiancée. No doubt that was as it should be, but it meant Val was no nearer the truth. Gradually it was forced upon her that Lord Torrington did not intend to help her out. He had brought her back to make peace with Val and considered he had done his part and the next move was up to her. But the situation had deteriorated due to Mrs. Harris's revelations, and she doubted if Val would even give her a hearing. He was firmly convinced that she was one of Torr's girls, and in face of all the evidence against her, she could hardly blame him. Yet it was up to her to make some sort of an attempt to placate him, it was the justification for her presence there, but she was at a loss to know how to approach him without risking a public snub.

Fernando brought in a tray of drinks at ten o'clock, the customary nightcap which was served to anybody who wanted one. The men took whisky and soda, so did the trousered girl and Cecilia. Lois declined.

"You should have something," the Earl said kindly. "Perhaps a glass of milk would be more to your liking."

He rang the bell and in spite of Lois's remonstrances, a glass of milk appeared. To her astonishment Val took it from Fernando and carried it across to her. She was sitting a little apart from the others on a seat in the window embrasure, and he stood before her holding out the glass.

"Here's your tipple," he said. "Innocuous stuff."

"It is, isn't it?" She looked at him appealingly. As he had not had time to change, he wore a tweed jacket over a cream shirt, the sort of garb he had worn in Italy, and last time they had been together he had embraced her passionately, but though her eyes sought his, full of wistful longing, his expressed as much feeling as a stone image.

"Milk for the kitten," she said meaningly.

His lip lifted in a snarl. "Snakes also like milk."

"Please, Val," she pleaded, "there's a lot I want to tell you. I...I'm not here for the reason you think. Couldn't we go somewhere private?"

"My dear Miss Lang!" He pretended to be shocked. "I'm under no illusions as to why you're here, and your conduct is outrageous, but we must preserve appearances—if we can. Incidentally, your lodgekeeper friend was quite convinced you were on your way to Gretna Green—she doesn't seem to be aware that immediate marriages over the anvil are no longer legal, but I don't suppose that would worry you. However,

I'm glad for Cecilia's sake that you thought better of it, or perhaps Torr did? He'd more to lose than you had."

The slow colour crept up under her skin.

"Val, please, don't say such horrible things!"

"Surprising that you can still blush," he drawled.

The colour receded, leaving her very pale, her eyes enormous, all black in her white face.

"I've been ill. I wasn't fit to go back to London, then I was offered a lift..."

"What a sad story, but your friend didn't mention any illness. She said you flew to Torr like a homing pigeon and it was a pretty sight to see you together. I would have called it something very different."

Miserably Lois thought that Mrs. Harris's flights of romantic fancy could not have been more ill-timed. It must have been she who had summoned Lord Torrington, and seeing her drive off with him had caused her to arrive at the wildest of conclusions, which Val had accepted as fact.

"Didn't your likeness to Torr hit her?" she asked eagerly, for if she had noticed it, it was a step towards disabusing him of his mistake. Then she bit her lip in vexation for she should have said "Lord Torrington."

Val shrugged his shoulders carelessly. "It was nearly dark in her passage, and she was too thrilled with her own news to look at me."

Definitely Mrs. Harris had been no help.

"But you came back from London to find me," she prompted. "Miss Anstruther said you thought you recognized a friend from Italy."

"And you thought she meant yourself? Bit self-centred, aren't you? I'm afraid I shall never find the girl I met in Italy, she doesn't exist. No, I came back to say goodbye to the family and have a last look around before leaving for Canada. I met a half-witted oaf in the grounds, who spun me a yarn about seeing a ghost several nights ago, who'd vanished into the lodgekeeper's cottage. Ghosts have always intrigued me, so I went to investigate, and there I learned the full sum of your indiscretions, my pet. I'll admit I had an urge to punch Torr's head, but upon reflection, you aren't worth it.''

Lois wilted under his biting words. This man could never have loved her, if he was so ready to believe the worst of her. She caught Torr's eye across the room, he was watching them approvingly, believing that she was straightening out the tangle, but without his co-operation it would be impossible to convince Val that she had been genuinely deceived by the likeness between them.

Val saw the direction of Torr's glance and sneered, looking exactly like the portrait of the fifth Earl.

"Since I don't want to be accused of trespassing, I'd better move to a less contentious vicinity.''

Anger surged up in Lois, for he had only come to speak to her for the pleasure of insulting her. His masculine vanity was wounded because he believed that Torr had succeeded where he had failed.

"Yes, you'd better go,'' she told him bitterly. "Since you can't even be civil.''

"You prefer Torr's suave insincerities? For your comfort, this is goodbye, Lois. I only regret I ever ran across you. Tomorrow I shall be going home, and I can't tell you how I'm longing to be back in my own country. The air seems cleaner and fresher out there, and I like to think that our girls are true.''

With which thrust he left her, strolling over to the girl in trousers, who welcomed him with greater alacrity than a married woman should have shown.

Lois hid her glass of milk behind the window curtain. Her throat was tight and closed with unshed tears. She could not drink it.

The evening was hot and close after the warm day, thunder was rolling up from the west, and the presage of the coming storm added to the tensions within the room.

Val was sitting on the arm of the girl's chair, non-

chalantly swinging one foot. She could not see his
face, but Lois could; it wore an expression of insolent
contempt, it was the way he used to look at Nella after
he had quarrelled with her, for he despised the women
who were avid for his favours. She seemed further
than ever from clearing up the misunderstanding between them, and she was beginning to wonder if Val
were not being deliberately obtuse. The news that he
was searching for her had seemed a hopeful sign, but
he had denied that such was his intention. Mrs. Harris's disclosures had given him an excuse to repudiate
her without a qualm of conscience. He was glad to be
going home, and still more glad to be returning unen-
cumbered.

She wished she could avoid spending the night at
Erne, but there was nowhere else she could go, and no
transport available. She must continue to endure until
she could slip away first thing in the morning. How
naïvely foolish she had been to return with Lord Torrington without having ascertained how Val would
greet her.

A distant rumble caused the sporting woman to say
nervously that she hoped the storm would pass Erne
by, as she did not like thunderstorms at night. Torr told
her gallantly:

"You can always come in to me, you know, my
room's next to yours."

"No need, I'll be with her," her husband said
frostily.

"You know you always sleep through thunderstorms," his wife complained. "Even an air raid
wouldn't wake you!"

Lois thought of her own vast chamber with misgiving. It was too much like a museum to be a comfortable
locale in a thunderstorm.

Lord Erne suggested making up a four for bridge,
but the majority of the company opted for bed. Lois,
who did not play, declined a perfunctory invitation

from Cecilia and said good night. As she passed Torr, who opened the door for her, he whispered:

"You don't seem to have made much headway."

She shrugged her shoulders helplessly. "It's hopeless, he won't listen to me. Look at him now."

Both glanced towards the bridge table, where Val was to be one of the players. He looked towards them with an evil glint in his eyes.

"A hard nut to crack," Torr said. "But don't lose heart. There's always tomorrow, and I'm sure he'll come round in the end."

Tomorrow Val was returning to Canada, and not only had he finished with her, but he was relieved to have done so.

CHAPTER EIGHT

Lois ascended with her fellow guests to the upper floor, parting from them at their doors with a formal good night. The sporting woman was still moaning about the possibility of a thunderstorm, the younger woman of the other pair had the sleek look of a well stroked cat. Val had been lavish with his insincere compliments. Cecilia and Torr had stayed to make up the bridge party, and Lois hoped the latter would get round to explaining the reason for her presence at Erne. Her companions seemed to have accepted her as a family friend in spite of the diversion Val had caused upon his dramatic entrance. That they had shrugged off as a private matter beyond their comprehension, it was doubtful if they had grasped the significance of the exchange, and the Earl's intervention had established Lois's position as being beyond reproach.

The Blue Room was the last to be reached, the corridor turning at right angles before she came to its door. At that juncture, the modernized part of the house ceased, and the long passage continued into the older part of the building. Lois paused on the threshold of her room to look down its seemingly interminable length. It was only lit at her end and it disappeared into shadowy darkness. It would, she knew, pass behind the soaring pillars of the Great Hall, surrounded by the stone balconies from one of which she had watched Lord Torrington receive his guests, and continue through the unused rooms beyond. The contemplation of all that vast emptiness was a little intimidating. There were several rooms adjacent to hers, their doors firmly shut, and she thought it was unlikely that they were occupied. Hers had only been opened to accommodate her.

She went in and switched on the light, revealing the impressive furnishings. The canopy of the huge bed reached to the ceiling. Someone, presumably Juana, had turned down the coverlet and unpacked the meagre contents of her case. Her pyjamas looked forlorn on the great expanse of the bed. Mrs. Harris had washed them out and ironed them dry while she was having her breakfast only that morning, which seemed to belong to another life.

It had been very kind of Torr to try to help her, she thought, as she walked over to the dressing-table; he had seemed genuinely concerned about the miscarriage of her romance, and he could not have foreseen how his plans would go awry, but he might have been more explicit about the reason for her return to Erne. That impish humour of his had served her ill, for she suspected that he had rather enjoyed her predicament and he had certainly amused himself needling poor Cecilia. He resented having to marry the Hon. Cis, and the knowledge that her suspicions were unfounded had given him a pleasurable sense of superiority while he teased her, but it would have been kinder to both of them if he had eventually told her the truth, which he had apparently not done. For she seemed to have reached a complete impasse with regard to Val.

Lois sighed, as she mechanically rearranged her humble brush and comb on the expanse of polished wood which represented the dressing-table. It seemed hard that she could not reach him after all she had been through on his account, and she had been forced to accept the conclusion that he had never really cared about her. She had been able to light him up, as the saying was, but the attraction was in reality entirely superficial, and now he feared that if he let her vindicate herself he would in honour bound have to redeem the half-promise he had made to her. So he continued to be wilfully blind, and there was nothing more she could do to undeceive him.

Tomorrow she must find transport to convey herself back to London. She had not notified either Joanna or her office when they might expect her, so they would have concluded that she was still convalescent. Tomorrow also, Val would start his journey back to Canada and that would be the end of the story.

The electric light was inadequate to dispel the gloom of the huge apartment, though there was another bulb over the dressing-table, and a bedside light, and Lois had snapped both on. She saw that everything had been provided for her needs. A carafe of water and a tumbler beside the bed, fleecy towels on an old-fashioned horse, and a brass can of hot water upon a still more old-fashioned wash stand to save her a journey to the bathroom if she wished to wash her hands and clean her teeth.

She wondered who had last tenanted the room. Titled heads must have slept in that bed in the days of Erne's glory, which was now about to receive her humble self. The bed hangings were of blue velvet worked with gold thread, now tarnished, which had given the room its name. Cecilia had said the four-poster was an heirloom.

Catching sight of herself in the mirror, she giggled. Her own appearance in shirt and trousers was so at variance with the apartment's sombre state.

"Cheer up, my girl," she said to herself. "It's an ill wind etc. I always was thrilled by Erne and I never dreamed I'd ever have a chance to sleep under its roof."

Her disposition was naturally sanguine and though she dared not examine her heart too closely, for it was sore from Val's bludgeoning, she began to appreciate her situation. It was not many girls in her position who had a chance to flutter a titled dovecote. She had been entertained by a live earl, given lunch by his son, and been accepted within the sacred precincts of Erne as a guest. It would be something to remember in her old age and tell to her grandchildren, if she ever had any grandchildren. Not being a sentimental fool, she supposed she would get over Val in time...a long time... and possibly marry someone else, though she could not at that moment conceive of being attracted to any man who did not possess the Daventrys' tawny eyes.

"Though I could probably find a more comfortable mate," she thought wryly, stifling the ache in her heart that the thought evoked.

Since she was unlikely ever to tenant such surroundings again, she began a detailed examination of the room, recalling as she did so that it was in this place that Val's origins lay. The irascible great-grandfather might himself have once occupied this room, before he took himself off to Canada.

There were few pictures, rather to her disappointment. She did discover in a corner a not very good oil painting of three children, two little boys in shorts and a girl in a white frock. Torr, his sister and the dead brother? Probably, for all three had the Daventry eyes, and the boys could have been Val in his childhood.

Lois sighed and continued her inspection. Heavy brass candlesticks holding wax candles and a matchbox in a metal container stood on the mantelshelf above the grate which was concealed by a brass firescreen on which was embossed the display eagle which she had first seen on Val's cuff-links. He did not seem to have revised his opinion of the British aristocracy, judging by what he had said after dinner, or was it only Torr whom he despised? The old Earl was a model of an English gentleman, she would never forget his courteous behaviour towards herself.

She went to the window and drew aside the heavy curtains. This side of the house did not overlook the lake. Sheet lightning flickered from time to time illuminating the fields and the low hills in the distance. The storm seemed to have passed over. Below her was an ornamental garden, revealed in a lightning flash, it was a long way below. She was high up in a corner of the great building like an eagle in its eyrie. The House of the Eagles, for Erne was another name for Eagle.

Lois let the curtain drop and began reluctantly to undress. Once she paused, thinking she heard something move, a faint rustle, and glanced apprehensively around. Such a place might well harbour rats or bats, or perhaps it was only a bird nesting in the roof. However, there was nothing she could do about it, she could only hope the creature, if it were a creature, would not emerge into the room.

Finally she approached the immense bed, to enter which was quite a feat. Once she had climbed on to it, she found it was quite comfortable and remembered Mrs. Harris's comment about goose feathers. She seemed to sink into them like a downy nest. With the passing of the storm the night had turned cooler, else she would have found them much too hot. She felt a little lost in the bed's wide expanse. It would have accommodated four persons adequately without overcrowding. She turned her head towards the pillow beside her and for a moment had a vision of a dark head dinting its smooth surface, a bronzed face, with inky crescents concealing its vivid eyes. Instantly she dismissed the fancy; that was something she must not dwell upon.

She left the bedside light on, for its glow relieved her loneliness and she did feel a little lost amid the magnificence of the Blue Room.

She fell asleep, to be awakened with a start as thunder boomed overhead. A second storm had come up and broken directly above the house. She thought of the nervous lady with faint amusement, wondering if her husband had woken up or if she had accepted Lord Torrington's invitation. She wished she were occupying less isolated accommodation, for the storm seemed to increase in violence, the thunder crashes being almost simultaneous with the lightning flashes, and the great room was eerie, the glow from the bedside lamp doing little to dispel the ominous shadows.

The light flickered once or twice and then went out, followed by a deafening crash overhead. The intense darkness, lit from time to time by a violent glare through the chinks of the curtains, was oppressive. Lois was not naturally nervous, she had experienced many Mediterranean storms, but she was enervated by her recent illness and shaken by the events of the previous day. She longed desperately for the comfort of a light. Then she remembered that she had seen candles and matches on the mantelshelf, provided it would seem for just such an emergency. During a lull in the racket overhead, she summoned all her resolution, and sprang out of bed with the intention of lighting them. Her foot landed on something soft and warm, which emitted a blood-curdling shriek. Startled out of her wits, she blundered across the room and overset a chair, which fell with a crash that seemed to reverberate round the room in the intense silence before the next thunder roll.

Lois stood trembling in the middle of the room, waiting for the next flash to get her bearings, and show her what animal was sharing her accommodation.

A beam of light cut a swath through the enveloping darkness, and she realized someone had come in noiselessly carrying a torch.

"Is anything the matter?"

At the sound of his voice, her heart began to gallop and her hands flew to her throat.

"There...there's a wild beast somewhere in the room..."

Val shone the torch round its immensity and on an arm chair by the fireplace, a large black cat glanced at him disdainfully, before continuing to wash its face.

"Oh, it was only a cat," Lois exclaimed with relief, "but it uttered a bloodcurdling yell when I stepped on it. How on earth did it get in here?"

He laughed. "Probably sneaked in while Juana was doing your room and hid under the bed. I heard its screech and apparently it, or you, knocked this over." He picked up the chair, which was a heavy wooden one with an embroidered seat. "It made an almighty thud, and I wondered if murder was being done. I'm next door to you, you know."

She had not known, she had thought the next room was unoccupied. His unexpected appearance had thrown her completely off balance, and she babbled on nervously:

"My light's gone—the storm, I suppose—and I was trying to get to the candles on the mantelpiece." He walked across the room and ran his torch over it. "Are you in another museum piece? It…it's a bit overawing, isn't it?"

"Mine is much smaller and has a modern bedstead. I think it was once connected with this one, a dressing room or a powder closet, and though the doorway has been bricked up, the partition is thin, that's why I heard you shriek."

"I didn't shriek, it was the cat."

"Poor pussy!" He lit the wax candles, and the wicks flared up, twin spears of light in the encircling gloom, and Lois gave a sigh of relief.

"Feeling scared?" Val asked. "Didn't Torr extend to you an invitation to join him, like Mrs. what's-her-name?"

"No, of course not. He's the last person I'd go to. It's been a bad storm, though it seems to be going away now." The thunder had sunk to a distant rumble, though lightning still flickered. "I didn't bargain for treading on a cat," she laughed shakily, but he made no rejoinder to her lightly spoken words.

He was standing by the mantelpiece, with his back to the light, and she saw he was wearing a dark robe over his night gear, and there was something slightly menacing about his figure.

To her discomfiture, he raised the torch, illumining her in its beam, and she became aware of her scanty costume, for her pyjamas were short-sleeved and short-legged. She crossed her arms over her breast in an instinctively virginal gesture, and glanced at him uneasily.

"It's very kind of you to come to my rescue," she told him uncertainly.

"A pleasure, I was glad to avail myself of the opportunity," he faintly stressed the last word. "Hadn't you better get into bed? You're shivering."

She was trembling, but not with cold.

To her relief, Val snapped off the torch and obediently Lois moved towards the great pile of the bed, but paused beside it, hesitating, as the full impropriety of the situation hit her. That Val had come to her aid was a legitimate excuse for his presence, but it would be more seemly if he left before she actually got into bed. It seemed to dominate the room with all its suggestiveness, for this was no discreet divan that could be disguised from its real purpose with an ornamental throw-over.

"Want me to come and tuck you up?" There was a jeering note in his voice from which she shrank. He was fully aware of the bed's significance.

"Thanks, but that won't be necessary."

Resolutely she climbed into the middle of the four-poster, pulling the bedclothes over her shoulders.

"Good night, Val," she said pointedly.

The thunder, as if loth to quit the vicinity, boomed

again, and the candles flickered. Involuntarily Lois exclaimed: "Oh, dear!"

Half-way to the door Val paused. "It seems to be coming back," he observed.

"I...I hope not," she said tremulously.

He turned to face her. "Do you want me to stay?"

"I...I'd be glad of company."

"Even mine?"

"I'd prefer yours to anyone else's." She became aware of a sudden tenseness in his attitude, and sat up abruptly, drawing up her knees. "I...I know I can trust you," she told him breathlessly.

He laughed mockingly. "Don't be too sure of that. I'm a man, you know."

"I do know."

"And as such, you're prepared to make the best of what's to hand?"

An ambiguous question with dangerous overtones. She stared at him wide-eyed, as he went to the mantelpiece, picked up one of the candlesticks and carried it over to the foot of the bed, lifting it high, so that its beam illuminated her. She was sitting with her arms clasping her raised knees; the bedclothes had slipped from her neck and shoulders, covered by the thin pyjama tunic. The candlelight turned her arms to old ivory and found flecks of flame in the hair curling softly round her face. Her eyes, very dark and intent, were fixed on the man standing before her, and she saw that his held the same glitter that she had noticed at dinner, golden points of light reflecting the flame of the candle. His breathing quickened, and his hand shook so that spots of grease fell on the coverlet at the foot of the bed. Outside the lightning still flickered, but the thunder had diminished.

"Do you really want me to stay?" he asked softly, "knowing what payment I shall exact?"

She quivered. "Yes...No...Oh, Val!" It was a cry from her aching heart. Then the full meaning of his words struck her. Believing what he did of her the suggestion was an insult.

"What do you think I am?" she asked sadly. "First Torr, then you?"

"Why not? We look very much alike, and all cats are grey in the dark."

"Val!" Sheer horror sounded in her voice. "Get out!" she said fiercely.

"Why? What's he got that I haven't? Except a coronet, but that he'll never give you. I'll admit you were making the running with the Earl, you little hypocrite, you don't know a cactus from a thistle, but it was wasted effort, my dear. Torr will never give up Cecilia for you, charm you never so wisely. He can't, he's got to marry money."

"I know all that," she said wearily, "and I don't want Torr. For heaven's sake put that candle down, Val, before you set the bed alight."

Obediently he placed it on the nearest table. The flame rose upwards in the still air of the room, illuminating the planes of his face, throwing into relief the carved bronze of his features, his dark brows jutting over the caverns of his eyes. Lois watched him yearningly; she felt no fear of him, though she knew what was in his mind. She wanted him desperately, but she would not surrender to his jealousy and scorn. If she could not have his love, she would remain virgin all her life.

He straightened himself and glanced at her with hooded eyes. She was unaware that she herself looked infinitely desirable, the love that she dared not confess, making her eyes luminous, and giving a soft glow to her skin. Her childish attitude, her slim arms clasping her raised knees, was both innocent and alluring. She said quietly:

"It seems that at last I've got an opportunity to talk to you."

He intervened contemptuously, with an arrogant lift of his head.

"Talk! We've got a unique opportunity. Why waste it in talk?"

"Because you persist in misjudging me, and I must explain..."

"Explain, explain!" he exclaimed violently. He made a movement towards her, but something in her stillness, her total lack of fear, restrained the mad leaping of his pulses. He turned away with something like a groan, and began to pace the room with long measured strides. "You needn't waste your breath with explanations," he told her. "I know you've used me more than once as a substitute for your emotional frustrations." Lois gasped; what new misconception was this? "But you needn't elaborate. Let me put you in the picture in plain black and white without any rose tinting from you. You were marking time out in Italy until Torr came to you, and when he didn't show up you came back here to look for him. Meanwhile I served to while away the time, and my likeness to him must have added piquancy to the situation. Not wanting to go any further!" He laughed unpleasantly. "And I, stupid sucker that I was, believed you to be all sweet innocence, too rare a blossom to be desecrated by my unruly desires. God, Lois, if I'd known then what you were, you'd have got more than a few kisses!"

He paused by the cat, stooping absently to stroke its head. The animal stretched and purred. The gesture wrung Lois's heart, so tender towards a dumb beast, so harsh towards herself.

"But surely at Diano Castello..." she began hesitantly, nostalgia washing over her, as she recalled the dim space before the church, the tall mast of its illuminated tower, the glittering points of light that marked the line of the coast, and Val, tender and loving, asking her to think carefully of what she must lose if she accompanied him to Canada, when all the time it was he who was doubtful, and had finally decided that he did not love her after all.

Val swung round to face her accusingly.

"That was your master stroke, my darling. You made a proper fool of me that night. When you begged me to come back, I really thought you meant it."

"But Val, I did..."

"So much so that when I returned, I found you'd vanished without a word or a sign." (Enrico must have lost her address, she decided.) "I didn't realize then that you were after bigger game than a mere Canadian nobody, not until I came to Erne and found you skulking around in that ridiculous get-up. Even then I still didn't see, until you hit my face down by the river. God, Lois," he clenched his fists, "when you had the audacity to come back with that heel, I wanted to smash his face in, but that isn't done in a gentlemen's house—besides, he can't help it, philandering is his natural bent. But you, you double-crossing little bitch," his hands went to his throat, pulling at the collar of his night-gear as if he were choking, or to demonstrate what he would like to do to her, "you've duped me all along!"

Lois continued to regard him steadily, seeking to find an opening in his passionate tirade to put her case to him. She said now:

"I've never duped you, Val, it's you who are duping yourself. You've twisted the facts to reach a wrong conclusion."

"You'd like me to think so, but you won't mislead me again," he told her harshly. He resumed his restless pacing, seeming to find in movement some relief for the pressures building up inside him. "I don't want to think ill of you, kitten," he went on, and his use of his pet name for her twisted her heart-strings, though she did not think he was aware that he had spoken it. "In Liguria you appeared so sweet and genuine, like a spring flower, and all that I could wish for in a wife. I thought you...cared...yet when at last I found you again you repulsed me." At her small sound of dissent, he stopped and shot her a barbed glance. "You struck me in the face," he reminded her. Again he returned to his pacing. "After that night, I thought things over and it occurred to me that there might be some misunderstanding. This extraordinary likeness between Torr and myself has caused quite a lot of confusion..."

Lois lifted her head eagerly; he was approaching the truth and his admission that she had been all he had looked for in a wife had raised her hopes to a high pitch of expectancy.

"So I came back with the intention of finding out where you were living and ascertaining the truth. Oh, yes, I know I told you a lie about that," as she gave an exclamation. He smiled wryly. "I didn't want to give you the satisfaction of knowing I took so much interest in you, but it doesn't matter now."

He halted at the foot of the bed, and his voice deepened to accusation. "That woman at the lodge stripped away any lingering illusions concerning you. She convinced me that you were infatuated with Torr, another of his troop of girl-friends, and if I needed any further proof, I got it when I came into the house and found you there, shamelessly flaunting yourself in his company. How dare you impose upon Lord Erne's hospitality and insult poor Cecilia?"

Lois winced at the fierce hostility in his eyes and voice and marvelled at the ingenuity with which he had worked out his totally false assumptions. Indignation stirred in her, he should have known her better than that, but she had in justice to him to concede that he had only known her for a fortnight before he had gone away.

Schooling her voice not to betray her rising resentment, she told him: "Mrs. Harris put me up for the night of the ball and I had to stay on because I'd contracted a chill..." He gave an exclamation of disbelief. "That's true, Val, she'll confirm it. Lord Torrington offered to take me back to London..."

Val's lips curled in a sneer.

"He conveniently happened to be passing, I suppose?" he cut in.

"He was on his way..."

"And you thumbed a lift?"

Again she felt a quick thrust of indignation at his misplaced facetiousness, and controlled it with an effort. A display of emotion would avail her nothing, and anger upon her part would fan the fires in him which she was anxious to bank down. She must somehow maintain her cool pose if she were to convince him she was speaking the truth.

"Of course not," she said disdainfully. "Do be serious, Val." She stared at his shadowed face, her eyes dark wells of supplication reflecting the candlelight. "I swear to you I'd never spoken to him until that morning."

Unwinkingly he returned her gaze. "Don't perjure yourself."

"Oh, Val," she cried desperately, "do try to listen without prejudice!"

He moved away, and sat down on the arm of the chair which contained the cat. Absently he began to caress it, and it expressed its appreciation of his attentions in deep-throated purrs.

"Go on," he told her, "I'm listening."

The remaining candle on the mantelshelf gilded the ebon thatch of his hair, and outlined his fine profile. He seemed more interested in the cat than in hearing what she had to say, nevertheless she persisted.

"I don't know why Lord Torrington called at the cottage yesterday morning, I think Mrs. Harris must have said something..." He shot her a significant glance, but he did not interrupt. "When I saw him, and it was for the first time, Val, I realized that I'd thought he was you when I saw him at the ball, and later, I believed you were he. I...I told him about us. He said you were on your way to Canada, but I might be able to intercept you if I went with him then and there; but when we got there, we found you'd returned. I...I came back to find you. That's all, Val, except that I..." She stopped, checking the words upon her tongue. She had been about to say that she loved him and he was breaking her heart with his cruel doubts, but in his present dark, inimical mood, he would take any declaration of love from her as a direct invitation. She dropped her head on her knees and gave a long sigh.

"What do you mean by saying you thought he was I at the ball? Why did you come to Erne at all if it wasn't to see him?"

"To...to find out." She realized then that he had no idea that she had thought he was his kinsman when she had struck him, and recalling the long line of deductions which had led her to that conclusion, it was going to be very difficult to explain her mistake with all its complications.

Val made an impatient gesture. "To find out if you still had a chance with Torr?" he insinuated.

"No. I keep telling you I never met Torr until yesterday morning, but I thought you were he..."

"This gets more and more involved. You're a poor advocate, Lois, you can't even plead your own case coherently. I think my version of your behaviour is much more consistent than your attempts at self-justification."

It was hopeless, she could not convince him if he did not wish to be convinced. She said with a flash of spirit:

"Believe what you want to believe, I've no more to say, and you'd better go back to bed."

"But I've something to say." At his tone she raised her head in alarm. He abandoned the cat, and springing to his feet, went on in silky accents which concealed a hidden menace.

"I'm aware that I lack the polish of an English milord to which you are accustomed, so you must excuse me if my approach is a little crude." He advanced to the foot of the bed, and even in the dim light she could see how his eyes were smouldering, and his muscles tensed, like an animal about to spring. "You aren't any unpicked flower, Lois Lang, for all your innocent airs, and I still find you maddeningly desirable." His voice became hoarse. "This is my opportunity to teach you a lesson, and perhaps when I've done with you, you'll think twice before attempting to play with a man's emotions. Such amusement is, you know, called playing with fire, and fire, my girl, can consume."

Savagely he flung the words at her, but she did not quail. She suspected he was threatening more than he intended to perform. Wounded by her supposed duplicity he was seeking to assuage his jealous hurt by frightening her, but she was not at all scared. Rather she was elated by the information that he still desired her. For all that the atmosphere was fraught with danger. The candlelit gloom was pregnant with the clash of their wills, the dark passionate man wanting to rend and tear, the still, pale girl who was confident that providing she kept her head, she could subdue the devil in him.

Unfortunately she was not as cool as she strove to appear; her pulses had leaped in response to the fire in him. She knew that any weakening on her part would hurl them into a vortex which could only sear them both. The Blue Room must have witnessed many kindred scenes of fiery consummation, when bygone Daventrys had asserted their seignorial rights, but Val was no lustful cavalier or Regency rake. He was a decent twentieth-century product, and though at that moment he was in the grip of a primitive lust, the aftermath would be bitter shame if he yielded to it.

She said quietly: "You can't do that, Val. Even though you persist in believing I'm what I'm not, you can't abuse yourself."

Their eyes locked; she met the smouldering flame in his unflinchingly, and continued to regard him steadily and without fear. Then he gave a strangled ejaculation, the glow died out of his eyes, leaving them dull and dark, and his muscles went slack.

"You win," he muttered. He pushed the hair off his brow. "Guess I was mad for a moment."

He walked to the window, and pulled back the curtain. The storm had moved away, and outside the rain was pouring down, soaking into the thirsty soil.

Lois watched his dark figure hungrily. She had not moved and her body was taut with longing. Every instinct was urging her to call him back, to surrender blindly to his will, to take the little he could give her without haggling. Her knuckles whitened as she clenched her hands round her knees. He would despise her even more if she offered herself to him now and reproach himself ever after for his weakness, while she herself would sink into an abyss of shame and regret for so desecrating her love, for the sake of a brief gratification. She had won her victory over him, and must abide by it, though the taste of it was bitter ash in her mouth.

He turned from the window and walked back to the bedside, and her heart knocked against her ribs, though her still face gave no sign of her inward turmoil. He stood looking down at her, but since the light was behind him she could not see his expression, though she sensed that the tension had gone out of him.

"You can still look like an innocent child," he said with a sigh. "Difficult to credit that it's all an act." He passed his hand over his brow and moved away from her. "For a moment I was crazy with hate and rage. I wanted to punish you, Lois, but it's no use. Though you may be a mercenary little bitch, I can't hate you, kitten, nor can I hurt you. I love you too much."

"Val!" Incredulous joy seeped through her, but without looking at her again, he scooped up the cat and went out of the room, carefully closing the door behind him.

She could not let him go after that confession without making a supreme effort to convince him of her integrity; an avowal of her own love for him might help. She jumped out of bed and stumbling across the dimly lit room, wrenched the door open. She was too late, for she heard his close and the click of a key turning in the lock. Looking round she saw that he had left his torch on the mantelpiece, and picking it up, returned to the corridor. She stood hesitating on the threshold of her room, for it would be wildly imprudent to knock upon his door, even with the excuse of returning the torch, but would she ever get another chance to put herself right with him?

She became aware that a faint light was showing from the angle of the corridor on her other side, and caught the sound of a guttural voice speaking in Spanish, and then Torr's impatient rejoinder.

"Damn it all, man, why must you wake me, even if the roof is leaking?"

This exchange shocked her back to sanity. To be discovered roaming the corridors of Erne at that hour would destroy what was left of her reputation, and if Lord Torrington encountered her, he would make a joke of her apparent indiscretion. She had little doubt about how he would have behaved under similar circumstances.

Reluctantly she re-entered her room and as she did so, something furry brushed against her legs. The cat, tail erect, preceded her into the room, delighted to have regained the refuge from which Val had evicted it.

Lois laughed and bent to stroke its head.

"Persistent, aren't you, puss? You're determined to get what you want."

She must persist also. Perhaps fate would be kind and grant her a chance to clear herself in Val's eyes before she left Erne next day. An appeal to Torr to corroborate her story would, she knew, be useless. Val would never accept evidence from such a source, but

Mrs. Harris could at least substantiate that she had been ill.

Meanwhile she had the comfort of knowing that the same roof covered herself and Val and the solace of his last words:

"I love you too much."

CHAPTER NINE

EXHAUSTED, Lois slept heavily for a few hours and woke to find the clouds had rolled away and the sun was shining. Although it was very early, she jumped out of bed and made her way to the bathroom, anxious to perform her ablutions before anyone else claimed it. She had no idea of how many people used it. A pail of dirty water under a drip in the passage was evidence of Fernando's leak. The downpour had found the weak spots in the fabric of Erne—another use for Miss Anstruther's money, Lois thought dryly.

Nobody else seemed to be astir, and she wandered outside into the brightness of the morning to ponder upon the events of the night, and consider if there were any possible way in which she could make a further appeal to Val.

The garden which she had glimpsed from her window was formally laid out in a pattern of well-kept beds divided by tiny box hedges, each being filled with summer blossoms. She walked down one of the gravel paths and through an arch covered with rambler roses, to find herself in an enclosed rose garden surrounded by a clipped yew hedge, and there to her consternation she saw the Honourable Cecilia Anstruther, wearing a neat blue linen trouser suit and examining the damage done to the roses by the storm. Lois would have retreated, if anyone had cause to dislike her, it was the Hon. Cis, but Miss Anstruther had seen her. She came briskly towards her, calling:

"Good morning, you're out early."

Lois returned her greeting, and Cecilia came to a halt

beside her. Her hard blue eyes studied the girl's figure, noticing that despite the disturbance of the storm, Lois looked as fresh and dewy as the flowers beside them and considerably less battered than the fragile blossoms. She sighed, for her own first youth was past, and she could in no way compare with Lois's delicate bloom.

"I hope the storm didn't keep you awake," she said frigidly. "It's the worst we've had for some time, and it must have been a bit eerie alone in the Blue Room." An edge crept into her voice, as if to imply that if Lois had not liked her quarters, she had only herself to blame for foisting herself upon her host.

"Oh, I didn't mind," Lois said quickly, a faint flush staining her face, for she had not been alone. She looked appealingly at the other woman and it flashed into her mind that she might be able to make an ally of this rather formidable person, if she could convince her that far from being a rival for Torr's attentions, she needed help.

"Miss Anstruther," she began earnestly, "may I tell you what really happened yesterday and why I came back with Lord Torrington?"

The Hon. Cis stiffened, and Lois sighed. Naturally Miss Anstruther resented her presence and the impulse that had prompted her request was a mistake. Sadly she turned away.

"I . . . I'll go back. You must be hating me."

"No, wait," commanded the Hon. Cis. She again studied the girl. She was not Torr's usual type, he liked sophisticated stylish women, and she had been secretly surprised when he produced Lois. She knew her fiancé very well and did not expect fidelity from him. She was prepared to put up with his amorous adventuring, providing he was discreet, but to bring this girl to Erne had been a definite affront, and it was unlike him to be guilty of discourtesy, unless as the girl had hinted, there was some other explanation besides the obvious one.

"Come and sit down," she said, "there's an arbour over here which may have proved watertight. We shan't be disturbed there and you can tell me all about it."

The arbour was a sort of summerhouse situated in a corner of the rose garden and being built of Italian marble had not suffered from the storm. Inside were several canvas chairs stacked up against the wall. Cecilia opened two of them and signed to Lois to sit down.

"Now," she said, "tell me everything."

"To begin with, I'm not the least interested in Lord Torrington," Lois informed her. "I never spoke to him until yesterday morning…" Cecilia raised her brows. "That's true, Miss Anstruther, it…it's Val Daventry." She stumbled over his name. "Him I met in Italy."

"Right, begin from there," Cecilia ordered.

Thus encouraged, Lois poured forth her story, and it sounded incredible in her own ears, but the alternative was even more so.

"You see, I felt I must explain to Val before he left for Canada," she concluded. "I never dreamed he'd come back here, and then when I turned up here with Torr—I mean Lord Torrington—you all thought the worst, including Val, and now…" her voice broke, "he won't listen to me, he…he called me a mercenary little bitch."

Cecilia was looking at her oddly.

"Truly love is blind," she observed. "Anyone with eyes like yours must be honest, but then I suppose he was mad with jealousy. What fools men are."

"You believe me?" Lois asked timidly.

"Entirely. Nobody could invent a story like yours, unless they were a romantic novelist, which I'm sure you're not. It's a case of truth being stranger than fiction. It all goes back to Val's great-grandfather. The Daventrys are a violent, stiff-necked lot, and if Gervase Daventry hadn't disowned his family, or been disowned by it, I'm not sure which it was, but had kept up with his people in the normal way, we shouldn't have had young Val turning up with a replica of the Daventry features to confound us all." She glanced with amusement at Lois's eager face. "I've studied the family archives since I'm going to marry into it, and there really was a Gervase Daventry who disappeared in Canada. There's a long history of quarrels and feuds—they're a most unforgiving race."

Lois sighed. "Do you think Val will forgive me?"

"My dear child, what has he to forgive? You've been the unfortunate victim of a very natural mistake. How could you know there were two of them, a facsimile of each other?"

"But I did smack his face, and not gently either."

"Do him good," Cecilia said unfeelingly. "The Daventrys are much too fond of acting as if they were the lords of creation. Well, what do you want me to do? Tell Val Daventry he's an unmitigated ass?"

"I don't think that would help," Lois giggled. "But if you could get him to listen to the facts, perhaps he'd believe *you.*"

"He'll listen to me," Miss Anstruther announced grimly. "And since apparently he considers I'm the wronged party"—she smiled, and her smile did wonders for her rather austere face. The Hon. Cis, Lois decided, was quite human after all. "He must accept your story if I do."

She looked at her watch. "It's still too early for breakfast, but Fernando will give you some coffee in the kitchen. You don't mind the kitchen?"

"I'm more at home there than in the drawing room, or..." Lois smiled mischievously, "with the cacti."

"You're too modest; you carried off the situation very well last night in extremely difficult circumstances. Lord Erne was very taken with you."

"I liked him, he isn't a bit like I imagined an earl would be."

"For a Daventry he's remarkably tolerant," Cecilia

observed, "and no fool. If you'd really been after Perry he'd have seen through you."

"But you thought I was?"

"Frankly, my dear, I was puzzled. Your appearance didn't fit the...er...part you appeared to be playing. But come along and get something to eat."

Though Lois was fairly certain that Fernando recognized her as one of the helpers at the ball, he made no reference to it. Nor did either he or his wife resent her appearance in the kitchen at that early hour. She was served with coffee, hot rolls just out of the oven and farm butter with the deference due to a duchess.

Cecilia, having drunk a cup of coffee, she would be breakfasting with the family later on, left her there.

"Go down to the bridge," she instructed her, "and I'll send Val out to you when he's had his breakfast." She touched the girl's shoulder lightly. "Good luck, my dear," she said.

Lois finished her meal leisurely, wondering if Val were up yet. She did not want to encounter him until Cecilia had spoken to him. Her heart was beating high with hopeful anticipation. If he really loved her as he had said last night, even though he believed she was a double-crosser, nothing could prevent a reconciliation once he was undeceived.

She went out into the brilliance of the morning, which seemed all the brighter for the storm. Raindrops still clung to the bushes and sparkled on the grass, but the sun was rapidly absorbing them. The pigeons that Torr had fulminated against circled round the towers of Erne; high in the air a lark was singing. Keeping off the wet grass, Lois strolled down the gravel path towards the bridge. In a short while Val would be coming to her and how would he greet her? Would he apologise for doubting her, but somehow she could not imagine Val abasing himself. A tiny doubt began to grow. Proud and stiff-necked, the Daventrys did not like to have to acknowledge that they were in the wrong. Perhaps he would not come, he would prefer to drive away and forget her.

Lois stepped on to the bridge and looked back at the piled masonry of the house. The week of closure was over and the red cord was being placed across the steps leading to the private rooms. A caterer's van drove into the forecourt, and men came out to carry its contents into the refreshment room above the water garden. The House of the Eagles was preparing to welcome its influx of guests.

But no tall, athletic figure came down the private stairway to search for her. That part of the place looked deserted. The dining room looked out on the other side and that was where the party would be congregated. Lois's trepidation increased. Would Cecilia find an opportunity to speak to him before he left, and if she did, would he be convinced?

She turned her gaze to the water running under the bridge into the lake, which stretched away into the distance, a smooth expanse of blue water reflecting the sky. Then her eye caught a diminutive figure among the reeds of the bank on the further side. Eric had escaped his mother's vigilance and come to the forbidden territory again. Lois glanced in the direction of the lodge, hoping to see Mrs. Harris's hurrying figure, but nothing stirred. There was no help for it, she would have to go and retrieve the truant herself. With a last look at the still empty steps, she crossed the bridge and walked down to the water's edge.

The recent heavy rain had made the approach marshy and muddy, and although Lois sought to pick her way from tussock to tussock, her feet in flimsy sandals were soon soaked.

"Eric," she called. "Eric, come back! You're being a naughty boy!"

The child gave her an impish grin and deliberately advanced further into the reeds; the ground was treacherous and at any moment he might slip into the lake.

"Eric!" she called again desperately. "It's not safe. Come back!"

The boy lost his footing and disappeared with a yell. Lois splashed in after him the water up to her knees. Eric had struggled upright, but he was frightened. He flung himself upon her, nearly knocking her over backwards. Covered in mud and ooze, the child clinging about her neck, Lois sought to regain firmer ground, splashing knee-deep in bog.

"Want any help?"

She pushed the hair out of her eyes and saw Val well beyond the reed bed, immaculately dressed in light fawn trousers and a primrose shirt, and shuddered as she thought what a spectacle she must present.

"I can manage!" she shouted back.

He started to take off his shoes.

"No, don't," she called. "No need for you to get messed up too," and floundered up through the reeds and marsh to the higher ground beside him.

Seeing that she had arrived unaided, Val pushed his foot back into his shoe. Lois disengaged herself from Eric, and feeling thoroughly cross and disgruntled, administered a sharp slap. He emitted a yell of mingled rage and astonishment.

"How can you be so cruel?" Val asked mockingly.

"He's a naughty disobedient child," Lois returned heatedly. "Now, Eric, you go straight back to your mother and get some dry things on. Do you hear me?" as the child gazed up at her. "Go home at once!"

"Aren't you going to carry me?"

"Certainly not. You're filthy."

Eric whimpered, "Mum carried me before."

"Then you were half drowned, now you're perfectly all right, only wet."

"Miss Lang is wet too," Val said gently to the indignant youngster. "She must change her wet things too, so suppose you run along?"

Lois was infuriated by his kindly tone, which seemed

to reproach her own sharp utterances. Eric's immersion was entirely due to his disobedience and she had wanted to appear before Val looking her best. Now her trousers were black mud up beyond her knees, her hair was rumpled by Eric's clutching fingers, and by the feel of it, there was even mud on her face.

Eric was nodding sagely.

"Last time she getted wet, she had to go to bed," he announced. "Doctor comed."

"Corroborative evidence," Val said.

Lois flashed him a questioning look. "You...you've talked to Miss Anstruther?" she asked eagerly.

"Cecilia has talked to me," he corrected her. "In fact I've had a lecture." He smiled at her ruefully. "There's mud in your eye, kitten."

"And everywhere else."

"Too true." He advanced purposefully towards her.

"Don't touch me, Val," she cried, backing away, "or you'll be covered as well. It would be a pity to mess that nice shirt and trousers."

"First things first," he returned. "If you're so concerned about my clothes, you can wash them for me." And he took her in his arms.

Eric, an interested spectator, asked: "Is she hurted so you kiss her to make it better?"

Val removed his mouth from hers. "I'd forgotten the kid," he muttered; then to Eric: "Still here, brat? Yes, she has been hurted, and I'm hoping to make it better." He smiled down into Lois's eyes. "Can you forgive me for being so dim?"

"Oh, Val!" She flung her arms about his neck and buried her muddy face in his neck.

"Apparently you can," he said softly. "But then you're not a Daventry, though you'll be one soon."

"There's Mum," Eric announced.

He looked left and right, and deciding that there was no way of evading justice, went to meet his mother.

"Mum, I's ever so wet and cold," and he sniffed

loudly, hoping retribution would be softened by concern. Val threw a disgusted glance towards the advancing Mrs. Harris.

"What a populous spot!" he exclaimed. "Come on, darling, scram!"

Hand in hand they ran laughing over the bridge, while Mrs. Harris watched their retreating figures with astonished eyes.

"Well, I never!" she ejaculated.

PINK SANDS

Pink Sands
Wynne May

It was a gem of a job, Barbara had to admit. As personal secretary to Sir Basil Harvester, she found the work challenging and Sir Basil a dear. One of the nicest aspects was living in his home, a genuine Scottish castle in coastal South Africa.

When she finally met Sir Basil's son, Gregory, he seemed to fulfill Barbara's dreams, for she fell in love with him on sight.

And then the nightmare began. Sir Basil's selfish and beautiful goddaughter, Reina, made it clear that she wanted Gregory herself. And Rod Haden, Barbara's ex-boyfriend, arrived to further complicate matters.

CHAPTER ONE

You came upon it suddenly. Two stone lions, crouching and waiting, at either side of intricately wrought-iron gates opening into a shadow-flecked drive which led up to its sheer walls and towers outlined against the sky.

The stone exterior which, with the passage of time, had lightened gave no promise of the excitement and colour within the Castle. From the battlements there were fantastic views of the Indian Ocean with its long white plumes falling to their knees on the rocks wrought, by the currents, into fanciful shapes and the great expanses of golden beaches which turned pink at sunset.

Sir Basil Harvester's chauffeur had met them at the airport in a sapphire-blue car and, after the long drive to the lower South Coast with its rolling hills and thick vegetation, on one side, and that dazzling dancing sea on the other, had brought the car to a smooth halt in front of the heavy door and handed them out.

Barbara, tired after the flight, moved her slim shoulders beneath the beautifully cut oatmeal-coloured suit she was wearing. They felt stiff and the nerves and muscles at the back of her head ached. Her auburn hair was taken loosely back from her face, just above the tips of her ears, and arranged in an expensively casual chignon which hours of jet plane travel appeared to have been given no opportunity of teasing into any kind of disorder. Her jade-green eyes, darkly lashed and clear, gave little indication that her body felt completely used up and that she felt almost ready to drop into a huddle at Sir Basil's feet.

Although her position as Sir Basil's personal secretary had projected her into a life as fast and as exciting as the jet age into which she had been born, it was also demanding and exacting. Constant air travel and staying at swish hotels or the private, and *very* remarkable homes, which were frequented by her employer in his capacity of president of Harvester International—the universally famed manufacturers of fine sculptured furniture—was the order of the day.

Back at the Castle, Sir Basil became a modern and lively host to a plentitude of—mostly—business friends. Tall, straight-backed and shouldered, with platinum-silver hair and keen blue eyes, he was notably unassuming and relaxed and smiling down at Barbara now, he said, "Tired?"

She gave him a small, tired smile. "A little, Sir Basil."

The sunset was a wisdom of colour which slanted over his deep tan and silver hair, emphasizing the blue of his eyes. That tan, and those blue eyes, had the power to promote envy in a good many much younger men—as did his loose-limbed frame. "You conceal it well," he said. "But then you always do."

Barbara's eyes flickered away from him in the direction of the silver-haired woman who was framed in the massive doorway of the Castle at the top of a shallow flight of fan-shaped stone steps. Lilian Harvester bore a strong resemblance to her brother and, coming down the steps, she smiled at Sir Basil and Barbara.

"Ah, Basil—Barbara! It's good to see you. How are you?"

Barbara had remained in the background, but then, in response to Lilian's warm greeting and radiant smile, she held out her hands. "You must be exhausted, Barbara," Lilian was saying in her deep husky voice which came as a surprise from one so petite. "You certainly don't look it, though—but then you never do, after one of these trips." She slanted a look at her brother and, laughing lightly, said, "You mustn't allow Basil to work you too hard now that you're back, Barbara."

"He's always most lenient, really," Barbara answered. "It was more like a holiday in Rome than a business trip. I think he has all the reason in the world to expect much more of me now that we're back." Even as she was speaking, however, she was thinking of the short, exquisite time by herself on the battlements where she could watch the mist as it came in from the sea before night finally blacked out the sunset. That climb, up the iron staircase which spiralled upwards, was well worth all the energy expended and, from experience, Barbara knew that later she would stretch out luxuriously on her water-bed—its plastic, water-tight mattress thermostatically controlled—and surrender herself to sleep.

Lilian, as petite as her brother was tall and elegantly angular, began to lead the way into the great hall which dramatically exhibited Harvester pieces in combination with exotic indoor plants. An antique Spanish figure and an iron crucifix, both seventeenth-century, looked at home with white sculptured chairs upholstered in glossy scarlet antique hide.

"Barbara must go straight to her room." Sir Basil always said this on their return from a business trip. "The child must be utterly exhausted." He glanced at Lilian, who smiled and said, "Of course. I heartily agree. But join us, Barbara, for a drink before dinner."

"Thank you. Actually, I'm a hardened traveller now," Barbara answered, although it was, quite suddenly, an effort to lift her voice. There had been a lot of responsibility on this particular trip—extensive shorthand notes to decipher, reports to type, and into the bargain, Rome had been hot, heavy and damp.

"I'll have a tray of tea sent along to your room," Lilian said.

Acquainted by now with the pattern of things at the

Castle, Barbara murmured, "Thank you, Lilian. That will be marvellous."

Occupying a commanding position above the river and lagoon and set in extensive and lush grounds which were terraced and balustraded and enhanced by stone statues and a temple-like folly, the Castle had been built by Scottish stonemasons for Sir Basil's grandfather who had arrived, from Scotland, in the vessel *Morning Glory* and who had wanted a *version—his* version—of a castle. The Castle had taken the stonemasons five years to build and, as Sir Basil himself expressed it, it was in architectural detail totally disordered. "The whole thing," he said, with that charming, momentary quirk of the mouth, "is completely absurd but belongs, nevertheless, to the Harvesters."

Barbara's room enjoyed a long vista down one of the many arched galleries that bordered the centre court where there was a magnificent swimming-pool because, of course, the entire Castle had undergone changes owing to the fact that its present owner took comfort very seriously.

Heavy glazed doors led from the room and, from her bed, she was able to look along an expanse of tiled flooring and six arches, beyond which were double doors, thick with carving, giving access to Gregory Harvester's rooms. She had never met Gregory, for the simple reason that their respective visits to the Castle had never tied up. However, she knew that Gregory was also in the Harvester business and that he travelled extensively and would possibly step into his father's shoes one day.

Against the walls of the arches exotic plants in urns cast designs against the walls and the entire scene had a Moorish touch, which was one of the many surprises. Barbara often found herself wondering what those Scottish stonemasons had been thinking of. From the outside, the Castle was as formidable as any chateau, but the interior, and the many "open" galleries, was like a Moroccan palace—done beautifully and excitingly modern.

On a table next to her bed, pink daisies had been arranged in a small ancient urn, and as she stooped to smell them Barbara relaxed her grip on the strap of her honey-coloured leather bag and let it slip to the bed with its silk melon-pink and lime cover. Then, with a little sigh, she undid the pins and clips holding her hair in place and allowed it to drop to her shoulders where it bounced against the shoulders of the elegant oatmeal-toned suit. As she caught sight of herself in the delicately melon-tinted mirrors on the built-in cupboard doors which lined one entire wall, she went to stand directly in front of one of them and gazed for a moment at her reflection.

She was not so much aware of herself as of the background to which she had grown accustomed. It was a background vastly different from the one she had known as a child—the farm which had always presented a problem to her father. Her father had left England for the sun, but had not bargained on the wind and the drought and the hail followed by torrential floods.

Barbara had been born in South Africa and, up until the age of thirteen, had been driven by her English-born mother across a wheel-rutted road, in a small car, to a school which, by South African standards, was considered to be "within easy reach" of the farm. Then she was sent to a boarding school and finally gained secretarial qualifications.

Before she had completed her studies her parents had died and when she was introduced to Sir Basil Harvester and, some time later, applied for—and secured— the position of personal secretary to this well-known man, her position was secure.

Now, with thoughts of the farm, she shrugged herself out of her jacket, kicked off her shoes and padded across the shaggy lime-green carpet to the long, low built-in dressing-table. A breeze moved the heavy melon-pink curtains which were drawn to either side of the glass doors, and she allowed her gaze to wander in the direction of the open gallery, past the six arches, down the expanse of tiled flooring to the heavy doors leading to Gregory Harvester's private domain. Up to the present time it had satisfied her that their visits had not coincided, because while she was at the Castle she had always had this feeling of utter seclusion and privacy and even at night she slept with the doors of her room wide open and, in the background, there had been the breezes and the pounding noises of the surf to lull her to sleep on her fantastic water-bed. Had Gregory Harvester been at home, however, he might well have done exactly the same thing—thus shattering this privacy.

A maid brought an antique silver tray bearing a small silver teapot and the items to go along with it. The scarlet uniform she was wearing reflected on the tray as she set it down on a small table. The china and the silverware were all exquisitely monogrammed.

"I can't tell you how much I'm going to enjoy that cup of tea, Theresa," Barbara said, smiling at the black girl.

"You are thirsty?" Theresa looked unbelievably cool and relaxed.

Shrugging, Barbara said, "I thought we'd never get here—the airport seems so far away when you're tired."

"It is a long way." Theresa's big brown eyes went in the direction of Barbara's case which had just been brought up. "You would like something ironed?" Her eyes went back to Barbara's face.

"No, thank you, Theresa. Tomorrow, maybe, when I get organized."

"Okay." The other girl almost sang the word out in her precise Mission way of speaking. Completely modern, a scarlet cap sat cheekily on her black hair which had been teased out until it framed her face. She was, thought Barbara, probably the despair of her grand-mother.

Somewhere in the Castle, dogs were barking and the barking turned to excited yelping. "Visitors," Theresa said. "You can hear. When the dogs bark, bark, barking it is visitors." The two girls listened for a moment and then, with a certain amount of tired despair and strain, Barbara said, "Yes—it certainly sounds like it."

Visitors usually meant that she would be expected to remain long after dinner, helping out with small talk, and she realized, too, that she would possibly be called upon now to go down some time before dinner to join Sir Basil and Lilian and their guests, which would mean having to rush her long yearned-for scented bath. Nevertheless, after Theresa had gone she took the tray through to her bathroom which was an essay in pale pink, lime and rose. The bath was in the middle of the shaggy carpet and, on the wide tiled surround there was another small ancient urn displaying tea-roses in shades of apricot and yellow. Barbara turned on the swan-shaped taps and found that she was tense as she half expected Lilian to phone through to ask whether she felt rested enough to join them a little earlier than for-merly arranged.

The scented water was relaxing and she gave herself up to it, sipping her tea in between lathering herself with the expensive soap provided for her use and, after-wards, as she dressed, choosing a sheer golden silk caf-tan which, according to Lilian, left one gasping at her auburn hair and jade eyes, she felt a lot less tired. Bar-bara's eyes made her outstanding in any company and she had astonishingly clear and golden skin to go with them.

When she had completed her toilet she decided to take a chance on Lilian phoning through and left her room, going in the direction of the iron spiral staircase in the external tower which led up to the battlements. The view from the battlements embraced the Indian

Ocean and the coastline on both sides and, at the moment, was capturing a mood of infinite tranquility and timelessness, along with the romance of the Castle which had been built so long ago.

Because of extensive grounds, dropping to the lagoon and the beach by means of rugged flagstone steps and retaining walls, the Castle could have been cut off from civilization. As it was, however, the lights of the coastline sparkled like clusters of priceless gems, reminding one that a lot had happened since Sir Basil's grandfather had been at the Castle. As it brushed the shore and thundered against the rocks the wash of the sea was plainly audible. Barbara's auburn hair blew across her face and the soft damp clung to her arms.

High above the smells of the earth but capturing the salty sea mist which rose up from the sea, she tried to close the doors of her mind and stood, putting out a hand to what the future had to hold for her rather than think of what had gone before—and of her loneliness. Close to the shore she could see the mellow golden lights of a liner as it made its way down the coast. It was a sight familiar to her and yet one which always filled her with more loneliness as she visualized the young people dining and dancing aboard or leaning against the rails to enjoy the swish of the vessel as it cut through the satin-black water. People in love—married, maybe—with families...

Realizing that it was time to go, she turned away and made her way back to the staircase which was invisible, except for a curve of railing, from the battlements. She stood holding on to the railing with one hand while she slipped into her shoes, which she had removed before walking across the floor for fear of damaging the almost soft material which covered it, and then as she fumbled her way down the stairs her shoes made metallic noises which rang out in the tower. At the bottom, a door opened out to a plant-filled foyer where more doors led to various sections of the building.

When she was back in her room she was aware of the dampness on her skin as she tidied her hair, sweeping it back into the sophisticated chignon she always liked to wear in Sir Basil's presence, unless she happened to be at the poolside.

There was the sound of soft music coming from the direction of the library. A girl, with a breathtaking voice—a voice too magnificent to describe—was singing soul. For some unknown reason Barbara had the feeling that she would remember that particular song for a long, long time.

How well she had come to know the library, a high, square panelled room, with its booklined walls, every book bound in chocolate brown leather which formed such a perfect background to the lengthy royal blue sofa with the apricot scatter cushions, royal blue curtains falling in folds from the ceiling-to-floor, small-paned window at the far end of the room, white lamps with dark blue shades and bowls of flowers. At the moment there were arrangements of apricot pink roses and pink, pale mauve and purple asters. The fitted apricot pink carpet was highlighted by a turquoise and apricot patterned area rug in front of the fireplace where Lilian's white cat sat cleaning itself.

"Ah," Sir Basil called out, "just in time for a cocktail, Barbara," and then she was suddenly, and overwhelmingly, aware of the other man in the room—a younger version of Sir Basil, devastatingly handsome in every way. He was tall, lean, with blue eyes and dark hair instead of silver, but, if anything, he was slightly shorter than his father because of course—and she did not have to be told—this was Sir Basil Harvester's son Gregory. She was caught completely off balance, nevertheless.

"Barbara," Sir Basil was saying, coming towards her, "although you've been my very efficient secretary for some considerable time now, you've never met my son—Gregory."

While time stood still something was happening to Barbara and, whatever it was it was disturbing. Something was also happening in the background and the girl with the golden voice was singing, "It's no secret any more...your finger-tips tell me all I want to know..."

The chords of the piano were so hauntingly beautiful that Barbara felt the muscles in her throat tighten and then she found herself saying, "N-no, we've always missed—somehow." She was amazed that her voice sounded so controlled.

With something like recognition Gregory Harvester's blue eyes went over her and she knew that, for that brief moment, she had stopped breathing, and then a curious intimacy seemed to have sprung up in the room.

Barbara's first impression of Sir Basil's son was that he was probably unpredictable, reckless to a point, but dependable—so cool and completely and utterly devastating.

He said, smiling, "My father didn't prepare me for this—shock."

"Shock?" She widened her eyes at him.

"I thought you were much older." She could feel his curiosity mounting as he went on, "As you say, we've always missed meeting. I guess you could say that's because I lead such a comprehensive and double life." His smile was mocking.

"Did I say Barbara was old?" Sir Basil turned to ask, as he went through the ritual of mixing drinks.

"No." Gregory lifted his shoulders. "I merely surmised that she was...well, certainly much older. I gained the impression from those perfectly typed letters—they appeared almost staid in their neatness." His eyes were still on her.

"You mean the ones your father dictated to me?" she asked stupidly and primly, then felt absurd and smiled.

"Where are you going to sit?" he asked. He was

alert, assured, like his father—easily smiling, and gave
the impression of being tanned from Bermuda and
Jamaica. Something told her, however, that, if the occasion so demanded, Gregory Harvester could be ruthless and unrelenting.

At that moment, Sir Basil came to where she was
standing and gave her a drink. "Feeling better?" he
asked.

"Yes." She gave him one of her usual polite smiles.
"Much better, thank you. It's amazing how quickly
one recovers from the kind of tiredness brought on by
air travel."

"That's because you're so young," Gregory said.
His eyes went to her glass and she knew, suddenly, that
her fingers were tight around it and she relaxed them
slightly. Because she felt a little out of her depth she
remained standing. She took a sip of her drink and then
Gregory said, "Tell me, what do you think of Harvester's sexy furniture, Barbara?"

She thought for a moment. "I don't know if I agree
with you," she said. "I wouldn't exactly describe it as—
sexy." While she was speaking she was thinking that
this was not strictly the truth. Harvester's furniture had
the power to quicken the senses and so, she supposed,
it could be described as sexy.

"The way I always figure it," he went on, "is that,
like all things in life, we can be depressed, uplifted,
excited or even calmed, warmed or cooled—by furniture. What does Harvester furniture do to you?" Before she could reply, however, he said, "It shocks
many, you know."

She watched him as he turned the amber liquid
round in his glass and bent his head to the bouquet. He
was perfectly at ease and yet she felt that he was just a
little tense.

Making herself innocent, she said, "I don't know if I
agree with that, either. I think that Harvester's have
created the kind of furniture that..." she broke off,

groping for words, and then went on, "creates a *need*. I mean, this is the age of space technology, after all, and people think—and live—along those lines."

In the background, the girl with the golden voice was still singing: "Don't whisper things to me you don't mean..." and the piano, taking command with its decisive chords, ingeniously syncopated phrasing, odd little arpeggios that always moved downwards, leading the other instruments on.

"Chairs, for instance," Barbara made herself go on, "chairs of perspex and fitted with leather upholstery could be said to be stretching the space age to the limit." She slanted her jade eyes in Sir Basil's direction. "However," she tried to look serene, "they can also be something which makes one want to feel part of them— just by sitting on them."

Rattling ice-cubes, Sir Basil said, "And that's precisely what Harvester's is all about, Barbara."

"I've often wondered," Gregory went on, also rattling the ice-cubes in his glass, "how Father felt when he made the changes, because, as you are no doubt aware, Harvester's wasn't always like this."

"I should have thought the changes would have come from *you*," Barbara laughed lightly.

"It seems to me," Sir Basil cut in cheerfully, "that I'm the only one around here who's conscious that we *do*, after all, as Barbara put it a moment ago, live in the space age. For all that though, comfort and beauty is something I take very seriously." His smile ignited his blue eyes.

The music had switched neatly into a kind of blues— a series of single, mournful downward-glissing notes— and it was at this moment that Lilian joined them. "Sorry I'm late," she gave one of her mischievously radiant smiles, wrinkling her nose slightly.

Walking into the Harvester dining-room was an experience. The Castle suddenly became a "Moroccan palace" in appearance. Pointed arches, fitted with pale ivory mesh screens that admitted a soft blue light, recaptured the past but blended successfully with Harvester-designed furniture. A huge Moroccan lantern with amber, iris and emerald tones was suspended at a point between the arches and in front of the screens two bronze bowls containing dark glossy green leaves stood on a wide ivory-coloured shelf-like projection in front of the screens. Exquisite green placemats did not hide the beautiful marble of the circular table top where a long container held bronze, gold and pale yellow marigolds—each flower a perfect specimen. Ivory chairs on slender swivelling pedestals and shaped like tulips were placed around the pedestal of the table and fully upholstered in the same colour green as the foliage arranged in the bronze bowls in front of the screens which formed the backdrop to the table. On the marble floor thickly piled ivory-gold carpeting completely muffled footsteps. Every piece, right down to the last marigold, was perfectly placed and it was a magnificent study in ivory, pale gold, holly-leaf green and lit from behind with that filtering misty-blue light and by the huge lantern suspended above the table at a point exactly between the two arches.

Once again, the feeling for Barbara was curiously intimate, and she felt suddenly overwhelmed at the immensity of her involvement with the Harvesters—it was almost as if she belonged with them.

The meal, from frozen salmon mousse to strawberries in champagne and eaten to the stereo sounds— very muted, of course—of Henry Mancini, was superb, and she found herself wondering how many girls were lucky enough to have found themselves in a position like the one she had secured for herself.

Not because she wanted to, but because she felt that it was fitting, she asked to be excused soon after dinner and, later, in her room, she saw that the huge doors leading to Gregory Harvester's private rooms were open to the breezes which filtered down the length of the arched gallery. Down below, in the centre court, water spurted from a fountain at one end of the swimming-pool, and she longed for the peace of the battlements where she could stand with the wind blowing through her hair and immediately began to remove the pins and clips from the chignon until her hair cascaded round her shoulders. While she was doing this her thoughts went to Rod Haden and she wondered what he was doing at this moment. Rod worked in Uvongate and she had been seeing rather a lot of him before going to Italy with Sir Basil.

Tall, with dark hair and eyes, there was an almost constant brooding expression about Rod, but looks were deceiving and Barbara had come to know him well enough to realize that this was his particular brand of ammunition so far as women were concerned. Rod was not above, given the chance, of course, experimenting with women, and that quiet attentiveness he showed them could give way to bombardment if he did not get his own way. With her, however, their relationship had progressed with a reserve on Rod's part which suited her very well, but something told her that he was feeling his way with her, and yet, in a way, she couldn't be all that sure. Rod was possibly too clever for any girl to be sure what it was that had happened to her until it was all over and he had turned, without a backward glance, to someone else. So far, however, she had enjoyed being with him and had promised to phone him directly she and Sir Basil arrived back, but the call could wait, she told herself until tomorrow. At the moment she felt unsettled and, sensing an emotional involvement so far as her feelings towards Gregory Harvester were concerned, she went into the adjoining bathroom and brushed her hair. Her green eyes followed the movements of the brush, and when she had finished she put the brush down on the long cabinet and whispered, "Barbara Knight, you knew perfectly well, when you took on this position as personal secretary to

Sir Basil, that you were going to *have* to be as tough as hide—the kind of hide that goes into the making of Harvester furniture. You knew that you had to be tough in order to take it should the position come to an end one day, and you would have to say goodbye to this luxury—but, quite apart from the luxury, the Castle which has become your home. Don't make it harder for yourself by falling in love with his very devastating son Gregory."

Turning away from the mirror, she allowed her eyes to travel round the gorgeous bathroom and the room beyond. "And you *are* tough," she whispered again, to strangle these feelings. "You *must* be tough, actually, if you can manage to hold an exacting position like this—hopping off one jet plane and on to another, constantly taking notes, constantly at Sir Basil's beck and call."

Sometimes she didn't think Sir Basil quite realized just how often he made demands of her. Anyway, something told her that she would have to be even more tough now. Gregory Harvester could go out of her life, just as suddenly and dramatically as he had entered it. She must not look for hidden meanings that did not exist and her motto was going to have to be "play it cool".

Somebody had turned down her bed, while she had been at dinner, and the sun-smelling apricot pink sheets looked inviting. Sometimes she felt tired to the point of exhaustion after one of these business trips. Although Sir Basil was more than twice her age he seemed tireless, and this was, she surmised, because he *was* more than twice her age and therefore, as a result of this, absolutely at ease, whereas she, on the other hand, often felt completely out of her depth and, because of this, tense, although she tried—always—never to show it.

The battlements waited on her and, as she stepped up from the iron staircase, she could hear the tossing and turning of the waves as they kept on coming in.

The sea would still be warm from the sun and the
breakers would be wild and free.

It was strange that she always yearned to come up
here, because this was where she felt alone and sad. Far
back, somewhere, a dog raised its eyes to the moon and
howled and, listening, Barbara was amused—for it was
not one of Sir Basil's dogs. They were far too well bred
for that.

Clasping her fingers about her elbows, she went to
stand next to the wall. Down below, to one side of the
drop of the garden, the river flowed into the lagoon
which was a huge pool without ripples...dreaming.
Alone, in the isolation she had created for herself
merely by climbing up here, she tried to close the doors
of her mind, thus shutting out the memories of her
parents and the farm...The night air felt cool on her
face.

When he spoke she caught her breath and turned,
her face reflecting the silver of the night.

He did not come immediately to her—the space between them deliberate. His long glance was calculating
and appraising and it had the power to make her feel
utterly beautiful.

CHAPTER TWO

"YOUR face looks young and wild," he said softly. "Coppery skin, tightly stretched and silvered by the night."

"I—I was thinking," she said, her auburn hair blowing about her face. In her consciousness of being Sir Basil's personal secretary she caught it and held it back.

"Leave it," he told her. "Let it blow about your face. When I look at you I get a lot of satisfaction."

Barbara gazed back at him and, struggling with the problem of having been caught there by him she said, "I'm afraid I find myself in one of these situations..."

"What kind of situation?" His tone was gently explorative.

"Well, I know I shouldn't be here. I've never even asked permission, actually."

Gregory came to stand next to her. "Don't keep clutching at your hair," he said, and she found herself more than eager to forget all her liberated thinking and allow herself to be dominated and dictated to by him. "In fact," he went on, "I've found myself wishing that I could set it free ever since I met you."

Realizing that he was very aware of her—as aware of her as she was of him—she said shakily, "It makes me feel more efficient taken back."

"But," his tone was mocking, "aren't you efficient? I understand that you're very efficient."

"I—well, I suppose so." Alone with him, like this, she was unsure of herself. Below them the waves kept coming in and receding on a sigh. There was a small pause and then she said, "I didn't think anybody else came up here."

She saw him outlined against the star-studded sky—

at ease and confidently handsome. The sea was pulling the clouds in from the hills, trailing wisps across the glitter of moon and stars.

"You looked so lonely, standing there," he said.

"You said—young and wild, I think." She laughed softly, embarrassed.

"Same thing."

"I don't think so," she said, trying not to be so aware of him. "But," she shrugged, "in any case, I was just thinking. Sometimes I walk in the garden. Sometimes I go to the Temple of Love."

"Ah, one of my grandfather's follies. I've been told that my grandfather was his own architect and I can well believe it. As a matter of fact, when I'm at home, which happens to be far too seldom lately, I also take a stroll in that direction."

"I'll keep away from there too—in future," she said on a little breath with just a hint of a smile in it.

"I don't get this. Why will you keep away from there too?" he asked, but she knew, just by the tone of his voice, that he knew perfectly well *why*.

"I don't want to encroach on all your private haunts." She felt herself becoming confused.

"I thought we'd got all that sorted out? You won't be." She heard the amusement, slightly laced with impatience, in his voice.

"Thank you—but in any case, I'll keep away..." She broke off and then said, "I must go now. I merely came up here to feel the wind on my face before going to bed. I was here earlier on and no matter when I come, it's always the same, always spectacular, and it's always the same—I'm *always* enchanted."

"Well, it's a place for dreaming," he said, "if you happen to like to dream. It's a place where the sky is the roof. What better place to dream?"

"I suppose everybody likes to dream—on occasions," she said, and was immediately aware of his interest.

"Was *this* an occasion?" His voice was soft and then he appeared to be waiting with a kind of impatience.

"That would be telling, wouldn't it? But in any case, on the battlements I experience a sense of escaping from the past," she said, before she could stop herself. Then she added, laughing a little to cover up, "And a little into the future. Well, I'll say goodnight." She gathered her long skirt up with her fingers.

"Here, let me help you. It can be tricky even though I see you've removed your shoes."

"I'm afraid of putting my heel through this covering, whatever it is," she told him, looking down.

He held out a hand.

"It's quite all right, thank you," Barbara stammered, starting to walk past him. "I'm used to it. I think I could almost go up here blindfolded." Glancing back at him, she said, "I suppose you think I'm quite ridiculous, coming up here, on my own, like this?"

"I'm just a little puzzled, that's all." He began to follow her. "Your caftan," she heard him say, "is made to order. Somehow it captures the mood of infinite tranquillity and timelessness that pervades the battlements. Is that why you wore it, by the way? Because you intended coming up here?"

She laughed. "I wore it for comfort and to be in the swing of things."

"Let me go first," he told her, after she had slipped into her shoes. "In that case, I'll be in a position to hand you down."

Biting her lip, she watched him as he went down several stairs and then he reached up for her fingers. "Actually," he was saying as with a tingling thrill she felt him take her hand, "I'd rather you didn't come up here—alone. Does my father know that you do? Does Lilian?"

"No—I told you, a moment ago. Nobody knows. At least, I don't think so. I've never asked permission to come." She groped for the stairs with her feet, praying that she wouldn't fall against him. "Lilian—your aunt—did say once that she's terrified of the place." Then she *did* lose her footing and stumbled down two narrow iron steps and clattered to a halt right next to him and they stood perched, together, on the narrow ledge. There was a moment's silence and then he said, against her hair, "Do you see what I mean?" She tried to steady herself and he held her closer. "Apart from the danger," he went on, "it's—no place for you up there alone. What would you do if a monster came upon you suddenly?"

Widening her eyes in mock concern, she said, "A monster? Where would it come from—the sea? A sea monster?"

"No." His smile turned the remark into the joke it was. "Didn't you know, Barbara, that there's a mad scientist living in one of the towers which he uses as a laboratory?"

She felt like suffocating—longing to move on, down the steps, and yet longing to stay. "No." Her voice was faint. "I didn't, actually."

"But yes—and he has assembled a monster."

"You frighten me," she laughed a little, her imagination leaping.

"And *that* is precisely what I had in mind. You could well have had a bad fall just now. It's dangerous."

His mouth brushed her forehead as he moved away from her, down on to the next step where he intended to break another possible fall. After the space of several quick heartbeats she began to follow, her fingers gripping the iron handrail.

In the foyer, she said, "Goodnight," and then, before he could reply, she fled.

The next morning she awoke to see a fusing of pastel colours as the dawn broke out, but fell asleep again, almost immediately.

When she awoke again the sky resembled blue velvet and the sun was casting amber hands across the full length of the gallery. Whoever had brought the antique silver coffee tray had also opened her doors and, from her bed, Barbara was able to see the doors of Gregory's suite. They were clamped back, against the outside wall—open to the fresh air.

Before pouring her coffee she slipped from between the sheets and closed her doors, shy and embarrassed, for all the long space of gallery which divided her from the man she knew had captured her heart. Idly, she found herself wondering why the doors on this side of the gallery—the doors to her suite—were of glass, whereas the doors leading to Gregory's rooms were wooden and heavily carved. She came to the conclusion that somewhere along the line the doors at her end had been replaced. Perhaps the sea air had finally had their way with them, for the wide gallery was open on one side to the weather.

As she sipped her coffee she was able to look through huge windows at one end of her room, across the sea, pale silver, now, in the morning sun.

She chose her clothes with her usual care for detail— a silk Schiaparelli-pink trouser suit which, strangely enough, merged with her dark auburn hair. Then, before going down to breakfast, she went out to the gallery and looked down on the centre court where the pool glittered in the sun.

It was a scene of sheer open-air luxury, and the pool was at Barbara's disposal whenever she wanted it, which was a wonderful thought, and as usual she marvelled at her good fortune. Wicker furniture and a magnificent iron candelabrum graced the area. Two ceramic elephant tables stood at each end of a long wicker sofa which was upholstered in a stark white fabric. Pink, lime, rose and mango and cocoa scatter cushions caused instant excitement. Urns with pink and blue hydrangeas growing in them were placed against the col-

umns of the arches. Chaka, one of the dogs, caught her
eye as it loped through the doorway into Gregory's
suite and Barbara turned quickly and made her way to
the breakfast-room where, familiar with the routine by
now, she ate by herself. Everybody at the Castle
seemed to breakfast at different times.

Afterwards she went along to the library where she
knew there would be stacks of unopened mail awaiting
her attention. Through experience she knew which letters to open and which to leave for Sir Basil to open
himself.

When Sir Basil finally came into the library, which
was where she worked and where he liked to dictate
letters, he said, "Well, have a good night's rest, Barbara?"

"Yes, thank you." Her smile was businesslike. "I've
sorted the mail, Sir Basil. It certainly piled up while you
were away."

"So I see." His eyes went to the huge desk and then
came to rest on her face again. "Well, all set for some
work?"

They had morning tea in the library and then Sir
Basil brought his dictation to an end by dictating a
lengthy letter to a well-known specialist firm of tan-
ners, who produced many grades and types of leather
in an impressive range of colours.

When he had gone she brushed her lips with the
tips of her fingers and yawned, as she surveyed all the
work she had to do during the course of the day. From
experience she also knew that she would work until
about an hour before lunch time when she would
change into a bikini and have a quick swim in the
pool. After lunch, which she usually had with Lilian
and Sir Basil, she would continue working, with a
break for tea, until about four-thirty, and after that,
unless Sir Basil needed her in the evening—sometimes he had businessmen to dine at the Castle and
needed Barbara to take notes or to play back tapes in

the library—she was free to go her own way and to do just as she liked. Outside, the sun blazed down, wilting the glorious dark blue and pink hydrangea heads. At this time of the year the sun lost little time in getting the better of everything.

Because she had promised to ring Rod Haden when she got back she glanced at the French clock and then dialled his latest number. Rod was always changing his position.

When she got through he said, "When am I going to see you?" He had the kind of brooding voice to go with his tall, dark and moodily handsome looks. He also had a slow way of talking and a way of pursing his mouth which women found attractive.

"I'm going to be busy all day, I'm afraid," she told him. "There's a stack of work—a huge backlog, if you know what I mean. I just can't see myself being free before tomorrow—late tomorrow, actually."

She wondered why she had said that. Why, all of a sudden, did she feel so indifferent towards seeing him? While she had managed to keep their relationship untangled she had, nevertheless, always looked forward to being with Rod.

There was a pause. "Why tomorrow—*late*?" he asked, and she could visualize those dark eyes narrowing as he gazed across his desk, that touchy shrug of the mouth.

"I've just tried to explain, Rod. That's when I'll be free. That's how it happens to be with me, right now. It's always like this after we've just arrived back from some place."

"Why can't I pick you up for lunch? You do have lunch, I take it?" There was that edge of nastiness to his voice which she had grown to know was never very far away if he did not get his own way.

"Of course I have lunch—but there'll hardly be time. It's always expected of me that I lunch here at the Castle with Sir Basil and Lilian—and any guests, of course, who might just happen to be present." Immediately she thought of Gregory and bit her lip.

"Talking about guests," Rod said, "didn't I see the son and heir in town late yesterday afternoon?"

"Possibly," she answered. "He does happen to be here." Surprised, she asked, "Why? Do you know him?"

"I belong to the same golf club, if that can be called knowing him. You must have met him by now, then?" There was caution behind the words, and something else—jealousy, maybe.

"Yes. Yes, I have, as a matter of fact."

"Then that would account, no doubt, for the—er—tomorrow, *late*." His voice was frankly sarcastic now and Barbara visualized his lower lip curling slightly and wondered impatiently why she put up with Rod Haden and his moods. He had a way with him that made her feel that she was often letting him down when he had expected so much of her.

"Not necessarily so." She found that she was snapping. "It's merely the order of things here. I happen to be Sir Basil's secretary, remember."

"Quite." His mood was decidedly snappish now. "Okay—tomorrow, *late*, it will have to be, then. As a matter of interest, just how late?"

"If you would like us to have dinner somewhere together—well, about seven-thirty, if that's all right with you, but if you'd intended..."

Cutting in, he said, "How long do you expect to be in residence this time?"

"Oh," her shoulders moved beneath the Schiaparelli-pink silk jacket, "for quite some time, I should imagine. Sir Basil has this new scheme..."

"What new scheme?"

"Well, there's this new creative showroom being opened up at Uvongate. There are going to be no fewer than—oh, I can't just remember at the moment, but say thirty to forty complete room settings. He's

also going to be tied up with that internationally famous colour and décor consultant, Lucas Hollander.
You must have read of him? He's the one who is joining Harvester's. There's also phenomenal expansion
going on in the factory complex in Uvongate. It's dou-
bled its size in the last couple of years, and this is
quite something for these parts. So I guess I'm going
to be here for some considerable time, before flying
off again." She laughed lightly, trying to put Rod in a
good mood.

"I didn't exactly ask for a bulletin," he said. "What
you seem to forget is that I haven't quite the same interest in Harvester's as you appear to have."

"Well, it's my work. It just happens that I *work* for
Harvester International." She wondered why Rod always sounded so petty when the name Harvester
cropped up.

"So?" she asked. "What's it to be, Rod? Dinner?"
Then she heard the tiny catch in her breath as Gregory
Harvester came into the library. She dropped her
lashes.

"Drinks and dinner," Rod said. "I'll pick you up at
six."

"Fine." She tried to keep her lashes still and not let
the fact that Gregory was in the room unsettle her. "I'll
be ready."

"You haven't told me what you did in Rome." Rod
seemed eager to talk now.

"I—well, in between working I did a little sightseeing. It was terribly hot, actually, and damp—a damp,
heavy kind of heat."

"I didn't ask about the weather. By yourself?"

"No, not by myself." She was becoming impatient
and embarrassed. "With a friend."

"Friend?"

"Yes—an air hostess. She was off duty. You'll have
to excuse me, I'm sorry. I have work to do. I'll see you
tomorrow...'bye!" Replacing the receiver, she ex-

pelled a short, impatient breath and then lifted her lashes. "Good morning." She found she didn't know what to call him.

"You didn't have to cut short your conversation," Gregory said. "I could have come back." As she looked at him she was aware of a touch of arrogance— the knowledge that he was a Harvester. Then, because it was obvious that he wanted something, she said, "Is there anything I can do for you?" She knew that she was tense and tried desperately not to show it.

"I wondered if you could type something for me," he said, "when you have time."

"Yes, of course."

"Unless my father has completely snowed you under with work? It certainly would appear so, judging by the desk." He grinned suddenly.

"Some of it's urgent, some of it—a lot of it—isn't," she told him.

"It's a Harvester report," he explained.

She was aware of his after-shave lotion. Moving her eyes away from his face she said, in a little voice, "Is— is that it—the report?"

"Yes." She watched him as he placed a folder on the desk. "I think it's pretty straightforward. If there's anything you don't understand—well, you know where to find me. By the way, you don't have to keep your doors closed."

"Oh," she said, at a loss. "I—sometimes it gets breezy."

"Does it?" His smile was mocking. "Well, if you happen to be allergic to breezes...About the report, though. Perhaps I should mention that from here— let's see..." He turned one or two pages over. "Oh, yes, from here—research and development into new materials down to here...Harvester's exacting attention to detail and their famed craftsmanship is..."

Desperately, Barbara tried not to be aware of him. She tried to focus her attention on what he was explaining to her and when he had finished she wondered what he had been talking about, but she said, "I see." Lifting her eyes to his, she asked, "How many copies? You didn't say."

Smiling at her, he said, "I thought we'd got that one sorted out? Three copies."

"Oh, yes, of course. I'm sorry, I'm dreaming this morning."

His eyes were on her hair. "You look very demure, this morning," he said. "The kind of pink you're wearing was made for this kind of red hair and," his eyes held hers, "this kind of green—jade."

Barbara fingered her chignon nervously and then said, "Well, I *am* demure."

"Are you?"

"Yes, I am. Very demure. Anyway, I wouldn't exactly call my hair red. It's just ordinary old auburn."

"That's not quite the way I would describe it myself," he told her.

"You'll have to excuse me," she said. "As you can see, I have work to do. I really must get started."

"I think what it amounts to is that you're trying to get rid of me." His eyes insisted that she look at him. She did, but said nothing.

"If my father keeps up this merciless barrage of work I'm never going to see you." Gregory still sounded relaxed, almost amused, but there was a look in his dark blue eyes which she could not quite make out. She sensed a change of mood, however, and knew that, regardless of the tone of his voice, he was no longer joking.

"Well, that's what I get paid for," she told him. "Besides, we've just got back from Italy where it was more like a holiday than anything else, and now I have to make up for lost time."

"I feel no consolation in this knowledge," he grinned, "but believe it or not, I too have work to do, so I'll leave you to it." He glanced in the direction of her notebook and all the files and pieces of paper stacked to one side of her typewriter.

After he had gone Barbara stood up and went to the window where she gazed out to the sun-dappled court-yard. Her fingers fidgeted with the heavy silver bracelet she was wearing. She had treated herself to it in Rome. Her dark auburn hair contrasted excitingly with the pink trouser suit. She had known that when she bought it. Her thoughts were confused as she allowed herself to speculate a little and then she came to the conclusion that, although she hardly knew Gregory Harvester, she had fallen in love with him.

Beyond the window, with its small square panes, the heat haze shimmered and her mind flounced away into the haze.

Her position at the Castle didn't cover this, she thought, and felt depressed. Gregory Harvester's teas-ing remarks and smiling eyes meant nothing. Even as she worked, later, however, her thoughts kept filtering towards those thickly carved doors at the opposite end of the gallery.

Later on, radiating energy, Sir Basil came into the library and signed the letters which she had already typed. "I should say you've earned a swim in the pool before lunch." He put down the pencil he had been using and leaned back. "Help you to cool off."

"That will be marvellous," she murmured. She felt tense, all of a sudden, aware of the mist which lay be-tween her and living with the Harvesters. She was after all, merely in the employ of Sir Basil—not a guest, or a relative.

Usually, when she was at the Castle, she knew that she would have the pool to herself in view of the fact that Sir Basil preferred to swim first thing in the morn-ing, before anyone was up, in fact. Lilian, on the other hand, preferred the afternoon, although she did some-times swim with Barbara before lunch. This was the first time during the eighteen months she had been working as Sir Basil's personal secretary that Gregory Harvester had been home.

The dogs started barking and yelping excitedly and then there was the sound of a girl laughing—a husky, thrilling laugh. "Down, naughty! Down, I say!"

The noises came from the big hall near the library and Sir Basil straightened from the desk and looked in the direction of the double doors. "Hello there," he said, "that sounds like Reina." He glanced at Barbara. "My godchild—my very unruly and very beautiful godchild. You didn't know, did you?"

"No." Barbara's mouth went dry and this, she knew, was because she was thinking of Gregory and the husky, thrilling laugh which had certainly not belonged to a child but a woman, young and exciting.

"Well," Sir Basil sighed, "you soon will."

For some unknown reason Barbara felt hollow and depressed. Somehow she knew in advance that Reina, Sir Basil's godchild, was going to be devastatingly beautiful—and she was. The girl who was walking into the library was all that.

Tall, slim as a reed, the heels of her low-heeled shoes click-clacked on the tiles just outside the library before she stepped on to thick carpeting. She was haughty, exciting and utterly devastating—a blonde girl, with hair loose to her shoulders. Her eyes, a kind of greeny-blue, went straight to Sir Basil. "Darling," she drawled, coming quickly towards him. "Tell me, how's my favourite godfather? Aren't you going to kiss me?" She stood back, mocking him, and it was the first time that Barbara had ever seen Sir Basil at a loss to cope.

Behind the girl, Lilian, petite and silver-haired, frowned and shook her fashionably styled head. Reina's cool eyes rested on Sir Basil's mouth and, beneath the silk shirt he was wearing, tailored to outline his good shoulders and lean frame, Sir Basil shrugged and moved slightly to one side. As though to take the sting from this, however, he smiled and said, "You're getting far too big, surely, to go around kissing godfathers and old uncles." But he placed his tanned hands upon her slim shoulders and said, "When did you arrive? Now?"

"Yes, *now*, darling." The girl's long legs moved restlessly beneath the pink slacks she was wearing. Both girls were therefore wearing pink—the only difference being in the material and style and the shades of pink. Whereas the pink Barbara was wearing seemed to merge with her hair the pink the other girl was wearing clashed wildly with all that blonde hair, but the effect was nothing short of magnificent.

"Where from this time?" Sir Basil asked.

"Why should I tell you?" Reina pouted, "especially if you're not going to kiss me, but," she shrugged, "in any case, darling, if it makes all that difference, I'll tell you...from not so far away. From the wilds of Zululand, if you must know—at a lodge there, with the atmosphere of a luxury safari. Darling, you know that old, old set-up-drum-beating Africa and all that jazz, drinks beneath a romantically star-studded sky and game reserves and game rangers."

Behind Reina, Lilian grimaced again, her small pert face tense, but when Sir Basil glanced her way she smiled, bunching up her chin and not showing her small perfect teeth.

"Well," Sir Basil looked coolly amused now, "that's great." He glanced at Reina. "We're glad to have you, *child*." There was emphasis on the child, although Reina must have been all of twenty-three. "You'll be good company for Barbara. Barbara," he turned, "do come and meet my godchild—Reina Geray. You'll discover that she also calls me Uncle—or rather, she used to, before she arrived at this 'darling' state. I'm not her uncle, of course, but this was always used as a mark of respect on her part. She's called me Uncle since she was about two bricks high. Her father was the best friend I ever had."

For a moment Reina's eyes clung to his face and then she said, "Darling, you'll never let me forget, will you? You believe in these square things—a mark of respect, for instance—I don't. It's time I called you Basil, or darling, as the moods change. Uncle is for the birds, let's face it." Her eyes swivelled to Barbara. "Hello," she said. Just that, but it was the way she said it.

"Reina Geray—Barbara Knight." Sir Basil's voice was curt.

"So this is the ideal secretary?" Reina's glance was a hostile inventory that assessed Barbara. "Somehow we always seem to miss out on meeting up—you know, when I'm here, you're not and when you're here, I'm not."

Chilled by the tone of the other girl's voice Barbara said, "Well, now that we've finally met I'm very pleased that we have."

Reina laughed lightly. "That seems to be an indiscreet thing to say." Her eyes went back to Sir Basil. "Where's Greg, by the way?"

There was a small silence and then he said, "Oh, so you know he's back, do you?"

"Well, of course. News travels, you know—and fast, at that."

"Apparently," he replied drily. "What are your plans before lunch?"

"What do you mean, what are my plans before lunch?" Reina's voice was peevish.

"Well, Barbara is going to swim. I thought you might care to join her."

"I was hoping to swim with Greg, as it so happens."

"Greg has gone into Uvongate," Lilian put in, with calm authority. "He'll possibly be late for lunch. I don't think there's much point in waiting for him. It would be as well for you to swim now—that is, if you really want to."

"I surrender," Reina shook back her hair and Barbara chose that moment to say, "Please excuse me. I'll go and change now. Oh, by the way, Sir Basil, here's that statement you were looking for."

"Oh, good." He sounded preoccupied.

While he was making a show of studying the statement in question Barbara left the library and discovered that Lilian had followed her. "She makes me so *mad*, that girl," she was saying in her deep, husky voice which always came as such a surprise. "She needs a jolly good spanking! She is absolutely man-mad, but for all that, would like to pin down a Harvester, and whether it be father or son makes no difference to her. When she was born her parents asked Basil to be her godfather." Lilian shrugged. "It would have been churlish not to—especially as Paul Geray was Basil's best friend. While Basil has always been fond enough of the girl I think, in recent years, he has found her a bit overpowering, but like you, Barbara, she has no parents—both having been killed in an accident. I suppose one should make allowances for Reina, but she's been difficult since a child. We've always tried to make her feel that she belongs here, and she does, really, but she irritates me so much, especially for the last couple of years, and what's even more disturbing is the fact that she appears to be irritating Basil. I have the feeling that one of these days he's going to say something nasty to her. Anyway, my dear, go and have that swim. This heat is absolutely crushing."

"Shall I wait for her—for Reina?" Barbara asked.

"I shouldn't think so." Lilian made one of her wry faces. "I sound like an old cat, don't I? I suppose I am, really, but I'm sure that if Paul were alive he would be utterly ashamed of his daughter, at times."

"Does—does Gregory like her?" Barbara asked, meaning Is Gregory in love with her?

"Men are such fools," Lilian shrugged. "Who's to know?—but no, I don't think so." Laughingly, she added, "The air is full of catty spite, I'm afraid."

Barbara found herself hoping that she would not have the other girl's company in the pool. Reina's hard, unpleasant look had not gone unnoticed. Sir Basil's attitude towards Reina had bordered on just this side of impatience, even though he probably looked upon the girl as his own daughter.

How Gregory felt towards Reina, however, was another matter and, amazed at her thoughts, Barbara was aware of dangerous emotions stirring in her. Dangerous—because she had no right to feel them.

She had the sparkling pool to herself and then Lilian joined her, although not to swim. "I've brought you something deliciously cold to drink," she called out to Barbara, who was in the water by this time, then she curled up on the long wicker, white-upholstered sofa with its brilliant scatter cushions.

After a while Barbara climbed out of the pool and began to rub herself with a towel, then she came round to the lounging area with the curved and comfortable white lacquered Hong-Kong sofa and chairs. To one side flowers spilled out of locally woven baskets, making more colour against the cool Portuguese tiled floor— one of the many alterations to the Castle.

Smiling, Lilian gesticulated in the direction of one of the chairs. "Sit down and relax," she said.

"I'm wet, Lilian." Barbara took the drink from the ceramic elephant table and remained standing, although her black and pink-flowered bikini did not hold much water and she had already towelled all the drops of water from her tanned legs.

"Darling, I've told you so often, these cushions are here to cope with damp bathing suits." Lilian looked absolutely stunning in her white slacks and blue and white tunic and it was difficult to believe that this was a woman who was probably in her fifties. As usual, her blue eyes were perfectly made up and with her pert, silver-hair-framed face she was the type who could get away with up-to-the-minute clothes whereas many women of the same age would tend to look overdone and a trifle ridiculous. Good looks, Barbara found herself thinking, certainly ran in the Harvester family.

There was a splash at the far end of the pool, and they both turned as Gregory emerged after having swum the entire length under water after his dive.

"I wonder how he managed to escape Reina?" Lilian whispered, and then, grinning deliciously, she called out, "Very good! Where do you get all that breath, Gregory?"

"No smoking," he called back, casting his eyes in the direction of Lilian's cigarette. "Just you think about it, my dear aunt."

"I *am* thinking about it," she answered gaily, "but I have no will-power."

Gregory hoisted himself out of the water and smiled at Barbara. "What about you?" he asked, and she was instantly aware of the brief flicker of interest in the expression of his eyes as they went over her near-nude body. "Do you smoke?"

"No. I've never felt the inclination to smoke, so I suppose I'm lucky," she answered, trying to keep her voice normal. As usual, the sight of him made her breath come a little fast.

"By the way, have you seen Reina?" Lilian asked.

"I saw her car outside," answered Gregory, and the face he turned to her was expressionless.

"She's been at a lodge in Zululand." Barbara knew that Lilian was keeping her voice easy.

"Oh? What's she here for?" He sounded as though his nerves had tightened up.

"Your guess is as good as mine, my dear boy. She went along to her room to change. She did say she was going to swim before lunch, but," Lilian glanced at her watch, "if she doesn't get a move on she'll swim—and eat—alone."

Gregory looked at Barbara. "I saw you from above," he said. "Quite a performance."

Normally she would have said jokingly, So you were spying on me? However, because of the way she felt about him and because he was Sir Basil's son she said, "The water was gorgeous."

"Let me take your glass," he said, "unless you'd like another drink?"

She gave him her empty glass. "No, thank you."

"Come in again." He glanced in the direction of the pool.

"I don't think so." She heard the stiffness in her voice. "It's time I went to change for lunch."

"Oh, go on, Barbara," Lilian cut in. "There'll just be time for a quick swim before we have to go and prepare for lunch. Go in with Greg."

"It will have to be very short, then," Barbara replied and, because she was embarrassed, took a neat header into the water and did a slow crawl to the other side and back just as he dived in.

He came up beside her. "I call that pulling a smart one," he said as he shook his dark hair from his eyes.

"Well," she laughed, "I *did* say it had to be short."

She saw his eyes go to the tendrils which had escaped the topnotch of hair she always wore beneath her cap. He seemed to be going to say something personal, but changed his mind.

Lilian, who had been watching them, stood up. "I'll see you two young things at lunch," she called.

"I'm getting out now." Barbara struggled to be non-chalant, but knew that she had failed. There was almost an edge of desperation to her voice. "Wait for me, Lilian."

Just at that moment Reina Geray appeared on the scene looking glamorous in a yellow bikini, "Well, don't let me keep you," she said sweetly, looking at Barbara, and then to Gregory she said, "I've been looking for you. News gets around fast, doesn't it? I heard that you were here and—well, here I am." Her eyes were glittering and excited.

Barbara left the water and gathered her towel and sunglasses together before she ran towards the sliding doors which led to one of the many foyers of the Castle. To one side was the magnificent pool house with its many arches and urns of plants and golden canvas curtains drawn to one side. Here it was difficult to visualize the face which the Castle presented to the world.

Reina was saying something, but her voice had dropped to a low whisper. Barbara felt the coolness of the tiles in the foyer, but even from here she could hear Gregory's reply, "Well, what am I supposed to be—impressed?" His voice was lightly mocking. He had made his masterful protest to Reina, she thought resentfully, but was prepared, no doubt, to play it her way.

CHAPTER THREE

As she changed back into her pink silk trouser suit Barbara asked herself why she was allowing herself to become so emotionally involved with Gregory Harvester and the beautiful girl who was Sir Basil's godchild.

Hating the tension she had built up for herself, she swept back her hair and began to arrange it expertly at the back of her head. She had a good position at the Castle, she thought. What more did she want?

The dining-room, with its ceiling-high, pointed arches, was filled with the golden, blue-tinged light which filtered in from the sea and sky where they merged together on the horizon. The huge gold and yellow marigolds had either been replaced by fresh ones or had remained startlingly beautiful in the water. There were deep green placemats on the gold-veined marble table top and they matched the cushions on the tulip-shaped chairs and the foliage of the leaves set in the bronze bowls before the screen-fitted arches.

Reina was already there. She had changed into a square-necked green voile dress and wore hooped earrings which were made up of tiny bright flowers. Her hair was loose. Turning as Barbara entered, she said, "You have a fabulous position at the Castle, haven't you? I mean, you even eat with the Harvesters."

"That doesn't mean to say that I don't know my place." Barbara's reply was quick with controlled temper.

"No?" Reina regarded her for a moment. "I often wondered what you were like. In fact, you've occupied

quite a place in my mind. Basil's last secretary was
nothing but an old bag—which, in my opinion, is exactly as it should be."

"In what way have I occupied a place in your
mind?" Barbara asked, wishing that someone would
come along.

"Oh, don't be mediaeval. Why does one girl occupy
a place in another girl's mind? I had heard that you
were young, that's why. Quite frankly, this had me worried. The way I worked it out was that, simply by being
young, you would fulfil a need in Basil and as a result
do disturbing things to him."

"What kind of disturbing things?" Barbara felt her
temper getting out of hand. "I consider my work as the
most important thing in my life, right now."

"Right now? And later? I mean, when a man, a
vital man like Basil, reaches a certain age he needs to
be reminded by a doting young thing that he doesn't
look that age and that he's still devastatingly handsome and virile. Basil is not the kind of man who's
content just to sit back and welcome old age with open
arms. An older woman, say about Lilian's age, would
hold exactly the same qualifications as you have—possibly more, through experience." There was a flash of
hostility in Reina's eyes. "You must be proud of yourself, that's all I can say, having arrived in this world of
style and distinction, and I suppose you want to make
sure you keep it."

Nervous and angry, Barbara said, "I'm not at all sure
what you're driving at, but I have a jolly good idea, of
course. I suppose it would be unnatural, with your kind
of brain, if you were not immature." She found that
she was trembling and was relieved when Lilian chose
that moment to come into the dining-room.

"This seems to be one of those disjointed days," she
was saying, cheerfully enough. "Basil will be late."

"How is the surf, these days?" Reina asked casually.

"I don't know. I haven't been in lately," Lilian

answered. "What are your plans, Reina? How long do you intend staying?"

"As I was saying to Greg a little while ago, I have no plans. I hope you don't mind?" There was an arrogance about Reina as she lifted one gold marigold from the centrepiece and sniffed it, before putting it back. "Why do you use these things?" she asked. "Revolting flowers. They positively reek!"

"There are marigolds *and* marigolds," Lilian said, with deliberately aimed sarcasm, "and these happen to be perfect specimens—too beautiful not to use in a flower arrangement. Ah, here is Gregory, so I guess we can begin lunch."

They were waited on by an African butler in an immaculate white suit.

"By the way," Reina glanced at Barbara, "it's a small, small world. Do you know who I met recently— the last time I was here, actually? It was while you were in Italy. I met Rod Haden. He told me all about things between you two."

Trying not to reveal her feelings, Barbara said, "Oh? Well, I can't think what there was to tell." As she spoke she was aware of a watchfulness on the part of Gregory.

"Oh, come now, Barbara. We're living in the permissive age, after all." Reina cast satisfied greeny-blue eyes round the table.

"You obviously have a lot of imagination," Barbara kept her lashes down and moved the spoon in her soup. "Or else he has."

The truth had not taken long to explode in her— Reina was trying to create a bad opinion of her. How did one cope with the catty behaviour of Sir Basil's god-daughter? How did one stand up for oneself without causing unpleasantness? and right now she felt like being unpleasant. The strain showed in her face as she allowed the butler to remove her plate.

Reina persisted, her eyes bland, "You know Rod

Haden, Gregory? He says he knows you, at any rate, although he didn't seem impressed. In fact, he seems to have a distinct grudge against you."

Cutting her short, Gregory said curtly, "You don't need to fill in the details—I know all about Rod Haden."

Full of resentment now, Barbara could not help saying, in a tightly controlled way, "I don't know why his name has cropped up." Across the table, Lilian made one of her little faces and shook her head.

"Oh come, Barbara, why not be frank?" There was a certain satisfaction in Reina's voice. "You'd be so much nicer if you were not so concerned with your public image. In any case, the bringing up of Rod Haden's name was well meant, on my part."

"Yes, I'm sure it was." Barbara felt determined to have the last word, although there was a hidden meaning to the sweet way in which she said this. The way in which she passed the remark also signified that she had no further interest in the subject, but she had been determined to make her point. Reina Geray was becoming a symbol of everything she disliked and, across the table, the eyes of the two girls met in a war of their very own. Something had also altered the mood of the meal and Barbara abandoned the dream that she would ever get to know Gregory Harvester better. Somehow she did not think that he would give her the chance to.

Afterwards she could not remember who had steered the conversation to safer channels, but she knew that she was grateful when Sir Basil came into the dining-room, apologizing for his lateness.

She spent the rest of the afternoon in the library working and her thoughts moved restlessly in and out of the letters she was typing back from her shorthand notes.

Up to now, she brooded resentfully, she had always felt in command of her position as Sir Basil's personal secretary. She had even felt that she had, in her own way, carved a life for herself for as long as she was required at the Castle—just in much the same way as the Harvesters had carved into the rocks and built themselves a fair-sized tidal pool. Now she wasn't sure any more. Something seemed to have gone wrong with the arrival of Reina Geray and, as a result of her conversation during lunch, Gregory Harvester's change in attitude towards her seemed to border on the hostile.

During the afternoon he came in and she glanced up and stopped typing. "I haven't had time to start your report yet," she said, "but I'll be free quite soon now. Will that suit you?"

"That will be fine. I just came to have a look at the Tessara file. Is it handy?"

Barbara got to her feet. "Yes, I'll get it for you. The files are in the next room."

She was aware of his blue eyes going swiftly over her, assessing her, and they sent out a message that was not lost on her. She wanted to say, I don't know what Reina's game is—or rather, I *do* know—but it's not the way you think.

He followed her across the thick apricot carpeting into a room which led off the library, at the far end, where there were a number of steel filing cabinets, bookshelves, another desk and a typewriter. From the windows there was a view of the courtyard which could be seen from the library. Conscious of Gregory's closeness, Barbara found the file and gave it to him.

"I gathered from your telephone call...I couldn't help hearing, by the way...and from the conversation which took place during lunch that Rod Haden is a friend of yours." He kept leafing through the file, but did not look at her.

"People meet people," she answered, "and I met Rod Haden." She wished her voice sounded easier.

"I once had the unpleasant task of telling Rod Haden to keep away from the Castle. He has quite a reputation down here in Uvongate." He still went on leafing through the file. "What's more important, he's also given a number of girls including my own sister, and a number of married women, a bad name." He lifted those blunt, black lashes suddenly. "He goes into each affair with unscrupulous calculation. He did the same with her—my sister."

Barbara felt a spurt of rage. "Are you worried about me, your sister or merely Harvester International?" She stared at him with wide, angry eyes. "Are you worried about what we might do to the name Harvester, in other words?"

Visibly annoyed, close to anger, he said, "I wasn't thinking of Harvester International. I didn't include it in this train of thought."

Somewhat inconsequently, she said, "What am I supposed to do when I'm off duty—sit at the Castle and knit?"

"How you behave in your spare time is no concern of mine," he snapped. "I thought I was acting in your own interest when I brought Haden's name up a moment ago."

"And, like Reina Geray, you 'mean well', I suppose?" Even while she was speaking she was thinking—well, here goes your job, Barbara Knight.

"Yes, but apparently I was wasting my time." He gave her a quick, cutting glance.

"You shouldn't listen to gossip," she said, wanting to tell him that what Reina had suggested about her was preposterous.

"It's all up to you. I'll take this file with me. There's something I want to sort out."

"All right." Her voice was almost a whisper and she felt terribly upset. Because she felt the sting of tears she turned away.

Back at her typewriter, she found it difficult to concentrate, and when Sir Basil came in some time later he said, "What, still at it, Barbara?"

Glancing at the French clock she was amazed to see that it was after five o'clock.

"These are ready for your signature, Sir Basil," she told him. "I wanted to get everything finished before I start on a report—for—for..." she broke off and groped for words, "your son," she ended lamely, hoping that Sir Basil did not think she had passed this remark as a feeler as to what she should do and what she should not do in the line of work for Gregory.

"Ah, yes. I meant to speak to you about that, Barbara. However, Gregory must have given you all the details. Well, that's fine. By the way, there'll be some people round this evening for a smörgasbord. I mention this merely so that you can make yourself beautiful." He gave her a smile.

"Thank you," she murmured, accepting this as an invitation but wondering at the same time whether she should phone Rod, at the last moment, and tell him that she would be free, after all, to go out with him.

Later, in her room, she wrestled with her thoughts and, to avoid more complications arising in her life, decided not to phone and to do as Sir Basil expected of her. She would attend the smörgasbord.

It was with a feeling of dread, however, that she looked through her wardrobe and decided upon a celery and pink dress with a high neckline and long sleeves, tightly cuffed at the wrists. When she was ready she went out to the gallery for a moment where she stood gazing down at the pool area which had already been prepared for entertaining with an air of sophisticated informality and then went downstairs. With a flip of a hip Reina spotted her and turned to say something to Gregory and Barbara felt outside of things—somebody unrelated to the way of life of these wealthy, leisured people.

She stood seeking some face she knew, feeling unsettled and nervous, but trying not to show it. And then, looking above the height of Reina's blonde head, Gregory caught sight of her and, for a brief moment, in the light which came from tall white galvanized iron lamps placed at intervals along the terrace in front of the pool house, they surveyed one another, then, with a remark to Reina, he came towards Barbara. "You look lost," he said. His smile was polite, nothing more. The sounds of the stereo leaked through from some-where—romantic, mood-setting. "Come along and join us."

Barbara raked her mind for something to say—some excuse. "I'm looking for someone," she said, "but thank you all the same. I'd—I'd rather not, if you don't mind."

His mouth quirked faintly. "Well, that's entirely up to you, of course," he said, and then she watched him as he turned from her and made his way back to where Reina was standing.

The lamps cast a blue-bronze light on the water and above the murmur of voices, as people stood around holding cocktails before going along to help themselves at the mimosa-yellow, frilly-clothed round tables, piled high with food, there was the murmur of the sea. Champagne bottles were being opened with deft twists of the cork and followed by carefully planned pops.

High above, the battlements waited for Barbara— when it was all over, quiet, detached from everything else. The sky the roof, as Gregory had said, and she found herself beginning to panic, wishing it was time for her to flee up there so that she might be alone with her unsettling thoughts.

Vaguely, she was aware that there had been a small, satisfied smile on Reina's beautiful face as Gregory had joined her.

"Ah, Barbara!" It was Sir Basil's beautifully measured drawl and, grateful, she turned, her face lighting up. "I've been looking for you," he said, and then Barbara's shocked green eyes flew to Rod Haden. Frantically she tried to work out whether she had arranged for them to meet this evening instead of the following night.

"H-hello," she said, worried and uncertain.

"Your young man has paid you a visit," Sir Basil was explaining cheerfully. "I've asked him not to take you away but to join us instead. After all, there's everything you need here—food, drink, people, music—so what do you say, Barbara?"

"Well, yes, thank you," was all she could think of, and then, stunned, she watched him, Scotch in hand, as he left her alone with Rod. Sir Basil had the knack of knowing immediately who people were and what they wanted, and he began to prowl among his guests.

In view of what had taken place at the lunch table Barbara felt like falling apart. "I wasn't expecting you," she said, looking at Rod. "Have we got something mixed up—our wires crossed, or something?"

"No. I decided to come and see you—to find out if you would change your mind and come out with me tonight," he answered.

Normally she would have been thrilled for this to happen. Up until now Rod had merely called for her in his car, driving right up to the heavy, studded door of the Castle, but each time she had been ready, waiting for him, and there had been no need to invite him in or to introduce him to Sir Basil or Lilian.

"You look put out," Rod was saying, and suddenly she was conscious of his tall, lean, dark looks—the good looks which lay in the shadow of a kind of sullenness always present about him. She knew that Rod was a man who wanted things to go his way, even if he had to play along for a while in order to get them.

"We arranged for tomorrow evening," she went on, "it's just that you took me completely by surprise. I mean, after all, I'm merely working for Sir Basil. I'm not in a position to invite my friends here—although I know they would always be made welcome. It just doesn't seem right, somehow—it *wouldn't* seem right, on my part."

Rod helped himself from a passing tray. He took two glasses and, handing her one, gave her a long look.

"The way I see it," he said, "you'd be better off in a flat."

In the background a trumpet seemed to be softly laughing its way down the scales while the rest of the orchestra swelled melodiously, mingling with the piano notes. Beneath the sound, people still continued to talk and laugh as they drank cocktails and champagne. Nearby, the Harvester staff were moving in on the tables, which resembled billows of yellow mimosa blossom, waiting for the first move.

"Tell me," Rod said, suddenly, "who's the chick with Greg Harvester? I seem to know her face."

"You sound as if you don't like Greg Harvester," she said.

"I don't."

"Why?" There was a kind of urgency behind her voice. "Why don't you like him?"

"I have my own reasons for not liking him." He turned to look down at her from his sulky lean height.

"Would it be because of his sister?" she asked, on an impulse.

"Don't remind me," he said. "If his sister wanted to make a fool of herself over me that was her affair. Do *you* like him?"

Feeling a small moment of power Barbara said, "Yes, I do. I have no reason not to like him." Around the fragile stem of her glass she felt her fingers begin to tighten up. Where along the line, she was asking herself, had she come to her own conclusion that Rod Haden was not to be trusted with women?

Before she could move away he placed an arm about her waist. "You have a tendency to complicate things," he said against her hair. "Why? Why are you always like this? Why can't you just relax and let things take their course?"

Moving out of his embrace, she took a sip of the drink he had given her and then, over the rim, she found herself looking across at Gregory Harvester, and she did not have to be told that he was putting two and two together. His expression told her all she wanted to know.

People were moving towards the tables now and there was a moment of tension on the part of the catering staff in their white jackets. Fat yellow candles flickered behind amber smoked glass and were reflected, along with the tall wrought-iron candelabra, in the black-satin water of the pool.

The music was now a subdued, but restless thudding of drums, exciting in its intensity. All round there were signs of immeasurable wealth.

"Well, this isn't the time to worry about weight," a passing girl said, laughing up at her escort.

People with cocktail-relaxed faces helped themselves to food, aided by the staff.

"I always wonder where Sir Basil manages to collect all his guests from," Barbara said to Rod. "So many of them are young. He seems to be one of those people who only grows more interesting as they get older—he's the kind of person that people of all ages like to be with. He's full of vitality, don't you think?" She had decided to be friendly. "Of course, I realize that a lot of entertaining revolves around the interests of Harvester International—but still, the way in which Lilian copes is fantastic. I mean, everything virtually depends upon the way in which she runs this huge castle. They often entertain on a full scale and this alone must take tremendous organizing."

"Well, they have the money to do it." There was a kind of resentful way in which Rod said this.

"Their wealth is something which has been built up through hard work and initiative, from what I've grown to learn," she answered, quickly on the defensive, because she had got to know Lilian and Sir Basil so well.

Rod showed only the mildest of interest in her remark as he helped himself to food.

When Gregory spoke Barbara turned quickly. "How

are you doing?" He glanced briefly at the food on the table and then his eyes met hers.

"Very well, thank you," she replied, and then Rod said, "Hello there. Long time no see—been overseas again?"

"I was in London for six weeks," Gregory replied. "Just got back, as a matter of fact."

"Business trip?" There was a kind of arrogance about Rod, as though he was aware that it was only through Barbara that he was here.

"Yes." Gregory's tone was curt.

At that moment Reina joined them. "Hello there," she smiled at Rod. "I didn't expect to see you here. I thought you were always kept discreetly in the background?" She laughed lightly and Barbara's heartbeat quickened. "You remember me, don't you?"

"You'll find that you'll keep on making discoveries about me all the time," Rod answered easily.

"I can well believe that," Reina laughed, and her eyes went over him and, beneath the casual look, Barbara could sense her interest. "Tell me," Reina went on, "are you walking with us to Pulpit Rock afterwards? You know, it's the rock right up the beach. A crowd of us are going to watch the moon come up over the sea."

"Is this an invitation?" Rod asked, and his dark eyes went to Gregory and his mouth lifted faintly.

"Everybody welcome," Gregory's voice sounded deliberately impersonal, "although, to be quite frank, this is the first I know of the walk." His eyes went to Reina, who shrugged.

"You don't listen," she said, and then glancing at Barbara she went on, "Just slip off your shoes and hoist up your skirt. No changing—and what's more important, no pairing off—absolutely no pairing off. I can't stand people who pair off. It's just not polite. Everybody must stick together—lovers included."

"I don't think you have to worry about that, so far as

Rod and I are concerned, Reina," Barbara said, in a tight little voice.

"No?" Reina's glance was mocking.

"Well, everything appears to be organized for a walk up the beach," said Gregory, "so we'll see you later. Right?" He glanced at Barbara and she nodded, but there was no agreement in her eyes.

Some time later Lilian came over to where Rod and Barbara were standing and Barbara introduced her to Rod, and it was obvious that Lilian had formed her own opinion about him. Her smile was small and polite—nothing more.

High above the sophistication of the pool scene the battlements clawed at the starry sky. A girl wearing a saffron and blue gown slid into the lamp-light and Rod's dark eyes automatically strayed in her direction even while Lilian was talking to him, and then when Lilian caught Barbara's glance her smile seemed to say, Take the advice of an older woman, Barbara, this man is not for you.

Once Sir Basil passed by, his hair silver even in the bronze light. "You young people go right ahead and make your own plans for what's left of the evening," he said, stopping next to Barbara and Rod.

"There's to be a walk up the beach to Pulpit Rock," Barbara replied, for want of something to say.

"What?" he grinned. "In that get-up? Hadn't you girls better change into something a little more suited to a walk on the beach? Who's going, by the way?"

"Reina, for one...Gregory..." Barbara broke off, still not certain how she should refer to Sir Basil's son.

Lifting his shoulders, Sir Basil said, "Well, you know what you're about, I suppose. I've forgotten what it's like to be young." There was a flicker of amusement on his face before he moved on.

"I can think of better things to do than walking up a damp beach in a suit," Rod grumbled.

"Well, we don't *have* to go," Barbara told him. "Actually, I'm terribly tired. I've been frantically busy since we got back from Rome."

"Forget about the beach and come for a drive," Rod said.

Resentment stirred in her. After all, he had turned up at the Castle without even consulting her about it. "I'd rather not." Her voice was strained.

"There's no point in staying on here if everybody else is going to walk up the beach," he said, with an irritable edge to his voice. "It would appear that only the old-timers will be staying behind."

"Either we walk or we stay here," she said. The words were lightly spoken, but there was a depth of meaning to them. "I hadn't arranged to leave the Castle this evening."

Suddenly Rod glanced in Reina's direction. "Oh, well, I suppose we'd better join in with the rest of them and walk."

Barbara's face was moody as they went down the stone steps which dropped down to the beach and lagoon. There was a silver smudge against the horizon where the moon prepared to rise and then the smudge gradually turned a bright copper, illuminating the sea. Great blue heads of agapanthus, silver in the night, brushed the skirt of her gown against her legs. She stopped walking. "Rod?"

Somewhere along the beach a girl laughed. The lagoon lay motionless in the shadows, just waiting on the moon.

"Yes?" He turned.

"I don't really think I want to walk. I'd like to go to my room and see you tomorrow evening, as we planned in the first place. Would you mind terribly?"

The moon started to hoist itself out of the sea. It was huge and unreal and, almost immediately, it began to climb the sky. The lagoon lost some of its blackness and Rod's dark face was suddenly clearly visible. "What's made you change your mind?" he asked.

"It just seems too much of an effort," she told him. "Besides, I don't want to ruin this dress, and as you yourself said, you have a suit on. I think Reina is being a bit ridiculous, arranging this walk."

"Most of the others—well, *all* of the others—are dressed in pretty much the same way," he said.

"Yes, I know. Had it been prearranged people could have made a plan and changed or dressed accordingly. As a matter of fact, this gown I'm wearing has a one-piece swimsuit to match. I could have worn it beneath, had I known."

"I suppose if you don't want to go, you don't want to go." He sounded peeved now. "How about making up your mind?"

"It's made up. We won't even be missed."

"You say we won't even be missed and yet you wouldn't go for a drive. It doesn't make sense." He sounded ready for an argument.

"That was different."

"I don't think it is—however..."

Behind them long beds of agapanthus, red, yellow and pink cannas, blue daisies, pink petunias, cornflowers, yellow cosmos, purple verbena, pink and red hibiscus were suddenly all lit by the moon.

Rod tilted his head. "Was that Reina's laugh?" he asked.

"I don't know. I don't think so. She and Gregory went on—well ahead, I think."

"In that case, we'll go back," Rod took her arm. "I'll see you tomorrow evening." They began to go back up the steps, brushing past the leaning stalks of the flowers which were damp with dew.

As they walked back to the Castle Barbara knew that Rod was annoyed with her. She had grown to know that he liked his own way about most things and she walked beside him with cool indifference, her thoughts busy with Gregory and Reina. They would be strolling along the beach and, more than likely, the golden straps of

Reina's sandals would be slipped through his fingers while his other hand would be clasping hers.

"I'll walk with you to your car," she glanced at Rod's moody face.

"Just as you wish," he said. Already his thoughts seemed to have taken flight as he planned his next move.

He got into his car and, in the moonlight, his dark assessing eyes went over her before he backed out of the parking area. With a flick of his hand he drove off, and Barbara stood trying to work out her own feelings and she found herself wondering why it was suddenly so very important that she saw through Rod. Up until Gregory Harvester had arrived she had taken Rod Haden as she had found him, seeing him as a man-about-town type who looked for the best in everything—clothes, food, cars. A man who chose his girls with care. However, on going back in her mind, in the short while she had known Rod he had changed flats and changed his position, not to mention his car and, no doubt, his girls. He tired of restaurants as quickly as he tired of the "special dishes" he had taken her there to enjoy. Perhaps Gregory had been right?

After his car had disappeared she thought about his careless flip of the hand which made her feel that he was not so much disappointed in having said goodnight as irritated at not having obtained his own way so far as taking her for a drive was concerned. She also knew, without being told, that Rod had played right into Reina's hands by arriving at the Castle tonight. The look in Gregory's eyes had confirmed that.

Her mind was over-active now and she knew that before she would be able to sleep she would have to unwind slowly by climbing up to the battlements where she could stand with the wind on her face.

At the top of the iron staircase she plucked at the clips and pins in her hair, and there was impatience in her movements. Her hair fell to her shoulders, then she slipped off her shoes and, stooping, dropped the clips into one of the shoes.

The moon was climbing quickly, overpowering the stars with its brightness. Some of the tension began to go out of Barbara. She stood shaking back her hair from time to time, her eyes closed, feeling the dampness and the wind.

At the sound of footsteps on iron she swung around quickly, drawing in a sharp breath. The wind flattened her skirt against her legs and ripped her hair back from her face. A dark head appeared and then Gregory stepped up on to the battlements.

"What are you doing here?" she asked, hoping that the sudden panic she had felt at seeing him had not shown. "I mean, I thought you were way up the beach—with Reina."

"I could ask you the same question," he said. "What are *you* doing here?"

"I thought you'd gone to Pulpit Rock?" she said, confused.

"Well, as you can see, I didn't go. Where's Rod?"

"We changed our minds," she replied. "We went as far as the steps, just above the lagoon—and then we turned back."

"And he left?"

"Well, of course. As you can see, I'm not hiding him." There was defiance in her voice. "Apparently I'm in for your customary sarcasm," she added. Her face and hair surrendered themselves to the falling dampness and she knew it was glimmering on her skin. Gregory gave her an assessing glance and she was aware of this too.

"The more you see of Rod Haden the more you stand to be hurt," he told her abruptly, "unless, of course, you don't *mind* being hurt? Perhaps it would be worth it?"

"No girl likes getting hurt," she replied stiffly, "and *I* don't particularly want to be hurt." She gave him a level look and their eyes held for a long moment.

They could hear the restless churning of the ocean as it was ordered about by the moon.

"Don't keep clutching at that red hair of yours," he said. "Let it blow. It changes you from my father's efficient secretary to the sly lynx-eyed creature you are."

"Let me give you one piece of advice," she began to work herself into a state of annoyance, "don't you say things like that to me. I know *why* you said it, of course. Behind Reina's remarks, however, there are hidden meanings which don't exist, and I would like you to bear that fact in mind, Mr. Harvester."

"I don't listen, much, to what Reina has to say, believe me," he answered lightly, "but like my father, I back my fancies to the limit."

"And you think I'm—sly?" Her mind was moving ahead to the moment when she could escape from him—escape his insults.

"Let's just say that I can't make you out." His face was hard.

"And do you call that backing your fancies to the limit?" she asked hotly.

He laughed.

"Just because I happen to be friendly with the man who made a fool—a *willing* fool, no doubt, of your sister, don't think you can go around making snap estimations of me!" Her breath was coming fast.

"You certainly know him well—well enough for him to come here, regardless of what has taken place in the past. I all but threw Rod Haden out, once, when my father and Lilian were overseas." Contempt filled his voice.

"All that concerns you is the Harvester name," she said. "Just as it did with your sister. You were worried, not about her, but about the name Harvester. Are you afraid Sir Basil's personal secretary will bring more disgrace to the name?"

"You're being childish," he snapped. "What you do in your private life has nothing to do with Harvester's."

"No? Well, what's all the fuss about?" she asked.

"I thought I made it clear to Rod Haden that he wasn't wanted here at the Castle?"

"I didn't invite him here," she said. "He just turned up."

"That's not the way I saw it, anyhow," he answered.

A plane arched moonward and whined out of sight, its ruby lights competing with the pearls of the moon, and it helped Barbara to regain some of her composure as she and Gregory automatically tilted their heads to gaze at it.

When the whine had died away she said, very softly, "I've never invited Rod here, apart from the fact that Sir Basil and Lilian have always made it clear that it would be quite in order for me to have my friends here. Up to now, however, I've only allowed my friends to pick me up in front of the door and drive off, without coming inside. It's been better that way—it was the way I preferred."

"You misunderstand me." His voice was a shade less hostile. "Your friends are naturally welcome here. However, Rod Haden is quite another matter. He led my sister into believing that he was serious with her and then, to put it into a nutshell, he ditched her. My father and Lilian happened to be overseas at the time. Like you, Barbara, Charmaine was insensitive to advice. It looked serious to me," he broke off and shrugged, "and, short of locking my sister up, there seemed to be nothing much I could do about the affair except perhaps to give Rod Haden the benefit of the doubt, *this time*, which is what I did, as a matter of fact. I can say that he seemed serious and I was even a little impressed, if reluctantly so. However, it all boiled down to the fact that marriage is not exactly what Rod had in mind. Expertly, and without fuss, Rod told

Charmaine this. She took it badly—she's not the type to react indifferently."

"And I suppose you think I'm different?" Barbara felt a rising anger, mingling with a terrible hurt. "Is that it?"

"Would I be discussing my sister's affairs with you if I thought you were different?" he snapped. "Think about it. Apart from the fact that I don't want *you* getting hurt I don't want Rod Haden coming here, for obvious reasons. He happens to be everything I dislike in a man, but in any case, my sister will be coming home shortly and I don't want her..."

"I'll tell Rod not to come here," she cut in. "Up till this evening, he's only been as far as the huge, studded door, where he's waited for me in his car—and that's where he'll remain—actually, I'll meet him in Uvongate in future."

"You intend to go on seeing him, then?" She sensed his anger.

"Well, of course. Taking people as *I* find them is something *I* take very seriously," she told him with sweet sarcasm.

"You believe in these things," Gregory said. "Rod Haden doesn't. If I haven't convinced you by now, you'll have to convince yourself."

"Well, of course," she went on in that same tone, "that follows."

Then, with tears streaming down her cheeks, she fled from him, picked up her shoes, scattering the hairpins and clips and fumbled for the top step of the spiral staircase.

CHAPTER FOUR

BARBARA made a point of avoiding Reina Geray during the days to come. She also worked out how to be out of the pool by the time the other girl was ready to swim.

Her thoughts were often divided as she worked in the library. Several times Gregory dictated letters to her and once, after a lengthy discussion on the subject, he got her to type a report.

Coming into the library one morning, he said, "It becomes quite a habit with you, doesn't it?"

Somehow she maintained a mask of composure. "What becomes quite a habit? I don't see much point in guessing about it. Suppose you tell me?"

"You're doing your best to avoid me. Right?"

Their eyes met and, aware of a heightening tension, she said, "Oh? And what makes you think that?"

"You've made it pretty clear." His smile turned the words into a sardonic statement.

Barbara was aware, suddenly, that they were playing a game, and a thrill of excitement ran down the length of her spine. "I don't know how you can say that," she said. "All I happen to be doing is going about my work in the usual way."

"With accurately timed planning as to how and when to use your leisure hours." He smiled at her more with his eyes than with his mouth.

"Well, of course. The world is full of people accurately planning their lives. Don't *you*?" She fought to keep her voice even.

Giving her one of his disturbing looks, he said,

"Yes, as a matter of fact I *do* plan my life—but that's not what I meant."

"Oh?" With her pulse going faster, she held the ballpoint over her pad, suggesting to him that he continue dictation and yet hoping he wouldn't. "What did you mean?"

Skilfully, without appearing to, he evaded her questions. "By the way," he said, "I saw you at the Bird of Paradise last night. You were having a late meal with Rod Haden. I wondered why you weren't at dinner, as a matter of fact."

"I didn't notice you there," she said, wondering why.

"You didn't notice me for the very simple reason that I wasn't eating there. I merely dropped in to see the cabaret. I'd heard it was very good." There was a pause. "There's no need to ask whether you had a good time. It was obvious at the time that you were."

Another second passed and then he observed, "I notice you don't say anything."

"No. What *is* it you want me to say?" She shot him an annoyed glance. "Sir Basil has never indicated that he disapproves of the way in which I spend my leisure hours. This is the first complaint I've had, actually."

"That's because my father doesn't know Rod Haden."

Barbara began to feel hemmed in by his arguments. "I know how to look after myself. Besides, I happen to like being with Rod Haden. Perhaps I'm not as easily devastated by him as your sister was. I'm perfectly able to handle our relationship the way *I* want it." She expelled an impatient little breath. "Do I have to lie and cheat in order to keep an appointment with Rod?"

The morning sun was making long bands of yellow across the apricot carpet. Beyond the huge window, which was open, the monotonous drumming of insects, worshipping the sun, could plainly be heard.

"Not at all. If you feel so strongly about it—well, I

guess that happens to be your affair. If you can't see through Haden now you never will. Let me remind you, however, that he works with the nonchalance of experience, so I guess it will take time for you to find out. I might mention that, in my sister's infatuation, she did exactly what you have just suggested. She cheated and lied with the cool determination of youth, in order to be with him. She wasn't the first—and apparently she won't be the last."

Barbara made no reply to this and, very pointedly, looked down at the notebook in front of her. "I've got everything down, by the way," she said, "if you want to start dictating..." She found herself thinking of Charmaine Harvester, who was twenty, the same age as she was herself. Charmaine, who, according to Lilian, was somewhere in Spain after having become "emotionally involved with a man while Basil and I were overseas."

Gregory lifted his shoulders in a small shrug and began to dictate.

When he finally left the library Barbara felt a sort of relief, and yet she found herself disappointed that he had gone.

She spent the rest of the morning at her typewriter and then had lunch with Lilian at the poolside. Lilian told her that Sir Basil and Gregory had gone out to lunch.

"Barbara," Lilian helped herself to a salad and sprinkled grated cheese over it, "I must confess that I was very frankly inspecting your friend the other evening. Rod—what's-his-name?—Haden, is it?"

"Yes, Rod Haden, Lilian." Barbara felt her nerves tighten.

"I suppose," Lilian's shoulders moved in a little shrug, "women go for that slow, brooding look. Rod Haden has the kind of looks that makes me think of that old saying—still waters run deep. I suppose it's something about his mouth, the expression about his mouth—but I know that I could be wrong." She ended on a note of bright reassurance.

"Rod is just a friend." Barbara's voice was distant, stiff. She felt a surge of impatience with the Harvesters in this sudden interest in her private affairs. She had no intention of discussing Rod with Lilian, and after waiting for enough polite time to pass before she could change the subject, she said, "Sir Basil is taking me to the new factory complex this afternoon, and then on to the creative showroom." The creative showroom was, of course, part of the factory complex. "Lucas Hollander, the colour and décor consultant, is going to be there."

"Ah, yes, a fascinating man. He'll be dining here tomorrow evening, as it so happens. Talking about the new complex—for the first time ever, Uvongate people will be able to select furniture after five o'clock. I think this is perfectly marvellous. People won't have to travel mile upon mile now if they want to select Harvester furniture, into the bargain. The wonderful thing is that this internationally famous colour and décor consultant will always be on hand. This is a great new step for Uvongate. I think Greg deserves a medal. This whole thing happens to be his brain-child. Did you know that, Barbara? As a matter of interest, seeing that you'll be going there this afternoon, let me read you the write-up in today's paper—unless you've seen it?"

"No, I haven't, as a matter of fact," Barbara answered. "Let me get the paper for you, Lilian. There it is—on that chair."

When Lilian had found the right page she began to read, in her deep, husky voice, "No fewer than thirty-five room settings have been furnished by Harvester International in their new creative showroom in Uvongate. The settings include lounge, dining, study, bedroom and patio furniture made by Harvester's and the displays will enable customers to relax as they go about choosing Harvester schemes on the Lower South Coast, without having to travel to Durban. The picture below shows a section of the showroom which has evoked favourable comment from other designers and visitors from large towns. Originally from England, Lucas Hollander has worked in design centres throughout the world before making his home in Uvongate." Lilian looked up. "This is another feather in Greg's cap. *He* was the one who managed to organize this." She continued reading, "Lucas Hollander served his apprenticeship as an interior decorator twenty-five years ago and thrived on decorating problems. He will be in attendance at the showroom during the entire week, when customers can discuss their colour and décor problems." Lilian tossed the paper on to a chair. "As a matter of interest, Barbara, is Gregory easy to work for? You should have formed an opinion by now."

"Yes." Caution lay behind Barbara's voice. "He's very easy to get along with, but I wouldn't like to cross swords with him."

Lilian laughed delightedly. "Oh, wouldn't you? Really? Talking about crossing swords, you should have heard him snap at Reina before lunch. He was very abrupt with her. She wanted him to take her somewhere—she's a very possessive young thing. She trades on the fact that Paul—her father—was Basil's closest friend. In the end she took herself off in a huff—that's why she's not having lunch with us."

Soon after lunch Barbara said, "Lilian, please excuse me. I really must go and look out a new shorthand notebook to take along with me this afternoon. I'm to take notes at the meeting, of course."

"When you get back, try to fit in a swim before dinner. You haven't been in today and I can promise you the water is gorgeous."

"Oh, Lilian, did I remember to tell you that this is my Yoga night? I'll be eating in Uvongate with the girls," Barbara said.

"I'd forgotten." Lilian laughed lightly. "How's it going, by the way? Still twisting your body into all those funny positions? I'm still deciding whether to join or not. I've heard such wonderful reports. These postures certainly seem to keep one loose-limbed and fit."

"I certainly feel on top of the world," Barbara answered. "You should join, Lilian."

"I'll think about it. All right, you run along, then." Lilian stretched languidly. "I'm going to relax here for awhile."

Barbara was in the library when Gregory came in and she glanced up quickly. "Well? Ready?" he asked.

"Yes." Suddenly she felt tense. She had not known that Gregory was to go along with them to the complex. "I'll just get my things together," she told him.

While she busied herself with opening and closing the drawers of her desk she was aware that he was regarding her coolly and she had a small side-struggle with her hands because they were trembling and she did not want him to see this.

They went out to his car and she stood hesitantly, waiting for Sir Basil to arrive on the scene. Gregory opened the door for her and she looked at him, puzzled.

"My father is not feeling well," he told her. "We had lunch in town and he mentioned that he had a headache, which steadily seemed to get worse. So," he shrugged, "he won't be going. Personally, I think he overdoes things all round. He just can't get used to the idea that he's not as young as he used to be."

"Oh." Barbara felt at a loss for words and, dismayed at this turn of events, she added, "I'm sorry."

It was hot and windy and the sloped streets of Uvongate were active. Capped with white, the sea looked dark and moody and the palm trees which lined the centre island of the marine parade appeared to be straining, leaning to one side, but they had in actual fact taken on that shape from the perpetual sea breezes which constantly buffeted them.

Gregory drove fast and made no attempt at conversa-

tion, so a silence settled between them. Barbara's eyes
went to the yellow scarf which had been caught in the
door of the glove compartment and, directly she saw it,
she recognized it as Reina's and her immediate sensation was one of jealousy.

Finally he was the one to break the silence. "By the
way, have you met Lucas Hollander?" he asked. "Has
my father had the opportunity of introducing you to
him?"

"No. I haven't been to the new complex yet, as it so
happens," she answered.

"I see." His blue eyes scanned the area for a parking
spot and then, when he had found one, he parked the
car and Barbara got out before he could come round to
her side and open the door for her.

The wind was having its own way about everything
and was being highly successful in creating unpleasant
conditions. Two girls walked past, their hair in a state of
complete disorder, and Barbara saw Gregory's eyes go
to her own hair which was taken back into its customary loose but firm chignon which ensured a sophisticated and well-groomed look even on a day such as
this. The style seemed to emphasize her youth and yet
it added a kind of mystery to her which made one think
that here was a girl who was used to travel.

They reached a gallery which was illuminated by a
tremendous crystal chandelier. The marble floor had
doors leading off at various intervals, and had been
given added beauty by the sculptured look of big-
foliaged plants growing in magnificent planters.

"In here, Barbara," Gregory took her arm lightly
and pushed open a door and Barbara found herself confronted by at least eleven men, heavily involved in
business talk. However, used to this sort of thing, by
now, she did not bat an eyelid but remained standing
next to Gregory, waiting for the next move.

He made the introductions easily and then, smiling,
said, "Don't be alarmed, Barbara. Everybody has a

card with his name on it in front of him, so you won't get mixed up so far as speakers are concerned."

Later, after the meeting, she was included in an inspection of the factory and room settings. As he led the way through the room settings, Lucas Hollander was saying, "Interior design has a—a sensory function. Like—er—like exciting cuisine, for instance, exquisite ballet, music or..." he broke off and smiled in Barbara's direction, "like the very tantalizing perfume worn by a very tantalizingly beautiful girl."

All male eyes were on Barbara, but, aware only of Gregory's, she felt tense, although she smiled. "Thank you," she said, easily enough. "Do you like it?" This kind of thing, too, was something inside her experience as Sir Basil's secretary and she had learned to cope well.

"Very much," Lucas Hollander replied, and there followed a murmur of approval.

The settings, treated with the most unexpected and highly imaginative colour schemes, were excellent. The men stood around, talking in clusters.

"I felt the lush South Coast of Natal—or should I say the *lower* South Coast—people do seem to stress this point—should call for *snap*." Lucas Hollander snapped his fingers and then went on, "A whole lot of snap." There was a polite silence. "The inside of rooms all swing open to views, so there should be a leaning towards colour—tamale-hot colours. Fiery orange, for instance, flaming fuchsia. What are your views, Gregory?"

"Well, I can see what you mean about colour," Gregory answered. "Those scatter cushions over there, those bedspreads—the tufted Mexican rugs over there...."

Lucas Hollander nodded his approval. "Exactly. See, over there, I've had everything set off with white walls, gleaming copper—most people go for that, in a big way, tin-handicraft hangings. And then, to cool the eye, there is space—openness. Rooms, quite suddenly and unexpectedly, give way to terraces, usually open to expansive views—as in this case where there are spectacular views to the ocean.''

Eventually the tour came to an end and when they were in the car Gregory asked, "Well, what did you think of it?''

"I thought it fabulous,'' Barbara replied. "I absolutely endorse the write-up in the newspaper. It's phenomenal expansion. Fortunately, Harvester's can afford to take a plunge of this nature. I mean, Uvongate is so far down the Coast, and although it's a busy town, it's nevertheless small.''

"Uvongate is growing all the time,'' he said. "The entire lower South Coast is going ahead in leaps and bounds.''

"Yes, I know, but all the same, a venture like this could misfire, but one just knows instinctively that it won't.''

His attitude changed subtly. "So we have a business head beneath that well-groomed hair?''

"Well, of course.'' She could feel his eyes travelling over her and she sounded, as she felt, ruffled. "I wouldn't be here if I didn't have some sort of business head. I mean, I wouldn't have qualified as Sir Basil's personal secretary. I have to have some idea as to what's going on.''

"Do you know,'' he started the car, "you haven't told me a thing about yourself.''

"Well, you haven't asked,'' she told him, turning her head away. The shadows were inky now. The meeting and the tour of the factory and showrooms had been lengthy. The first lights of the town were coming on. There was the kind of pink sunset which exploded behind the hills, turning the beaches pink—the kind of sunset Lucas Hollander had referred to.

"What was it you wanted to know about me?'' Her voice was very quiet, guarded.

"Whatever you choose to tell.''

"I...'' she broke off and then started again, "I met

Sir Basil. His secretary had just left him and I was lucky to secure the position. I still can't believe my good luck, actually.''

"Well," Gregory said, "you have the necessary qualifications. Mrs. Semple left Harvester's because she wanted to go and live with her daughter in England. In view of the fact that Mrs. Semple happened to be in her fifties I was staggered to find that her successor was about nineteen." She heard the grin in his voice.

"Twenty," she said. "I'm twenty."

"I stand corrected. You're twenty. So, beneath that cool, sophisticated veneer, you're only twenty." There was a pause and then he said, "Lilian tells me that your parents were tragically killed in an accident?"

"Yes." Her voice was small and contained. "They were. It makes all this seem so wonderful—my position with Harvester's. I—I feel as if I belong somewhere again."

He did not say anything for several long moments and then he said, "Barbara, will you have dinner with me tonight? In town?"

"I can't." She felt dismayed. It was her Yoga night and Cynthia would be calling for her at the Castle to drive her into Uvongate where they would meet several other girls and go along to the hall to attend their classes. After Yoga they always went to a Steak House for a meal. It was a standing arrangement between them.

"Why not?" There was undisguised impatience in his voice.

"Because I happen to be going out to dinner—in Uvongate. I have an appointment."

"With Rod?"

"No, not with Rod." Her voice was cool. "I'm going to have dinner with three girls."

The sun was splashing the sea with last rays from way back of the bush-matted hills. Gregory turned to give her a quick glance. "I find that difficult to believe."

"Well, it happens to be true," she told him.

"How about a drink, then, before going back to the Castle?"

She glanced at her watch. "All right. Thank you."

To hide her feelings she gave her attention to the colours shifting about the sky as they drove in the direction of a palm-fringed hotel which stood out against the dark blue backdrop of the sea. Gregory led the way to an expansive glassed-in terrace where the white chairs were upholstered in hot pinks and limes and a crystal chandelier floated down from a tented ceiling. Beyond the glass, the sea was all tumult and movement. A scrap of paper blew past the windows.

Barbara found that she did not know what to say now that she was about to have a drink with her employer's son. A steward came to their table and bent slightly, looking at Gregory enquiringly and then, after taking the order, left them, his footsteps making absolutely no sound on the deep-piled carpeting.

"What were some of your other views on the complex?" Gregory asked suddenly.

"I kept thinking that it was difficult to believe that we were not visiting a series of magnificent homes," she said.

"Or some playboy-executive penthouse, maybe?" He gave her a smile.

"Well, yes, now that you come to mention it." She returned his smile.

"Most of the furniture you saw there is so easy to maintain," he went on. "I'm referring to some of the fibreglass stuff. It happens to be non-burn, non-rust, corrosion-resistant and practically every patio cushion you saw there can remain outside in all weathers. That's saying something, with our climate."

"I agree," she said, less unsure of herself now. Then she went on, "I've often wondered how Harvester's started on this latest trend. I know quite a lot, working for Sir Basil, but not that side of the story."

"Having been in the field of plastics, my father could see the trend was going from traditional to modern furniture, but although in the age of space technology, it was only recently that manufacturers became orientated to production. I might mention that when Harvester's first started out on this particular venture we couldn't get anyone interested in our range of products. Now, large as we are, we can barely cope with the demand. One just has to travel to Europe to see that fibreglass furniture is the coming thing."

"It's staggering visiting the factories," said Barbara. "It's odd to think that the 'furniture' comes in drums and goes out in pantechnicons. In other words, from liquid to solid," she said.

"Yes—virtually the very next day," he answered. "It's in the moulding for a matter of hours."

"And yet," she sat back, finding that she was beginning to relax with him, "although much of it is..." she groped for a word, "futuristic, so much of it makes sense."

"So much of it?" Gregory laughed outright and she could feel her face turning pink.

"What I mean," she went on, "it seems to belong in the Castle, for example—just as it belongs in other environments. Actually, by comparison, I think, it makes other furniture look almost dull—or it *can* have that effect. Not always, of course." She was beginning to feel out of her depth again.

"That's the fate of being beautiful." He gave her an amused glance. "And I believe that Harvester pieces *are* beautiful. Some call it sexy."

"I suppose it's because of the purple bunny-pile gyrochairs and low, fur-covered double beds," she said, then wondered whether the pink in her face showed again. For some unknown reason she found herself saying ridiculous things.

He laughed again and then said, "Change your mind and have dinner with me." The unexpectedness of the change in conversation took her completely by surprise.

"I'm sorry," she stammered. "I can't. It's impossible. This is one date I can't break. I wouldn't like to, as it so happens." She was about to tell him that she attended Yoga classes when he said curtly, "I see. Well, I guess that's explicit enough."

The great white-capped waves flung themselves at the rocks, smashing into pieces, then rushed up the pink-tinged sands. Although the light had practically faded sea-birds still ran along the tidal strip and, along the coastline which they could see from their chairs, the lights were glittering as they began to show up more.

Barbara found herself tense and listened to the kind of babble which stems from sophisticated boredom at sundown in a hotel.

Finally Gregory said, "If you're to keep your dinner date you'll be anxious to get back and change, no doubt. You'll want to get into something a little less businesslike, I should imagine."

"It's not that kind of date," she said.

"You're a hard girl to trap." He stood up and came round to her chair.

In the car, he said, "I still know very little about you, except that you work for Harvester's and that you are — alone."

"My father came out from England to farm in South Africa," she said. "With my mother, of course. I was brought up on a farm—I was born in this country. He— they—weren't very good farmers, I'm afraid. Nothing ever seemed to pay off..." Her voice trailed away.

"It's not always easy," he said.

"We were happy, though, for all that," she went on. "I often think of the farm, which had to be sold, of course—afterwards. I was thinking of it only a moment ago. The beach out there reminded me of the sandy road leading to the farm. Very sandy, very full of potholes, but sometimes, in certain lights, it looked absolutely beautiful, turning a deep pink—some mineral, I should imagine. I don't know. Perhaps just the light—at dawn, or sunset, or before a storm. Whenever I look at a pink tidal strip I think of home."

"You have an attractive way of talking," he said. "Like your parents, no doubt—very English, very charming."

"I hadn't noticed really." Her eyes rested on his lips and then, realizing it, she glanced away. "The Harvesters have very English accents, for that matter."

"My father and Lilian have very slight Scotch accents," he said. "Just a slight broadening here and there."

The steep, winding streets looked windblown and, above retaining stone walls, flowers and shrubs were being nudged around. The cafés were busy.

"I can see that guilt has set in," Gregory commented, breaking the silence which had settled between them.

Widening her eyes, Barbara turned to look at him. "Guilt? What do you mean, guilt has set in?" Her little laugh was confused.

"You're feeling guilty about turning me down tonight. Right?"

"You're being fanciful."

"I don't think so. I don't believe you're going out with three girls."

The Castle waited for them, its battlements outlined against the dark sky. A huge star hung near the horizon. Gregory parked the car and then turning to her, he said, "Well, Barbara, have fun tonight. Think of me—disappointed."

She had the urge to remind him that there was a very glamorous blonde by the name of Reina staying at the Castle, and the thought of it made her jealous.

"Now I know you're kidding," she said lightly. "Now, where have I put my notebook?"

"You put it into your bag," he told her.

"Of course. Well, thank you. Lilian knows I won't be here for dinner."

"Somebody calling for you?" His voice was casual, too casual, and she knew that he had Rod Haden in mind again.

"Yes." She tried to think of something flippant to say about Cynthia calling for her in her old car, but she couldn't.

They walked in the direction of the huge studded door and, inside the great hall, Barbara said, "Well, thanks again—for the drink."

He shrugged and gave her a faint smile. "I'll be seeing you. Be good."

Although the boisterous wind had been hot it was now laced with a clammy kind of dampness which created a feeling of chilliness, and for this reason Barbara decided to wear a pink V-necked cardigan over a short black pleated skirt. Beneath this she wore her black leotard and wide-mesh pantie-hose.

She was ready waiting in the drive when Cynthia arrived in her car. "Hop in," Cynthia called. "I don't want to stop this stupid old crate. It wants to stall all the time. I don't know what it's about. I'm picking the others up at the Glass Bubble, by the way. They're having a milk shake, or something. I only hope it doesn't curdle when they do their Yoga!" She shot Barbara an amused glance. "Do you know what you look like in that outfit with that red hair, green eyes and black-patent shoes?"

"No." Looking down at her black, mesh-encased legs and patent-leather shoes, Barbara said, "What *do* I look like?"

"You look like a tart," Cynthia laughed. "I've never seen you look like this. What possessed you?"

"I didn't feel like wearing slacks," Barbara answered.

"Well, all I can say is that I've never seen you look like this before."

"Well, that's something, anyhow." Barbara felt the slight edge of peevishness.

"You look like a tart," Cynthia said again. "Honestly."

"When you put it like that," Barbara shrugged.

"There's no other way to put it."

"Thank you." Barbara answered, with an amazed laugh.

"My pleasure. No, but jokes aside—you just don't look like *you* tonight, Barbara. No offence meant."

"I'm sure." Suddenly Barbara laughed. "What about that old dame who comes to Yoga? She always wears a frock over her mesh pantie-hose and *she* gets away with it."

"I nearly phoned to tell you that I couldn't make it," Cynthia said, changing the subject cheerfully. "This old bus has me worried. There, did you feel that? Jibbing?"

"Yes." There was tension in Barbara's voice now. "I did. Perhaps the carburetor is dirty. Can you clean a carburetor?"

"No."

"Neither can I." Both girls laughed.

"I do wish you'd phoned, though," Barbara said. "It seems risky to have to drive me back to the Castle after the class and then drive yourself back home. This part of the road is lonely."

"Oh, we'll make a plan, Barbara, don't panic."

They picked up the other girls at the Glass Bubble and then drove to the Neomark Hall where Yoga exercises were performed once a week. Afterwards they drove to one of the Steak Houses on the beach front and, windblown and in high spirits, they ordered steak and chips with salads, followed by coffee with blobs of cream.

It was on the way back to where Cynthia's car was parked that they met Rod Haden. "Ah," Cynthia said, "the very person I was hoping to see. Now you can take

Barbara back to the Castle for me. My car is giving trouble and I wasn't looking forward to that drive."

"Sure." Rod's dark eyes went over Cynthia and then he glanced at the other girls. "What about you two?"

"No," Cynthia cut in. "I have to pass their way. It makes no difference. It was the drive to the Castle and back here that was worrying me."

Wishing that Rod would offer to look at the engine of Cynthia's car, Barbara said, "Cynthia, I'm really worried. Perhaps you should leave the car here and let Rod take you home as well?"

"If it gets any worse—the jibbing, I mean—I'll phone my father from Anne's place," Cynthia replied. "It's as simple as that."

When the car had driven off Rod said, "Come for a drink with me before we go back."

Barbara looked down at her black mesh stockings. "I'm not dressed to go places. I've just come from Yoga, as you can see. You should have heard what Cynthia had to say about my get-up. I usually wear slacks. I don't know what possessed me this evening."

"You look fine," he said. "We'll go to the Ladies' Bar at The White Caps."

"Were you on your way to have a drink?" she asked, not wanting to interfere with his plans.

"I was going to have a nightcap, followed by an early night. Now the early night can wait until tomorrow." He regarded her with cool appraisal.

"I feel a sight," she said, "but at least the lighting is dim there."

"It isn't unusual to wear lacy black stockings with a black mini-skirt." He sounded irritable. "So what's the big panic?" He raised his dark brows.

"It isn't unusual, I know, but it's not particularly the way I like to be seen. I didn't expect this turn of events. Usually we have a grill after Yoga and then go straight home."

Rod took her arm. "If you could be seen at the Steak

House you can be seen in the Ladies' Bar. Come along,
and stop arguing.''

She had to adjust her black-stockinged legs to his
long stride and, looking down at her, he began to walk
faster, teasing her.

"You're in a hurry," she laughed, and then, on an
impulse, clutched at his arm with both hands. The wind
whipped her hair across her face and she shook it back.
"My slide came out," she said, "and then I dropped it
on the floor at the Steak House and couldn't find it.
The light's dim there too.''

"I like it the way it is," he said. "It's time you forgot
the fact that you're Sir Basil Harvester's personal secretary and let your red hair down. You're always so afraid
of any disorder in your life. I'd like to change all that."

"You haven't a chance," she answered breathlessly.
"I like things just the way they are…" and even while
she was talking she looked up into the cold eyes of
Gregory Harvester.

Taking her hands from Rod's arm, she stopped walking and, out of breath, said, "Hello." She watched his
blue eyes travel over her chunky-heeled patent-leather
shoes, black-mesh stockings, black-pleated mini-skirt
which was topped by the pink V-necked cardigan, before they came to rest on her face and her hair which
was going wild in the wind.

His expression provoked her into saying, "Well, Mr.
Harvester, you seem to delight in throwing me off my
guard. Will I do?"

His face was hard. "No comment," he said, and as
he walked away, the thought struck her that, had he
been amiable, she might have asked him for a lift back
to the Castle, seeing that he would be going that way.

CHAPTER FIVE

ROD drove her back to the Castle and brought the car to a stop in the shadows. He tried to take her into his arms, but she said, "Rod, I'd rather not."

"Why not?" He released her and looked down into her pale face. "I can't understand you, Barbara. You're one of the hardest-to-get girls I've ever known, do you know that? What's the matter? Aren't you in love with me—not even a little?"

"No. No, I'm not. I'm sorry." Her voice was soft. "I..."

"Don't go on," he said. "I know—I like you, Rod, but I'm not in love with you. How corny can you get?"

"I thought...."

"What did you think? Did you think we could just be good friends?"

"Yes, I did."

In an almost bored voice, he said, "Oh, come on!"

"I *do* like you," she made a helpless gesture with her hands. "I *like* being with you, and I'd hoped...."

"What had you hoped?" he snapped. "That I would be immune to your charms?" He tried again, stroking the back of her neck with his fingertips. "I'll tell you what I was hoping," his voice was soft. "I was hoping you were going to spare me a bad time. I'm mad about you, Barbara."

Trying to keep the situation light, she said, "Actually, Rod, it's the other way around. You seem bent on giving *me* a hard time. I don't fall in love easily...I mean, this sort of thing doesn't come easily to me. That's the way it is with me. I'm sorry."

Towering beneath the sky the Castle seemed to ring with silence—a palpable breath of the past. Barbara longed to get out of the car and close those great studded doors on Rod Haden for good.

"We've known each other for—let's see...." Rod's voice was mocking now and she cut in, with some impatience.

"I don't like sitting out here—right in front of the Castle, like this."

Before she could argue he laughed lightly and started the car. "Okay," he said, "we can put *that* right. We won't sit right in front of the Castle. We'll sit somewhere else." He swung the car round and drove back down the long avenue in the direction of the gates with the crouching lions.

"Now you're being stupid." Her voice was firm, although her heart was hammering beneath the pink jersey. "Please turn back, Rod."

At the gates he stopped the car and turned to look at her.

"Take me back this minute!" she demanded.

"Let me educate you," he said.

"Don't you dare touch me! This has gone beyond a joke, Rod. Can't you see that?"

Headlights lit up the crouching lions on the gates and they both looked up. A car drove into the grounds, slackened speed and drew up next to Rod's car, then Gregory Harvester said, "I'm sorry—I just wondered who it was parked here."

Barbara felt like collapsing into a heap on the floormat of the car and she heard the sharp intake of her own breath.

"I guess this had to happen sooner or later," Rod called out easily. "If you have any objections to our parking inside the grounds now's the time to name them."

"No objections," Gregory replied. "After all, Miss Knight doesn't seem to have any, and that, I guess, is the main thing."

His car slid forward and Barbara sat in stunned silence. Then in a hard little voice she said, "Take me back, please, and—I'd rather not see you again, Rod. How could you have done this to me? Do you know what you've just done? You've allowed Gregory Harvester to believe that this is a regular occurrence—my parking in your car with you."

"Aren't you being rather absurd? What difference does it make what Gregory Harvester thinks? After all, you work for his old man, not for him. What do you do in your private life, regardless of who you work for, is your own business." She heard the spite in Rod's voice.

"What I do in my private life doesn't come under the heading of sitting necking in a car. It never has done, and it's not likely to take a turn in that direction. I'm absolutely furious! Take me back, before I get out of this car and walk."

He started the car and Barbara resigned herself to her humiliation.

Rod dropped her off in front of the massive door of the great hall. "I'll see you round, no doubt," he said carelessly, "but if you'll accept a piece of advice, Barbara, try not to do everything the impossible way—and I'll tell you this much, it's impossible to expect a man to go on seeing a beautiful girl and remain merely friendly."

"Your type of man, maybe." Her voice was wild and unrestrained, as she tried to gather her shattered pride together. Immediately she spoke she found herself thinking of Charmaine Harvester who had fallen for Rod. Perhaps—just perhaps—if Gregory Harvester had not come along she, Barbara Knight, might well have found herself out of her depth with Rod.

Rod allowed her remark to go with a small expressive shrug and she was aware of tears stinging her eyes as she turned away and walked in the direction of the stone steps. Sir Basil's night-watchman opened the great door for her. "Thank you'" she said. "Good-night."

In her room she studied her pale face in one of the rose-tinted mirrors and then allowed her eyes to go slowly over the skirt and jersey she was wearing over the black leotard and open-work black pantie-hose worn for Yoga. Moodily, her jade eyes went back to her face, her hair, dishevelled, even though she had done her best to tidy it hastily in the powder room of the hotel. She looked, as Cynthia had teasingly called her, a tart—a word she always hated and never used. Tonight, however, the immaculate Barbara Knight had, quite unwittingly, turned herself into a sex-kitten, and Gregory Harvester had to be in the scene. She took the slide which she had found in her bag at the hotel, from her hair and shook the auburn tresses about her shoulders while her thoughts turned to the healing wind on the battlements. Suddenly she craved to get up there—to feel the wind on her face.

She knew that she would never again be able to go to the battlements without the possibility that Gregory might be there, so when she reached the top of the spiral staircase she looked up cautiously, then slipped off her patent-leather shoes with the chunky heels and walked across the floor in black-stockinged feet to her favourite viewpoint.

The enclosing walls kept the wild wind from her body but blew her hair about her face. As she stood there in the silence, except for the thundering of the breakers far below, she felt young and vulnerable and indescribably lonely.

There was a sound and she swung round just as Gregory stepped up from the iron staircase. Barbara felt her thoughts splinter.

"Well," he said, and she was aware of a hardness in his voice, "this *is* nice." In the light of the moon and stars he condemned her with his eyes.

"I didn't think you would come up here at this time

of the night," she said, lifting her shoulders. "After all, it's pretty late."

He began to walk towards her. "You should know by now that I come here at any time."

"I was just going." She tried to keep her voice steady.

"You don't have to go," he told her, still in that same hard tone. "In fact, I'd like you to stay."

"I can't think why." She fingered the neckline of her jersey.

"No? Well, I'll tell you. You present a very stimulating challenge." She was aware of his eyes going over her.

"I can't think why," she said again. "Might I ask what you're driving at?"

"You could work that out for yourself, if you wanted to."

This set her back, but she tried not to show it. "I'm not going to beat about the bush," she answered. "I don't like being made a fool of, and that's exactly what Rod Haden did to me tonight. You don't have to regard me as a challenge just because you saw me parked in his car with him. I didn't encourage any advances from Rod and I certainly don't desire any from you."

"No?"

He studied her for a moment and then she said, "No."

"I won't beat about the bush either," he said. "I don't think you need play a game with me. What you do," his eyes went slowly over her again, "in your leisure hours has nothing to do with me—or with Harvester's, for that matter. In other words, you don't have to lie. If at any time I happen to ask you out to dinner just be honest and say that you have an appointment with Rod Haden. You don't have to invent a lot of girls."

He stood silhouetted against the sky and something told her that his presence here was no accident and that he had seen her as she left her room to make her way to the staircase which led up to the battlements.

"Think what you like," she said.

"You remind me of the Castle, Barbara—and the Harvester pieces which go towards garnishing it," he told her.

"Really?" Her voice was tight. "In what way?"

"Well," his voice was mocking. "We'll take the Castle first. It's not the exterior but the interior that's so hard to credit—rooms treated with that unexpected sexy furniture. As I once remarked, the interior comes as almost a shock to many."

"Meaning?" She looked back at him steadily.

"Meaning," he went on, "that beneath the usual sheer elegance of the exterior which you present to the public, in your role as personal secretary to Sir Basil Harvester—beneath that cool little fortress, which looks as if it would resist the most handsome of lady-killers, there's unexpected sexiness—like the Harvester pieces. I guess one could say that in your own way you're something of a genius. You certainly had me fooled."

Outraged, she said, "I see." She remained silent, feeling as though he had actually invaded her, and then she looked down at the lacy stockings. "In other words," she said, "had I worn soft voile or crushed muslin and a fruit-circled straw hat, you wouldn't have regarded me as a challenge?" Her jade eyes looked immense in the starlight.

"Now you're exaggerating, of course. However, taking everything into consideration, I seem to be wasting my time in warning you about Rod Haden. You appear to be," he broke off and hoisted one shoulder, "a hardened young traveller—in more ways than one."

Barbara had a sudden impulse to slap his face. "How dare you!" Completely staggered by his insult, she put out a hand to steady herself against the wall and then, before she quite knew what was happening, he took hold of it. He was so close to her now that their bodies touched.

"Let go of me!" she exclaimed, then found she was running in the direction of the spiral staircase which, although hidden from sight, was marked by the hand-rail which ended in a half-circle on the floor of the battlements. Her shiny shoes glinted on the floor and she stooped to pick them up before, shaking, she let herself down on to the first step.

When she reached the lobby below she turned quickly to see if he was following her, and when she saw that he was not, she dropped the shoes and nudged her feet into them before she began to walk in the direction of a door which led to a thickly carpeted staircase with golden hand-rails. From there she made her way back to her room. Beyond the arches of the gallery she could see that the thickly carved doors leading to Gregory's private rooms were open, and with a small cry of humiliation and rage, she closed the doors of her room and drew the curtains across the plate glass.

In the morning, after a restless and broken night of wondering about her future, she chose her clothes with her usual care for immaculate detail, then breakfasted alone before going to the library.

She was uncovering her typewriter when Reina walked in. "Aren't you being transferred to the new complex, now that it's ready?" Reina asked. "I should have thought that would have been the most obvious thing, instead of having you work here in the library." Her eyes swept the room with its books and magnificent flower arrangements.

Trying to keep her voice pleasant, Barbara said, "This arrangement seems to be the one which suits Sir Basil best."

"I find myself thinking about this—this—*position* of yours," Reina continued, with an ill-concealed hostility. "I must confess that my thoughts keep revolving around one thing."

"What would that one thing be?" Barbara was aware of her facial muscles beginning to tighten.

"Well, let's face it—most girls only accept this sort of position when they happen to be looking for a good time. It's as simple as that—or rather, if they happen to be on the make."

"Perhaps you've been mixing with the wrong type of girl," Barbara tried to hold on to her temper.

"I don't think so." Reina shrugged beautifully. "Sir Basil is very handsome. He's the type of older man who would present quite a catch to any girl. He's a gorgeous man, actually—that tan, that silver hair and dark-blue eyes and, above all, that flat, flat tummy."

"Nobody could disagree with you on that point," Barbara replied in a cold little voice.

"No, I didn't think you would disagree, actually. But tell me, what about Gregory? Clearly, you're out to humour, for want of a better word, both your employers."

"What about—Gregory?" Barbara's voice had given way to sarcasm now.

"He's always so busy lately. Why? Surely he isn't busy all the time?"

"He happens to be very busy," Barbara said. "For one thing, he's compiling a long report. As a matter of fact, I've typed a stack of papers and there are more to come, I'm told."

"I could have typed them, for that matter," Reina answered, "while I'm here."

"I have no say over these things," Barbara replied.

"Well, couldn't you suggest something? Couldn't you mention that you're absolutely snowed under with Sir Basil's work?"

"No, I couldn't suggest that."

"Would you like me to?" Reina asked.

"Please, whatever you do, don't." Barbara surveyed the other girl coolly.

"While we happen to be on the subject," Reina went on, "just one more thing—who is it you *are* interested in? Father, son—or just Rod Haden?"

"I'll make it short and sweet, while we happen to be on the subject," Barbara said swiftly. "I find your remarks nothing short of insulting." They stood in unfriendly silence for a moment and then, seething, Barbara sat down and began to type.

Later, Lilian came into the library. "I just want to arrange another bowl of agapanthus," she said. "Aren't they gorgeous?" She buried her nose in the great blue heads. "By the way, Basil isn't feeling terribly well again, Barbara. He had dinner in his room last night, which is unusual for him. Gregory was out somewhere and I ate with a very sulky Reina." Suddenly Lilian laughed her low, throaty laugh. "I'm a cat, I know, but when Gregory mentioned that he wouldn't be home to dinner I didn't enlighten Reina. She's far too possessive, that girl. When she found out that we were to dine together she didn't even try to hide the fact that she was just a little more than put out. After all, that's not why she turned up at the Castle—to keep *me* company."

"I hope Sir Basil will feel better soon." Barbara's eyes were troubled. "As you say, it's not like him. He's always so fit."

"He's been working too hard. He's been overdoing things. It's as simple as that." Lilian began to place the flowers in a bronze bowl, which was filled with water and ready for her to begin. Slanting in through the windows, the sun caught her silver hair and gave life to her small, almost unlined face. Her eyes—those Harvester eyes—were very blue and carefully made up. She looked slim and glamorous and there was a youthful look about her. "By the way," she said, "come and have your morning tea with me next to the pool."

"Thank you," Barbara answered. "In the meantime, I'll just go on with the work I have on hand."

When, some time later, Gregory came into the library she was still typing, and she waited until her heartbeat had dropped to normal before she looked up.

"I think Lilian must have told you by now that my father is feeling out of sorts. There are several letters and one or two odds and ends he's asked me to attend to. If it's convenient, I'll dictate them now—unless, of course, you would prefer to finish what you're doing?" His eyes went to the paper in her typewriter. "In that case I'll come back later."

"It's convenient now," she told him, having no choice but to pretend that nothing had happened between them.

"Okay," he said. "Shall we get started?"

Her green eyes scanned her desk for her notebook. "I'm ready when you are," she told him.

"You'll have to put me wise as to the speed you like to keep to. How does my father dictate—fast? Slow?"

"Fairly fast," she replied.

"And you keep up?" She was surprised when he smiled.

"Yes." She did not return his smile.

"Well, in any case, I'll keep mine easy until we get used to each other."

"Just as you like." Tenatively, she fingered a strand of auburn hair which had worked loose. She tucked it into the chignon at the back of her head, feeling frustrated and helpless at this turn of events.

While he dictated to her his voice assumed a detachment that made the situation easier and for a while she almost forgot who he was as she concentrated on getting her notes down.

When Theresa brought their tea into the library Barbara made no reference to the fact that Lilian had asked her to have tea next to the pool. She surmised that in view of the fact that Gregory was dictating Lilian had decided to send the tray into the library.

Eventually Gregory said, "I suppose we'd better have tea."

"How do you like it?" Barbara asked, preparing to pour.

"Very little milk—no sugar, thank you." His blue eyes held hers for a moment and then he seemed to relax. Leaning back in his chair, he said, "How much longer can this heat last? Isn't it time we had some rain?"

Barbara noticed with dismay that her hands were shaking. "It certainly is dry and hot," she answered. Where was the cool and collected Barbara Knight? Where was the Barbara Knight who had always remained calm in her role as Sir Basil's personal secretary? The girl who had learned to hop a jet plane as easily as she hopped a line on her typewriter or who had learned to pour tea with a steady hand?

Gregory Harvester had destroyed that girl. Gregory Harvester and Rod Haden between them.

"What's the matter?" There was a slightly mocking tone to Gregory's voice.

"Nothing's the matter." She glanced quickly at him. "Why do you ask?"

"Your hands are shaking." His eyes went to them.

"I don't think they are. Well, *if* they are, anybody's hands shake when they're making an attempt not to spill something—which is what I'm doing, right this moment."

She passed him his cup and saucer and then she stiffened when he said, "Permit me to disagree. People usually shake when they're nervous."

There was a silence. She took a sip of her tea and replaced the cup on the saucer with a little click.

"*Are* you nervous?" he asked finally.

"People shake for a good many reasons." She was determined not to look at him and allowed her eyes to stray in the direction of the walled court beyond the huge window with its small panes of glass. Stone urns filled with blue and pink hydrangeas made the area exciting.

There was another silence and then he said, "This morning you look such a nice girl that I feel I have to mention that with Rod Haden love is only a game. My sister, if she happened to be here, would tell you that."

"What's your definition of a *nice* girl?" Barbara took her eyes away from the walled court with its stone urns filled with blue and pink hydrangeas. "One who doesn't go in for black lace stockings topped by a black mini-skirt and a Schiaparelli-pink cardigan?" Her long, delicately tinted nails played up and down her arm and then, when she realized what she was doing, she dropped her hand and splayed her fingers on the top of the desk.

"They're worn all the time, I know," he said, lifting his cup and studying it before putting it down again. "On you, though, they invite trouble. They become dangerous."

"Let me take your cup," she interrupted, "if you're finished?"

"I am." His blue eyes mocked her.

He dictated several more letters, and when the telephone rang he stopped abruptly while Barbara used her free hand to lift the receiver.

"Hello, Sir Basil Harvester's secretary speaking."

"Hello? Got over your mutters?" It was Rod, and she took a sharp impatient breath. When she had recovered her composure she said, "I happen to be right in the middle of dictation. I'm afraid I can't talk now."

"Well, in that case, there's nothing for it but for me to phone later." He sounded pettish.

"Please don't. I hardly think it will be worth it—you see, I have nothing to say to you," she snapped, and before he could reply, she replaced the receiver.

"That was mean of you," Gregory said, but she saw that he was grinning.

"I've always made it perfectly plain that I'm not to

be phoned round about this time of the day," she said. "I'm sorry about that." She turned a page in her note-book and looked up at him. "You said—upholstered in a glossy antique hide—I'm ready to go on, if you are."

"Ah!" For a moment Gregory sounded just like his father. Then he slumped back in his chair and crossed his legs and the tips of his fingers met. Smouldering slowly, Barbara watched him and waited on him to re-sume dictation.

"Scrap that," he said finally. "Leave that one over. I've got to think about it."

After he had gone she tried to dismiss him from her mind as she continued working, and when it was time to prepare for lunch she stood up. Her mind felt com-pletely used up.

When the ivory phone hooted again she instinctively held her breath, believing it to be Rod. However, it was Lilian. "I insist that you break it off now," she said. "There's just time for you to go and change into your bikini and take a swim before lunch."

"I'll be with you in minutes," Barbara said. "Thank you, Lilian."

Gregory was at the poolside, with Reina stretched out beside him, her tanned, half-nude body gleaming against a lime-green sun-bed. Lilian, already in the pool, called out, "It's wonderful, Barbara. Come along!"

Barbara's feet made slapping noises as she ran in the direction of the deep end and then she dived in, send-ing up a spray of water which looked like splintered glass in the sun. She surfaced right next to where Lilian was standing.

"I get so *mad* at that girl," Lilian's voice was soft, "and I guess I don't have to supply you with a reason, Barbara. When Gregory made it quite clear that he in-tended working she went out, but I'd no sooner phoned you when she arrived back. I was looking for-ward to just the three of us—Gregory, you and me."

After swimming several lengths they got out and stood dripping water. "There'll be time for a long, deliciously cold drink," said Lilian, her breath coming fast.

"Relax while I pour them," Gregory stood up and went in the direction of a cane trolley.

"If you want to swim before you have a drink, Reina, you'd better go in now and get it over," Lilian said, beginning to rub herself with a towel.

"I'm waiting for Greg." Reina's voice was lazy.

Giving her a sideways glance, Gregory said, "I've already been in."

Reina sat up. "Oh? Have you? That was mean of you. Now you can just come in again... with me."

Busy with their drinks, he said, "I'm not going in again."

Reina unfolded herself from the sun-bed and went to stand next to him. "Why didn't you have the grace to tell me?" she asked.

"For the simple reason that, a long time ago, I promised myself never to tell you anything." He did not look at her and then he passed Lilian her drink. As Barbara accepted the drink which he had prepared for her, he said, "This should cool you down," and, aware of the sheen of health on his tanned skin, she thanked him through her lashes. Glass in hand, he lowered himself into a chair. Teasing Barbara, he said, "Nice work. You have a good style."

"Thank you." She inclined her head slightly.

"Your irony is absolutely lost on Barbara," Reina's voice was very light—too light. "She doesn't twig that you don't really mean that."

"Before it gets too late," Lilian cut in, "you dive in, Reina, and give us an exhibition."

"Okay, I'll do that." Reina's voice was sharp now, and then she ran to the deep end and propelled her body almost into the centre of the pool. She then did a fast, showing-off kind of crawl to the other end and then swam over to the side, where the others were sitting. Clinging to the coping tiles, she blinked her eyes. Water cascaded from her blonde hair and, shaking it back, she said, "Pass me my drink, beloved."

"To what do I owe the title?" Gregory asked, handing down her glass.

"*You*," Reina said sweetly, "are taking me out this afternoon."

"When was this arranged over my head?" He settled himself against the cushions again.

"I'll make it short and sweet," she replied. "I've just thought of it now."

"Well, I'll also make it short and sweet. I have work to do." The mockery had gone from his voice now and Barbara was almost ashamed at the surge of satisfaction which swept over her.

"And I could disagree with you, on that point," Reina persisted, pouting. She took a sip of her drink and then said, "I think it's a fairly safe assumption that you might just change your mind."

"You haven't a hope," he told her. "If I haven't managed to convince you, you'll just have to convince yourself. I'm going to be busy for the rest of the day."

It was obvious that rage and humiliation succeeded one another as Reina stared back at him.

"Come along, everybody," Lilian called out cheerfully. "Time to break it up and change for lunch."

Sir Basil joined them for lunch and, with considerable abruptness, said, "Just an upset. Nothing to worry about." The alert, assured Sir Basil Harvester was not accustomed to being let down by his body and to being confined to his unique tower apartment with its huge private terrace and unobstructed views, and wanted nothing more than to change the subject.

Towards the end of the meal he said, "Doc Lindbergh thinks it might be a good idea for you to do the Port Elizabeth trip for me, Greg."

There was a small silence before Gregory replied. "Were you flying?" he asked.

"No. As a matter of fact, I was going by car, for the simple reason that I wanted to see Adrian Price in Grahamstown. You can see him for me."

"Well," Gregory shrugged, "that can be arranged, I guess."

"As you're aware, there are to be several conferences in Port Elizabeth and Barbara will be going along to take the necessary notes and so on," Sir Basil went on, and something changed in Gregory's face while Barbara felt her mind going a blank. Then she struggled to keep the panic she was feeling from showing.

"But couldn't the conferences be taped?" Reina cut in swiftly.

"They could be and they will be." Sir Basil sounded annoyed. "That's the usual procedure, but Barbara also takes notes. Several other secretaries will be attending for the same reason, as a matter of fact."

Before leaving the dining-room, Sir Basil said. "So be prepared, will you, Barbara, for a motor trip to P.E. within the next week or two." He gave her a smile. "Don't look so worried, child."

Barbara knew that her face had blanked again and then she said, "I'll start preparing right away, Sir Basil."

"If you're stopping over for a night in Grahamstown," Reina said, "I wouldn't mind going along with you. I'd like to buy some dresses in that fabulous handwoven material made by the locals there. I could always make a plan about getting more time off work."

"The stop will be a matter of hours," Sir Basil told her. "It wouldn't be worth your while going. In any case, this is strictly a business trip. Perhaps some other time. How's that for a deal?" His tone was cheerful.

"It's as tough as some of your hide. I suppose that's what this trip is all about—leather, and all that."

"I see you're all clued up." He remained cheerful.

"Yes, but what I'm *not* clued up on is how I'm going to survive here with you sick and Greg away."

"Oh, you'll make a plan. You usually do," Sir Basil sounded off-hand now.

Listening to them, everything seemed to be shattering down on Barbara. Apart from the fact that she was to travel alone with Gregory Harvester, she was thinking about the forthcoming trip to Port Elizabeth which was going to take her so close to the farm where she had been brought up. She knew every bit of the road and she asked herself how she was going to bear travelling along it again without turning her head to look in the direction of the turn-off where the rickety gates were situated at the beginning of a sandy road which turned pink in certain lights.

CHAPTER SIX

DURING the next few days Gregory continued dictating letters on Sir Basil's behalf, and Barbara felt a little of the tension begin to go out of her as she adjusted herself to this arrangement.

With deliberate tact, Gregory left her alone and conversation revolved around Harvester affairs and nothing else. A kind of companionable relationship had, in fact, sprung up between them as they worked together.

On her afternoon off Barbara got into her bikini, slipped a pair of white slacks and a bronze top with tangerine coloured poppies over it and went in search of Lilian before going to the beach. She found her relaxing at the poolside. Casting her infectious smile at Barbara, she said, "Hello, you look very glamorous—not that you don't always look that way. Afternoon off? Are you off to the beach?"

"Yes. I thought I'd just let you know, Lilian. I'll probably swim in the tidal pool."

"Why doesn't Gregory take you?" Lilian asked bluntly.

Laughing, Barbara said, "Why should he? I left him in the library, as a matter of fact, signing letters."

"Basil is simply furious with Doc Lindbergh," Lilian told her, chuckling. "Doctor has insisted that Basil take things easy for a couple of weeks at least. So it's fortunate that Greg arrived back just when he did. Reina has gone into town, by the way, to meet Rod somebody-or-other. The name rings a bell, don't you think?"

For a moment Barbara wondered whether Lilian had told her this on purpose, but on looking closely at her, she felt that for the moment at any rate the name Rod hadn't registered.

"Tell me," Lilian went on, "have you seen that new boutique in town—the one with red and white striped awning and wrought-iron lanterns? It's in Lucienne Arcade."

"No," Barbara answered, "I haven't."

"Well, you should take a visit there. It's like a small piece of London transplanted to the sub-tropics. I bought a patio gown there, as a matter of fact."

"I must make a note of it," Barbara said, her mind busy with Reina and Rod.

"Well," Lilian waved cheerfully, "look after yourself."

The quiet, sandy beach was hot and the palm trees on the banks of the lagoon sweltered in the glare. An ancient and twisted tree had collapsed during a storm at some time in the past, and it lay across a ridge of rocks next to the greeny water, its trunk bleached silver by the sun. The sand was scorching hot, so Barbara walked along the tidal strip, carrying her gold sandals by the straps. The cold wet fingers of the sea kept stealing up the beach, gently caressing and easing her problems from her mind. Eventually she retraced her steps and walked back to the tidal pool where she stood on the rocks and slipped out of her slacks and top. Then she searched in her big bag for the black and pink cap which matched her bikini and put it on, her jade eyes slightly shut against the sun and the small pain as the cap caught at the roots of her hair, tugging it.

When she dived into the sun-shot water it closed in on her and she gave herself up in sheer delight. Strangely enough, the water felt cold, but this was no doubt because her body had been so hot. Panting a little, she swam to the side of the pool and hoisted herself out to sit with her slim, tanned legs dangling into the water. She ripped off her cap and the water which had been captured in the pink petals and green leaves splashed out. Her auburn hair bounced about her shoulders, slightly damp even though she had worn a cap, for it was more decorative than protective.

"Hello, mermaid."

It was Gregory's voice, and Barbara swung around, trying to adjust herself to his presence. His dark-blue eyes went over her and she found herself thinking how fabulous he was—his eyes a dark blue, his skin wonderful, with a burnt-in South African tan. He had a way of making other men pale into insignificance beside him— like his father. He kept standing where he was and, aware that he was probably wearing swimming trunks beneath the pale blue jeans and darker blue shirt he was wearing, she said, "Are you going in?"

Drops of water still glistened on her eyelashes and she could see them shining like tiny jewels in the sun. She tried to blink them away.

"How about coming in with me?" he asked.

"I've been in," she stammered.

"I know—but come in again."

"I don't think so." She turned her face away and then there were small rustling movements as he began to remove his jeans and shirt. One of the leather slip-on sandals he was wearing fell down on to some rocks below where he was standing, and before it fell into the water, he scrambled down after it.

Barbara turned to look at him and, when he straightened up, they both began to laugh, discovering quite suddenly that the pleasurable thing right now was being together. "Come on," he said, "what about it? Keep me company in the surf."

"No," she said.

"Why not?"

She searched around for an excuse. "Because of sharks. I'm afraid of sharks."

"There are shark nets. Didn't you know?" he asked, with a momentary quirk of his mouth.

"Well, come to think of it, yes." Barbara gave him an impish grin.

She sat there, undecided, her pulse going faster, wanting to be with him and yet still uncertain of him—uncertain of herself. The fact that they had worked in harmony during the last few days meant approximately nothing, but she said, "All right," and began to adjust her cap.

"Leave your things where they are," he told her, "but hang on, while I put mine along with them."

While she struggled to tuck her damp hair beneath the wet bathing cap she watched him and hoped her yearning thoughts did not reach him.

He came back for her and she jumped across the rocks and back on to the sand and then the mood of body surfing overtook them as they plunged beneath the first breaker. Eventually, with arms outstretched and faces submerged in the water, they surfed towards the beach, and when they stood up the water swirled and receded around them. Their clothes contrasted with the purple flowers of crawling, succulent Hottentot figs and Barbara's eyes went to them. "We'd better rescue our clothes from that dune before they get blown away," she said. She pulled off her cap and the wind, which was suddenly very strong, whipped her hair across her face. "I'm glad I went in," she panted. "It was wonderful. The sea's so *rough*!"

Closing the distance between them, Gregory stood so close to her that she felt his nearness. Their eyes met and it was as if both knew, and accepted, that this was not the first time that they had known they existed for each other. There had been another time—when a girl with a husky, exciting voice had been singing soul to the accompaniment of an exciting orchestra.

The sand, whipped up by the new force in the wind, stung their legs. The sea looked curdled. "I think I'll go back. The weather is changing," said Barbara.

"Don't go back," he said. "Let's go for a drive instead."

"Where to?" Her voice was strained.

"What about the river tea gardens? It will be protected there, if nothing else. We'll go back up and get straight into the car. There's no need to change. There's a pool up there. We could swim again—or sunbathe, have something to drink..."

"Honestly, I don't think so."

"Why not?" he asked. It seemed ridiculous to brood on what had gone between them—to remind him of the way in which he had insulted her, to play hard-to-get when all he was offering was friendship. Perhaps, she thought, if she went with him he would draw his own conclusions about her and not allow Reina's remarks to influence his decision. She might even find the right moment to laughingly explain about the Yoga outfit and her meeting up with Rod, after the class and subsequent drive back to the Castle in view of the fact that Cynthia's car had given trouble. Certainly it could help to clear up a lot of things and make working for Gregory, while his father was not well, more pleasant.

"All right," she murmured. "I'd like to."

They climbed the stone steps up to the Castle, brushing past huge blue agapanthus heads, on tall leaning stalks. "Shall I go and tell Lilian?" she asked, in a breathless little voice, when they were at the top.

"No. Why should you tell anyone?" His smile was mocking.

She waited for him while he got his car from the garages and, aware of her wet bikini beneath her slacks and top, slipped into the seat beside him. Her face felt stiff and sticky from salt water and she longed for the moment when she could go to the powder room at the river tea gardens where she could splash her skin and apply the cream which she always carried with her to the beach.

They headed in the direction of Uvongate and then, before they reached the town, Gregory swung the car off the National Road on to a rough gravel road where mirages danced in the heat haze. "This happens to be a short cut," he told her. "There's a bridge higher up. If we took the better road of the two—over the causeway, that is—it would take much longer. Just so long as you don't mind the dust?"

"I don't," she assured him.

They passed a Zulu maiden, as she walked towards them, proud and innocently naked but for some bead-work and a scrap of vivid silk draped about her swaying hips. Gregory slackened speed to protect her from dust and possible flying stones which spurted up from the wheels.

"It's still fairly wild up these parts," he said, changing down, "it's just one place that's never gone ahead, somehow. However, it's one of the few places left down the coast where one still has the feeling that time has stood still."

"Except the Castle," Barbara answered. "The grounds are so extensive it's hard to credit that nearby there's a busy and sophisticated town with an abundance of hotels, holiday flats and bungalows, shops and so on. All this is new to me, as it so happens. I haven't been up the river."

"I didn't think you would have—it's not sophisticated enough for Rod Haden," he said.

"Why bring that up?" she asked. "I don't see why Rod Haden's name should crop up."

"I don't see why his name should crop up, either, but," he shrugged, "there you are. It's a name constantly with me."

"It exhausts me just to think of it," she said, with considerable feeling.

Gregory parked the car in an area provided. A troop of vervet monkeys emerged from the surrounding bush and they sat around, scratching themselves with neurotic fingers fighting, now and then, over fleas. On the veranda of the tea room a grey parrot dozed, with one eye open, and then it shrieked, "Hello, darling!"

The lawns sloped down from the steps of the building to the river which was trembling in the blinding haze of a sky which had grown feverish. Now that it had got going, the parrot shrieked again and Gregory said mockingly, "It must be a woman."

"I don't see why," Barbara said, "but maybe." She laughed.

When they were on the veranda he asked, "What are you going to drink?"

"I'd love a Coke," she answered.

The roof of the building was of thatch and almost hidden beneath an avalanche of purple and mauve bougainvillea. Instead of having a cooling effect the wind, which was beginning to force its way through the foliage, only seemed to be intensifying the heat and Barbara longed to wash her face and cream it. She rubbed her fingers across her cheeks. "I must find a tap," she said. "This salt is making me shrivel."

"I'll have a Coke waiting for you," he said, pointing to a table, "over there."

"Wonderful!"

"And then we'll swim again. How's that?"

"Fine," she answered, aware of the stifling heat and her damp bikini which had begun to cut into her beneath the slacks. Something told her that if they were going to swim there would be no time to dry off before a storm broke.

In the cloakroom she thought about Gregory as she washed, creamed and touched up her face. Combing her hair, she wondered what he was really like beneath that confidently efficient shell.

When she went to the table he said, "I've ordered the Cokes. They should be here presently." His eyes went over her. "You look deliciously cool."

"Well, looks are deceiving. I'm feeling anything but cool."

"I know looks are deceiving. I keep reminding myself. However, looks are also something to be enjoyed, not to be examined, so I intend to concentrate on just that.''

Disappointed in him again, Barbara sat back and regarded him with uneasy displeasure. Her eyes flickered round the veranda and, beyond it, the tea-room where thin bamboo matting covered the walls, upon which crude paintings, in vivid splashes of colour and depicting South African scenes, were hung. African curios in the form of bright beadwork, woven baskets and vases and figures moulded from clay were exhibited in a small alcove. There was a fragrance of straw about the place which conjured up pictures of sun and tall grasses swaying in the breeze. Lizards, tiny, arrow-thin creatures, clung to the exposed roof beams above them and she smiled a little as they darted away out of sight.

"Mamba Paradise would be an appropriate name for this place, I should imagine," said Gregory, following her gaze.

"I—it's so—so untamed," she replied. "I agree with you."

"Imagine spending a night in one of those rondavels," he mocked, and for a moment she regarded him thoughtfully, then she asked, in a small tight voice, "Do people come here for holidays? I mean, it looks so—abandoned. Besides, it's not very big—only a couple of rondavels and this building, which appears to be mostly veranda and tea-room."

"They cater only for visitors who happen to want a mixed grill—tea, coffee, cold drinks—that sort of thing, I understand," he said. "One used to be able to hire a rowing boat here. I don't know if that still goes."

The air was thickening. It was pregnant with wind and electricity and even the birds in the garden were twittering with a kind of excited apprehension.

When they had finished their Cokes Gregory said, "What about a swim? Are you game?"

Not really wanting to, she said, "Do we have to buy a ticket?"

"I've already approached the establishment. The pool is open to visitors and, taking everything into consideration, it's in pretty good condition."

Barbara's smile was strained. "All right, then. I think there's going to be a storm, though."

"It will probably pass over," he told her.

The water, as they entered it head-first, was tepid. There were a number of cream and gold frangipani flowers floating on the surface. Barbara swam three lengths and then turned on her back, and what she saw made her gasp. "There's going to be an awful storm," she called, turning over and swimming for the side of the pool.

"Let it storm," said Gregory. "Who cares?"

"I do." She hoisted herself out of the water and sat on the terrazzo tiles. Her eyes went to the monkeys as, chattering among themselves, they swung themselves into the surrounding bush, grabbing monkey babies as they went. There was a wild flurry of leaves and dry twigs. Some of the leaves blew into the pool and were bobbing about on the churned-up surface.

Barbara stood up and went to her bag and beach towel and, panting a little with exertion, began to dry herself. Her mood became one of uneasiness as she regarded Gregory who was still doing a lazy crawl up and down the length of the pool. She turned as the Indian waiter who had served them on the veranda came out to collect cushions from the chairs. "The wireless says we can expect unsettled weather conditions," he said, "and I think it's right." He looked up at the sky. "It is coming sooner than they think. There have been a lot of violent storms in the Transvaal and the Orange Free State. I think we are in for it now. Soon, too."

As he climbed out of the pool Gregory said, "It will break the heatwave." He began to look around for his towel.

Barbara stooped for her bag. "I'll be back in a minute," she said, then started to run in the direction of the main building. In the cloakroom, because there was nothing else for it, she shrugged into her slacks and top and immediately both garments absorbed the dampness of her bikini.

Gregory was waiting for her on the veranda. He had ordered two more Cokes and he seemed to be in no hurry. Barbara felt herself getting excited. "Don't look so keyed up," he grinned. She saw that he had changed back into his jeans and shirt. His wet trunks were rolled up in his towel and she thought, with some resentment, that he was not being subjected to the discomfort of wearing a wet bikini beneath them. She promised herself never to rely on her bikini as undies again.

"I'm not really keyed up," she told him, trying to laugh lightly, "but honestly, I do feel we should be getting back. If it rains that road will be terribly muddy, for one thing."

"Well, take it easy," he drawled.

"For how long?" she mocked him. "That's what I'm worried about."

"One would think you'd never seen an approaching storm before." He sounded amused.

"It's not that." She took a small sip of her drink and looked up.

"What is it, then?"

Disconcerted, she murmured, "It's hard to explain. I just have an inexplicable thing about staying here."

"Perhaps you have a date tonight—with the girls?" His smile suggested a lot of things.

"No, I haven't." Her voice was tight and she gave him a serious look. "Actually, there's a story attached to that."

Before she could continue there was a brilliant flash of lightning followed by an ear-splitting crack of thunder and she jumped, spilling a little of her drink. "Oh, that was *close*!" Her voice was shocked now.

A heavy drop of rain hit the steps outside and then

another, and soon there was a solid curtain of water, separating them from the garden.

"Perhaps you'll dine with me now?" Gregory gave her another of his mocking smiles.

"Where?"

"Here. They advertise mixed grills here, after all. By the time we've finished the storm will have passed over."

Against her will she felt a surge of excitement but it was not the kind of excitement which she had felt about the approaching storm.

There was another flash of lightning, followed by more crashing thunder. Barbara flinched openly, her eyes wide and scared.

"Would you like to go into the tea-room?" he asked.

"Yes. I don't like it out here."

"What protection do you think the tea-room has to offer?" he asked as he came round to get her drink. "Come on, I'll carry these."

"No one likes being told they're stupid," she said, when they were inside.

"I didn't say that." He shot her a smile.

"No—but you implied as much. I just don't happen to like storms very much. I guess that applies to most women."

"You're still a little girl." His tone was more gentle than mocking.

She made no reply and they sat, without talking, listening to the thunder and the tossing and turning water noises and while Barbara flinched at every orange flash, Gregory did not bat an eyelid.

At last she said, "There seems to be a flood going on."

"Nonsense!"

"Listen," she told him. "Listen to the river. Why is it making such a noise?"

"Why not? As soon as the lightning eases off I'll phone Lilian and put her mind at rest. In the meantime, I'll go and tell them we'll be having a meal here later on. How does that suit you?" he asked.

"If you think so." Her thoughts took flight into the time when the storm would have passed over completely and the stars were out and they were eating, by candlelight, on the veranda. Even if the stars were not out she visualized a soft, sighing rain and then, later, the drive back in the coolness which had come with the storm. It was an attractive thought.

It was a long-drawn-out storm. Just when it appeared to be diminishing it started again in full fury. Barbara watched in alarm as Gregory, long-legged and casual, left her to go to the phone, and when he came back he said, "Well, I've told Lilian where we are and I've also told her that we'll be eating here. I spoke to the owner, a Mrs. Gordon, by the way, and I've made the necessary arrangements to have grills later on. My father came on the line—I forgot to mention that."

Barbara's eyes widened. "What did he say?" she asked quickly.

"What do you mean—what did he say?" She saw the flicker of amusement in his eyes.

"About us—being here together?" she answered.

"We spoke about the storm. He mentioned that the rivers are up. The sea is discoloured."

"So soon?"

"Apparently it's been raining further up in Natal. The rivers are full."

Their eyes held and she said softly, "What's wrong?"

"Why do you ask, Barbara?"

"Suddenly you look—cagey."

"You might as well know," he said. "I was thinking of the causeway."

Barbara searched her memory. "The causeway? But I didn't see a causeway on the way here, did I?"

"Don't you remember, I mentioned the short cut? You didn't see the causeway owing to the fact that we came over the old bridge. The road across the causeway happens to be tarred, but the causeway might be under water. The road to the bridge, on the other hand, will be knee-deep in mud. So I guess you could say we have a problem on our hands." He sat back and regarded her with some amusement.

"Oh, no!" she exclaimed, and there was undisguised dismay in her voice.

"Anyway," he said, "let's face that when we come to it."

"But we *have* come to it," she pointed out, with some annoyance. "Haven't we?"

"We'll consider the position after we've eaten," he told her.

Nearby, the waiter was setting a table for two. Finally he beckoned to them. "All ready for you now, sir." They moved over to it and while the waiter hovered about serving them he said, "By the way, the causeway will probably be under water, sir, and the other road will be very muddy. You might not be able to get back."

"In that case," Gregory replied easily, "we'll just have to seek shelter in your rondavels out there. We shall also have to equip Miss Knight here with a stick in case she has to dispose of a snake during the long and very dark night."

"Oh, you're so callous!" Barbara interrupted, laughing, but feeling alarm at the same time. Something told her that the chances of having to spend the night here were not all that remote.

Glancing at the waiter, she said, "Do you get many guests up here?"

"Guests? You mean—to stay?" The waiter sounded puzzled.

"Yes."

"No guests, miss. Visitors during the weekends. People come here to swim and boat. Our grills are very popular and so are our cream scones. We also serve cold meats and salads, but we don't see many people

during the week. Holiday people prefer the beaches and
the shops and hotels. The local people like to get away
over the weekends. They are usually the ones who
come up here." He laughed. "They let the holiday
people take over."

"So you don't have people staying in the rondavels?" she asked.

"No, miss. Those rondavels are for Mr. and Mrs.
Gordon's two sons and their families... for when they
come down from the Transvaal on leave."

"I see." She looked down at her plate.

"What will you have after your grill, sir?" The
waiter transferred his attention to Gregory, who said,
"Fruit salad and ice-cream. Or would you prefer fresh
cream, Barbara?"

"I would, thank you," she murmured, her mind active with the rondavels outside. "Cream would be very
nice."

When the waiter had gone they sat in silence for a
while. There was a kind of tension between them now
and then Barbara said, in a strained voice, "We should
have left here before the storm broke. There was no
need to swim." Her lashes flickered and she looked
across the candlelit table at him. "That would have
been the reasonable thing to do."

"Men don't reason things that way," he shrugged.

"Don't they?" Her thoughts were chaotic.

"No." She watched his eyes travel to her mouth and
then back to her eyes. "They don't."

Afraid of the expression in her eyes, she tilted her
head forward and her hair fell partly over her cheeks.
The water had got beneath her cap and her hair was still
damp. Beneath her clothes her bikini pants clung to her
and were cutting into her flesh. She looked up. "What
do men reason with?" she asked very softly.

"With their desires, usually," he said, and Barbara
felt a rising anger. Had he foreseen this turn of events?
she asked herself.

The waiter brought their fruit salad, topped by a foam of whipped cream. Beyond the darkening windows they could see that the shawls of water were growing thinner. The rain was slackening away. Suddenly Barbara felt her heart begin to lighten. They might still make it.

For a while they just sat there drinking their coffee and listening to the rain. The air was smelling of damp earth. The waiter came back to the table. "Have another cup of coffee," he suggested amiably. "I'll take it out to the veranda for you. It's nice out there now. Just mind the puddles of water."

They had to sit far back from the low white wall and pillars, which ran across the length of the veranda, dividing it from the garden. The rain had driven in and lay in glimmering pools on the cement floor.

"Tomorrow the sun will beat down as mercilessly as ever," Gregory said. "If anything, it will be even more humid."

Feeling ill at ease again, Barbara agreed, "Yes, I suppose so." She was aware of tension building up all the time. "Shouldn't we be making some kind of effort to get back?" She cleared her throat. "It's practically dark. I'm thinking of the—er—mud and—water."

"What else are you thinking about?" he asked, his eyes on her face.

"I've just told you—the mud, the water. I'm also thinking about Sir Basil and Lilian."

"Is that all?"

"Well, of course."

He stood up suddenly, and smiled down at her. "Come along, then. We can always make the effort, I guess, if nothing else. Ready, Miss Knight?"

They both turned as Mrs. Gordon came out to the veranda. "Well," she was wide-eyed with concern, "I've been thinking about you two young folks out here and I have a nasty feeling that you're not going to get back to Uvongate tonight—it is Uvongate, I take it? There's been a proper cloudburst. Not only that, but the weather has been bad in most of the other Provinces and it must have finally caught up with us...and you know what that could mean? It could mean that the road to the bridge is washed out and the causeway is under water." She stood back and surveyed them.

"To be perfectly frank, I've been thinking along those lines myself," Gregory replied.

"Well, it's a bit late in the day for that," Mrs. Gordon replied, merely stating a fact, but without sounding aggressive.

"Anyway, hold thumbs for us," Gregory said cheerfully. "We're just about to leave."

"I'll do that, certainly, but I don't hold out much hope, I can tell you that. If you can't get across then you'd better come back here and I'll see what I can do about putting you up for the night."

"I hope there'll be no need for that," Gregory told her.

"If the worse comes to the worst," Mrs. Gordon said, "it will have to be in the rondavels. Unfortunately, there's no electric light at the moment. You see, we're having the place re-wired—the rondavels, I mean. They were a threat, so far as breaking into fire was concerned. So the electrician said, anyway, but you can never trust that bunch. The lights *were* flickering, mind you. I'll give him his due."

It was still raining when they went out to the car. Barbara found that her nerves were tight with tension. Cutting into her thoughts, Gregory said, "Relax, Barbara."

"I am relaxed," she answered. "I'm just thinking."

"What about—of having to spend the night with me in some lonely rondavel with no light?"

"There were two rondavels," she answered quickly. "I counted them."

"All two of them?"

She made no reply. Then he said, "Did you observe that they were joined together? There might be an interleading door—or there might not be one, on the other hand."

"How do you know they were interleading?" she asked, and he laughed.

"By the roof. You're not as observant as you think you are."

"You sound so amused," she said bitterly. "It's not a joke."

"I didn't say it was. It's very serious, as it so happens."

"Well, let's keep it that way," she said, as he opened the car door for her.

When he got in beside her he said, "It sounds as if you don't trust me, Barbara."

"I didn't say that."

"Well—" she could hear the grin in his voice, "maybe you *should* have said it."

"You've done this on purpose," she snapped, "haven't you?"

"Now you're being silly. *I* certainly didn't *invent* the storm."

"No, but you could foresee this turn of events, couldn't you?"

"What kind of talk is that?" He had become abruptly impatient. She held her breath while he started the car, terrified that the engine might cut out in view of the fact that it had been out in such a deluge. Gregory seemed preoccupied with his own thoughts now and they drove to the causeway in silence.

The headlights picked out the churning water.

"Where is the causeway?" asked Barbara in a flat little voice, knowing very well where it was.

"It's under water," he told her. "As you can see."

"That means we're cut off, doesn't it?"

"I'm afraid so. The other road will have been wiped out," he answered.

She sat back and closed her eyes. She knew she was shaking. A bitter resentment was building up against him. Had he done this on purpose? Had he postponed leaving the tea gardens before the storm started, with this sort of thing in mind?

CHAPTER SEVEN

THERE was no sign of Mrs. Gordon when they got back to the tea-room, but the Indian waiter was still about. Moodily Barbara watched Gregory as he explained the position to the other man.

"I'll call Mrs. Gordon," the waiter said. "She is just fixing Mr. Gordon up for the night. He is in bad health—in a wheelchair, as a matter of fact."

While they waited Gregory stood at the low wall of the veranda, staring out into the darkness.

"So it's under water, is it?" said Mrs. Gordon, coming out to the veranda. "Just as I thought. Well, we'll just have to make a plan, that's all—and it wouldn't be the first time. Now, I can put you up with pleasure, but I'm not going to be as two-faced as to say that it won't present a problem, because it will. You see, here in the main building we have a little lounge—private, I mean—and one bedroom and the tea-room, of course. But, like I said, there are the rondavels, and the electricity has been cut off while we have the re-wiring done. Then there's another snag—but come along and I'll show you. We'll have to watch the mud and slush. What a storm!" She began to lead the way and they followed. "You know," she said, over her shoulder, "we had these rondavels built for our boys—well, they're men now, of course, and their wives and children for when they visit us during their holidays. The trouble is, they're interleading, but I'm sure you won't mind that too much. They're not rondavels in the true sense of the word, although we call them that because they're thatched. Mind you don't slip there. However, to get back to putting you up. I guessed you were engaged. Are you?'' She did not turn, obviously not wanting to be confronted by another snag, but Gregory said, ''Yes, we are engaged, as it so happens.''

Barbara felt her eyes widen with shock, but kept quiet.

''Ah, well,'' Mrs. Gordon kept on walking, ''that certainly simplifies matters to a great degree. Your young lady will have no worries. By now she'll have grown to trust you. Mind you don't slip.'' Her ample posterior was a vague white shape in the darkness.

Nearby, the roar of the river was an awesome thing. Mrs. Gordon turned the knob of the door and it made a rasping, rusty noise.

''Everything smells musty,'' she was saying, ''but it's only the result of humidity and from the place not being lived in at the moment. I'll have the beds made up for you while you're having a cup of coffee. I'm sure you could do with one. Good, here's Chetty with lamps. Did you bring candles as well, Chet?''

Chetty busied himself in the room. Mrs. Gordon rubbed her hands together. ''This is it, folks. I'm afraid it's all I have to offer, but I feel sure it will be better than sleeping in the car. It's turned quite nippy now.''

''You're very kind, Mrs. Gordon. I'd like you to know that we're most grateful,'' said Gregory. ''I must apologize for the inconvenience caused by our own carelessness, especially as Mr. Gordon is in poor health.''

''So you know about that? Well, it's just one of those things. He's not in pain, that's the main thing. Now, you'll want a bath, if I know the fads of young people, and at least you will be able to have piping hot water. We have a chip geyser down here and very efficient it is, too. Don't make any bones about that. Chetty will get someone to bring wood and light up. When Tina brings the bedding down she'll bring the towels and soap.''

Because she felt it was time for her to say something Barbara smiled, "Thank you. You're really very kind."

An inspection of the bathroom revealed that it had an unlined corrugated roof, but everything was spotless. Trailing bougainvillea scraped its thorns on the roof, and Barbara's nerves tightened and her eyes flew to the window.

Aware of the look, Mrs. Gordon said, "Don't be alarmed if you see some big spiders about. They're just harmless house spiders. But now comes another problem. What about something to sleep in? You see *me*." She laughed heartily. "Mr. Gordon isn't much better, and you two haven't an extra bit of fat on you."

"Please don't worry about anything for me," Gregory told her. "I'll get by. It wouldn't be the first time, but," he cast an amused look in Barbara's direction, "my fiancée, perhaps? Barbara?"

"I'll manage, thank you, please don't worry." Her smile was small and stiff—for Mrs. Gordon's sake.

"Well, anyway, I'll have something sent along—for both of you. They'll be clean, that's the main thing. Well, I guess that's all. No, no, Mr....?" her voice trailed away, "I can manage my own way back."

"I beg your pardon," Gregory said, "Gregory Harvester—my fiancé, Barbara Knight."

"I've heard of the Harvesters, of course, who hasn't?" Mrs. Gordon laughed. "This doesn't come up to the same standard as your Castle, I know."

It was very silent after Mrs. Gordon and Chetty had gone. The door was open to the darkness and a soft, deceivingly soft, rain.

"I'll sleep in the car," said Gregory. "You can begin to relax."

There was a shaky moment when Barbara almost shouted at him, almost broke down and wept from rage and humiliation, but when the moment had spent itself she said stiffly, "There's no need—after all, there *does* happen to be an interleading door."

"No key," his tone was mocking again. "Not on this side, anyway." Wide-eyed with annoyance, she watched him as he went to the door. "None this side either." He remained there smiling at her and the candles cast spluttering shadows across his handsome, taunting face.

"You're trying to rile me, aren't you?" She took a sharp breath. "You're trying to rile me in just the same way as you *cheated* me."

"Steady on!" He came to stand near her and she moved away. "In what way have I cheated you, Barbara? What do you think I am? A built-in barometer?" He laughed lightly.

"No, that's not what I think at all, but you saw the storm coming, and if you didn't see, I kept warning you. Later, you could see for yourself that it was going to be a bad one. There was time—there would have been time—to leave before it broke or, at the very least get across the bridge before the rain turned the road to slush. There would have been time to get across the causeway, no doubt, before the water rose, but..."

"But what?" He leaned against the white wall and crossed his arms. "But what, Barbara?"

"You dawdled. You drew your swim out—you *wanted* this to happen. You wanted to prove something to yourself, didn't you? You wanted the chance to try and prove that I—that I'm a—a—some sort of tramp—subway woman. You think I'm—easy game..."

She broke off as an African woman, accompanied by an African man, arrived. The man was carrying a bundle of bed-linen which had been slipped into a huge polythene bag in order to protect it from the rain. "Plenty rain," he grinned. "More coming."

"I certainly hope not," Gregory replied. "I think we've had enough, don't you?"

"The rain is good for planting."

"That's so—yes." Gregory nodded in the direction of a small table. "We have a lamp and candles—but I see you've brought more."

"It will make the room warm," the man answered cheerfully. "Tina will light them." Already the room was being transformed to a pink glow which threw more fantastic shapes and shadows upon the rough white walls.

"Mrs. Gordon said coffee is waiting," said Tina. "Up there. You can drink it while we make the beds."

"In that case, we'll go up," Gregory told her. It was obvious that both beds were about to be made up in the room in which they were standing. "One bed in here and one in there," he added, and there was a small silence before Tina said, in typical blunt African manner, "You are not married?" Her frankness had nothing to do with rudeness.

"Not yet. One day, I hope." Gregory's smile was easy. "Ready to go up for some coffee, Barbara?"

As they picked their way across the rain-soaked lawn he said, "Take my hand, in case you slip."

"I can manage on my own," she told him, and promptly slipped.

In the darkness he reached for her hand. "Don't be stupid. Do you want to fall?"

"I admit I *am* stupid," she replied bitterly.

The coffee calmed her a little, although her clothes felt damp and uncomfortable and she had begun to shiver. The lights of the tea-room were still burning, but there was no one about.

"I'll go and phone Lilian before they shut up shop here." Gregory stood up. Barbara found herself beginning to breathe differently just at the thought of how the news would affect Sir Basil. How irresponsible he would think her!

When Gregory came back he said, "I spoke to Lilian."

"What did she say?" Barbara's face was taut.

"She sounded frankly amused, as a matter of fact."

On the way back to the rondavels she jumped as

something swayed in the wind and brushed against her arm.

"It's only a creeper. Forget all that talk about snakes. I was just kidding you." Gregory sounded almost kind.

In silence she watched him open the door and then he stood to one side and she entered. "Although this is the most attractive one of the two," he was saying, "you'd better sleep in there." He nodded in the direction of the other rondavel where lamp and candlelight flattered the faded floral curtains and bedspreads which apparently were always left on the beds even when they were not made up.

On the defensive, she asked hotly, "Why? Why should I have that one?"

"For the very simple reason that this place is not equipped with keys, for some unknown reason. If I sleep in here I'll be between you and the door to the garden—not that I imagine it makes any difference. However, I should imagine that most girls wouldn't care to sleep in an unlocked room in a strange place. Are you with me or against me? It's entirely up to you." He sounded faintly irritable.

Against her will she found herself looking at his bronzed throat and the dark silky hairs there and on his arms. Suddenly their eyes met and, for one swift moment, the look in his was unguarded.

"Well?" His voice was soft.

"With you." She swallowed.

"Good. By the way, I forgot to check the car windows. I'd better see whether they're closed in case it begins to pour again during the night. You're not going to be nervous, are you?"

Barbara was, in fact, terrified, but she said, "No."

When he had gone she gathered towels and soap together and ran across a short expanse of soggy lawn to the bathroom. In view of the fact that the chip geyser had been lit for their convenience, she felt obliged to use the hot water. Although she was craving for a bath or shower she very much doubted whether she would have braved it otherwise, especially as she had cream and tissues in her bag. She decided to shower, and afterwards was glad she had put her fears of snakes and spiders to the test.

The sound of music greeted her when she got back to the rondavels. Her eyes went to Gregory, who was sprawled out on his bed, and when he saw her he sat up and swung his legs over the side. "Well? Feeling better? I remembered there was a transistor in the car. I thought that a little music could be a good thing." He smiled.

"The water's piping hot," she told him. "I had a shower."

The music sounded out of place, the chords striking violently on the piano and the instruments of the orchestra surging in to take full command of the melody.

Barbara felt herself beginning to shiver again. Her shower had been spoilt by the fact that she'd had to slip back into her bikini and slacks and top again. She'd scooped her hair up in a topknot and secured it with a rubber band, but damp tendrils were escaping and clung to her cheeks.

"Do you think the rondavels are far enough back?" she asked.

"Far enough back?" He sounded puzzled.

"Yes—from the banks of the river. I'd hate to be washed away in the night, down to the sea, if the water rises."

"That's not very likely."

"I think it is."

"But then, Barbara, you have a mind that jumps to far too many conclusions."

"No," she said softly, "it's you who has a mind that jumps to far too many conclusions." Her throat felt dry. He continued to watch her with that dark blue gaze which betrayed nothing—and yet everything. Why not face it? she thought. She was furious with him. She hated him—but she was also in love with him.

"Do you mind if I go through to my rondavel now?" she asked.

"No," he said, "not unless you have any better ideas." She took a sharp breath and he went on, "I appreciate that we have problems, you and I. I won't pretend, I want to kiss you—but that happens to be my problem. You look so very innocent, standing there with your hair caught up like that. It's difficult to think of you as Rod Haden's girl. It's a knowledge I could well do without, actually."

"I *am* innocent," her voice was furious and laced with hurt, "make no mistake about that! No matter what Reina has to say, no matter how I dress on occasions, no matter how it looks to you when I happen to be in a parked car—I'm innocent, and what's more, I intend to remain that way!"

"I'm jealous," he told her, "and being jealous I have the compulsive urge to hurt you. Please dismiss my remarks—with my sincere apologies."

"I've learned enough about men by now to realize that when a man says he's jealous that's his way of trying to break a girl down. It's his way of trying to lead her on..." She did not recognize her own voice and knew that if she did not get away from him she would probably break down. Turning, she went into her room and slammed the door, then stood for a moment, aware that on the other side he was doing the same thing, then she heard the other door closing and knew he had gone to take a shower.

Tina had draped an outsize cotton nightdress over the pillows on the bed which had been made up and turned down for her to slip into, and with a huge feeling of despondency Barbara picked up the garment. She felt utterly drained.

The sheets smelled of the sun and wind which had dried them and she bunched the top one against her chin, feeling the sting of tears, but before she could even begin to cry, she fell asleep.

The sun was spilling its liquid colours across the red floor when she awoke in the morning and the rondavel, with its whitewashed walls and floral curtains, seemed a different place and a sense of peace enveloped her until she realized why she was here. Her eyes flew to the door at the very same time that there was a slight tapping noise. "It's Tina!"

"Oh," Barbara sank back. "Come in, Tina."

"I bring your coffee," Tina said, coming into the room. "The rain is finished." She stood regarding Barbara with polite interest. "He is up already and he is on the veranda and he say you must come for breakfast when you are ready, but you mustn't hurry."

"I see. Thank you—and thank you for the coffee, Tina."

When the other girl had gone Barbara sipped her coffee, then got up and went to the windows, drew the curtains and opened the windows wide. She caught her breath when she saw Gregory. Obviously he had left the veranda and taken a walk down to the river and was on his way back. She saw his eyes go to the faded cotton nightdress which Mrs. Gordon had sent along, and she drew the curtains closed and started to dress, beginning to hate the sight of her damp bikini.

Gregory was on the veranda when she went up to the main building. "The causeway is impossible," he told her.

"Still?" Her green eyes widened.

"Yes. However, I'm going to try and make for the bridge. I'm going to take a chance on the mud. By the time we've had breakfast and given the sun a chance to get going there might be an improvement in the road. In any case, to put your mind at rest, I intend to try."

Nearby a bush palm rattled and shook its stiff leaves in the brisk breeze. "How do you know the causeway is under water?" Barbara asked.

"I know because I've been there. I was up at the crack of dawn, taking a look. I'm just as anxious, for reasons of my own, to get back." His voice sounded curt.

They had breakfast on the veranda at a table with a scarlet and white gingham cloth and the smell of bacon and toast was almost reassuring, Barbara thought, although the meal was eaten in an atmosphere of almost hostile tension. Once she met his eyes and for one mad moment she thought she could see tenderness in his face.

After morning tea they left, and the drive back to the National Road was nothing short of a nightmare. By rights, they should have given up and turned back, but Gregory seemed determined not to give up as the car slipped in the mud. Once he got out and Barbara watched him moodily as he put branches and stones in front of the wheels, refusing all help from her.

Reina was the first to greet Barbara on their arrival at the Castle. "Hello," she said, "so you finally got back? Do you know, I've been divided between a sort of grudging admiration and envy?"

"Really?" Barbara's voice was short.

"Yes. You certainly know how to plan things, don't you? Right down to the last detail. How very clever of you, Barbara, to get Gregory to take you up to that remote, cut-off spot when there was such a storm brewing. We all saw it. Any fool would have."

Lilian saved the situation by coming into the hall. "So you made it?" Her smile broadened on being impish. "Where's Gregory?"

"He went to make arrangements about having the car washed. You can't see it for mud," Barbara replied.

"Which way did you come? Don't tell me that dilapidated old bridge is standing after that storm? And the causeway must surely be under water?"

"It is," Barbara answered.

"Come and see what the early morning papers have

to say on the subject." Lilian began to lead the way into the drawing-room, to the sophistication of Harvester furniture, valuable paintings, exquisite flowers, thickly piled gold carpeting on marble. Barbara felt like collapsing as she looked into Sir Basil's face and as his eyes went briefly over her.

"Good morning, Barbara—or is it good afternoon?" He glanced at his watch. "I do believe it is. I should say you're fortunate to have got back. According to the weather forecast, the rain isn't over, although it dawned fair enough this morning. I noticed a moment ago that the clouds are blowing up again." He looked almost boyishly unsure of himself in his endeavour to put Barbara at ease.

"I'm sorry about last night," she said.

"See what the headlines have to say." He glanced around for the newspaper and, when he had found it, held it up for her to read. *Hall Roof Collapses Under Heavy Downpour.* Sir Basil started reading aloud, "Driving rain and thunderstorms have brought flood damage to a wide area of the Natal South Coast, causing rivers to burst their banks and cutting the main road in several places. Part of the roof of Uvongate's new Neomark Hall collapsed in the early hours of this morning after torrential overnight rain. The road bridge at Umtwalumi is impassable, with swirling flood waters making driving conditions hazardous. Many motorists found themselves marooned." He looked up and smiled. "And there you have it. You can speak from first-hand experience."

Later, as she lay in a hot scented bath, seeking her lost peace and confidence, Barbara thought about the newspaper report. Although the article had eased her humiliation she was still feeling as if she had been connected to a high-tension wire.

In the late afternoon she worked in the library and found it difficult to concentrate. She had not seen Gregory since he had dropped her in front of the fan-

shaped steps leading to the heavy door and driven off
without a word in the direction of the garages. The sun
had disappeared again and clouds, heavy with the threat
of more rain, were banking up.

Later, Sir Basil came in to see how things were going.
After a while he said, "You appear to be coping with
Gregory's dictation."

"Yes." She struggled to be absolutely casual.

For several minutes Sir Basil scanned letters which
she had typed and which were now ready for Gregory's
signature. "There were just one or two points I wanted
to check," he said. He cleared his throat. "Er—about
this Port Elizabeth trip, Barbara. As you are aware,
there will be several conferences down there. The point
is that Gregory will now be in command. Doctor Lindbergh is emphatic that I remain here. There doesn't
seem to be much point in arguing with him, especially
as he so accurately pointed out Gregory happens to be
on hand." There was an awkward silence and then he
said, "How do you feel about this, Barbara?"

Feeling herself begin to tremble, she said, "H-how—
how do you mean, Sir Basil?"

"You don't experience any—problems? I don't want
to be instrumental in—er—any ill-feeling on the part of
that young man of yours, or any kind of embarrassment on your own part."

"He's not my young man, Sir Basil. That is, if you're
referring to Rod Haden, and I imagine you are. Rod is
merely a friend. My work and my personal life have
nothing to do with him, in other words."

"I see." He appeared to be thinking. Then he cleared
his throat again, which was completely unlike him.
"And—er—Gregory? You must feel free to be perfectly frank with me. How do you feel—what are your
feelings about travelling with him? I thought you
looked a little upset this morning, on your return."

Her face showed no expression, but she was pale.
She could even *feel* the paleness.

"I—don't mind, in the least," she said, in a little
rush.

"We can take it as settled, in that case?"

"Yes, of course. If this is what you want, Sir Basil."

"That doesn't quite answer my question, does it?"

"I think it does. I'll have everything ready, Sir Basil.
It's quite all right."

By the time Gregory came into the study the rain had
started in earnest again and she had turned the reading
lamps on. "Just as well we took a chance on the mud,"
he said, easily enough. "This looks like a set-in."

"Yes, it does." Barbara started to type again.

Out of the corner of her eye she could see him leafing through a report which she had just finished typing
and then he said, "Well, we seem to be saddled with
each other for the P.E. trip."

When she felt that she could answer with reasonable
calm, she said, "It would appear that way." She
glanced at him, through her lashes. "I'm sure, however, that your father would be open to suggestions."

"Are these ready for signature?" he asked curtly.

"Yes. These are also ready for you to sign."

A slow anger was burning away inside her and, into
the bargain, she felt utterly depressed. It was a long
time since she had been so depressed with life.

"By the way," his voice was very casual, "you'd better pack something glamorous for the trip. We might
be expected to join a party, somewhere, at one of the
night-spots. Certainly the end of the conferences will
be marked by a cocktail party."

"I'd better mention that I don't accompany Sir Basil
to night-spots or cocktail parties at the end of a business trip." Her voice was sedate.

"What kind of talk is this, Barbara? You're deliberately misunderstanding me. This time you *might well* be
called upon to accompany *me*—in the interest of Harvester International." The tone of his voice discour-
aged argument.

"In that case, I'll make a note of it," she told him in a precise, stage-like kind of voice, and he let the remark go with a small, but very expressive, nod.

Although Barbara was seething she made a big show of looking through her work, wondering whether she should go to Sir Basil and try to sort something out. Why hadn't she been frank with him when he had given her the opportunity to express her feelings? Had things been different, she thought bitterly, she would have been fascinated by the thought of being called upon to accompany Gregory Harvester—whether in the interest of Harvester International or not.

After he had gone, she went on typing, and by the time she finished work for the day it was dark and the rain was pelting down from a shrouded sky. With a last look to see whether the desk was completely tidy, for this was where the Harvesters liked to gather before dinner, she made her way back to her room, determined not to become involved in joining them for a sherry.

To her dismay, however, Theresa came up to her room to say that Lilian had sent her to ask why Miss Knight had not joined them in the library before dinner.

"I'll be down shortly, Theresa," Barbara said.

When she got to the library there was no sign of Reina and the sight of Sir Basil, Lilian and Gregory made her freeze because of the hint of intimacy. This was one time when she would have welcomed the other girl's presence. She even experienced a huge sense of having been let down by Reina.

Was it coincidence that the girl with the golden voice was singing? The music did nothing to steady her.

"Your dress goes beautifully with this carpet, Barbara," Lilian was saying. "Had you noticed? It's exactly the same shade of apricot. How well it goes with that glorious hair of yours and those enormous green eyes. This room could have been made for you."

"Thank you," Barbara murmured. "I—I hadn't noticed, actually."

"So the roof of the Neomark Hall has gone," Sir Basil said. "Tell me, Barbara, isn't that where you young things, and not so young," he grinned, "go to divert your tensions? I'm referring, of course, to your Yoga classes—this—this seemingly curious art where people tie themselves up in knots."

"Yes, it is." Barbara tried to dredge up a smile. "I suppose we'll have to either skip a few weeks, until the roof is repaired, or find another hall."

"Talking of Yoga," Lilian stood up, "at last, Barbara, Geraldine Denuhin has been successful in talking me into joining. As a matter of fact, I went shopping this morning and I bought my leotard. It's here somewhere. I shoved it into one of the drawers of that chest. Let me show you—I got the one with the high neckline."

While Lilian was busy at the chest Sir Basil said, "Yoga was at one time a predominantly Eastern pastime, I understand? However, it seems to have gone West. Tell me, Barbara, do you honestly feel it does good? What about hidden dangers?"

Barbara took a tiny sip of her sherry and then, smiling dutifully, she said, "Most enthusiasts don't go beyond the elementary stages, Sir Basil." While she was speaking she was aware of Gregory watching her. "Speaking about our class, we merely concentrate on a few—just a few of the—I *think* it's eighty-four classic postures to tone up muscles and glands. Actually, there are no rigorous exercises."

"No?" Sir Basil sounded faintly amused. "What would you call it, then?"

"The emphasis is on control," she told him.

Lilian came back to where they were sitting and began to open a small box which was lined with purple tissue paper. "Take a look at this," she said. "It looks just like a black swimsuit with a high neck. I didn't get the long-sleeved one, it's too hot. Here are the mesh pantie-hose to wear beneath it. I'm either going to look like a French Follies girl or a tramp!" she laughed delightedly.

Barbara was aware of a watchfulness on Gregory's part.

"Don't tell me you go into Uvongate looking like *that*?" Sir Basil's tone was mocking.

"Of course not." Lilian gave him an impatient little look. "You cover it up—with slacks or something. Isn't that right, Barbara?"

"That's so, yes, although I've been told I resemble—a hardened young traveller, before today, so you'd better watch out." Barbara felt herself shaking.

"Obviously I'm missing something," Sir Basil laughed a little. "What do you mean, Barbara, by a hardened young traveller?"

When Gregory spoke Barbara felt her fingers tighten about her glass. "Barbara now finds herself in one of those situations," he said. He turned to Lilian. "What has decided you to become a Yoga enthusiast?"

"Oh," she laughed lightly, "a number of things—tension, loss of concentration, aches and pains, lack of self-confidence, the environment, the air we breathe, the strain of modern living."

"You sound like a teenager," Sir Basil mocked. "By the way, where's Reina?"

"She's gone out," Lilian told him.

"Obviously—but where?"

"She's gone out with Rod Haden," Lilian's expression told Barbara nothing.

During the course of the evening Barbara found herself beginning to unwind very slowly. Gregory continued to watch her with that dark blue gaze of his. No mention was made of their stay at the river tea gardens. They dined at the marble-topped table while outside the Castle surrendered itself to the rain. There would be no visit to the battlements tonight, Barbara thought. Whenever her eyes happened to rest on Gregory's face she was aware of the faintest of amused lights illuminating his eyes and her mind moved ahead to the time when she knew he would refer to the black lacy stockings. He was the type who would play a part to the full. She condemned him with her eyes, and once he said, "Tell me, Barbara, why are you looking at me like that?" while there was an almost startled silence on the part of Lilian and Sir Basil.

They retired to the library where coffee was served. The room was fragrant with woodsmoke from a lazily burning log in the huge grate. With the heat had come the havoc of the storm, following by a set-in rain and chilly conditions.

Barbara's mood changed. Her thoughts were becoming chaotic again as she thought of the impending Port Elizabeth trip. She knew, however, that if the trip had to be cancelled she would feel more regret than relief. She was sufficiently in love with Gregory Harvester to harbour these feelings.

CHAPTER EIGHT

A DECEIVINGLY soft rain screened the sea and the hills for several days. Barbara worked in the library and prepared for the Port Elizabeth trip. Gregory had flown to Johannesburg on a short business visit, but the arrangements remained the same—he was to go to Port Elizabeth in Sir Basil's place.

Reina was restless and often out, and when she did happen to be at the Castle she roamed about with a grace that was almost animal, obviously resenting the fact that Barbara was to accompany Gregory on the trip.

One morning she said, "I feel like a deranged ant. I'm in an acute state of misery. I managed to get leave from the Salon, and this took some working out, I can tell you, as I'd only just returned from that lodge place in Zululand, and I arrive to discover that everybody is in a tizzy over some P.E. trip. All this *mad* activity. Surely Basil isn't that sick, Lilian, that he can't go?"

"My dear Reina," Lilian said, "your godfather happens to be adhering to the advice of his doctor." Lilian and Barbara had been having morning tea together in the library when Reina had joined them.

"Have some tea," Lilian suggested.

"No, thank you. And this rain!" Reina hugged her elbows and went to stand at the huge window where she gazed out at the sullen mass of dark cloud. Moodily, Barbara watched her, then her gaze went beyond her to the tiny tree frog which was flattened against a pink-veined leaf on the other side of the glass. The leaf gleamed as rain drops clung to its furry sides. She had been admiring both the frog and the leaf on and off all morning from her desk. Reina, however, did not even notice them. "I'm depressed," she sighed.

"Well, I'm sorry, dear, but we can't help the rain. We badly need it, as a matter of fact." Behind Reina's back Lilian raised her eyes to the ceiling and then grinned at Barbara.

Reina swung round. "Why did Greg fly to Johannesburg without telling me?"

"He'll be back tomorrow," Lilian told her. "It was a quick business trip."

"And the very next day he leaves for P.E.," Reina said resentfully.

"Yes." There was a little pause, and Lilian said, "But what about this young man you've been seeing lately?"

"Which young man?" Reina's expression was cagey.

"Rod—Haden, I think?"

"Rod? Oh…" Reina shrugged. "Actually, he's Barbara's boy-friend. Rod and I happen to be birds of a feather, right now—ask Barbara about it." Effortlessly beautiful, she shrugged again and then pushed her hands into the deep pockets of the pantsuit she was wearing. "I've been seeing Rod merely to show certain people that I have a mind of my own."

Barbara stood up and placed her cup and saucer on the silver tray. "I'd better get on with my work," she said. "I have a long report to type. It has to go to P.E." She went back to the desk where a huge splash of shaggy yellow chrysanthemums created an illusion of sunshine.

"Nothing to offer but the birth of another wet day," Reina went on. "I'm sick of it! Basil is as hard as rock formation, doing this to me—sending Greg away. I don't want to go back to my flat. In fact, there are two people in it at the moment. I gave them permission to use it while I was away. Frankly, I should say," her voice contained deliberately aimed spite, "that everything which is happening around here is the result of very, very clever planning and foresight on the part of someone."

"Oh, nonsense, Reina!" Lilian sounded impatient now.

Barbara tried to force her mind away from the conversation taking place and went on with her typing, and was thankful when Reina and Lilian finally left the library.

After dinner she completed her packing. She had chosen her clothes with care, giving attention to the last detail. When she had finished she changed into a caftan, undid her chignon and, feeling safe in the knowledge that Gregory was in Johannesburg, went up to the battlements. The rain was over and the stars were out, but the roar of the tumultuous and rebellious tide was a reminder of the storm and heavy rains. The soft damp clung to her arms and she shivered, for the weather had not yet warmed up. She realized that she should have worn something warmer than the caftan she was wearing.

Although she had come here to try and regain some of the serenity she had known before Gregory came on the scene, she knew that after the Port Elizabeth trip she would either have to learn to live with the fact that she was in love with her employer's son or she would have to leave the Castle and find other employment. Both ideas filled her with dread. If she stayed on, she would always be looking for hidden meanings in everything Gregory said or did, and if she left the Castle she would always be looking for him, somewhere...She knew she was not a girl to love lightly and began to have last-minute flutters about the forthcoming trip. The thought of travelling all that way with Gregory filled her with panic. What had she been thinking of? Why had she allowed herself to be caught up in this net? Suddenly she was staggered at the trap she had set herself.

She was aware of a noise and turned, just in time to
see Gregory as he stepped up from the iron staircase.

"I know you, don't I?" he said, his tone slightly
mocking. Adjusting slowly to the shock of seeing him
there, Barbara made no reply and then, after a moment, she stammered, "I thought you were due back
tomorrow."

"I made up my mind on the spur of the moment,"
he told her, still in that same light voice. "My business
was finished, so I took an earlier flight."

The thought that he had flown back immediately his
business was completed filled her with pleasure, but
here again she knew that she was seeking a hidden
meaning to his return. Possibly he had come back because of Reina.

"I was just going," she said, but she did not move.

"You must be cold," he said, and before she realized
what had happened, he had taken off his jacket and
draped it around her shoulders. From sheer unprepar-
edness, she moved away from him and slipped the
jacket from her shoulders. She held it out to him. "It's
not that," she murmured.

"What is it, then?" He came to where she was
standing and taking the garment from her placed it
about her shoulders. "Keep it on," he told her.

"I was about to leave—just as you came on the
scene."

"I don't believe you."

"In any case, it happens to be true." Her skin was
beginning to absorb the expensive warmth of his
jacket.

"Are you packed?" he asked. "For P.E.?"

"Yes."

"Everything a secretary should need on a trip like
this?"

"Yes. I'm used to this sort of thing."

"It's all in the game, then?" Her words seemed to
amuse him.

"Yes, you could say that—if you care to refer to a career as a game."

This was the way he liked it, she thought bitterly—able to destroy her with a remark or a glance.

"Have you packed something glamorous?" he asked.

"I've carried out your instructions to the best of my ability. In other words, I've packed suitable clothes for the trip and in the interest of Harvester International."

"Tell me," he enquired, "how do you feel about this trip?"

There was a pause and then she said, trying to keep her voice under control, "I'm—I'm—neutral, as it so happens."

"It's impossible to be neutral," he said.

"I'm devastated, then."

He laughed. "Insults won't help the situation."

Her immediate reaction to his remark was to walk away and leave him, but quietly, almost in a whisper, she said, "I have no way of defending myself against you."

"Do you *have* to?" he asked, taking the lapels of the jacket and holding them together just beneath her chin. "You're shivering, do you know that? We'd better go down. By the way, just how prepared are you?"

"I don't know what you mean," she replied, aware of the warmth of his fingers beneath her chin.

"What did you think I meant? But in any case, I'll brief you, Barbara. Are you prepared to leave a day in advance? In other words, are you prepared to leave for Port Elizabeth in the morning?"

She thought for a moment. "I am, as it so happens, but I don't understand. Sir Basil mentioned nothing of this to me this evening."

"I quite appreciate that. I think I made it clear when I got up here that I finished my business in Johannesburg earlier than anticipated. On my arrival back I had a talk to my father and we came to the conclusion that if you were ready we'd leave a day early. That's why I'm here, as a matter of fact. Lilian sent Theresa to your room to ask you to come down, but you weren't there. I had an idea you'd be on the battlements."

"What's the idea of wanting to leave earlier than previously arranged?" she asked.

"Well, for one thing, I'll have longer with Adrian Price in Grahamstown."

"I see. Well, yes." Her pulse quickened. "I'm packed and ready, as it so happens—more or less, anyway. Just last-minute things to attend to."

"Good. And you don't experience any problems?" He was relaxed, or rather, he *sounded* relaxed, but she knew he was watchful.

"What problems should I have?"

"You figure it out, Barbara."

"It doesn't matter to me." She could feel his eyes on her face.

"Why kid around?" he said. "What I mean is, are you prepared to trust me?"

"Yes, of course."

"Why of course?"

"As you said a moment ago, why kid around? I've already spent one night in your company. I've said yes—what else do you want me to say?"

"You're shivering," he said. "We must go down." He took his hands away and Barbara drew a long breath to steady herself.

When they were in the foyer she said, "What time do you plan to leave in the morning?"

"Six-ish?"

"Very well. Is it necessary for me to see Sir Basil tonight?"

"No. By the way, Lilian told me to tell you to go straight to bed. I mentioned that you'd probably be up here, daydreaming," he smiled. "She also asked me to find out what you would like to have sent up—tea, coffee, milk? You name it—Harvester's have it."

"Tea, please. I'd love some tea."

"Tea it'll be, then. Goodnight." He brushed her chin with his knuckles and then she watched him as he left her.

The sky was pink, salmon, gold and silver when they left the following morning. A light breeze was laced with the tang of the sea. Barbara found herself shivering slightly, but she knew this was not merely because the air was still fresh after the rains.

As they sped along the National Road they caught glimpses of the surf as it sent up white plumes which curled slowly over on to the pink sands.

"Look at the dew," said Barbara. "It's been tinted to a pale shimmering gold."

"By the way," Gregory said, "I owe you an apology. I know now that black openwork stockings are worn along with a garment referred to as a leotard. This garment is worn by acrobats, ballet dancers and—Yoga enthusiasts." When she made no reply he said, "Right?"

"That's so." Her voice was stiff.

"Why didn't you tell me?"

With some impatience, she said, "I don't have to explain myself to you. Let me say this, though, while we happen to be on the subject—you seem to think I'm insensitive to insults. There's a cold streak in you."

In the distance, the sun was pulling the morning mist off the sea and the hills on the other side of the road were collecting it.

"I was hasty," he replied, "but then Rod Haden is everything I dislike, and you were with him, dressed in an eye-catching get-up. Rod Haden evaluates the women who interest him with a cold-blooded calculation and you seemed to be playing right into his hands. I saw red."

"You thought I was playing into his hands, just as your sister did, in other words?" she asked, and saw his face change.

"Yes." He shot her an annoyed glance. "Lilian and

my father don't know who the man was. All round, I don't think my father would have been quite as lenient as I was, but I was thinking of Charmaine."

Instinctively Barbara decided to say nothing. At one time, this very silence would have had the power to make her feel vaguely disloyal to Rod, but now she felt nothing.

For some time they travelled in silence. The sea was hidden now, by undulating bush-matted hills. Eventually Gregory broke the silence. "Would you like some music?"

"It's pleasant the way it is," she answered. "Don't you think? The scenery is beautiful. It seems a pity to break it by listening to music."

"I think we can arrange to keep it that way." He gave her a smile, and suddenly Barbara felt wildly happy.

They stopped for morning tea and then later they lunched at a small country hotel smothered in the usual purple bougainvillea. Towards the late afternoon Barbara felt compelled to say, "Wouldn't you like me to drive? You must be tired, and after all, I do drive and I also happen to know this road very well."

"Fine," he said, "I'll be able to sit back and watch you."

"I don't like being watched. That's not the object."

"In that case, I'll try to concentrate on the scenery," he answered. When the change-over had taken place and she was in the driver's seat, he said, "So you know this part of the world?"

"I used to live near here." Her voice went suddenly flat.

"I see." There was a kind of concern in his voice, as though he sensed how she was feeling.

The car took the next pass easily and then they had reached the top. Before them stretched the countryside she knew so well. There was the wide curve in the road. Barbara's fingers closed on the wheel. She was becoming impatient now, wanting to see it and yet not wanting to see it—the turn-off to the farm. The rickety old farm gates which opened to the private sandy road. In certain lights—early morning, sunset or before a storm—the sand appeared almost pink.

The silence in the car was beginning to get on her nerves. By the time she realized she was going too fast, it was too late. Unable to keep her eyes from the turn-off, she felt the car begin to sway and then there was nothing she could do about it. The whole road seemed to be lifting and she knew she had lost control. Her last impression before the car left the road was of Gregory's tanned hand, with the gold wristwatch gleaming on his wrist, grabbing the wheel and trying, no doubt, to put matters right. The car broadsided and then there was a jolt and her last thoughts were that she had broken her neck.

When she recovered consciousness she found herself in his arms on the side of the road. The bank loomed up behind them.

"Barbara," he was saying, smoothing back her hair, "Barbara?"

Vaguely, her eyes went in the direction of the car and it was a relief to see it standing on four wheels.

"I'm sorry," she whispered. "Look what I've done. I couldn't help myself—I had to look at the turn-off." The whole world had declared itself against her. She closed her eyes and when she opened them again he asked, "Are you in pain, Barbara?"

"No. I'm amazed I can turn my neck, though. I honestly thought I'd broken it." Pale with fright and shock, her jade eyes looked immense. Trying to sit up, she said, "But what about you?"

"I'm fine—nothing. Worried about you, though."

"No, I'm all right. I'm sorry about the car. There's a dent." She felt herself shaking.

"Forget about the car. It's not the car I'm worried about, Barbara." He held her, trembling against his chest and she found herself clinging to him.

"I could have killed us." She began to cry softly.

He kept stroking her hair, and when she was calmer, he released his hold on her and looked down at her face which was covered by a tangle of auburn hair. Her wide eyes remained on his face as he smoothed back her hair again, then he bent his head and kissed her mouth. She closed her eyes and then felt him tense. "A car," he said. "There's a car. I'll wave them down. Afterwards I'll try the engine, and if for some unknown reason it refuses to start we might be able to cadge a lift."

From where Barbara sat she could see the light indicators of the approaching car. "Believe it or not," Gregory was calling out, "but they're going to turn here!"

The car slackened speed to take the bend and then, a little further on, stopped. Both doors opened at the same time and a man and woman ran back.

Threatened by faintness as she tried to stand up, Barbara sagged to the ground again. Vaguely she was aware of the couple talking.

"She appears only to be suffering from shock. She'll be okay as soon as we get her to the resort."

"Oh, no!" Barbara began, "*not* the farm—not the farm!" Blackness engulfed her again.

Somehow she found herself in a car. Gregory held her to him and she was grateful for the feel of his strength. She made a huge effort to concentrate when they reached the farm which, even in her state of collapse, she could see was not the same any more. There was a splendid entrance. Wrought-iron gates set in thick white walls which looked like three pillars with a red-tiled roof running the full length of it. Wrought-iron lamps were suspended at either end. This entrance to the farm alone resembled an old hacienda. There were a few landmarks, though...the big tree...

The elaborate gates were opened for them by an African man. It was obvious that he had an office in the main centre pillar where there was a circular window which was set into the thick white wall and made ornamental by more wrought-iron curving around it.

It was terrible to be creating all this nuisance and not being able to help herself, Barbara thought as another black wave hit her with devastating precision. When she opened her eyes again she stared up at a beamed ceiling and wondered where she was, before the details of the accident crowded in on her. A woman's face, young, somewhere in the mid-thirties, came into focus. "I'm Moona Burgess," she was saying. "Remember me?"

"Yes," Barbara murmured.

"Do you remember the accident?" Moona Burgess asked. Her hair was dark, her eyes brown and she had a wide, generous mouth.

"Yes." Barbara had difficulty in raising her voice.

"Do you really?"

"Yes. It happened at the turn-off. I was trying to see if the old gates were still there."

"You seem to know about this place?"

"I should do. It—used to be my home," Barbara explained. "W-where is Gregory?"

"He's busy phoning your father-in-law," Moona answered.

Barbara looked blank. "My—father-in-law?"

"Yes. He said he was going to phone his father, so I guess that makes him your father-in-law—or doesn't it?"

"It doesn't. We're not married. We were on a business trip to Port Elizabeth. We were to attend a series of conferences."

"Oh, I see. I'm sorry. I just jumped to conclusions—but then I always do. Anyway, he has been madly worried about you. I guess that's what made me think he was your husband. You passed out cold when we arrived here—but cold!" Moona laughed. "In the end I had to push Gregory—you see we've got down to first names—out of the room and close the door. He was becoming a nuisance. I know how to deal with people who've passed out. I could cope better without him hanging around."

"I never expected to see this part of the world again," Barbara said. Her eyes went round the room with its tiled floor, white walls and black-beamed ceiling and woodwork. "Everything is different." The room was tremendous and wonderfully furnished in what appeared to be Mexican style. "You must have knocked down the old farmhouse? Did you? Or did you just add on somewhere?"

"The entire house was demolished," Moona told her. "We've converted the farm into a fabulous—well, *we* think it's fabulous, anyway," she laughed again, "all-the-year-round resort. We have a private game reserve—but we'll talk about that later. The main point is, how do you feel now? You've had a shock. Gregory was set on rushing you to Grahamstown, but Miles, my husband, has sent for our doctor who happens to be fairly close."

"I feel fine now. It was such a shock. I didn't really need a doctor, as it so happens," Barbara smiled.

"It could have been so much worse," Moona answered.

The doctor expressed the same opinion. "Your fiancé," he said, "was worried about your neck, but I can assure you there's nothing to worry about there. You must have jerked it."

As he prepared to leave he said, "I've left something for you for those shakes by the way."

Moona came back into the room. "Must she stay in bed?" she asked.

"No, not unless she feels like it." He glanced at Barbara. "How are those legs?" he asked. "Still dancing?"

"A little. It's wearing off now."

"I understand," he went on, "that Moona and Miles are putting you both up until you make arrangements about your car. You'll be the first couple to stay in the plush new resort, so your accident has its lighter side."

After he had gone Moona said, "I'll have your cases brought in here. I had you put in a double room because I thought you were honeymooners—you *look* like honeymooners. So you might just as well stay here. What a pity you aren't married. Don't you adore this room?"

"It's fabulous," Barbara replied, feeling embarrassed. "His father—Gregory's father—happens to be my boss. I should be on this trip with him, as a matter of fact, but he's not well. Moona, we seem to be putting you out no end. I feel awful about it."

"We're thrilled to have you." Moona ran her fingers through her dark hair. "Miles and I seem to have done nothing but fight, these past couple of weeks. We're so tensed up about the opening gala. Company will do marvels for us. Please believe this and, in the knowledge of it, relax, Barbara. Tell me, would you like a bath before dinner? There's a fabulous bathroom through here. Honestly, I do wish you were married. This is one of the nicest rooms."

"I'd love a bath."

"Well, be careful and don't lock the door, just in case you have another fainting spell. If I think you're taking a long time over it, I'll pop my head in." She laughed lightly. "But, don't go yet. Gregory wants to see you. He's been pacing about since he finished his phone call. Will it be all right if I let him in now?"

Barbara's eyes flew to the ornately framed mirror. "I—I suppose so. I look a sight, though."

When he came in he asked, "Well, how do you feel?"

"Fine. The shakes are going."

"I'll leave you two," said Moona. "I hope you don't mind, but I have things to do."

After she had gone Gregory said, "When you passed out again I wanted to rush you to a doctor in Grahamstown, but the Burgesses reckoned on getting a doctor quicker, which surprised me, I must say. We seem to be cut off here." His eyes lingered over her. "This is *it*, then? The farm?"

"Yes, but Moona tells me that the house was demolished to make way for this resort. I'd heard rumours about the people who'd bought it. I'd heard about the private game reserve, but I didn't realize that it was going to be an all-the-year-round resort."

"Wait until you've seen the rest of it," he told her. "The way *I* see it is that Acapulco is on the way to capturing international favour."

"Is that the name? Acapulco?" she asked.

"Yes. I guess things have got to go on, Barbara. Scenes change."

"I know. I keep telling myself that. I feel devastated at what I've done to the car... apart from the delay I've caused. What did Sir Basil have to say?"

"He was terribly concerned. So was Lilian." Suddenly he sat down on the side of the bed. "I want you to promise me one thing."

"What's that?" She widened her eyes.

"I want you to promise me that you'll stop worrying about the car. The damage is very slight. I tried to start it before the Burgesses drove us here, then I noticed that there was a hole in the radiator—caused by a flying stone, no doubt. Miles is having it towed here and a Grahamstown garage is sending someone to collect it in the morning. It will be delivered back here when the necessary repairs have been carried out."

"And what about us?" Her green eyes were troubled. "Adrian Price?"

"We're going to remain here, unless this will cause you unhappiness. In that case, I'll hire a car. I don't know if you're aware of this, but Miles and Moona Burgess have asked us to stay on here for a kind of opening gala. It's a publicity stunt... members of the Press and so on, and a selected number of guests."

"I'd gathered as much. When is this gala?" She was thinking of the Port Elizabeth conferences.

"The Press people and guests arrive tomorrow—to stay over, I understand. They'll be followed almost immediately by the first bookings."

"But what about the conferences?"

"Leave that for me to attend to." He looked intently at her. "Will all this make you too unhappy?"

Barbara thought for a moment before she said, "The whole place appears absolutely changed. I suppose there'll be landmarks. It might help me to forget a lot of things. It might even help me to get over everything—make my visits to the battlements more bearable, sometimes."

"That's precisely what I had in mind, as a matter of fact. What are your plans, right now? Are you going to remain in bed? Are you having dinner here? What had you worked out with Moona?"

"First, I'm going to have a wonderful bath and then I hope to stay up." There was a little pause and then she said, "You've been so marvellous to me over all this. I—I want to thank you."

"Well, go ahead and thank me." She felt his dark-blue eyes possessing her.

"Thank you," she said softly. Suddenly she was gripped by a nervous and excited fear.

"Like this," he said, taking her into his arms. He turned her face up and kissed her mouth; very gentle with her. When he released her he said, "I'm suffering from reaction—at seeing you alive and well."

"No broken neck," she said shakily.

He kissed her again. There was nothing she could do to stop him—nothing she wanted to do.

"I—er—you'll have to be patient with me," he said. "I've been out of my mind with worry." He became casual. "From what I gather," he stood up, and she watched him with her eyes, "the Burgesses are really very busy, right now, as they see to the final preparations for this gala, and while they've made me feel we're more than welcome I gather that tonight, anyway, we'll have to amuse ourselves after they've dined with us. Moona has suggested that we try out one of their cuisine menus."

"It sounds more like a dream than the disaster it is." She couldn't keep her voice steady.

"The disaster it started out to be," he smiled down at her.

After he had gone Barbara lay back against her pillows, strangely content, then got up and went into the bathroom and turned on gold-plated taps. While the water ran into the yellow bath she went out to the patio and gazed at the dusk, amazed that she was back and that she was actually looking at what used to be the farm. Even as she stood there she realized how adapted the land was for an all-the-year-round resort and a private game reserve. The curve of the hills were as she had known them and yet there was an unreality about everything. Her eyes swept the patio with its Victorian-inspired white lacy Hong-Kong cane chairs upholstered with yellow. It was almost impossible to believe that she had grown up on this very spot where, instead of the shabby old farmhouse there sprawled a magnificent holiday resort which, something told her, would be all brick, terra-cotta, carved wood, pueblo-glaze tiles and wrought iron—a place of excitement and infinite luxury.

After her bath and when she had changed into something glamorous she would see it all for herself...and she hoped she would be able to veil the pain in her eyes.

CHAPTER NINE

By the time Moona Burgess knocked and came into the room Barbara had bathed and changed into a long white terrace gown.

"I'm glad to see you've made a comeback," Moona smiled. "Miles drove Gregory back to the car and it's now been towed here. In the morning someone from a Grahamstown garage will collect it. As soon as the menfolk have had a bath and changed we're to meet in the brand-new pub for a drink before dinner. After that I'm afraid we're going to have to ask you and Gregory to amuse yourselves." Her dark eyes slanted at a rakish angle. "I don't think that will be too difficult, though."

Barbara decided it was best not to argue on this point and merely smiled. "Fine, Moona. That sounds wonderful."

They had drinks in the main bar, which had a magnificently vaulted ceiling. To get to the bar one had to go through a thick Mexican arch where tall potted trees stood at either side. The barman tried not to look sheepish as he served behind the counter for the very first time.

"To Acapulco," Gregory raised his glass.

"And to our very first guests," Moona replied cheerfully. "May they return to Acapulco in the not-so-distant future."

"Hear, hear!" Miles' laugh was one of satisfaction.

"Tomorrow, you two can amuse yourselves by looking over the entire resort," Moona said, "and then Miles will lend you the Land-Rover so you can drive out to the game reserve. We even have rhino, by the way. We're really very pleased with ourselves—you know the feeling. Aren't we, Miles?"

Grinning his approval of his beautiful wife, Miles said, "That we are. So here's to us—and all those who frequent Acapulco as our guests."

"This is fun," said Moona. "It's helped to break the tension we've been carrying around for weeks. We've been fighting like cat and dog over the least little thing." Smiling widely, she went on, "We thought you might prefer the romance of outdoor dining, so we're dining in the outdoor dining area. But, quite apart from the romantic side, we thought it would be a mistake to dine in the main dining-room with its huge dome and sea of tables and chairs. You know, just the four of us. We'd be utterly lost. Don't you agree?"

"Heartily agree," Gregory answered.

"We lured our chef away, I'm ashamed to say, from a leading Madrid hotel," Moona laughed lightly. "How we worked it, I'll never quite know. By the way, Barbara, I simply must show you our kitchen. It has brown and black damask wallpaper, which blends suberbly with the copper hood over the tremendous electric stove and with black iron hanging lights. It has a beautiful Mediterranean-tiled floor."

"Here's to our kitchen," Miles raised his glass, enjoying himself.

"And while we're about it, let's drink to our aim for a beauty salon, sauna, massage—the lot," Moona laughed.

"Hear, hear!" Gregory clicked Barbara's glass with his own. "Let's drink to Moona and Miles."

"And to Barbara and Gregory," Moona said.

The meal, which was outstanding and eaten in an atmosphere of gaiety, finally came to an end and Barbara waited for an opportunity to ask Moona whether she could use the telephone. The least she could do, she thought, was to ring the Castle and express her regret at what had happened, even though Gregory had already phoned home and spoken to both Sir Basil and Lilian.

"Go right ahead," said Moona. "Use the one in reception, if you like. There's absolutely nobody to listen in. Tomorrow this time will be a very different story, however. Miles hasn't studied advertising for nothing."

There were no hitches getting through and Barbara found herself listening to Reina's, "Hello—Sir Basil Harvester's residence."

"May I speak to Sir Basil or Lilian, please?" Barbara found herself beginning to shake.

"Who is that calling?" Reina's voice was affected.

"This is Barbara Knight, Reina."

"I thought so." Reina's voice seemed to snap over the line. "You're becoming quite a performer, aren't you? Because I've heard, by now, that you happened to be driving."

Barbara's nerves registered protest. "Reina," she said, "I don't want to waste time. This happens to be a trunk call and I'm anxious to speak to Sir Basil or Lilian. I also happen to be very tired and—well, not quite with it. I don't feel like an argument over the phone."

"That's not the way I would put it myself. I would say, Barbara, that you're pretty much with it. You certainly know how to go about getting your own way— even if you have to practically turn a car over to get it. You make an ordinary gold-digger look like—like an impostor."

"And you make me feel *sick*!" Barbara snapped, dizzy with disgust. "Will you kindly get off this line?" She passed a shaking hand over her forehead.

"I suppose," Reina went on, "you've decided that Rod Haden doesn't have enough to offer?"

"It's not for you to judge. Your opinion doesn't matter much to me, Reina—now will you get off this line, please?"

"My opinion will matter to you at the very first opportunity which happens to present itself, let me tell you that. I don't intend to stand by and let you ease yourself into the Harvester establishment, that's for sure. It's astonishing what money can do to a man's cheap little steno—especially when there's a handsome son to fall back on when things don't quite work out with the boss."

With a gesture of abdication, Barbara replaced the receiver and sat staring at it in shocked disbelief that such things could have been uttered by one girl to another. She closed her eyes, forcing her mind to switch off for a moment, and when she looked up again from the huge black intricately carved desk, her green eyes widened with panic as she found herself looking into Gregory's eyes.

"What is it?" he asked. "You look upset."

"It's—nothing," she stammered. "I was trying to get through to—to someone and—couldn't, that's all."

She watched his eyes change, for a moment as he listened to her, and then he said, "Let me dial the number for you."

Her response was quick. "No, I'll try later on—not now."

"Were you talking to Rod Haden?" he asked bluntly.

"No, of course not." They exchanged a long glance. She wanted to tell him about Reina, but thought it best not to. After all, Reina happened to be Sir Basil's godchild.

"You didn't phone him, Barbara?"

"No. I've just told you."

"It couldn't have been my father—or Lilian—on the line to upset you like this?"

"No. Besides, I'm not upset. I couldn't get through, that's all. It was a wrong number." She stood up, feeling suddenly weak. "I'll try again—when the lines are better. Tomorrow, maybe."

"The lines should be better, this time of the night,"

he told her, somewhat impatiently. "Let me try again. It will make you feel better, if you get through."

"No, honestly, I'd rather not."

He shrugged. "Well, if that's the way you feel..."

She was aware that he did not believe her. There was a short silence and then he said, "Miles and Moona are sorting out last-minute affairs for the big day tomorrow. There appears to be great panic in case the flowers don't arrive in time. They should, in fact, have arrived from P.E. today. I understand, however, that they've been assured and reassured that the flowers will arrive in good time. Let's hope so, for their sake."

"Isn't that just typical?" Barbara murmured, her mind still brooding over what Reina Geray had said over the phone.

"Isn't that just typical—of what?" he asked. "You sound so detached. Would you like to go back to bed, Barbara?"

"No," she answered, fighting to think calmly. "What I meant a moment ago is the way in which things go wrong at the last moment. It's just typical. There's always something to cause an upset along the the line. Plans have a habit of going wrong."

"Well," he shot her an amused look, "it isn't compulsory to allow things to upset one—or to get the better of one. Shall we go and listen to some music?"

She made herself look into his eyes. "That will be lovely."

Moona was in the discotheque when they got there. "This place happens to be soundproof, although goodness knows why," she laughed, "unless our architects thought the noise might disturb the animals in the reserve. I've sorted out a lot of soul stuff. All here, on one side. I don't know about you, but I adore soul. If, however, you want something to really send you, look over here."

"You've been to so much trouble over us, all round," Barbara said.

"I've already told you, we're delighted to have you. I mean that, really. You helped us to keep reasonably sane. Miles and I will join you for a nightcap. I might mention that we're going to need one. It's a miracle that we're still together. I've threatened to walk out on him and he's threatened to walk out on me. You'd be amazed at all the little items which keep cropping up—items we never even thought of until the last moment." Moona looked around briefly. "Well, I'll leave you to it. You have the entire discotheque to yourselves."

The tiny floor was stepped down from an aqua-blue carpet and the chairs and bar stools were upholstered in a darker blue while coral scatter cushions created the necessary drama.

"The architects went to town on vaulted ceilings," Gregory said, looking up at the revolving light fitment which was punctuated with blue and coral bulbs. There were the same kind of bulbs set into the edges of the dance floor.

"I can hardly believe I used to live here," Barbara said. "Perhaps in the daylight I'll be able to identify myself with the exterior, although I very much doubt it, somehow. So much appears to be changed—except for the hills in the distance, of course, and the odd tree or shrub, if any have been saved. I suppose many of them would be—they were beautiful."

"Right now," Gregory's voice was soft, "I want you to forget everything and identify yourself with the present—with us." He came to where she was standing. "You can't go back, Barbara, only forward."

"Yes, I know." Her voice had a small hurt sound to it. "That's what I've always tried to do, as it so happens. I always try to propel myself, utterly and completely, into the role of being Sir Basil's personal secretary. I've tried to look ahead. My work has helped."

"You try to look ahead, except when you walk on the

battlements," he said, and she was amazed at the tenderness in his voice.

She made a little gesture with her shoulders. "Yes, I'm afraid so."

"That's where you feel your loneliness." He smiled. "You see, I'm beginning to understand you."

"Beginning? I'm very easy to understand. In fact, too easy, sometimes." She looked down and she knew he was compelling her to lift her eyes, and then, when she did, they stared at each other for a long moment.

"I wouldn't exactly say that," he replied.

"Why not? It happens to be true."

"To me, you've come up with several different images," he told her.

"Well, I find that—surprising. What are these images?"

"The first—a girl in a sheer golden silk caftan which did exciting things to her auburn hair and jade eyes, and which seemed to go with gold shaggy carpeting on marble floors. A girl I shall always identify with my home and with the very fitting music which Lilian, no doubt, had chosen. I looked up and saw you standing there..."

"You're very fanciful," she said, her heartbeats beginning to hamper her breathing. She bit her lip as she watched him choose a record from the pile and then, without looking at her, he said, "And then, Barbara, there's the image of a girl on the battlements—her face looking young and—wild, almost, in its loneliness."

Her eyes looked immense. This was a side to Gregory Harvester she had not known existed. "S-sometimes I need to be alone there," she confessed.

He straightened and balanced the record carefully between his fingers. "There's a girl behind a desk, much too big for her. Immediately I saw her there I made up my mind that my father was going to have to find another secretary."

Her startled eyes followed him as he placed the rec-

ord on the turntable. She sensed the tension in him as
he went to the bar and poured them each a drink, and
when she had taken the glass from him she immediately took a little sip, merely for the need to do something to hide the way she was feeling.

The music was just as Moona had promised it would
be—pure soul. "There's also the image of a girl,"
Gregory went on, "in a black mini-skirt, topped by a
sweater of the finest jersey in the kind of shocking pink
that took electricity with her golden skin. A girl in black
lacy stockings. A girl I had to try and identify with Rod
Haden and couldn't, somehow, until I was forced to
when I found her parked in his car with him. In fact,
I've never quite worked that one out."

"I don't want to talk about Rod Haden," she said
swiftly.

"No?" He raised dark brows.

"No."

"Well, neither do I, as it so happens, but to get back
to my girl. The girl with red hair and jade-green eyes.
This time I'm thinking of her as she appeared in a black
and pink bikini. As a sudden sand storm on the beach
blew up she danced about as the sand stung her legs,
making her look curiously childlike. This childlike appearance was particularly noticeable as she came to the
windows of a rondavel at the tea gardens, because she
happened to be wearing a cotton nightdress several
sizes too big for her. The shocked expression as she
saw me contrasted strangely with the permissive times
in which we live."

Suddenly Barbara laughed, trying to keep the laugh
casual. "How many images are there, for goodness'
sake?"

"Let's not fool ourselves," he said, and put his
misted glass back on the counter. With a kind of panic
she watched him come towards her. He took her glass
from her numb fingers and set it beside his own. "Barbara, I'm sold on you," he said softly, and she felt his

physical presence like a shock. A kind of warmth seemed to leap up between them in the space which separated them. "I'm in love with you."

When he kissed her she made no resistance, and then, as her urgency met his own, she responded eagerly to him.

After a while they broke apart. "I d-didn't know," she whispered softly.

"You didn't kiss like a girl in love with Rod Haden, Barbara." He spoke with sudden impatience.

"I'm *not* in love with Rod Haden," she answered. "I'm—in love with you. It's surprising you didn't guess, actually."

They danced for a while until he said, "I don't think this is a good idea for a girl who was suffering from shock a few hours ago."

"I'm feeling remarkably fit," she said, "taking into consideration the way I felt after the accident."

"Well, let's keep it that way," he smiled. "I don't want you to have a relapse."

When Moona and Miles Burgess joined them for a nightcap Moona said, "You look like two people in love."

"I can understand that," Gregory lifted Barbara's hand and kissed her fingers. "We *are* in love."

"Well, congratulations!" Moona looked delighted.

"This calls for a toast," said Miles.

Later, Gregory saw Barbara to the private patio which led to her room. The sky was jewelled with stars and dew glimmered on the lawns.

"Goodnight," he said, tilting her face up. "Will you be all right? You're not going to brood, are you?"

"No. At least, I don't think so. I find I can't identify myself with Acapulco. It's like a dream—the whole place has changed so." Looking at him, she felt overwhelmed at the immensity of the turn of events. After a moment she said, "What about you? After all, the car has been damaged, your appointment with Adrian

Price will be late and you'll have to get in touch with Port Elizabeth explaining our lateness. The first conference will have to be postponed, won't it?''

"You leave all the worrying to me," he told her, "but believe me when I say I'm not going to brood." He took her into his arms and she thrilled to his touch. The mountains in the background receded, floated away, like the waters of the lagoon at the Castle, forming circle after circle. The circles ended in one rippling arc. He took his lips away but still continued to hold her, then he released her suddenly. "Sleep tight," he said softly and, turning, went down the shallow steps. Barbara was aware of the scent from yellow roses growing in white tubs and she inhaled deeply, not wanting to think of anything but his kisses and the touch of his hands.

As she prepared for bed she knew she was devastatingly tired. Gregory had been right when he had called a halt to their dancing. Everything she did she did as though in a dream. Twice she went to the doors and gazed out into the night. Had she really been brought up on the spot? Had she gazed, dreaming, on those distant mountains?

With a dread that she would suffer from insomnia she got into bed, but fell asleep almost immediately.

In the morning she sighed before she was properly awake and, for several moments, lay like a child in strange surroundings, wondering where she was. And then, one part of her hurting and the other wanting to sing for happiness, it all came back to her and she sat up. Apart from a feeling of stiffness and a slight headache there was nothing to suggest that she had practically turned a car over the day before. Her morning coffee arrived and she got up and went through to the bathroom, swallowed two headache pills and then got back into bed. Glancing at her watch, she saw that it was seven o'clock and there was a strange quiet about the building. Without being informed one would know, instinctively, that most of the rooms in the resort were unoccupied. It was an unusual experience as she lay back on her pillows listening. Now and then there were noises like doors banging in the distance somewhere, and the merest hint of expensive cutlery and crockery clattering. There was the drone of what might have been a tractor, although she very much doubted it, or the traffic on the National Road. Birds twittered and, for a moment, Barbara felt a heartbreaking sadness.

A maid in a gay floral uniform came in for the tray and while she was in the room she opened the doors to the patio. Barbara turned her head. It was a wonderful day. She thought of Gregory, the man she loved and, remembering, touched her lips with her fingertips.

It had been with a certain resentment that she had packed her most glamorous clothes, but she was thankful, now, that she had as she chose the white loose-knit top to wear with celery-green slacks.

The ebbing and flowing of tension was almost a physical thing with Moona and Miles Burgess.

"Darling," Moona said, "I know you two aren't going to be put out if we don't breakfast with you. You're too much in love for that. I'm putting through one mad phone call after another. The flowers should be arriving shortly and the Press and publicity people, not to mention the first guests, will be arriving about an hour before lunch..." She let her voice trail away and lifted her hands, "Oh, do you begin to see what I mean? But the offer still holds—the Land-Rover is there for you to use, Gregory. Go and have a look at the game reserve. You have heaps of time before the garage people come to collect your car. In any case, you don't have to be here when they come. Miles can see to everything for you. It's just a case of letting them tow it away."

"Surely there must be something we can do to help, Moona?" Barbara asked.

"No. Don't take it amiss, Barbara, but much as we adore having you—you've helped to relieve so much tension—we want you nicely out of the way, right now."

After breakfast, which they ate at the same blue-clothed table with the pink floral arrangement, Barbara went to get her white linen sun-hat which she usually packed when she went away because it was one of those hats that just folded into a case. When she went outside Gregory had already brought the Land-Rover around to the main entrance and was waiting for her. Suddenly she was wildly happy. He smiled at her and she savoured the moment. "Ready?" he asked, his eyes going over her.

"Yes—I went to get a hat," she said.

"I was going to remind you to bring one—if you had one."

The lawns were still glistening with dew in colours of copper, sapphire, emerald and silver, depending on the angle of the sun. Before leaving her room Barbara had made up her mind that nothing was going to jeopardize her happiness—not even the old familiar landmarks which she associated with her home and her parents. It was almost as if her parents were near, insisting that she did not give way to depression. However, she paused, uncertain now that she was going to drive to a place which had once been familiar farmlands.

"Well," it was almost as though he could sense her thoughts, "let's go and see what Miles has in the line of big game."

Turning quickly so that he would not see the tears which had sprung to her eyes, she tried to dismiss the memories from her mind and to live for the moment, as she had promised herself.

In the Land-Rover she said, "Miles didn't mention big game, did he? I take it you mean lion, elephant, by big game?" She laughed lightly. "I mean, the rhino are big enough for me!"

"I understand the reserve contains a large number of impala, eland, black wildebeest, warthog, zebra, six white rhinos and ostriches," he told her.

The game reserve included grassy scrub-dotted plain, some forested patches and a river. There were bush-clad valleys, which she remembered so well and which had provided habitats for many different kinds of birds and mammals, even in her father's day. There was a thin wispy mist over the area, but it was lifting with the sun. Gregory reached for her fingers and kissed them, and Barbara's nerves reacted immediately. Her green eyes went to his dark hair, to the way in which it grew down to his neck. How little she knew of him, and yet, in such a short space of time, how much. Each line of his tanned face, the shape of his hands—strong and slender.

The breeze was laced with scents, giving the feeling of quickened senses. At any minute they would see game.

"Miles has a ranger, I understand," Gregory told her. "He has a house out here somewhere." Suddenly he slackened speed, and then Barbara noticed two rhinos. Thinking about a film she had seen, when a Land-Rover had been charged and attacked by one of these unpredictable beasts with their cunning, almost mean little eyes which seemed to see nothing and yet so much, she caught her breath. "Be careful," she whispered. "Don't go too near. Rhinos have a habit of charging when you least expect it."

"That presents a stimulating challenge," his voice was teasing.

"Frankly, I don't think so," she answered, and was relieved when, after a few moments, the animals lumbered off into some long grass.

A plane roared overhead and then whined out of sight.

"In no time at all," Gregory said, squinting his blue eyes against the sun as he looked up, "this peace will be shattered by tourists—so we're fortunate to have enjoyed it first."

"Money makes such a difference," she answered.

"In my father's time everything was such a battle. If only he'd been able to think of something like this! He might have made some money." She was silent for a moment and then added, "In any case, there was none to start a venture like this. There never seemed to be enough."

After a while Gregory switched off the engine so that they could watch a small herd of impala grazing. Nearby, zebras drank from a water-hole, their striped reflections shivering in the water.

"At least there are no lions here to hunt them down," Barbara said. "Here they can go down to a water-hole or bask in the sun without any fear." Beneath the brim of her hat her skin looked firm and golden.

"Do you know what I keep thinking?" he asked.

"No—what?"

"I keep thinking that when we get back to the Burgesses', I shall have to share you with a whole lot of people." He placed his fingers on her chin and turned her face up. Their eyes met for a moment, wide, searching, interested, before his gaze dropped to her mouth and he kissed her. Her lashes flickered and she closed her eyes. "On second thoughts," he said, against her mouth, "I have no intention of sharing you. You'll find, Barbara, that I'm very possessive. I knew from the start that I wanted you."

In the background the impala continued to graze and the zebra, satisfied, began to leave the water-hole. "I suppose we'd better be getting back." Gregory turned the ignition key and started the car. For a moment the animals looked up, startled, and then, one by one, they bounded into the grass.

The flowers had arrived by a special delivery van when they got back and the poolside had been transformed with purple umbrellas against the sun. It was a magnificent sight as king proteas, anthuriums, huge tea-roses in shades of apricot, pink and yellow, combined with azaleas and copper beach, were lifted out of the van and carried inside. Fruit and nut arrangements complemented exotic red and white-striped amaryllis. More soft pink roses were lifted out, more orchids and sprigs of marguerites. For the terraces and patios splashes of sunny yellow, bronze, lavender and white chrysanthemums, brilliant blue irises and masses of white guelder-roses. Looking at them, Barbara knew the thrill of colour.

Moona and Miles Burgess had indeed gone wild with one big splash of colour and, no doubt, one big florist account. Although there would always be beautiful flowers gracing the resort this was a special publicity stunt. Photographers would soon be arriving to capture this beauty.

At last Barbara found herself able to help Moona. The arrangements had to be taken to various parts of the building and the maids giggled as they also assisted. "These should have arrived *yesterday*," Moona wailed, exhausted. "You're a gem, Barbara. I don't know how I should have coped at the last moment without you to supervise where these arrangements should be placed."

"The main thing is, they've arrived, Moona," Barbara consoled her.

"Yes, there is that to it, I suppose. Darling, will you bring those pink roses along here, please? Aren't the containers out of this world?"

Rooms became suddenly flower-laden and beguiling. Finally there was time for a quick shower before changing into a slack-suit for lunch. There was to be a champagne party at the poolside. Barbara discovered that some of the Press people had arrived. There was also a smattering of girls in bikinis and men in bathing trunks sitting on underwater seats sipping chilled champagne at the pool bar. It was a scene of sheer luxury and sophistication. Photographers began to move in on it and, trying to appear very casual, girls in scant bikinis or attractive trouser suits and long patio gowns, posed languidly in the golden glow of the sun.

The lunch was superb and served without any noticeable tension on the part of the new staff. Moona, looking stunning in a cocoa and pink patio gown, appeared coolly relaxed, apart from a patch of colour across each normally pale cheek. Miles gave himself up to having a good time—after all he had been through to get to this moment.

During the afternoon more people arrived, but these were paying guests, people keen to be among the very first to book in for a holiday at the new fabulous Acapulco.

"Your secret is perfectly safe with me," Gregory whispered once, his dark-blue eyes mocking Barbara.

Looking at him blankly for a moment, she said, "My—my secret?"

"Yes—that you're in love with me."

"Oh." She felt the colour come into her face and then laughed shyly. "I'm sure it must show."

"Do you really love me?" he asked.

"You know I do. You *must* know, by now."

"Too many men have their eyes on you," he said.

"You have a wonderful imagination," she laughed, "with all these beautiful girls gracing the poolside they don't have to look at me."

"No? That's where you're completely wrong. You're the most beautiful girl here."

Barbara felt wildly happy, especially as she had been able to get through on the telephone to Sir Basil and had also spoken to Lilian. They had both been wonderful, going out of their way to assure her that the accident could have happened to anyone and that they were concerned only with the fact that she and Gregory were safe.

In the afternoon they swam. Out of habit, Barbara and Gregory, seasoned travellers that they were, had packed swimming gear. Later they strolled to the shop in a red-tiled courtyard and bought African handcrafts. In the centre of the courtyard there was a tremendous wrought-iron bird cage, but instead of housing birds, it was filled with flowers while exotic plants in urns made splashes of green against the white walls. Looking at impossibly coloured sunset clouds, Barbara found herself thinking that this was almost like being on honeymoon.

They were having pre-dinner drinks in the main bar when Reina Geray arrived, a small smile of triumph on her lips.

CHAPTER TEN

"You're consistent, I'll say that much for you," Reina was saying, raking Barbara's face with her eyes. "If you don't succeed at first—well," she shrugged, "try, try, try again. Is that your motto?"

Gregory regarded Reina blankly for a moment before he slid his long-limbed body from the stool. "What the devil are you doing here?" he demanded.

"I'll tell you. By chance, utterly by chance, I found out that *Rod Haden* was coming here. I'll leave that for you to work out, Mr. Harvester. Anyway, I cadged a lift because I decided there and then to treat myself to the opening gala. I happen to have heard all about it."

Barbara sat in stunned silence. For a moment she was paralysed with shock at the other girl's words. Rod? Here?

"After hours of driving in that hellish heat," Reina went on, "I'm practically insane and I'm longing for a bath. In case you happen to be wondering where Rod is, Barbara, he's garaging the car. I figured it out that you two would be in here before dinner just as everybody else seems to be. Her eyes swept the bar. "I'll be seeing you," she said as she walked away.

When she had gone Gregory slid back on to his stool while, wide-eyed, Barbara looked at him. "Obviously," he said coldly, "I've been missing out on something. What is all this? Have you any idea?"

"I've no idea at all." Barbara tried to keep calm. "I'm utterly bewildered."

"No idea at all?"

"None. I've been sitting here trying to work it out."

"Perhaps this is the result of your telephone call last night?"

"Last night?" Her words were jerky. Blinking with confusion, she said, "But last night I phoned the Castle."

"Did you? And again today?"

"Yes. I thought I explained about the call last night. I—I didn't get through."

"No, of course you didn't. You got through to Rod Haden, didn't you? That's more than just a little obvious now. Were you upset when Rod told you he'd be bringing Reina along with him?"

Barbara stared back at him with dismay, then she gasped, "Gregory, how can you believe that?"

"You mean you don't know why Rod Haden is here? Why else would he be here, if it were not for the fact that you let him know where you were?"

"I've told you, I don't know why he's here. I certainly didn't invite him here. It just doesn't make sense."

"I'm afraid I happen to be more realistic, Barbara. You phoned Rod, and although you might not have actually asked him to come here, this is the result. I happen to be familiar with the way in which Reina enlarges upon things when it suits her. However, you and Rod were obviously arguing on the phone last night, and I'm beginning to put two and two together. You certainly wouldn't have been arguing with my father or with Lilian. No doubt Haden made mention of the fact that he would bring Reina along. His way of getting even with you for being here with me."

In a sudden movement Barbara got to her feet. "I refuse to sit here and listen to these insults another minute," she said furiously. "Reina must certainly be congratulating herself on scoring another triumph. I—I could write a thesis on Reina, actually. I could tell you a few things—but it's quite obvious you wouldn't listen.'' She became conscious of people watching her. ''So think what you like,'' she whispered.

From his stool Gregory condemned her with his eyes, then stood up beside her. ''What else am I to think?'' he asked very softly. ''Am I to accept that Rod is here for any other reason but to be with you?''

''Accept whatever you like. I don't particularly care.''

For a moment they looked questioningly at one another and then, with a kind of wildness she couldn't control, she turned and fled from him. Vaguely, she was aware that he was following her.

When she got to her room she turned the key and ignored his knocking. Eventually the knocking stopped and soon after it stopped her telephone rang. She took it off the hook without answering it, then put it down again, thus severing the connection.

Completely shattered that the man who had told her that he was in love with her should condemn her like this, she started to pack her two small cases without even stopping to ask herself how she intended leaving Acapulco. The main thing was that she had made up her mind to leave the resort at the first possible opportunity.

Finally she changed out of her long dress and into a trouser suit, and when she was ready, she opened the door and went in the direction of the arched corridor which was adjacent to the outdoor dining area and pool in the hopes that she might find out whether any of the Press people or photographers were leaving. Perhaps not all of them were going to spend the night at the resort. Even if she got as far as Grahamstown, she thought, trying to reason things out, she could book in at one of the hotels there and make the necessary arrangements to get to Port Elizabeth by herself in time for the conferences. The main thing was to leave Acapulco now.

There were one or two people standing about talking.

It was too early for dinner and most people were still either in the bars or lounges or in their rooms changing. From the pool there were splashing noises and a lot of laughter.

Eventually Barbara decided to approach a bearded young man she had seen taking photographs earlier on. "Excuse me," she said, forcing a smile, "but do you know of anybody who might be able to give me a lift to Grahamstown, or even better, to Port Elizabeth, which is where I'm heading for?"

There was something terribly disconcerting about having to ask a stranger for a lift, even in these hitch-hiking days. The situation, however, was foreign to her.

"You've come to the right person," he told her, grinning down. "I'm leaving for P.E. in about—er—let's say half an hour."

"You are?" Staggered, she actually laughed with the relief she felt. She had not known it would be this easy.

"Yes, why?" He continued to look down at her, mocking her lightly. "Don't you believe me?"

"Yes, I do believe you," she smiled back, liking him, "I just can't believe my good luck, that's all. By the way, may I bring two small cases? They're quite small and very light."

"Bring as many cases as you like," he told her. "I'm going back in an otherwise empty Fiat. It will be a pleasure."

"Thank you. Where shall I meet you?" she asked, nervous now that she would be found out.

"Here, if you like."

"I'll do that. I'll meet you here in just under half an hour." She took a little breath. "Please, don't go without me. I'd hate to cadge a—I mean I hate to cadge a lift like this, but it's terribly urgent. I wouldn't like to—start all over again..."

"You won't have to, and don't give it another thought. It's done all the time by all the best people.

You just have to look on the roads." He grinned. "By the way, you'll be travelling with Bill Mackenzie, at your service, ma'am." He inclined his head and clicked his heels.

"I'm Barbara Knight," she told him, "and I can't tell you how grateful I am. You see, something has cropped up. Something has gone haywire with my arrangements and I've just got to leave here as soon as possible."

"Well," he went on smiling, "if you have to call it something, ma'am, I guess you could call it that."

Back in her room Barbara wrote a hurried note to Moona and Miles Burgess, thanking them for their very kind hospitality and begging their forgiveness for running out on them, then she wrote a letter to Gregory in which she stated, quite simply, that she had managed to secure a lift. She would, she added, be attending the conference, in the interest of Harvester's and in her capacity as secretary to Sir Basil. "However," she wrote, "I shall be submitting my resignation to Sir Basil upon my return to Natal, and I'll leave that for you to work out." She also mentioned that she would phone him from Port Elizabeth directly she arrived there, for she intended finding her own accommodation and had absolutely no intention of staying in the same hotel as he would be. By doing this he would be in a position to brief her as to the times and her duties in connection with the conferences. Finally she addressed two envelopes and handed them in to the reception desk, then went back to her room for her cases.

Much to her relief, Bill Mackenzie was already waiting.

"Here, let me take those," he said, taking the cases from her, and beginning to lead the way to his car.

All at once she knew that she wanted to weep as she had never wept before. Everything, past and present, crashed down on her. Fighting to keep calm, however, she followed her bearded friend.

"Some place," he mumbled from the depths of his beard. "Must have cost them a pretty packet, that's all I can say. Just let's hope they get their money back—but I should say they will."

"Yes," she replied, and her voice was almost inaudible.

"Super position, of course. Quite a lot of game too, including white rhino—not that I know the difference."

"Yes," she said again.

As they drove through the dark in the direction of the National Road she tried not to look back and she tried to make her mind a blank. The headlights of the car picked out familiar landmarks, and in the end she sat back and closed her eyes against the tears.

The journey was uneventful. Bill Mackenzie drove too fast, but not necessarily recklessly so. He made no demands upon her and did most of the talking himself. At Grahamstown they stopped for coffee and he phoned a Port Elizabeth hotel for her and booked her in so that she would experience no bother on her arrival there. Gregory, she knew, had intentions of hiring a car to make the journey in the event of his own car not being ready to make Port Elizabeth in time for the first conference.

Bill Mackenzie finally dropped her off at her hotel and, once she was alone in her room, Barbara permitted herself to cry. Her happiness had retreated as fast as she had captured it. Love had been the end of loneliness, but she was back where she had started. To allow herself to fall in love with the handsome son of her employer had been her mistake—the greatest of all her mistakes. The life she had built up for herself as Sir Basil Harvester's personal secretary was slowly beginning to crumble, because of course she knew that it would be impossible to carry on where she had left off. There could be no going back. Even Gregory had said that. She was far too involved with Gregory Harvester to continue working for his father and living at the Castle.

She waited until six o'clock the following evening before she phoned the hotel where she was supposed to have been booked, and asked for Mr. Gregory Harvester.

Directly he heard her voice he demanded, "Where are you speaking from?" There was concern in his voice.

"Never mind where I'm speaking from. There's no reason for you to know," she told him abruptly. "I've phoned, just as I said I would. You'll now be able to brief me. If you tell me...."

"I'll pick you up," he sounded impatient. "Where are you?"

"I'll take a taxi," she told him stubbornly.

"I have the car now. You're being unreasonable, Barbara."

"*I'm* being unreasonable?" Her voice was sarcastic. "I don't think so."

"Well, that's a matter of opinion. I've been practically out of my mind about you," he said, and because this kind of talk could go on and on, Barbara let his remark pass.

"I have no intention of having you pick me up," she said, after a moment, "and that's final. So will you brief me? I'd like to make *one* thing clear, however—I intend going back to Natal by plane. I haven't got the slightest intention of travelling back with you."

"You'll do no such thing."

"I can assure you, that's exactly what I'm going to do."

"We'll talk about that when the time comes. However, if you insist upon taking a taxi take one. There are a whole lot of things I'd hoped to say to you, Barbara, in the car, before the conference."

"There's nothing I have to say to you. Nothing. I have no wish to see you again, in fact. It's just that I have no option. I can't back out now, not until the conferences are over." Her jade eyes were wide with unshed tears.

"Barbara..." she sensed the tension in him and could visualize him standing up, pacing a little—as far as the cord of the telephone would permit.

"Don't Barbara me," she said bitterly, sensing an involvement. "You behaved shockingly towards me."

"Put it down to jealousy...I'm sorry. I want you to know that I got to the bottom of Rod and Reina's visit to Acapulco. I was hasty, I can see that now. I jumped to conclusions."

"It took you a long time to find out. Long enough for you t-to..." Her voice trailed away. She had been about to say "long enough for you to have lost me," but she was not sure whether he had ever really wanted her. "I have to go now," she said.

"Don't ring off yet. Let me tell you how Rod happened to turn up at the resort. Your guess as to why he allowed Reina to tag along with him is as good as mine. Frankly, he didn't even know you were there, and Reina didn't enlighten him. How she intended to play it from there I haven't the faintest idea."

"I'm not being paid by Sir Basil to speculate on the motives of his goddaughter," Barbara snapped. "If you don't give me my instructions you can hire a steno and let your father know the reason why."

"As I don't happen to think that's a very good idea, I'll ring off," he said. "I want you to know, however, that I love you."

She felt herself beginning to shake and she knew that for the rest of her life she would be depressed, cheered, excited or calmed merely by news of this man.

"Tell me where you are, Barbara."

"No," she said, struggling with tears, "I'll meet you there. I don't want to be confused any more than I already am. I'm utterly humiliated and devastated."

He was waiting for her in the elevator gallery of Harvester International, Port Elizabeth, and the mood of the natural travertine floor with its perimeters in marble, moiré-covered walls and recessed domes, lined with burnished gold leaf, reflecting the crystal chandeliers which were suspended from them, set the mood for their meeting.

As Gregory came towards her the sound of her heels on the floor stopped immediately. Taking her arm, he said softly, "I combed Grahamstown for you. Do you know that? Your letter wasn't clear."

As she looked into his face she found herself filled with conflicting emotions.

He glanced at his watch. "There's not much time to talk, but I want to make it clear—you're not going to fly back."

"Aren't I?" Her soft voice was sarcastic. "Just so long as I get back to work my notice it doesn't matter how I get back."

"That remains to be seen." There was a cold note of authority in the tone of his voice.

Reluctantly she allowed him to take her arm and to usher her in the direction of the lift and, finally, the reception room which had all the graciousness and atmosphere of a drawing-room.

A number of men, in dark business suits, were already there—gathered round in clusters, talking, and there was a smattering of elegant girls who were obviously the secretaries of men who were present from other concerns. The necessary introductions took place, and this was followed by a general milling about before the board-room doors were opened.

At one end of the room a geranium-red urn, flanked by white vases in which white chrysanthemums had been arranged, stood on a gilt console with a marble top. Above the console there was an eighteenth-century Chippendale mirror. This setting formed the backdrop to Gregory Harvester's chair at the head of

the table, and Barbara's heart contracted as she saw
him take his place. From then onwards, so far as Barbara was concerned, it was a case of concentrating on
the task on hand.

When the conference was over tea was served in the
reception room, and there was a drone of male voices
broken by the soft voices and laughter of the girls present.

From experience, Barbara knew that there would be
letters and telegrams to go off and she felt a wave of
despair, mingled with a kind of relief, that she would
have to stay on with Gregory after everybody had left.
She was still too much in love to feel otherwise.

Eventually, apart from the catering people, who were
still busy clearing up, they were alone. It was very
quiet, after all the babble of conversation, except for
the tinkling of cups and saucers as these were being
cleared away.

"We'll use the office which is reserved for my
father." Gregory's voice was very quiet and full of authority. He led the way into a beautiful room, and in it
she looked utterly beautiful and utterly sad.

Without preliminaries Gregory took her notebook
and pen from her and put them on the table. Then he
took her bag from her and placed it next to them.
"Make no mistake about this, Barbara—I *love* you."

She gave him a stricken look. "Don't," she begged.
"Please, don't. I don't even want to think. I—
I'm—tired of everything." Reaching for her notebook,
she said, "I'm ready when you are," and saw him
flinch slightly.

"I wasn't aware that you had left Acapulco until I
was handed your note," he said, "and by then it was
too late to do anything. Somebody told me you'd been
seen leaving with a bearded man. I thought perhaps
you'd managed a lift to Grahamstown and I cadged a
lift myself. I combed Grahamstown for you and finally
had to accept the fact that you'd got a lift as far as here.

As soon as I was able to take delivery of my car from the garage in Grahamstown I came on here.''

"You don't owe me an explanation," she said.

"Hear me out," he said, with some impatience. "I want you to know that before I left Acapulco I was able to make some sense out of the arrival of Ron Haden."

"Well, I don't want to talk about it. The fact still remains that you took Reina's word against mine, and yet you professed to be in love with me," she said bitterly.

"I *am* in love with you. When Reina walked into that bar and told me that Rod Haden had turned up my first reaction was one of blind fury. So far as Reina was concerned, it wouldn't have been the first time she'd done anything like that on being told of my whereabouts. She happens to be completely unpredictable. The fact that her father happened to be my father's best friend is neither here not there—it doesn't necessarily make Reina a pleasant girl. My father was landed with an impossible godchild, and I would go as far as to say that Reina has been a constant source of worry and embarrassment to him."

Woman-like, Barbara turned away from him. "Why go on? It's over and done with. You proved your—your—so-called love for me, Gregory."

"On the contrary, my love for you is anything but so-called. The fact is that Reina and Rod have been seeing a lot of each other, lately. Apparently she met Rod when you were in Italy this last time." There was a small pause and then he went on, "Barbara, do you know where Rod works?"

"No, I don't. I only know his telephone number. He used to work for Erskine's, but then he changed his position—Rod didn't confide the goings on in his life to me." She felt like shouting, Don't you know I'm in love with *you*?

"You didn't know he worked for a tourist bureau?"

"No, I didn't," she answered. "What difference does that make?"

"Rod was sent by the bureau in Uvongate to the gala opening which, as you know, was a publicity stunt on the part of the Burgesses. When Reina heard this everything clicked into position for her. She got Rod to take her along with him. She knew there would be no snag in getting accommodation at Acapulco—after all, it's not fully open to the public yet."

Curiosity got the better of her. "Did Rod know that we were at the Acapulco—that there'd been an accident?"

"I thought I made that clear. He didn't, right up until the time of their arrival there. This time Haden had nothing to do with anything. Why do you think Reina sought us out first? It was to give her a chance to have her say. After that it would have been your word and Rod's against hers. It was as simple as that."

As she listened to him Barbara's face was as remote as an image on a golden coin. Her thoughts, however, were in a complete muddle. When Gregory made an attempt to take her hand she snatched it away. "I've got to sort myself out," she said.

"Isn't it sorted out?" he asked abruptly.

"No. No, it isn't. Not for me. I should never have allowed myself to become involved with you." She saw the hurt. "I'm not interested," she said.

"Not interested?" His voice had grown hard.

"No. I've—I've been a fool. I guess I was carried away..."

She turned away and he took her by the shoulders and turned her around so that he could look down at her. "I don't suppose I was the first girl to imagine herself in love with her boss's son and I don't suppose I'll be the last," she said, feeling suddenly very pale.

"Was?" The question rang with apprehension. "*Was* in love, Barbara?"

"Yes. You see, I'm not in love with you, so you don't have to go on and on. I thought I was, but not now."

"That's something, anyhow." His voice was hard.

While part of her remained aloof her mind was screaming somewhere at the back of everything for her not to say these things. She found herself praying that he would take her into his arms and silence her. But he didn't. Men like Gregory Harvester didn't do these things.

"Perhaps you're in love with Rod, after all?" he said finally.

"Perhaps. Certainly we were perfectly happy before you came on the scene. I went out with him and..."

"Parked with him," he cut in hardly.

"Yes. I parked with him in his car—you saw that, didn't you? You never let me forget it. At any rate, Rod and I had pleasant times together. Everything changed when you came along. Since then, everything's changed." She tried to cover up the small break in her voice by clearing her throat. She wanted to hurt Gregory as much as he'd hurt her. "I'll be thankful when these conferences are over and I can get back," she told him.

"To Rod?" he replied curtly.

"Are you ready to dictate those telegrams?" she asked, glancing at her watch. "Time is going on, and if you want them to go off today you'd better do something about it. There are letters too, you said."

"By the way, you have a room with a balcony and bathroom waiting for you at the Golden Oriel," he said, "so when we've finished here I'll take you back to collect your things and take you there—back to the Oriel with me."

"There'll be no need for that. I'm perfectly comfortable where I am. I intend to stay there."

"You'll do as I say, Barbara. I mean that. Now, cut it out!"

A shock of something like excitement went through her. She had been going to argue, but shrugged her shoulders instead. "All right," she said on a furious little breath.

She had always known he could be abrupt, but there was something about his brusque superiority now that silenced her. He went behind the desk and she watched him with sombre eyes. The room was intensely quiet and she wondered if he could hear the frantic thudding of her heart. His voice, as he dictated to her, was cool. There was nothing in it to suggest that he had held her in his arms and kissed her, only hours ago. When he had finished she said, "Where do I type these?"

"Through there," he told her, and she followed him as he showed her into a small office at the far end of the room. "There's a telephone in case you want to use it," he said sarcastically. "When you've finished bring everything through for signing. I'll still be here. After that, give me the name of your hotel and we'll take it from there."

While Barbara worked at the typewriter her thoughts kept straying. It had been in her power to accept his love, regardless of the fact that he had hurt her. What man didn't hurt a girl when he was jealous—and Gregory had admitted his jealousy over her. However, she had chosen to remain cold and aloof—outwardly, at any rate. Inwardly, she had found herself longing to be in his arms.

From the window she could see clouds obscuring the sunset and she felt depressed and lonely. When she had finished typing she sat back in her chair and closed her eyes for a moment before getting up and taking the work she had done through to Gregory. The interleading door was closed and Barbara knocked lightly and then went through. He did not glance up, so she went to the huge table and placed her work to one side. "Thank you," he said, still in that same cold voice. "I won't be a moment." When he glanced up there was nothing in the expression of his dark-blue eyes to show what he was thinking. "Did the telegrams go?" he asked, and she had to search for her voice before she could answer him.

"Yes," she told him. "Immediately you looked over them I had them sent off."

"Good."

Barbara went through to her office until they were ready to leave. The building was quiet. The crystal chandeliers, suspended from the recessed domes lined with burnished gold leaf, glittered magnificently.

"This way," said Gregory. "My car is in the basement." In the car he said, "Now, where to?" and she gave him the address of her hotel.

"How did you know about this place?" he asked her.

"I didn't. Bill Mackenzie did."

"Bill Mackenzie?" His brusque superiority annoyed her, and yet thrilled her at the same time. "The chap who drove you here?" The question was hostile. She made no reply and he demanded, "Why don't you answer me, Barbara?"

"I usually hesitate for a good reason. In this case, because I don't think it concerns you."

"No? As it so happens it concerns me very much. I happen to be responsible for you. If you make a habit of accepting lifts you could hang yourself and not even know it."

"Well, I guess that's entirely up to me," she replied.

"Not while you happen to be in my care," he snapped. "Is this the hotel?"

"Yes."

"Well, I'll arrange to have your cases brought down," he told her still in that brusque way.

"I happen to be in a state of—I'm only semi-packed. I didn't know I was going to leave here. You'll have to wait."

His hotel, of course, overlooked the ocean. In the main lounge traditional ambience was created with oriental rugs, period style furnishings and soft colours.

Barbara was shown to a suite which opened on to a balcony where there was a view of the sea. There were flowers—pale yellow gladioli—on a side table in her room. The page had turned on the lamps, which had pale yellow shades. She went to the glass doors and opened them and went to stand on the balcony. She knew that she was utterly depressed. Then, because she would be occupying her suite until the end of the conferences, she unpacked before she had a bath and dressed for dinner.

The telephone shattered her brooding thoughts. Hesitantly she lifted the receiver.

"I'll meet you downstairs in ten minutes," Gregory said. "We'll have a drink before dinner." Because of something in the tone of his voice it seemed useless to argue.

"Very well," she answered in the kind of precise tone she would use for Sir Basil.

He was coldly polite while they sat in the lounge, but, without looking at him directly, Barbara knew he was studying her reflectively.

Conversation revolved around matters concerning Harvester's. Now that their outburst was over Barbara had herself in hand.

During dinner Gregory said, "Barbara, allowing for errors on my part, I feel you behaved unreasonably when you left Acapulco. We might have been able to sort things out between us, had you stayed on. Certainly we would have got to the bottom of Haden's appearance."

"Yes—but would you have believed it?" she asked. "I don't think so. Looking back, you've always been quick to criticize me. You've never given me the benefit of the doubt. And so," she shrugged, "I guess there was nothing to sort out and there never will be. So let's forget it."

It was true, she found herself thinking miserably. There could be nothing to sort out. He was the son of her employer and he had found himself involved with her, that was all. Had he really loved her he would not have been so quick to condemn. She had made up her mind and she wanted it to stay that way.

"There's nothing more to say," she lifted her lashes and then dropped them again as she made a big show of studying the menu.

CHAPTER ELEVEN

OUTSIDE the conference room the words CONFERENCE IN PROGRESS burned, in red lights, for the next three days. Barbara, elegant in one of the attractive knit-suits she had brought along to wear at the conferences, found her mind staggering beneath the weight of her work. Although she often felt the strain of business trips with Sir Basil it was never quite like this—but then she wasn't in love with Sir Basil!

The memory of Gregory's kisses kept flooding every corridor of her mind, and the problem of continuing to work for his father, under these conditions, presented itself at the most inconvenient moments. Reluctant as she was to give up her position, she was certain she was doing the right thing in preparing to tell him of her desire to leave soon after she and Gregory got back to the Castle. If she changed her mind and stayed on as Sir Basil's secretary, she realized that she would have to learn to harden herself to practise indifference to all matters concerning Gregory when all she felt was be-wilderment and a longing to have him love her. She would always be affected by him. There was therefore no other way out but to give up her position and get away from Uvongate.

Twice Gregory had to ask her to change a letter, and when she checked her shorthand notes she discovered that the mistakes had been entirely her own.

On the second night, after they had had dinner to-gether at the Golden Oriel, he said, "Barbara, is there a anything you'd like to do?"

"H-how do you mean?" she asked, lifting her eyes to his.

"Would you like to go out somewhere? A show? A nightclub?"

"No, thank you. I'm feeling a little tired, actually."

"I see. Well," he shrugged, "just as you like." His reply had been abrupt and she was filled with angry disappointment, before she asked herself what was it she had expected. Men like Gregory did not beg. Had she expected him to beg her?

"I'd better warn you," he said, breaking into her thoughts, "that the conferences will terminate with a cocktail party, followed by dinner and dancing at the Supper Club. You'll be expected to attend, with me."

Barbara imagined that she could detect a mindless, uncaring aloofness, so she said quietly, "I see."

After dinner was over she went to her room and was filled with a wild restlessness. Going out to her balcony, she stood watching the traffic on the street below and, further back, the black waves topped by that faint luminous glow as they turned over to crash on to the pale, shimmering beach.

Why hadn't she accepted Gregory's invitation to go out with him? she asked herself despondently. How was she ever to find out whether he really cared for her if she did not give them a chance to be together? Other questions kept flashing through her mind . . . and then, from where she was standing, she could see him as he walked to where he had parked the car. Directly he had driven off she went back into her room and lay on top of her bed staring wide-eyed at the ceiling. Eventually the tension which had built up relaxed under a shower of tears. It was so unlike her, she thought, sitting up and groping for tissues. Years ago she had learned to handle her tears until they played absolutely no part in her life.

After a while she calmed down and went through to the bathroom where she splashed her face with cold water, applied a light make-up, combed her hair and went downstairs. She walked into the main lounge with an air of self-assuredness, something which she had learned over the years of being on her own. Several men looked up and followed her with interested eyes, while she chose a comfortable chair and reached for a glossy magazine from a small table. Later she ordered coffee.

"Hello there, Miss Knight." Barbara looked up. It was one of the men who had been attending the conferences and she could not even remember his name.

"Hello." She smiled mechanically and tried to keep her voice easy.

"You look very lost," he said, smiling down at her, then his gaze slid sideways to the vacant chair beside her. "May I?" he asked.

"Of course."

"I would have thought you would have been out painting the town," he said, as he took a cigarette case from his pocket. He shook one free and offered it to her.

"Thank you, but I don't smoke."

She watched him as he took one and hung it on his mouth. He reached for his lighter and then he quickly removed the cigarette from his lips. "I'm terribly sorry—may I? How very rude of me."

"Of course," she said again. "Please go ahead."

"I find it gives me something to do with my hands," he told her, smiling. "Actually, if I set my mind to it I could stop smoking tomorrow." He glanced up over his hands as they cupped the flame, and grinned.

"I guess they all say that—and never do." Barbara gave him a smile.

The air around him moved with little convolutions of smoke and he laughed outright. "I suppose they do. Hey," he looked at her cup, "what have we here?"

"Coffee. I'm afraid I can't offer you any. There was only enough for two cups. I had one cup, and as that happens to be some time ago, what's left in the pot will be cold. Nobody has been to collect the tray yet.''

"Are you waiting for anyone?" he asked.

"No. I was just about to go to my room, as it happens," she told him, and saw the look of surprise in his eyes.

"The night is young," he said. "How about doing something together?"

"I'm terribly tired," she said. "All those notes, you know. It tells on one, in the end. Actually, I brought some work back with me." It was a white lie.

"Well, what about a drink, in that case, before you do go?"

Barbara tried to think of his name, but couldn't. "What about you?" she asked. "Why aren't you out painting the town?"

"For the simple reason that this happens to be my town. I can paint it any time I like, but you happen to be a visitor. It seems a pity not to see the sights." He broke off to signal a steward.

When Gregory came into the lounge they were laughing over something and for a brief instant he looked straight into Barbara's eyes and, brief though the instant was, his displeasure and annoyance showed, direct and unrestrained. Barbara watched him as he turned and walked in the direction of the bar.

"That was your boss," her companion said.

"Yes, but only at the moment. I happen to work for his father, Sir Basil."

"Oh, I see. He's ill, I understand?"

"Yes," Barbara's voice was tense. She longed to get away. "Nothing very serious. I think he's been overdoing things. Well, I really must ask you to excuse me." She still could not think of his name. "It was nice of you to come and chat to me."

He saw her to the lift and as she got into it she said, "Thank you again. I'll see you in the morning."

The episode left Barbara unsettled and she slept badly.

In the morning Gregory said, "So you recovered last night? Enough to join Barry Woods for a session." They were in the car going to the final conference.

"I wouldn't call it a session," she replied stiffly. "We met by coincidence and, as it so happens, I can't—I couldn't even remember his name."

"So you met him by chance?"

"Yes. I decided to go downstairs and order some coffee and he asked whether he could join me and..." she shrugged, "since misery likes company, I said yes."

"You didn't look particularly miserable."

"Well, I was. How should I announce the fact? By means of thudding drums and shouting and chanting?" she asked.

"What are you miserable about?" he asked. "Are you missing Rod Haden?"

After a pause, in which bitterness washed over her, she said, "Yes, as a matter of fact I am."

They drove into the roaring business-hour peak. Their stay in Port Elizabeth, which had been nothing short of a disaster, was practically at an end.

"I must see about a seat on the plane today," said Barbara, and held her breath.

"You'll do no such thing. You're coming back with me in the car. I thought we'd settled that?" Gregory gave her a furious glance. "You can dismiss going back by plane from your mind."

They reached the building and he parked the car in the basement. Their footsteps echoed on the natural travertine floor with its perimeters in marble as they walked in the direction of the lift. "I want you to know," he said suddenly, "that I think you've done a wonderful job here. I can see why it is that you're indispensable to my father."

In the tumult of feelings that swept over her she said, "Thank you, that's very kind of you. I do appreciate it."

The fact that she intended walking out on Sir Basil

soon after her return to the Castle filled her with a terrible feeling without a name. "I've got used to this sort
of thing," she told him, after a moment. "At first,
though, I thought I'd never manage, but one soon
learns the ropes."

They went into the reception-room, with its clusters
of men in dark business suits and the smattering of
girls with notebooks, and Barbara willed her mind to
switch off matters not concerning the conference. By
the end of the afternoon she had finished all the minutes, but there was a small stack of letters to do. Finally
these were typed and awaited Gregory's signature. She
had also spoken on the phone to Sir Basil.

The end of the conferences was marked by the usual
kind of cocktail party where people stand around in
clusters talking. The wives of several men present had
arrived and there was a general air of making up for lost
time as their husbands helped themselves to drinks.
Everybody seemed satisfied with the conferences.

Handing Barbara a drink, Gregory said, "Well, I
guess you could do with one, after all that."

"Yes, I could." She looked down at the glass. "What
is it?"

"I know so much about you," he said, "including
what it is you like to drink."

"Oh." There seemed to be nothing to say to that and
she looked away. The conferences were over—they
were going back. He knew so much about her and yet
they were going back as strangers, she thought bitterly.
While she was thinking along these lines her eyes met
his and she saw that there was no denial of the memory
of what had happened between them. Gregory's expression changed. "Cheer up," he said, "you'll soon
be back in Uvongate. You'll soon be with Rod." After a
moment he added, "That is what you want, isn't it?"

"Yes," she said, trying to match his tone although
her breath was hurting her. "If you say so."

By the time they left the cocktail party the lights of the city sparkled and trembled and, in the distance, the sea was black, except for the phosphorescent shimmer where the waves broke along the shore. Far out, a ship reflected lights in the water.

At their hotel Gregory said, "I'll come up for you."

"That will be fine," she answered, her mind flitting ahead to the Supper Club where they were to dine and dance. She thought of the glamorous dress she had packed, at his suggestion, before leaving the Castle. She had folded it and placed it in her case with mixed feelings and she was going to wear it with mixed feelings—one part of her longing to be loved by Gregory Harvester and the other half bitterly disillusioned by him.

She had only just completed the final touches to her hair when there was a knock on her door. When she saw Gregory standing there she said, "I'll just get my bag."

"Have you been comfortable here?" he asked. He glanced into her room.

"Yes," she stood to one side. "Have a look for yourself. I'm in the middle of packing, of course. I don't want to leave everything until the last thing in the morning." She gesticulated in the direction of frocks and garments and tissue paper in the stages of packing.

"I'm on the floor above," he said. "The set-up is very much the same." He went out to the balcony and stood looking down at the evening traffic. The doors were open and the smell of the sea was warm and strong.

"By the way," he came back into the room, "have the flowers arrived regularly?"

"The flowers?" Barbara felt confused. "I'm sorry—I didn't know they were from you. It's—it's not customary for me to receive flowers..." her voice petered out.

"I thought they might cheer you up." The remark

was offhand. He was standing so close to her that had either of them made one move they would have touched each other.

"Right." It was he who moved away. "Let's go, shall we?" She could tell nothing from his voice.

A long table had been reserved for the entire party at the Supper Club. Barbara looked very sleek and very fashionable and there was nothing to show that she was trying to clear up the wreckage of a love affair. The food and the cabaret were excellent and so was the band, although the floor was the usual postage stamp affair.

Gregory had been nothing more than polite the entire evening. However, he commented, "You're looking stunning, but then you always do."

"Not always," she replied. "I think you must have forgotten."

At that moment a photographer hovered near the spot where they were dancing and there was a blinding light as a flash bulb popped. Barbara blinked, caught unawares and Gregory laughed lightly. Then he said, "I hadn't forgotten, actually."

Although it was late people never seemed to stop eating. The air was thick with smoke. Barbara was beginning to feel the strain of everything and was thankful when the time came to leave.

The muted golden warmth of the hotel foyer greeted them and Gregory saw her to her door. "We'll leave soon after breakfast," he told her, "but don't stir too early. You look exhausted."

"I'll be ready," she replied. Her self-respect had been redeemed somewhat by having slipped back into the role of the efficient secretary. On the whole, she thought, she had coped rather well, once the conferences were under way. She regretted her reminder about the black stockings, however, and she saw herself degraded by it.

She was awakened in the morning by the ringing of

the telephone. "Sorry to break this up," Gregory's voice sounded almost tender, "but how's it going?"

Barbara's startled eyes flew to the little travelling clock she always carried with her. "Oh!" she gasped. "I'm sorry. I've slept in, I can see that. I didn't even hear the knock on the door for coffee. They must have given up and gone away and I just went on sleeping. I'll be with you in a jiffy."

"Don't let it worry you." His voice had a quiet authority. "Take your time. I've had breakfast, by the way. Shall I arrange for yours to be sent up to you?"

"It might save time—thank you." Her mind raced ahead to all the last-minute packing she had to do.

Later on, in the foyer, she said, "I'm sorry. I've made us late in leaving, haven't I?"

The staff hurried about, carrying their bags outside to the car. "I think you misunderstood the position," Gregory said lightly. "There's no urgency, Barbara. In fact, I suggest we take our time driving back." She saw his eyes going over her white slacks which she wore along with a black top. Her auburn hair was loose about her shoulders.

"We'll stop somewhere tonight," he said, after a moment.

"At the Acapulco?" she asked as casually as she could, but regretted the question immediately.

"No." His voice was suddenly abrupt. "Not at the Acapulco. With me there's no going back."

Barbara experienced a moment of disappointment. Even now, she was still hoping that they would be able to sort something out between them...she longed for another opportunity of testing his love for her, but it seemed hopeless. They exchanged a quick glance, then he said, "Well, our cases have gone...we'd better go."

They went out into the sun. The sea glittered lazily beneath it. Traffic was already beginning to slacken after the early morning peak hour. The journey was uneventful. Barbara willed herself not to look in the direction of the turn-off to Acapulco and a sideways glance at Gregory's profile told her that he was doing the same thing. Would they ever see it again—together?

They stopped at a tiny town which untidily straggled the length of its main street. The sun was beginning to set. Gregory had driven slowly. Perhaps he was also tired, Barbara thought. After all, he'd also been snowed under with business affairs.

"Will you tell me one thing?" he said, looking at the hotel.

"Yes—if I can. What is it?" she asked.

"If you don't like the accommodation, tell me, and we'll drive on to the next town."

"I see. It should be all right. These country hotels, right on the pavement, are surprising, sometimes," she answered.

Her room was right on the other side of the hotel, right next to the street bar, and there was a double bed in it and a cot. It was a depressing room and she knew that if Gregory were to see it he would have insisted that they move on.

Dinner was served in what appeared to be an old section of the hotel, which had been built on here and there over the years. The explanation was forthcoming when they were told by the waiter that there had been a wedding in the small town and that the main dining-room was being reserved for an after-sunset reception. Most of the rooms were occupied by wedding guests, from neighbouring farms, into the bargain.

"I did wonder at all the activity and the cars parked outside," Gregory said. "Tell me, Barbara, what kind of room have they given you?"

"It's quite comfortable, thank you," she murmured, reluctant to tell him and yet dreading to go back to the room at the end of a long, cheerless and creeper-shrouded veranda. "And you?" she asked.

"That's precisely why I asked."

They continued with the meal. Barbara allowed her

gaze to wander round the wood-lined room which looked ready to burn down at the flick of a cigarette lighter. It would, she thought, have been a good film set for a cowboy film.

After dinner Gregory said, "I want to see your room."

"Honestly," she said flustered, "there's no need. It's all right."

"I insist." The note of authority was back, reminding her of Sir Basil.

When he saw it he said, "Why the devil didn't you *tell* me, Barbara?"

"It's only for one night."

"I will not have you spending a night in this room. Dammit, apart from the state of it you happen to be right next to the pub. Get your things together. We're leaving."

After he'd gone unwanted questions flashed through her mind. Was he doing this because of her or was he doing it because he happened to be a Harvester—above putting up with such service?

They stayed at a small Tudor-style hotel which looked at home set back from the main street of the next small town. Before retiring they had coffee in the lounge. "You should have told me about your room," he said. "You know me well enough," and Barbara felt like telling him that she did not know him at all—that she had only thought she'd known him.

The Castle awaited them the following day with its romance of the past and furnishings which came as such a surprise but blended so excitingly and daringly with shaggy golden carpets on cool marble floors.

Sir Basil looked tanned and relaxed, his silver hair shining and contrasting with his alert, dark-blue eyes.

Lilian, small and petite in her white slacks and blue top, surprised Barbara by kissing her. "You look done in, child!" she exclaimed.

"That's not exactly surprising," said Gregory. "Barbara has worked flat out almost since we left here."

Giving Barbara a mocking look, he went on, "We've experienced a lot of events together—the tolerance of travelling together, an accident, little secrets shared, long hours of work and—bitter arguments...Right, Barbara?"

"I suppose you could say that." She made an attempt to smile naturally, and was aware that Sir Basil and Lilian both looked puzzled.

"Well, you'll feel better after a delicious soak in the bath," Lilian said, "and a good night's rest. I'll have a tray of tea sent up to your room, Barbara, while you settle in."

"Thank you," Barbara murmured. Things were back to normal again—but not quite.

Theresa, the maid, interrupted her thoughts as she came into the room with the silver tea tray. At the far end of the gallery the thickly carved doors were open now, and when Theresa left the room, Barbara went over to her own doors and closed them.

She was sipping her tea when there was a tap on her interior door. It was Lilian. "I came up to see how you are," she said. "I've never seen you looking so washed out and dejected, Barbara. Has the accident upset you so much? Are you sure you weren't hurt?"

"No, of course not. Gregory got a doctor to attend to me."

"Well, darling, you must put it out of your mind— that is, if you are brooding on it, and somehow I think you are. It could have been so much worse. Basil is terribly worried about you. He remarked on the way you look."

"Well, it was a shock," Barbara said. "I'll admit that, Lilian, especially as I happened to be driving. Apart from the shock, I felt awful, of course, for damaging the car and for wasting valuable time. Gregory's time with Adrian Price was cut short."

"He did all his business with Adrian Price in the time available to him." There was an awkward pause and then Lilian said, "Has there been—anything else? Anything else to upset you, Barbara?"

Barbara's panic grew as she looked back at Lilian. "No, of course not. There was an amount of—of strain. Conferences always produce that kind of tension. It's only natural."

"And—Gregory, Barbara?"

"What do you mean—and Gregory?"

"I mean, child, was he considerate?"

"Of course. Very considerate. He—we even moved on last night after he took one look at the accommodation put at my disposal."

"That's not what I meant, actually."

"He was most considerate, Lilian, all round."

"You both appear to be under considerable strain. You don't think he's fallen in love with you?"

"Why do you ask?" Barbara dropped her lashes.

"There's something in the way he—the way in which he keeps looking at you. His remarks are—are—*barbed*. He talks like a man who's in love with a girl and who wants to hurt her, for some reason or another. I'm pretty broadminded, but I don't think Basil should have allowed you to go off with Gregory. Talking about Basil, I can't begin to tell you how he missed you. They sent a Miss Rainback up from the complex and she didn't come up to his expectations at all. She just didn't seem to be able to cope."

While Lilian was speaking Barbara found herself thinking—please, don't make it harder for me, Lilian. I'm going to leave Sir Basil, regardless.

"By the way," Lilian continued, "Reina has gone."

"I wondered about Reina," said Barbara, her voice distant and stiff.

"Yes. She seemed all keyed up after she heard about the accident. I heard her on the phone in the library. She appeared to be ringing Rod Haden and then she informed us that she was leaving. What puzzled me was the fact that she left her car here and then, when she called for it again, after a couple of days or so, she offered no explanation and cleared off in a huff."

"I see." Listening to Lilian, Barbara experienced a sense of helplessness as she found herself wondering how much to tell her. The situation produced in her a feeling of constraint and a desperate need to be alone for a few days to sort herself out.

After Lilian had gone she went into her bathroom and turned on the swan-shaped taps, and she was suddenly so tired that she could have wept.

In the morning Sir Basil dictated several letters to her in the library, and twice she had to ask him to repeat the last sentence and twice she tried to tell him that she intended resigning her position, without success.

There were the usual magnificent arrangements of flowers, mostly all from the gardens—apricot-pink roses and dark-blue delphiniums, the same colours as the long-line sofa, apricot scatter cushions and apricot carpet.

When Gregory came into the library some time later, a thrill of half excitement, half fear ran down her spine. She had not seen him since their arrival back from Port Elizabeth. They shared a long look before he said, "I've come to say goodbye, Barbara."

"Goodbye?" She tried to keep the shock out of her voice.

"Yes. I'm leaving for Durban in about an hour's time and for Italy in a couple of days."

"I see." Her voice was small and businesslike. "How long will you be away?"

"I intend settling in Italy."

Her mind began to spin and when it had stopped spinning she said, "You—make up your mind quickly, don't you?"

"Yes—you should know that by now." His voice was hard. His expression told her nothing.

"What about Sir Basil?" she asked.

"What about him?"

"He hasn't been well lately. Won't he need you here?"

"On the contrary. If I decide to settle in Italy this will cut down on his visits there and, in turn, cut down the strain entailed by these visits."

So she wasn't even going to be able to see him on a trip to Italy, she thought despairingly. But then wasn't she planning to leave Sir Basil anyway? Perhaps she could stay on now? Perhaps things would be bearable. An uncontrollable part of her mind blanked out.

"This arrangement should suit you," Gregory was saying, from a long way off. "You could almost say that you're back where you started."

"Yes." Her voice was almost a whisper. "You could say that."

She had the insane feeling that it needed only *one* small movement from one of them, to put matters right, but she had no intention of making that move—in case she was wrong.

After he had gone Barbara covered her face with her hands.

CHAPTER TWELVE

In the weeks to come Barbara asked herself why she did not leave the Castle when everything reminded her of Gregory. She savoured those moments with a bitter sweetness, when Lilian made mention of his letters.

Somehow, however, she managed to pull herself together and tried to fill her mind with work. Every time she went up on the battlements the thought that Gregory was in Italy struck her with devastating effect.

Sir Basil was concentrating more and more on the complex. Lucas Hollander was now a constant visitor to the Castle and it was obvious that he and Lilian enjoyed being together.

Rod had left Uvongate for an up-country town.

"You look unhappy, Barbara," Lilian said one day, at the poolside. "Are you?"

"No, Lilian, of course not."

"You're not still brooding on the accident, are you?"

"No."

"Gregory told me, of course, about the—farm—where the resort is now. I've read about it, as it so happens. There was a big write-up in *Swinging Set*—you know that glossy magazine?"

"Yes, it was difficult to believe that it stood on land that I once knew so well," Barbara replied. "It made things easier for me, as it happens. It was hard for me to really identify myself with Acapulco—or rather, with the farm which used to be there."

"I believe you were made very welcome there?" Barbara had the feeling that Lilian was trying to draw her out. "You stayed there while the car was taken away to a garage in Grahamstown?"

"Yes—we did." There was a strange awkwardness between them, and then Lilian said, "Is it—Gregory, Barbara?" Both were aware of the constraint now.

Finally Barbara managed a laugh. "Lilian, you sound like a detective!"

"What happened on the Port Elizabeth trip?" Lilian asked abruptly. "Apart from the accident?"

Her mind reeling with panic, Barbara answered, "Nothing, Lilian, except that we—we—thought we were in love."

"The way I see it is that you *are* in love. Why else would Gregory clear off to Italy? Why else would you be looking the way you are? What, then, stands in the way?"

Barbara felt calmer now and suddenly it was a relief to tell Lilian about it.

Later she said, "But if Gregory had really been in love with me, Lilian, he wouldn't have been so quick to doubt me—to condemn me."

"But, darling, he told you—you *said* he told you in Port Elizabeth that he had acted hastily. He confessed that he was jealous and he tried to reassure you that he loved you. Am I right?" There was a silence and then she said again, "Well, didn't he, Barbara?"

"Yes, he did. The way I saw it, though, was that he found himself involved with me and decided to see it through. He did try to convince me, but..." she broke off, "he became sarcastic and cold. This convinced me that he wasn't really in love with me at all."

"In other words," Lilian sounded a little impatient, "you wanted him to go on convincing, go on reassuring and reassuring. Darling, isn't it typical of a man to treat a girl that way, when he happens to be in love with her and believes that she's not, after all, in love with him, which *is* what you told him? A man always lashes out at a girl he loves and thinks he has no chance with. Believe me, *I* happen to know. I had a similar experience. Neither of us would give, and so here I am." She shrugged. "You didn't know that, did you? Not many people do."

"I intended resigning directly we got back to the Castle," Barbara admitted. "I felt I couldn't go on working here, after having become so emotionally involved with my boss's son. I was merely giving it time— I didn't want to spring it on Sir Basil right away—and then I didn't have to. Gregory went away and I let things drift on and finally decided to keep my position for as long as Sir Basil wants me."

At that moment Sir Basil arrived on the scene. "I've come for a swim before my lunch," he said cheerfully. Impeccably courteous, he stood to one side, contemplating the water, while Lilian said, "I didn't mean to give you a hard time, Barbara. It explains a lot of things, though. Thank you for telling me."

After a moment Sir Basil said, "Well, I didn't hear you two splashing about. Haven't you been in?" He was wearing white slacks, horn-rimmed sun-glasses and an imported purple Italian shirt, and as he bent over to ease one bare foot out of its sandal there was not a scrap of extra flesh on his body. He unbuttoned his shirt, and although the hair on his head was pure platinum, the hair on his chest was still black. Looking at him, Barbara found herself thinking that Gregory would look like that, one day...Sir Basil's charm was incalculable. The refusal to be harassed or rude was only part of his charm. Had he, however, in his younger days been like his son? Had he been impatient and sarcastic and masterful towards the women he supposedly loved?

The weeks went by. The weather was changing subtly— the days getting shorter all the time. Barbara went on enjoying the infinite luxury of the Castle, to the best of her ability. Sir Basil and Lilian were entertaining lavishly and she was nearly always included in these affairs. She also spent a lot of time at the complex with Sir Basil who was taking an active part in supervising the sets, along with Lucas Hollander, and he appeared to be enjoying himself immensely.

Lilian continued to watch Barbara with a new thoughtfulness, and Barbara, aware of her silent scrutiny, was determined not to allow Gregory's name to crop up again.

The weather was definitely cooler now and often necessitated the wearing of warmer clothes. Behind the low mustard exterior of a new boutique, Barbara shopped extravagantly, giving herself up to the delight of choosing new clothes. Trying not to think of her loneliness, she browsed around the boutique, her footsteps making no sound on the rich chocolate shaggy carpet. She delved into alcoves containing evening gowns in such exciting colours as oyster-green, bronzed-brown, cerise. More alcoves revealed snug day dresses in cheerful citrus colours, lime and khaki, bitter green and orange. She had trouble making her choice and then, alongside rough-surfaced walls, reaching to a pine-wood ceiling, where chromed downlighters were suspended above containers of French perfumes arranged in pyramid formation on the counter, she gave considerable thought to her choice of perfume. For once in her life she spent lavishly, but when she had finished buying, she felt a different person.

"You must be getting married, surely?" The sales-girl sounded envious. "All this is perfect honeymoon stuff. Imagine going off to the Sani Pass Hotel with all that—on an exciting honeymoon. *Are* you?"

"No," laughed Barbara, with studied casualness. "I'm strictly a career girl."

Around about this time Sir Basil was arranging a businessmen's cheese and wine party at the complex and Barbara was to act as hostess. Having acted in this capacity in the past she knew exactly what was expected of her—nothing much, except to look glamorous and to see that empty glasses were replaced by full ones and that everyone had enough to eat.

For the occasion she decided to wear a dusky-pink trouser suit because it happened to be bitterly cold. The trouser suit made her look sophisticated and business-like.

At the complex a long table had been formally set in one of the sets. It was one of the few sets which had not yet been changed—the one where pink sofas and chairs exploded into pink sunsets, as Lucas Hollander had laughingly described it. Beyond the pink sofas and chairs there was the mock terrace with its giant ferns and pot-plants. The set reminded Barbara of Gregory, and her thoughts went to the time when he had invited her to sit on one of the pink chairs and, trying not to be aware of his dark-blue eyes following her movements, she had carried out his instructions.

Long-stemmed wine glasses glittered against the white cloth and a low flower arrangement was illuminated by a cluster of candles.

The caterers had been selective when choosing the cheeses—a flavour for every mood, every palate. Smooth mellow cheeses, creamy spicy cheeses, crumbly piquant cheeses... The selection of wines, too, was excellent—all full-bodied red and white wines. The entire table arrangement had a fresh clean appearance and a tantalizing aroma pervaded the set.

Businessmen stood around in clusters next to the giant ferns and bold pot-plants. Beyond the immense windows the sea was picking up the last rays of an explosive sunset. The plate glass kept the cold, brisk wind at bay and Barbara enjoyed the luxurious touch of her soft wool trouser suit as she busied herself with trays and glasses. She tried to close her mind to the time she had visited this same set with Gregory. Although she had been working at the complex with Sir Basil over the weeks it seemed ironical that this place she remem-

bered so well was the very set which had not been
changed.

As she moved about her trouser suit stood out excitingly against the olive-green leaves of the potted plants
and yet it blended so well with the pink-upholstered
furniture. Was that why she had chosen to wear it? she
asked herself.

Later on, she thought idly, there would be a cold
moon, its pale eerie light changing the mood of the sea.
Winter had at last come to the heady South Coast, but
even then it was an unpredictable thing. Log fires glimmered in the fireplaces at the Castle and while at the
moment they were certainly needed there would be
times when they wouldn't be.

Lucas Hollander broke into her thoughts as she held
out the tray to him and he exchanged his empty glass
for a full one. "The only rose amongst thorns, eh?"

"You get used to it," she said. "I'm always having to
do things like this in my capacity as secretary to Sir
Basil. Actually, I enjoy it."

"Just as long as the men leave you alone?" he
asked.

"They always do," she laughed, turning away.

The sight of Gregory hit her with the force of a
physical shock. She felt her eyes going wide and then
watched with a look of disbelief as he crossed the mock
terrace and came over to where she was standing.
"Here, let me take that—before *all* the glasses slip
right off," he said, as one glass crashed to the floor. He
took the tray just in time to stop the whole lot slipping
off the edge. "That was close!" He smiled down at her.
"Say something," he said.

"I thought you were still in Italy?" Barbara watched
him as he looked for a place to set the tray down and it
gave her a little time for her heart to regain its usual
beat.

When he turned round his blue eyes were suddenly
turned on her, full force.

"Does Sir Basil know you're back?" she asked. "He didn't seem to know." She shrugged in bewilderment.

"No. Nobody knows—just Lilian told me where to find you, as a matter of fact. I came straight here."

"*Me?*" she echoed.

"Yes—you."

After a moment she said, "Did Lilian write and ask you to come back?" Her voice was tight. She felt suddenly humiliated.

"Lilian might have been instrumental in my coming back a little earlier than I had planned." He took her arm. "Come," he said, "let these individuals fend for themselves."

She allowed him to lead her away. "I'm not supposed to," she murmured. "I'm supposed to be handing out wine and seeing that everybody has enough to eat in the line of..."

"I don't care what you're supposed to be doing. In fact, I'm not sure that I like the idea of the girl I'm going to marry waiting on all these men."

Barbara experienced another moment of terrible panic. Just what had Lilian Harvester been up to?

"Is Lilian responsible for this?" she asked. "I'll never tell her another thing!"

"Barbara," he said, "let's clear up all past misunderstandings in one go and once and for all, shall we? I think we've wasted quite enough time. I'm in love with you. I mean it—I meant what I said at Acapulco when I said that there was a beautifully calm girl, behind a desk much too big for her, and that I'd made up my mind there and then that my father would have to find himself another secretary. It was a girl I fell in love with at first sight."

"A man in love with a girl doesn't make snap decisions about her—the kind of snap decisions *you* made about me," she said. "When Rod and Reina turned up at Acapulco you connected Rod's arrival with a telephone call I'd been trying to put through to Sir Basil—

or Lilian. You gave me no chance to explain. Actually, it was Reina who answered the phone. There was always that—that critical side of you, wanting to attack me," she added.

"If you look back," he said, "you'll remember that when I spoke to you on the phone in Port Elizabeth one of the first things I said to you was that I'd been out of my mind about you. I admitted that I'd been wrong. I said—I want you to know I love you. I still want you to know!"

"I was filled with conflicting emotions then, and I'm filled with them now," she told him.

"Why didn't you tell me about Reina on the phone?" he asked. "You didn't tell me, so my own imagination went to work. That's natural, isn't it?"

"No, it isn't," she said. "*I* don't think so, anyway."

"Let's put it this way," he went on. "To take it further—what does a man do when a girl, with her face as remote as an image on a golden coin, tells him she's not in love with him? What does he do when she tells him that before *he* came on the scene she used to have pleasant times with another man? Those were just some of the things. Let me remind you of the others. What does he do when she states, quite flatly, that she should never have allowed herself to become emotionally involved with him, that she's not interested in him, that she's been a fool—that she was carried away, that she doesn't suppose she was the first girl to *imagine* that she was in love with the boss's son? I'll tell you what he does, Barbara—he takes her word for it. Sometimes he gets traditionally drunk. Sometimes he clears off."

"Well," she went on, punishing him, punishing herself, "who made up your mind, for you? Lilian?"

"I had absolutely no intention of settling in Italy," he told her. "I went there to simmer down. I went there in the hopes that you would keep on at the Castle and that you'd be there when I got back." There was a mixed feeling of amusement, anger and frustration in his voice. "Haven't we got this all mixed up?" he asked. "Barbara?"

Suddenly everything was giving out and she felt the longing to tell him how she had missed him. "Anger and hurt got the better of me," she told him. "I wanted to—to lash out at you. Isn't that a woman's reaction? You—you've told me of the man's reaction...it's—it's the same thing..."

Nobody appeared to be noticing them as he took her into his arms. The fronds of a potted palm rattled as he brushed past them to reach her.

"I've been so lonely," she said, against his mouth. "Gregory, I've been despairing, bewildered...I felt that only part of me was alive."

He released her to say, "How do you feel now?"

"I feel complete..." she closed her eyes and then opened them again, "anyway, *nearly* complete."

"That's more like it," he said very softly. "And it's something I intend rectifying in the not-so-distant future."

RETURN TO BELLE AMBER

Return to
Belle Amber

Margaret Way

Her mother was dead. The long years of bitterness and unhappiness were over for her now. Karen meant to go on and care for her young brother herself, but Guy Amber's impeccable logic and forceful personality took them back to Belle Amber, to the place and people her mother had grown to hate.

But in the beautiful atmosphere of the Australian vineyard estate, it didn't take Karen long to forget her hatred of Guy or to renew friendships with her relatives. All except Celia.

Celia was a beautiful, selfish, ambitious woman—with her mind set on Gregory. She saw Karen as a threat not to be tolerated.

CHAPTER ONE

THE gold was fading from the sky. It was turning imperceptibly to a delicate green, like cool, running water. A capering wind whipped up with the dusk skeining her long black hair across her face and throat. Karen roused herself from a world of random little thoughts and hurried on home. Soon it would be dark and Philip would be waiting. She turned up the collar of her coat, her long slim legs flashing, her heels on the pavement tapping out the same urgent message: Philip will be waiting: Philip will be waiting.

In her own quiet cul-de-sac the roar of the traffic, the relentless procession of cars, buses and darting taxi-cabs was suddenly obliterated. The fine old houses stood in a world of their own; a world of silence and gentle stability. The winter-into-spring blend of atmosphere was brisk and invigorating and in every garden the wattles were bursting into fluffy gold blossom. The sight and scent of them prodded her memory and induced a bitter-sweet nostalgia, a fragrant reminder of days long past. Karen gave an involuntary gasp, for an instant suspended in time.

In front of the old wine cellar stood a magnificent acacia. With each spring it burst into dazzling blossom: masses upon masses of softest yellow constellations that swayed against the whitewashed stone building. A very long time before someone had built a circular bench around its broad base, and there the children loved to congregate, in plain sight and scent of the mysterious and wonderfully spooky old place—the cellar. It was haunted, of course, by old Matthew Amber, who had built it and stocked it and loved

*it and gone there to die. How many childish fantasies had
they woven around him—the tall spectral figure that
roamed the gloomy underground tunnels stacked high with
dusty old bottles—bottles that glowed ruby and amethyst
when rubbed off and held up to the light.*

*At the back of the cellar was a squat stone wall trailing
ivy, with a background of camelias and low-growing azaleas, and beyond that the glasshouses crammed to the ceiling with exotic plants from all over the world. Aunt Patricia
favoured orchids and was the possessor of an enviable
"green finger". As soon as the temperature dropped a few
degrees she would rush off to the greenhouse to check the
humidity for her beloved cattleyas, for once the orchids bud-
ded they would bloom on for weeks at a time.*

One lovely image after another flashed across Karen's
mind like slides on a projection screen. Faster and faster
they flew, absorbing her entire attention. *At the foot of the
embankment, approaching the vineyards, was a small pond
guarded by willows, where fish liked to dart, leaving flashes
of silver and gold. Rikki got spanked once for trying to fish
there. Rikki was always the rebel, a small boy with silver-gilt
hair!*

The breeze tugged at her hair, pulling her out of it.
Karen blinked her eyes fiercely. It all seemed a million
years ago, anyway. The golden days of Belle Amber!
The days of her childhood; the halcyon days that could
never be recaptured.

Nearing her own front gate, great ferny fronds
groped through the fence towards her and caught at her
coat. Karen bent down and broke off a few with her
hand. Despite all her efforts the garden was getting too
much for her. She could cope with the lawns, but the
long-established flower beds were beyond her. She
shifted her gaze to the rambling old house, almost a
mansion. A light shone dimly through the living room
curtains. The house was getting too much for her. It
was too big, too lonely, but at least it was hers. She had
high rates but no rent to worry about. Even so, the next

few years would be a battle to make ends meet. She braced her slender shoulders, warding off a sudden burst of depression. She was tired, that was it. Wednesday was always a long tiring day with a straight run of dull pupils and theory classes after school. Responsibilities always seemed more overwhelming when one was tired. Characteristically she bega to hum quietly under her breath, fighting off the plague of doubts and self-recriminations that seemed to close in with the dusk.

The front door of the house opened and a boy of about ten careered down the stairs. Karen's face changed as she watched his swift flight, and an imperturbable gaiety spread over her lovely mouth. Philip was a handsome child with dark hair and dark eyes, his skin a clear olive. She dropped her music case and heavy shopping bag prepared for the high-spirited launch he made at her.

"Karo! Karo, guess what? I've busted my knee again, would you believe it?"

His sister looked down at him, the lovely gaiety still on her mouth. "I would, and you'll survive, my pet. Did you put any disinfectant on it?"

Philip nodded his head matter-of-factly. "Sure. But you should see the dents in the bike. I don't know how I'll ever get them out."

Karen clicked her tongue in commiseration and the two of them walked up the steps, flanked by stone jars overflowing with massed *Alba Magna* azaleas. Their arms were entwined, their dark heads together. They were very close. It had always been so. Even before their mother had died Karen had been everything to her small brother—mother, sister, brother, confidante. Eva Hartmann had spent the last eight years of her life mysteriously an invalid, a strange and bitter woman with an impenetrable protective veneer, aloof from her own children, obsessed with the past, obsessed with the Ambers, her own wealthy clan and the family who had contrived in so many ways to ruin her husband.

As a very young girl Karen had suffered recurrent

nightmares from her mother's tales of Amber mis-
deeds and machinations. The expression on that once
beautiful face still disturbed her dreams; the expression
Karen came later to recognise as a deep and implacable
hatred.

One of the few legacies Karen had of the past eight
years was a courageous independence of thought and
spirit, an aspect of her character that was fostered by
nature, and strengthened by the events and environment of her life.

Inside the house the hall light was blazing. The letter
was there again! Karen picked it up carefully, her hands
trembling. She glanced down at Philip.

"Go and wash your hands and set the table for tea."

He looked at her patiently, his dark eyes alerted.
"I've already done that, Karo. What's in the letter?"
He searched his sister's pale face. Her skin gleamed
opalescent under the bright light.

"Start on your homework, then," she murmured ab-
stractedly, her eyes already on the typewritten page, the
huge cheque that accompanied it. She separated them
uneasily while Philip went off, unprotesting without
trying to divert or offer comfort. He was already something of a philosopher. Karen was worried. He could
always read the signs, but she was not prone to airing
her worries. He would start on his homework. Besides,
every term he seemed to get more of it.

His sister walked into the living room, gazing down
at the letter. The house seemed very still around her,
almost as though it were listening. So they wanted
them. The almighty Ambers! Her eyes moved down
the page to the black forceful signature, as distinctive
and vigorous as its well-remembered owner—GUY
AMBER.

Lessons painfully learnt are forever remembered!
Karen lifted her dark head, her great tawny eyes flashing like topazes in the light. No wonder her mother had

hated him. What an insufferable style he had, though the technique was flawless, almost surgical in its clean sweeping thrusts. She could almost applaud his easy, positive assumption that she would fall in with his wishes. Her soft mouth held a sobering maturity. No, not wishes, precisely—commands. That was it. Commands, and he was a man long used to giving them.

So the great Guy Amber had come forward to look after the orphans. Eight long years later he would look after the orphans. He would take care of Pip's education. Philip was, after all, an Amber. He would go into the family business. Perhaps take his father's place... never!

The thoughts in her mind were clear, clear and cold and precise. Karen screwed up the sheet of paper with a single convulsive movement and pitched it into the fireplace with stunning accuracy, her young, almost breakable body taut with fiery disdain.

She would look after Philip. She always would, for as long as he needed her. She was nineteen, not ninety, and she was earning a good salary—her Conservatorium diploma saw to that. She was already assistant music mistress at St. Hilda's, the exclusive girls' school where she was once a pupil. All those years of study had paid off.

Her mother had kept her hard at it, though she derived no great pleasure from her daughter's accomplishment—"A necessary investment"—Eva Hartmann had called it as she paid out the high fees. Karen's undeniable gift, an inheritance from her father, had done the rest. Karen's eyes swung round the living room, fixing details. It was a beautiful room really, faded but still beautiful. A woman's room, highly individual, with each piece carefully selected by her mother. It still held her essence. There was no lingering trace of their dear dead father, no element of masculine intrusion, save the piano. Only the piano remained to remind the children of their father.

Stephen Hartmann had been a highly gifted pianist.
The piano, a six-foot concert grand, had been his own
cherished possession.

The French Impressionist paintings that shimmered
from the walls were her mother's favourites and over
the piano hung a fine Dégas print, so deeply familiar
to her from long hours of staring at it, the little dancing
girl's tutu caught in a halo of light. Even the books
were her mother's—a whole wall of them, beautifully
jacketed, with separate niches for display pieces of porcelain and china, crystal and ivory, coloured glass objects that winked in the light.

Karen's eyes came back to the piano, open as usual,
her music scattered helter-skelter all over the top from
the morning's frantic search for a Debussy *Arabesque*.
How often in the past when she practised had she
looked up to find her mother's eyes fixed on her...on
the piano; seeing and unseeing, her expression fixed,
her fine dark eyes clouded with remembrances.

Ever sensitive to her mother's moods, Karen had
only once broached the subject of her father. Then her
mother's taut answer, the queer tone she had used,
made Karen forever back away from the subject: "We
won't speak of your father, Karen. For me, at least, it's
a kind of peace without him."

Karen had never forgotten it—had she allowed herself to dwell on it, never forgiven it. Her father had
been very dear to her. She was, after all, made in his
image. To have lived all her life so close to her mother
and then to discover in one painful instant that she
really didn't know her at all came as a shattering realisation, part of the disillusionment of growing up. Something dreadful had happened to Eva Hartmann, but
when or how it had happened Karen had been too
young to tell. It was impossible to pinpoint the exact
period of time, though she had gone over and over it.

One thing was certain, the Ambers were up to their

necks in it. On their shoulders lay a great measure of the blame for Eva Hartmann's disenchantment, the great ache that gnawed away her fragile bones. Only with approaching maturity did Karen come to glimpse the exquisite pleasure her mother derived from her suffering, the implacable bitterness she wore like a shield. Her death was a shock, complete and absolute, but after the first rush of grief came a sense of release, a lightening of the burden that Eva Hartmann had knowingly or unknowingly conferred on her children.

Abruptly, Karen came out of her reverie. She hurried out of the room and ran up the stairs to her bedroom. The white bobbles on the high canopy danced as she threw her coat down on the bed. She pulled her dress over her head and reached into the wardrobe for her slacks and a sweater. It would only take ten minutes to heat the casserole through. She was a clever and capable young woman, but she thought little of her own varied talents. She hadn't the time. The days and nights spun by endlessly, none of them free from some form of anxiety.

Inevitably, her eye fell on an early framed portrait of her mother and father, and she checked in her stride to look down at it. Two handsome young people gazed back at her; her mother looking directly at the camera, her face, despite the outdated hairstyle, striking, imperious even; her father looking slightly past the camera, both of them caught at a high point in their lives, eyes and mouth smiling, happy and confident, facing the future with the assured arrogance of the young and secure. And they had been secure—then.

Her father's family, the Hartmanns, had been among the colony's earliest pioneers of the vine with a small but excellent vineyard and winery, and her mother's family—the Ambers, then a big wine-making firm, now controlled twenty of the finest vineyards in three States and a great trading company.

A merger between the two families had been inevitable. The Hartmann vineyards adjoined the Amber estates. It was only a matter of time before they swallowed them up. Stephen Hartmann played right into Amber hands. His land was ripe for the taking. In a major industry of the country, the small vigneron had a poor chance of survival. It was regrettable but certainly inevitable.

Of course as "family" he was given a place on the board and an excellent salary, but this was the artistic temperament. He was no tycoon. The Ambers were the tycoons: Luke, and his two sons, Richard and Guy. Richard, the elder, was killed when his horse fell and rolled on him on his father-in-law's property. The news, so sudden and tragic, heralded his father's massive stroke, though Luke Amber hovered on for several months between life and death before finally relinquishing his slender hold on life. After that, Guy Amber reigned supreme, second to no one, a position calling for courage, initiative and strong will. He possessed more than enough of all three. From all accounts, a man without a chink in his armour; a brilliant and successful business man, high-charged and ruthless, a ravening wolf that ate up timid little sheep.

But tragedy was not done with the Ambers. It ran its full cycle, striking in threes. Within a year Stephen Hartmann was killed, his death giving spate to a series of newspaper articles on the wealth and misfortunes of the Amber clan. The facts were printed, a few theories advanced. There had been a party at Belle Amber, which Stephen and Eva Hartmann had attended as a matter of course. They left early for a reason no two guests seemed able to agree upon. Yes, there had been some slight dissension, but certainly no blazing row. But no one, not even her mother, had known what was in Stephen Hartmann's mind when he piled up his silver grey sports car less than four miles from the house. The evening that had started out so brilliantly had ended literally and horribly—in a crash. Stephen had been killed instantly, his wife thrown clear, suffering multiple minor injuries.

Arguments were forgotten, and young as she was Karen had been aware of them. The family crowded around the bereaved widow, her two bewildered young children: Guy Amber and his sister, Patricia, almost desperately unhappy; Aunt Patricia, the children called her, though she was really their mother's cousin. Mark Amber, Luke Amber's only brother; Aunt Celia, Richard's widow, with her two children, Rikki and Liane. The uncles and the aunts and the cousins, all Amber shareholders and wonderfully eager to lend their wealth and support. Their mother had rejected them. With the ruthlessness and abandon of grief Eva Hartmann had cut herself off from her family, living out her life a bitter recluse. Karen's memories of her mother were based more on wishful thinking than reality, but her memories of her father were sweet. She stared down at his lean, handsome face, her dear father who had gone out of her life so quickly, so tragically. Something about his eyes gave her the feeling she was looking into a mirror. They were so much like her own, the same golden colour, slightly tilted under winging brows. His thick black hair was hers, the set of his head, the same cool elegance of bone structure.

It was then Karen knew a moment of sheer desperation. Her father had been such a champion of the young Guy Amber. He had liked and admired him, constantly applauded his extraordinary business acumen, far more pronounced than that of his tragic elder brother. Could Stephen Hartmann have been such a poor judge of character? Could she and Philip be the victims of their mother's warped judgment? Instantly Karen refuted the thought, and loyalty to her mother swung back like the tide. No, it couldn't be so! The letters proved it. Guy Amber was the black-hearted villain she had always thought him. His image flashed be-

fore her eyes and her anger subsided like a pricked
bubble. No, not always. Once in her childhood, he had
been a sort of demi-god to her, with an aura of brilliance and sophistication. In those days he had fascinated her, though she had been careful to steer clear of
him, for he was a merciless tease, fond of pulling her
hair and calling her "cat's eyes".

She was torn between weeping and the desire to hate
him. Memories one after the other thrust their way up
from her subconscious and the past sprang to life again.

She was back at Belle Amber; the colour and shape
of her existence, the most beautiful place on earth to
her. Where the great vineyards stopped there was the
house, white and enormous under its great curving
roof, glowing with pride in its beauty and bounty. She
had no resistance against the onslaught of its remembered fascination, and warmth flooded through her like
a hot sun through the vineyards.

Once, every weekend, every school vacation had
been spent at Belle Amber. All the children loved it—
Karen and Rikki, Liane and Pip, the baby. How well
she remembered the excitement at vintage time when
visitors like pilgrims descended on the famous old
show-place, eager to be initiated into the delights of the
vintage; the ritual and the magic that attended the occasion—the right approach to good wine, her father had
called it. In her mind's eye she could still see him, laz-
ing back nonchalantly, his lean body relaxed watching
the visitors holding their wine glasses, peering and
frowning, gyrating the wine around, some of them
spilling it, the experts taking great thirsty gulps of it,
the novices sipping, some smiling knowingly at some
dazzling revelation, others full of fanciful descriptions
that made his long mouth twist in a smile. Often he
turned to Aunt Patricia with a quick witty comment,
waiting for her answering smile; a smile that brought
into play the most fascinating dimple at the side of her
mouth.

Her mother never cared for showing visitors around and always avoided it by staying up at the house. Aunt Patricia loved it. So did her father and so did the children, ever eager to show off their knowledge, formidable enough for mere children. Even Guy Amber thought nothing of carrying a few flagons of Amber red out to a waiting car, his manner was charming and natural as any visitor could wish for.

Karen stood, faintly smiling, her thoughts turned inwards. In her fancy she could smell the odours of sweetness that emerged from the cellars; of fruit and soft oils and delicate ethers; acid smells and bitter smells, the sickly smell of fermenting juice, the vigorous bubbling and gurgling in the wax-lined concrete tanks, thickly capped with skins, pips and stalks—The Amber dry reds, the straight Cabernet Sauvignon, a wonderfully delicate table wine, made only in small quantities when conditions were favourable, and the more "forward" Shiraz-Cabernet, a "big" red, full bodied and fruity, but still retaining the distinctive Cabernet "nose"...

Philip had to call three times before Karen heard him. The thread of remembrance was snapped. She ran to the door, calling with sisterly conscientiousness— "Coming, pet, it'll only take a few minutes to heat up the casserole."

Two evenings later when Philip was long settled and Karen was busy correcting theory papers, the phone jangled. Karen put a paperweight over her work and went to answer it.

"Hello, Karen?" A woman's voice, clear and well modulated, came over the wires, a voice not entirely strange to her.

Karen answered politely. "Yes, Karen Hartmann speaking. Who is that?"

The mysterious, unidentifiable voice gave a slight husky laugh, one might have thought emotion-laden.

"Patricia Amber, my dear. Surely you remember me, Karen?"

"You have the wrong number, I'm sorry," Karen said with shocked disbelief, and hung up. The telephone rang again immediately, but she felt too depressed to answer it. Gently she took the receiver off the hook. It was no friend after all, she thought with a pang of regret. Meanwhile she was wasting time. She moved back into the living room. She had at least ten more papers to correct. As a teacher, at least, she thought rather sadly, she was successful. The overall standard was high.

She sat down again, to be startled twenty minutes later by the door chimes, shivering through the silence. Her head jerked up. There was no need for alarm; there was a chain on the door. She went to answer it, not even pausing to smooth back her dark, tumbled hair.

A man stood on the threshold; thirty-five or thereabouts—a tall, powerfully built man, but lean. A man there was no question of passing unnoticed, for he had a kind of dark splendour on him; the nose straight and classic, the cheek and jawline angular, too strong for easy good looks. Power and self-assurance seemed to flow from him and showed itself in the set of his head, and his shoulders, even more in the alive intelligence of his face, the alert and brilliant dark eyes. Karen almost recoiled in astonishment, her breath coming jaggedly. All her life, whatever else she forgot she would always remember this man. His eyes glittered over her. She felt the jolt of their impact right through her body.

"What the devil do you mean by hanging up on Patricia? You upset her dreadfully." His deep, arrogant voice almost struck at her physically, as compelling as a hidden current. "Open the door, Karen. I must speak to you." His tone was urgent, but there was nothing welcoming about his appearance, she thought bleakly. Those black brows and high cheekbones portrayed an alien, rather inhuman quality.

Her heart gave a great lunge and antagonism raced in her blood.

"How dare you come here!" she burst out passionately, her emotions ravaged to the point where she thought she couldn't stand it. "This is my home and no Amber will ever set foot in it. There's no magic formula to wash away the years... the tears that have been shed for you. Please go away. There's nothing to say. How could you think otherwise?"

His tone was impersonal. There was an ironic aloofness to the twist of his mouth.

"I see the blood line hasn't weakened over the years. Eva speaks through her daughter. Open this door, child. I'm not prepared to lay myself out on your doorstep." His eyes flickered over her stricken young face and his voice underwent a distinct change, became subtly insistent, easing the tone of authority. She almost gave him an "A" for adjustment.

"Please hear me out, Karen. I only want to help you, though you've been well taught to loathe and resent me."

Karen shivered on a great wave of helplessness. The quiet, level tone had more authority than a shout. He was so very smooth, so convincing, she knew it would be futile, even undignified to put up a further show of resistance. He was a man quick to rouse and she knew without question that his temper would be something to watch. It was too much! too much! too much!

She shot back the lock and he was through the door as swiftly as any hunter, towering above her. She was trapped, with the momentary impression of a magnificent black panther absolved from the ordinary rules and customs. The light shone down on his raven head. His dark eyes pinned her gaze.

"You haven't changed. You're like Stephen... to look at! You have his eyes, his bone structure, his good looks distilled. One day you'll be beautiful." His brilliant dark gaze shifted. "Let's go in, Karen. I've things to discuss with you." He held out his hand and with the force of her outraged emotions Karen retreated from him, avoiding contact. The woman was born in her, fully formed and ready to fight him, even if it proved fatal.

He was unused to opposition of any kind. His steely grip encircled her wrist as he stopped her retreat. She had the frightening sensation that anything Guy Amber wanted he would never let go of. His voice almost crackled with impatience as he gazed down at her tumbled dark head.

"Don't be afraid, Karen. I'd never hurt you!"

"I'm *not* afraid!" she muttered fiercely, looking him over deliberately with the same piercing appraisal he had bestowed on her.

He looked down into her over-bright eyes, observing every small detail of her upturned face.

"No, damn it, I don't believe fear comes easily to you. So much the better for both of us. In here, then, you colourful child." He drew her into the living room as though she and the house were already his chattels, then gave her a slight push into an armchair and sat down opposite her, his eyes not ungentle, but piercingly intent.

"Now, let's try to clear up all these distortions and confusions that are troubling you. Why did you never answer my letters? Surely common courtesy hasn't gone out of style?"

She gave a short, jerky laugh, gripping the arms of her chair.

"Oh, really, this is insufferable! You force your way in here...into my home. Surely you weren't planning on an effusive chat? It's been so long and all that... Well, let me tell you you've materialised a little too suddenly for my comfort. There's no kindness or sentiment in you, only a devilish cunning. You're hard and unyielding, a real Machiavelli, with an ominous face and black brows drawn, and I just know you could be violent and wild given the chance." Tension and excitement curved about her like a bright banner.

His voice cut across hers with the incredibly quiet command.

"Stop all that fanciful nonsense and get a hold on yourself, child. You're becoming over-emotional." There was a hint of real concern in his searching dark eyes. "For once in your young life, listen to fact and not preconceived notions. This is painful, I know, but it can't be glossed over. The old days are past. Your mother has gone. Eva was the victim of her own difficult nature. She was a bitter, unhappy woman who punished herself and punished us all in the process. She would never allow us to see you, you and Philip. You must remember how much the family loved both of you. She cut you out of our lives, yet she had no qualms about taking the money I sent her."

His words were a bright lick of flame towards dynamite. They exploded in her ears, sharp and vivid as lightning. She sprang at him then, the hectic colour staining her cheekbones. He came to his feet precipitately at the sight of her slight flying body, catching her under both elbows, and she felt the steely strength of his fingers through her thin sweater, a curious throbbing where his hands touched her.

"You're lying!" she blazed up at him, her face vivid with outraged pride. "I simply don't believe you. Mother would never take money from you. Not money ... not anything. I know. We've had to struggle for years, I tell you."

His dark face was formidable, a muscle moved tautly along his jawline. "I never lie, little one. There was no struggle, believe me."

Her heart thumped erratically, as though it could not contain itself within the confines of her body. He was too tall, too powerful, too able to reduce to nonsense her most deeply rooted opinions.

"You're the enemy, I know," she said coldly, "but you'll never daunt me. I'll be no pawn in your power game. My mother *was* a bitter, unhappy woman, I know that. She was weighed down with grief and regrets. She lived out her life withdrawn from society, but she carried her own burden, isolated from her family—a family she could no longer trust. I have the same pride, the same sense of dignity, and I absolutely demand my own privacy.''

He studied her for a long moment, faintly intrigued as though she was something quite unique in his experience. When he spoke his voice was almost indulgent.

"I can see you believe in taking the devil by his horns as though there were no other way.''

"There *is* no other way,'' she burst out impetuously. "Surely you can see that? You're a business man. Cut your losses. You'll gain nothing from me, though you'll do anything to achieve your purpose. Lie about it if you have to, as you've done in the past!''

A strange expression flared in his brilliant dark eyes.

"What an insolent child you are, Karen. The prospect of taking you in hand begins to appeal to me.''

She wore a soft, ironic smile. "I make no apology for saying what I think.''

"You'll find I'm without apology either.'' His hands tightened on her experimentally. "Just remember, my little firebrand, hot tempers are a characteristic of the Ambers, so our skirmishes won't be always this one-sided.''

Her response was commendably cool for a young girl. She moved back and away from him, curling up in an armchair, her expression brightening with triumph.

"Perhaps not. But I'll always fall outside your circle of influence. Being a male and an Amber you won't recognise it, I know, but it's a fact all the same, an unshakable fact of nature.''

She looked very young and very graceful against the gold velvet of the old wing-backed chair. A smile, white and transforming, crossed his sombre dark face.

"And what would you know about 'unshakable facts of nature' my little innocent—and you *are* an innocent, for all the exotic tilt to your eyebrows. The closest you've ever come to nature is a school project, by the look of you. You've never in your life seen a man as an individual, only as a symbol. Right now, I'm the symbol of tyranny in your young life, the hateful Guy Amber, the villain in a melodrama. Well, let's make a bargain, my stubborn young relative. I'll allow you to go your way entirely at Belle Amber, of course, if you'll allow me to do my best for Philip. As I remember, he's *all* Amber.''

"He has the family cast of features, if that's what you mean," she said cuttingly. "But thank God, that's as far as it goes."

"Karen, Karen!" He gave a mocking sigh, his hand slowly clenching. "Young as you are, you almost demolish me. Quite an accomplishment! Now listen, you temperamental young woman. However well you've been brainwashed, it can't all be true. Surely you've collected a few facts along the line? It just can't all be true. My sister Patricia is a wonderful woman. You must remember her. You were very fond of her when you were a child. Even if you would never come near me. I remember very well a ponytailed little brat with great golden irises, the exact colour of cognac." He was smiling at her in the old remembered way, his beautiful dark eyebrows arching.

She looked at him strangely, swinging to hide a sharp deep breath.

"Don't turn away from me, now, Karen," he said softly.

The colour drained from her ivory skin. He was too strong for her, his brand of charm too compelling. His speaking voice was very beautiful and her musical ear was fast succumbing to its dark velvet tones. No doubt he found it an invaluable aid in his big business ventures.

He studied her profile, then leant over and picked up her wrist, turning her hand over to examine her slender, oval-tipped fingers.

"Your hands have a strange vitality to them," he murmured, "almost as though they had a life of their own. You use them so much when you speak. Stephen used to do that." Abruptly his voice recaptured its usual pitch. "Don't waste your life for a shadow, Karen. I want to look after you, you and young Philip. I've always wanted to, though I don't expect you to believe me right now. You've been conditioned to hate me in your formative years."

A deep flush swept up from her throat. He was too near the mark. His lean, long-fingered hands against her skin were sending warning signals to her brain. The queerest sensation like excitement threatened to catch her up in a vice. It was making itself felt throughout her whole body. She knew with finality that he was the most sensual man she would ever be likely to meet.

Her pride made her cry out in resistance. "But I do hate you, there's no question about that, and you're only seeing the tip of the iceberg. There are fiercer, deeper resentments I'm hiding."

His face changed subtly.

"You're not meant to hate, little one. Not with your eyes and mouth." He released her hand lightly. "You know in your heart that you and Philip need my protection. You're only a young girl, alone, trying to rear a small boy. Even if I take care of all your expenses it's still not enough." His eyes swung about the mellowed beauty of the room. The light fell along his dark profile, remote and strongly aquiline. He had the look of a man deep in reverie, the dark head arrogant, the mouth sensuously beautiful, somehow conveying an impression of faint sardonic amusement. Yet there was a suggestion of something completely devoid of amusement about him as though the face could contain, at one and the same time, two powerful conflicting forces. It was, Karen concluded almost fearfully, an unforgettable face.

His voice jarred her out of her dream world.

"You must play for me," he said quietly, almost under his breath, his eyes on the gleaming Steinway.

"You assume rather a lot, don't you?" she made her voice sound light and amused. "I never said

I *could* play. That was my father's piano, remember?"

His dark eyes came back to her, narrowing.

"*You* play," he said with quiet emphasis. He took in her young classically oval face, ivory and intense with the promise of great beauty. His eyes fastened on her full, deeply moulded mouth, trembling with barely concealed emotion. "Strange how sadness points up beauty," he said almost musingly. "There's a great deal of hurt and a great deal of tenderness in those great golden eyes. But you're only awaiting a touch spark of some challenge to burst into flame. Do you realise it, I wonder?" He used a tone that implied a certain tenderness and Karen moved restlessly, frightened and wary of his easy mastery.

She had no wish to respond to such provocation, so she withdrew from it. She swung her eyes away from him, deliberately fixing her attention on a curtain that swayed erratically on the night breeze. He seemed to be making a conscious effort to taunt and tantalise her. She hadn't the experience to cope with it.

He looked at her for a long moment, her dark eyes unfathomable, noting the expression on her young face at once moody and sad. Abruptly his voice picked up.

"Now how long will it take you to finalise things here, Karen? Your job, etc. I'll arrange the sale of the house. It's in need of attention, but it's a beautiful old place and the site is excellent. I'll have no bother at all disposing of it and it should bring you in a nice little independence. Send the piano on when you're ready, and I'll settle the account at the other end. Have it tuned before you arrive."

All at once Karen felt the tears threatening. It was the final humiliation. All her old feeling for him, for Belle Amber crystallised into an intense longing and need. But it had to be denied. The words bubbled painfully, desperately, to the surface.

"I can't possibly agree. It's all wrong, I tell you. Mother would turn in her grave. If you knew... Mother... the Ambers... I can't bear all your convincing diplomacy. It's too studied, too dangerous." She broke off half chokingly and found herself in his arms. Her head found the curve of his shoulder and her body quivered pathetically against his lean, powerful frame. Suddenly she knew the most overwhelming compulsion to draw strength from this hard, vital man. All the world spun around in a circle with the two of them its pulsating centre. The silence was so complete it rang in her ears. Gradually, awareness closed in on her, the almost relentless magnetism that was emanating from him. She pulled away frantically, biting hard on her underlip, She tasted blood in her mouth and came to her senses.

"I'm sorry," she said curtly, sounding just the opposite.

His mouth compressed slightly.

"There's no need to apologise, though that's the first time I've ever been able to endure a weeping woman. But you're not a woman yet, are you? Just a girl-into-woman—a dangerous combination." He swivelled her to face him again. "Don't fight me, little one. Not now, not ever. I'll always look after you if only you'll let me. Think of Philip even if you deny your own right to security and happiness. Philip, I remember, used to love Belle Amber though he was only a baby. It's part of his heritage, after all."

"But surely you're married...have children. You used to be so..."

"Sought after?" he supplied, his hard mouth ironic. "I still have my moments, little one, but I can't say I've ever met the woman to hold my attention...for as long as it's necessary, anyway." His dark eyes were worldly and glittering. "We may never be exactly *simpatico*, but at least give me your promise of loyalty."

"I give it where it's due," she said cuttingly. A fierce sort of tautness held her immobile. She was fully prepared for this moment. It had been a long time coming.

Harsh sardonic humour leapt in his eyes.

"How you do play havoc with my ego, child! I can see I'll have to move warily."

"At least it's nice to know you *do* have a weakness," she countered smoothly. "You seem so incredibly steely. I take heart from it."

His hand closed over the tender slope of her shoulder.

"I was thinking of finding you some nice young man to cope with your humours, but I can see that would never do. I'm not at all sure a nice young man would survive that débâcle. You definitely need a master."

Some instinct made her shake herself free of him, angered and confused by her response to physical contact.

"I think not," she said hardily. "That kind of man would only meet with unrelenting resistance."

His eyes, long-fringed, gleamed with cool speculation.

"Do you think so? You look extraordinarily young and tormented at the moment, as though opposing forces were conspiring to tear you apart. You're going to take life hard, little one. That's why I want to be around."

She looked up at him, her black brows arching, her white skin curiously incandescent under the light.

"To give a devil his due, you do know how to manage your affairs. You almost have me persuaded. But then your voice is a powerful weapon, as I'm sure you've been told by that train of inadequate ladies who failed to hold your attention. Philip as a potential heir is a nice touch, too."

His eyes deepened to jet and a sudden menace glittered in them.

"Don't tempt hell fire, little one. I'll take just so much from you."

She didn't move her great golden eyes from his face. "Why the sudden flare-up?" she mocked him silkily. "Surely you've been insulted before?"

"By experts," he drawled, his eyes on the tell-tale pulse, that beat in her throat, "among whom I wouldn't concede you a chance."

"I've managed up until now," she managed with an air of youthful bravado, the colour flaring in her cheeks.

"That might change at any moment." His hard mouth relaxed. "Don't trade too hard on your sex, little one. Try to handle its privileges discreetly."

"To please whom?" she retorted swiftly.

"Me!" His dark eyes were amused. "It would be a step in the right direction." His eyes flickered over her tempestuous young face. "With the right clothes, the right make-up, that dark mane of yours under control, you'll be quite an acquisition to the family, a rather exotic sophisticate."

Surprise jerked her to a standstill.

"Have you ever contemplated a course of action that excluded personal gain?"

He flicked a hand to her cheekbones, his eyes deep as rapids.

"You defeat me entirely, child. It's a new experience. But let's sink our differences, if only for Philip's sake. He needs a man's hand, a man's discipline, not so much now but in a year or two. Make your break and return to Belle Amber. I promise not to stamp out all that marvellous fire."

Her lashes were heavy crescents on her cheek.

"I'm sorry. You make it sound very enticing, but I can't answer. I need time. I can't adjust so rapidly." Already with a sick heart Karen knew she was weakening. To pledge her loyalty to the Ambers would be to turn her back on the past. Yet how could she subdue this overwhelming sense of guilt, though her mother was no longer there to be distressed and affected by it? She felt suddenly as if she were a child with a child's ideas of right and wrong, rigidly separated. But nothing was so clear cut as that: there were always the fine shadings, the blurred edges. Grand gestures had a habit of turning self-defeating. Her mother had virtually destroyed herself with her implacable attitude.

He was quick to see the confusion of thought in her face.

"Don't think too deeply about things, Karen. It's an exhausting sport at the best of times. Right now you're suffering from a first reaction. Tomorrow you'll be over the crisis, adjusted to the idea. Then one day when you're in a more receptive mood I'll try to explain what really broke up our two families. Family quarrels are the worst quarrels of all, but you're not ready to hear about it yet." His voice ran on, disarming as a lullaby. "You can be as independent as you like. It's your nature, I can see that, but not for twenty-four hours a day, my child. It's too much, and you're only a girl. I want to look after you. Perhaps we're two of a mould. If we are it's in the logic of things that we should pull together. It would make a certain kind of sense from all the chaos. Come back to Belle Amber, Karen. It's even more beautiful than you remember."

She raised her faintly tip-tilted eyes to him with almost drugged acceptance, conscious of the frightening pleasure his presence gave her. But his attractions were not to be trusted.

"I'll come," she said quickly, not giving herself a chance to turn back. "But only for Philip. He deserves a great deal more than I can give him, though I'd try very hard. He's my reason for living, the most important person in the world to me."

His gaze swept over her, strangely insistent. "You're so young," he said almost wearily, his dark face taciturn. He moved swiftly, then drawing her with him to the front door. He paused with his hand on the polished knob looking down at her. "Don't keep me waiting, Karen. It's already been far too long!"

For an instant she looked up at him, caught into a moment of deep familiarity. His face had haunted her for so long and now he was here in front of her. He took her hand, his fingers tightening a little.

"You have to win in the end, don't you?" she said softly, the irony creeping back into her tone. "It's not very fair!"

"Life is never very fair, Karen," he said, looking directly into her eyes. "But couldn't you be honest for once, little one, and admit you're winning too?"

A sudden warmth sparked in her cheeks and her heart flipped half crazily. How frightening he was! Yet weren't all exciting people rather frightening? She was sure her jumble of emotions must show in her face.

"I think we'll be able to tolerate one another," he said lazily, his mouth curving.

"In small doses," she amended, and slanted a smile at him, her hand making a charming and provocative little gesture. Some force in her went rushing out to meet him compulsively, elementally, trapped in the quicksand of his strange fascination. Always imaginative, she couldn't suppress the strangest conviction that she was being guided in an inexplicable manner towards her destiny, some very queer intention of fate that brought Guy Amber back into her life again. The moment spun out, snatched out of time and fraught with significance.

His eyes shifted to the lovely curve of her mouth.

"No, a nice young man won't do at all, Karen," he said briefly, then opened the door and walked down into the night, one hand raised in a parting salute.

Karen stood for a long moment looking after him. She felt a stranger, even to herself, with a calm she could not understand, almost complete in itself. The garden was a blue-black jungle after the blazing shimmer of the house, and the air had a special sweet freshness of a cool night with an expected overnight shower. Against the white fence the yellow forsythia's sprays were silvered by moonlight. The magnolia tree in the corner was no more than a dark shadow waiting for springtime. In another month it would be heavy with flowers and fragrance. Even the grass was springing to new life. A solitary willy wagtail let fall five crystal-clear notes like a cascade of broken glass. It was the final touch of magic. The whole world was awakening from a long sleep!

CHAPTER TWO

SPRING had come to Belle Amber. The sun shone gold and benign on the ripening young grapes, line upon line, plunging on the vines, their shiny leaves, healthy and luxuriant, rippling like a vast green sea. Two hundred acres flourished in the foothills, set to the heavy bearing Shiraz and the "shyer" Cabernet Sauvignon, the aristocratic grape of Bordeaux.

The timing of the first green pruning had been perfect, a combination of experience and instinct, and the weather at the spring flowering free from high wind with just sufficient rain to fill out the berries without swelling them—with water, not flavour. All that remained was a spell of hot weather to ripen the grapes and develop the sugars—the potential alcohol. With any luck at all it would be a vintage year.

The great wrought iron gates leading to the house stood open and Guy Amber stopped the car at the entrance. Karen caught her breath, profoundly stirred. The high arch of lacy grillework hung on tall formal pillars and framed a long sweeping driveway, flanked by poplars; poplars that wore the traditional delicate green of spring. Up ahead was the house. Karen was filled with the urgent desire to see it. The man at her side turned to study her profile, her dream-shadowed eyes. He slid his arm along the back of the seat, amused and indulgent at the effect the first sight of the estate was having upon her.

"I can see from your face that Belle Amber is working the same old magic."

Philip's clear young voice piped up on the silence.

"I'll say it is, it's beaut, Uncle Guy! I swear I remember it." He leaned over from the back seat and thrust his dark head between them. "Do you mind if I walk up to the house, Uncle Guy? I've got a cramp in my foot—wouldn't you know it! A bit of a run might fix it."

Guy Amber laughed and swung his arm back to open the door.

"Go right ahead. This is your home now, Pip. I want you to enjoy it. Get to know every inch of it."

"Gee, thanks, Uncle Guy." Philip's young face reflected his liking and admiration for this re-found relative. He dashed out on to the pebbled drive and began banging his foot strenuously a half a dozen times. When his circulation was restored to his satisfaction he gave his sister a quick grin, then ran up ahead, disappearing into the bend of the drive with a backward wave of his hand.

Karen was silent, feeling curiously deserted. An awareness of the man at her side closed in on her thick as a cloud. He smiled at her averted profile.

"I was determined you would see it now when it's so beautiful with the spring flowering. The estate is beautiful at any time, but never quite like this."

She gave him a quick glance, fighting off an inexplicable surge of emotion at this obvious sign of his desire to please her. Illogically she resented it. She let her glance rest on him with cool intent, reflecting that there were three qualities that exactly personified this man: an almost regal assurance, determination and an aura of intense masculinity.

She gave him a swift unpremeditated answer: "Beware the gift that's laid in your hands—the frightening gift of happiness." Her eyes flicked his dark face. "Under that facile charm I sense a certain ruthlessness. Your *words* charm me, but I know I ought to mistrust the man behind them."

He gave a derisive little laugh. "How wonderfully

direct you are, Karen!" The quality of his laugh, amused and forbearing, fired her temper, and indignation made the words come tumbling out.

"Diametrically opposed to you, perhaps. I wonder what category you'd fall into. I'd say you were clever and devious and..." she broke off in alarm, stirred and excited, as one lean hand encircled her throat.

"You were saying?" he inquired pleasantly. "Clever and devious and..." The broad shoulders moved slightly nearer her.

"There are some situations in life one must just accept," she murmured obliquely, a lingering after glow in her cheeks from his touch.

"And this is one of them." He let the seconds tick by, then tapped her cheek lightly.

"It is funny how things work out though, isn't it?" she persisted, not very humorously.

A smile tugged at his mouth. "Funny is hardly the word, Karen. It's utterly amazing."

"And I simply have to rise above it, though it might just prove too much for *you*." Her voice danced over the tension that flared between them.

His dark eyes were coolly confident.

"I never undertake a venture I'm not capable of handling, little one. It might help you to remember it."

Her red, passionate mouth was ironic. "I could hardly fail to, could I? Your voice is loaded with conviction." She sighed elaborately. "It must be wonderful to be so self-assured. Then I imagine you sprang from the cradle fully armoured."

The laugh he sent across to her was sardonic.

"If you're not careful, my little cat, you'll finish with a tongue like carbolic acid."

She had the grace to blush. "Making me therefore a completely undesirable female."

His glance licked over her like a flame. "Did I say that? No, Karen. With a little wisdom, a little maturity you'll draw men like candlelight draws moths."

She moved her shining dark head in denial. "You make that sound an unworthy accomplishment. In any case, you're speaking to a girl only too anxious to avoid trouble."

"And men are trouble?"

"Some men," she murmured under her breath. "There are others, good and kind and generous."

"Good gracious, that sounds like an obituary!" he taunted her lazily.

"You mustn't heed my sense of humour," she said crisply.

His dark eyes gleamed. "For a girl who's anxious to avoid trouble, you seem to court danger as a matter of course. I'd better take the car up the drive, if only to avert another of your haymakers."

She glanced over swiftly at his arrogant dark profile, letting her gaze travel over the casual perfection of his jacket, the elegant cut and beautiful fabric.

He turned his own head, pinning her gaze, and some dark force, some probing light in his eyes held her still. Ashamed and grieved, she recognised her sensuous delight in the sight and the scent of him, the very sound of his beautifully timbred voice. But it was the traitor touch! She dared not raise the curtain on her own blossoming instincts or their implications. Guy Amber was simply a man, handsome and successful, with a sexual radiance that most women would instantly recognise. Once she accepted this self-evident fact she would be able to put it safely out of her head. She took a deep, even breath, pretending a casualness she did not feel. "Anything you say, oh, stern-faced lord of the manor!"

He smiled and leaned forward to switch on the ignition. The engine purred into life and his lean, strong fingers closed around the wheel. The car started and the pebbles crunched and sprayed out from under the tires. They swept up the tree-shaded drive and Karen sat forward a lovely, eager light in her eyes. This was where she belonged! Aware of her rising excitement,

Guy changed gear to let the car cruise gently through vast spreads of sloping lawn that led to a crest. On the crest stood Belle Amber; the dream had materialised and the magic she had counted lost returned.

It rose, up ahead, snow-white and perfect; a colonial mansion built in the early days of settlement by Matthew Amber, a wealthy Englishman, for his French bride, Julienne. When the colony of South Australia was first advertised, Matthew Amber sold up his Californian vineyards and migrated, along with his entire household, to this vast new-found continent. Within a month he had purchased fifty acres in the Adelaide foothills and set the land to the vine. As the years went by he acquired more land, more prestige; planted more vines; made still better wines and devoted himself through a long lifetime to the art of the vigneron. Such was the beginning of the great trading company of Amber Estates Ltd.

Softly Karen held her voice steady under her pounding blood.

"Already I love it...."

"More than yesterday and less than tomorrow." He flicked a glance over her creamy face, at once dreamy and burningly alive. The very curve of her neck spelled enchantment. His voice was almost tender. "Welcome back to Belle Amber, Karen. You look quite different, do you know that? Young and terribly eager, completely untouched by conflict, the way you were meant to look. The way I like you to look."

She could feel her heart beating rapidly. Stop it, she thought. Look away from those dark eyes, the splendid dark head. Unsell your own senses if you have to. It can be done. It has to be done. He's just a fascinating man, older and unattainable. Besides, he wasn't to be trusted. She looked away with a sense of purpose, deliberately veiling her eyes with a faraway look.

"A penny for your thoughts?" he said lightly, then smiled at her flicker of discomfort. "Ten cents, then."

"They're not worth the first offer, I'm afraid."

His dark eyes met hers across the space that divided them.

"Do something for me, Karen. Meet Patricia again without any preconceived notions. Just greet her naturally. She's longing to have you and young Philip. Be kind to her."

She looked over at him, her great eyes reproachful.

"What a strange thing to say to me! Surely you don't imagine I'll play the proud lady. Marie Antoinette condescending to the mob."

He laughed gently. "What a graphic child you are! No, Karen, I didn't mean quite that. But you could be a cruel little cat with someone's heart in your hands."

She withdrew from him visibly. "You do me an injustice. I have no taste for such things, unlike the ladies of your acquaintance."

"Perhaps not, Karen, but we're only at the beginning of rediscovery. Patricia is different...strangely vulnerable. You and Philip will be special to her. If it's any comfort at all to you, you're really needed at Belle Amber."

Her eyes registered every detail of his dominant dark face.

"How clever you are! You've hit on the lure by which we are all irresistibly trapped...to be needed. Just the one phrase—you're needed, Karen."

"And so you are, little one. All you have to do is let time clear up your past impressions. It takes living with people, seeing them involved in the process of day-to-day living, to give them their true dimension."

She looked at him steadily, her topaz eyes gleaming. "We all have a sprinkle of saint and sinner."

He intercepted her line of thought exactly. "Now *you* have the makings of a rather spectacular temper. You should make a formidable old lady."

Karen shook her dark head in denial. "You invest too much meaning in my casual word."

He laughed softly. "Karen, Karen, even you don't believe that. Already you see yourself as a flaming sword between me and all worthy cause."

Suddenly, with a shrug, she yielded.

"Forgive me, Guy," she said slowly, speaking more sweetly than she intended.

His smile was sardonic. "That *Guy* was more potent than wine. I can see you don't play for playing—but for winning."

She shrugged rather helplessly. "We seem to have been having this kind of conversation since we met."

His eyes smiled at her. "You mean we've cut through all the polite preliminaries. One day you'll be quite a woman, Karen!"

"Praise indeed. But in my own mind at least, I'm already a woman." Her tone, young and ardent, settled all arguments.

His handsome face was disbelieving. "Never, child. A woman's not really a woman until she's had a man's arms round her." Instinct made her move back against the seat, her head bent, her cheeks colouring.

"You're far too worldly for me."

"Beyond all question." He smiled at her with elaborate taunting courtesy, making her look away excited and confused. Guy Amber was dangerous with an almost relentless magnetism. The conviction had come and come for keeps.

"Relax, little one," he ordered briefly, "you're as taut as a bowstring."

Obediently Karen rested her head against the plush, expensive-smelling upholstery, releasing her pent-up breath.

As they drew abreast of the house Guy veered to the right where an enormous four-car garage presented three closed doors and a yawning black maw. As they eased into the garage she had the clear impression of orderly kept tools and gardening equipment and a long low sports car wedged between two much bigger cars.

Guy opened the door and came round for her, taking her elbow. They walked from the garage around towards the front of the house and mounted the wide shallow steps to the colonnaded porch that ran the entire length of the two-storied central wing.

Through the open entrance hall Karen glimpsed the patina of lustrous veneer, the gleaming parquet floor and the beautiful curving stairway that sprang up from the centre of the hall and wound its way into the upper storey. From the high-flung plastered ceiling hung a great chandelier dripping crystals that made ghostly music in the breeze.

Karen was aware of her own mounting tension and tried to relax it. Unconsciously she moved closer to Guy Amber, who encircled her wrist imposing on her the lightest restraint.

"You're poised to spring like a doe in the forest, Karen. Relax. I promise you this will be easy."

She suppressed her half-formed wish to flee.

"Now I'm here I dread it as much as I desire it."

"Hush now!" he held her still.

Even as he spoke a woman emerged from the interior of the house, hurrying towards them with swinging grace. She came on swiftly, smiling as she came.

"Karen!" her voice made Karen's name a sound of purest delight. Trembling slightly with a jumble of emotions, Karen stared at her, seeing a tall, over-slender woman in her early forties with the ageless kind of beauty on her, and whose strong physical resemblance to Guy Amber instantly proclaimed her his sister—Patricia Amber.

Instantly Karen's mind was stormed with scenes from her childhood; scenes in which this woman had played so large a part. The dark, luminous eyes were fixed on her face, seemingly trying to look into her very heart. Patricia Amber, the faintly sinister, illusory figure of the past eight years, existed no longer. She had not the remotest connections with this dark-haired,

graceful woman who wore charm and humour and
great personal dignity like a cloak.

She stood holding out her hand and for a second
Karen hesitated, then her instincts took over from her.
She was impelled forward and found herself caught in a
warm embrace, betrayed into a depth of response she
found herself helpless to conceal. The dark eyes that
looked back at her were blurred with emotion.

Patricia Amber stood back a little, surveying her
young relative with sparkling, totally approving eyes.
"Why, Karen darling, didn't I always say you would be
beautiful, and you're so like..." she took a deep steadying breath, half laughing, half crying, "so like..."

"Stephen!" Guy Amber intervened gently, putting a
hand on his sister's shoulder.

She brushed her cheek against it, drawing comfort
from his touch, so it seemed to Karen. The dark eyes
were glistening. "Pip has just rushed out after Uncle
Mark. He wants one good look at the vineyard to be
sure he's not dreaming. They'll be back shortly. I'm so
grateful Guy was able to persuade you to come back to
us, Karen."

Karen tilted her head, her eyes narrowing. "I don't
suppose it occurred to Guy for one moment that he
wouldn't succeed. He seems to be confident as few
men are confident that he always gets his way."

"It's only a front, little one," Guy replied smoothly,
though his eyes gleamed through their thick dark
lashes. His sister caught hold of Karen's hand to draw
her into the house.

"Come in, dear. I've so much to show you. We've
had a whole suite redecorated for you, with Pip close
by. I do want you to be happy here."

In the living room masses of fresh flowers were
everywhere, conveying a deep sweet sense of home-
coming. Dark polished wood contrasted with the ice
blue sheen of damask-covered walls, while tall windows hung with a matching brocade, sent patterns of

light over beautiful needlepoint rugs, velvet and silk upholstered pieces of mahogany and rosewood, and two beautiful Chippendale sofas. The whole effect was of elegance and a muted liveable beauty as though it had always been like that. And indeed it seemed to Karen as though nothing had changed. Paintings hung on the wall, expertly placed to enhance their colour and quality; landscapes, genre paintings, all very valuable, and an excellent portrait of old Matthew Amber. Karen felt a thrill of pride in that remarkable old face, with its strong angular cheekbones, the piercing dark eyes and silvery mane. It was a remarkable face, full of character and a splendid life force. He looked what he was: a man of vision with the practical qualities to make the vision a reality.

Karen's eyes swept on round the room with increasing pleasure. Objects both striking and delicate were strewn around the room like so many jewels adorning low tables and chests, and lending warmth and personality—the intimate touch—to the great formal room.

Patricia Amber followed her eyes, smiling. "Everything beautiful is made of a mixture, so Plato tells us. As a family I think we've followed the idea through. We're all of us addicted to our 'pieces'. By the way, dear, Celia and Liane will be home Friday evening. Liane has just got herself engaged, but I'll let her tell you all about it. Rikki is here, of course. He's not as strong as we would like him to be after that bout of rheumatic fever when he was a child. He spends most of his time painting. Celia's equipped him with a first class studio, but we're not often favoured with the results. He's very secretive about it all." She turned to her brother, whose dark eyes were for once expressionless.

"Would you mind giving him a call, Guy?"

Karen intervened quickly, "Please don't bother on my account. There's no need to disturb him. Most artists hate an intrusion into their private world."

The short laugh Guy gave was unmistakably sardonic, but he turned away without comment. Patricia
Amber watched him go, then turned back to Karen.

"I told Uncle Mark to be back by lunchtime. He's
taken Pip on a tour of the vineyards." Her eyes brightened. "Oh, Karen, it is lovely to have you here!"

Karen's eyes never left her face. "You really mean
that, don't you, Aunt Patricia?"

The dark eyes melted. "My dear child, having you
and Pip is a great joy to me. Pip, I think, is like all our
family, but you are your father. He lives on in you,
Karen. You're extraordinarily like him. The same
bones...the tilt of the eyes and the brows, even his
trick of the hands. You bring him back so vividly." Her
face was grave. "I was grieved by your mother's death,
Karen. I want you to believe that. Eva had a most unhappy life, yet had circumstances been different she
would have made an outstanding woman. She had it in
her. We were very close as girls. I knew her so well."
She sat for a moment seemingly lost in reflection.
Karen looked at her downbent head, and wondered,
not for the first time, at the exact part Patricia Amber
had played in her mother's life. It was obvious that she
was very devoted to her brother and he to her.

At that moment Guy Amber came back into the
room, followed by a slender young man wearing paint-
daubed jeans and a vivid blue shirt exposing a smooth
golden expanse of chest. His hair was an authentic
silver-gilt and tumbled artlessly-artful over his forehead and almost into his eyes, the exact colour of
aquamarines. He looked a golden boy, intense and picturesque and to Karen's eyes astonishingly healthy.
The vivid eyes found Karen's, slid over her with truly
professional interest, before he broke into an appreciative whistle.

"Karo, Karo, I'm not sure if you haven't grown into
the most beautiful bird in the world!" He covered the
length of the room in the shortest possible time, grasp-

ing both of her hands. "Welcome back, little cat. That's what Guy used to call you, remember. Or was it cat's eyes?"

"Something like that," Guy Amber drawled lazily.

Rikki was talking, the words tumbling out enthusiastically. "What a wonderful subject you'll make for me, Karo. The vivid contrast between your hair and eyes— it's quite stirring. Fancy picking a winner, and on my own home-ground. It's truly amazing!"

"You look wonderful to me, too, Rikki," Karen intervened gently, and on an impulse leant forward and kissed his cheek. It was smooth and golden and smelled faintly of turpentine. To her surprise he turned his head swiftly and kissed her mouth, his own mouth warm and surprisingly sweet.

"Your affectionate nature does you credit, Rikki," Guy Amber drawled his words lazily. "Now I can safely leave Karen under your wing." He glanced over at his sister. "I won't be able to stay to lunch, Trish. I'm cutting it fine as it is. I may stay overnight in town and ring you in the morning." He gave Karen a charming half smile. "This time tomorrow, little one, you'll be fully absorbed into the household."

The gallantry of his words belied by the mocking light in his eyes. She met those eyes briefly.

"Thank you for meeting us. I do realise you have many demands on your time."

He tut-tutted gently. "That sounds excessively correct, Karen, and not at all like you." He reached for his car keys and jiggled them nonchalantly. "Walk out to the car with me, Trish. I've a few things to tell you. Rikki will look after Karen." The dark eyes veered towards his nephew. "Don't *overdo* it, Rikki."

Rikki coloured furiously. "You're the very devil, Guy!"

"So I've been told." He took hold of his sister's arm and guided her out into the hall, with a brief "goodbye."

Rikki returned to his silent scrutiny.

"Now we're alone, I want to tell you, I really mean what I say. You've grown very beautiful, Karo, and best of all you don't seem aware of it. Fantastic, that! Especially in this household. I've been racking my brains for weeks for the right subject for the Havilland Prize—you know, for portraiture. I'm determined to have a go at it and now you've arrived. A gift from the gods. Guy, of course, would have been marvellous. He's such a splendidly arrogant devil, but he'd never sit for me, not in a million years."

"Why not?" Karen found herself asking, hanging on the answer.

"You said it yourself, girl, he has too many demands on his time. He's really big business. I'm simply floored he went out of his way to pick you and Pip up. By the way, Pip's not unlike him, is he? The Amber features, I mean. I caught sight of him with Uncle Mark. He was dancing up and down firing questions. A bright sort of kid, thank God! Just the right sort for this household."

Karen decided to redirect his attention. "How good an artist are you, Rikki?"

He grinned deprecatingly. "Some days I think I'm damned good, well a cut above mediocre, other days I feel I've no show at all. But I'm ambitious, though I don't show the family much of my work. Not for a long time now. 'Rikki's little hobby', Celia calls it, and lets fall a crushing little tinkle of laughter."

"Celia? Your mother, you mean?" Karen's eyebrows shot up disbelievingly.

There was a wicked little grin on Rikki's face. "No one else, my sweet innocent. No one, least of all her own children, would dream of calling the exquisite Mrs. Celia Amber Mother. It's aging, dear child, and too damn fundamental. Liane, poor thing, had to have it drummed into her. For me it came naturally. Still, I can't complain. She did set me up in the studio. It's safer to keep Rikki occupied, so he won't go gallivanting, pick up with girls, especially *pretty* girls. The Queen Bee doesn't tolerate competition. She can't take it, you know."

"That's absurd!" Karen protested faintly, feeling genuinely shocked.

Rikki's eyes narrowed sagely as he contradicted her. "No, it isn't. There are women like that. Surely you've heard of them. Millions of them all over the world, dedicated to themselves—the Grand Order of Queen Beeism."

"Rikki!" Karen's protest was half laughter. "How much of this is nonsense? It's quite fascinating, of course, but it's a wee bit implausible."

He crinkled his eyes at her. "You'll learn, kiddo, in time. But I'm glad you're here. You're straight and absolutely direct, and Liane needs a friend. I'm fed up with the deal she's been getting. She's trying so hard to be a carbon copy of Celia and the effect is disastrous, as Celia well knows. The funny thing is Lee could be highly individual once she's thrown off the shackles. Celia doesn't want men staring at her daughter—she might catch some of that gratifying admiration. She actually prefers Liane a mess, so she can steal the show. Vanity, thy name is woman. Hideous, hideous vanity!"

Karen stared at him, completely nonplussed. He winked at her and she began to laugh. Was this purely an act? Rikki always did like to shock.

"You needn't laugh," he said severely, his eyes on her face.

"Rikki, you're being ridiculous. Come on, admit it!"

"Ridiculous?" Karen sat speechless, struck by the inflection he gave the word. "No," Rikki replied, picking his words carefully. "Mothers are sometimes jealous of their own daughters, Karo. It has been known to happen."

Karen looked down at her hands. Despite his words

and their implied disloyalty, she felt moved to a quick sympathy. Ever sensitive to people, she sensed in Rikki a long-established hurt he was at pains to conceal with a facetious manner. But she had some experience of the fraudulent heart. Rikki was in his own way suffering.

His bright eyes slipped over her, compelling her attention.

"You know, Karo, with your lovely face and true woman's compassion, I'm crazy about you already. I think we'll get married."

Her face lit up with startled laughter. "You're joking, I hope."

"I'm not, can't you tell by my eyes?" His smile was very sweet, giving her a quick glimpse of the boy he was all those years before. "Don't take me too seriously, Karo. I talk a lot of nonsense. Fundamentally I'm a warm-hearted, affectionate boy with normal instincts. Any slight deviation can be explained or excused by the circumstances of my childhood." He sat back and regarded her. "Now you're something else again. Whatever kind of life you've had, it's made you fearless—those beautiful, clear eyes. I can see right through to your soul. There's nothing twisted there. No plotting and planning...the endless conniving."

Karen stood up with some agitation. "If you're trying to intrigue me, Rikki, you're succeeding a little too well. I've a picture of seething discontent. Who's at the bottom of it...Guy?" she hazarded.

Rikki looked up in genuine astonishment. "Guy? Good God, no! Why should it be Guy? Guy is as direct as you are. I have a shot at him occasionally, but I could no more bring him down than an eagle. He really is the most extraordinarily vital man. He resembles ordinary human beings like a tractor resembles his own Jaguar. Pure *machismo*, of course."

"Good grief, what's that?" Karen looked startled.

"*Machismo*?" Rikki snorted. "Spanish for a sexy forceful male—the big power game player with just a

dash of playboy, and the merest suggestion of ruthlessness all you females seem to go mad for."

"Leave me out of it, please," Karen said repressively.

"Well, all the others, then, doll. They waft through
his life trying to make the big impression, then wham!
flat on their face."

"I'm not surprised, he reminds me distinctly of one
of the Borgias."

Rikki laughed uproariously. "Well, I'm exchanging a
scion of the Borgias for a captivating child."

Karen smiled, showing her small, pretty teeth. "I'm
honoured, Rikki. When do I get to see your work?"

"When the mood takes me," he grinned conspiratorially. "I'm rather like a new mother at the moment.
You know, frightened to let anyone take a peek at the
baby in case they don't agree I've produced something
wonderful."

There was a quick rush of light footsteps and they
both looked towards the door. Patricia Amber came
into the room, speaking with gentle vivacity. "Well,
Karen, what do you think of Rikki, after all these
years?" Her luminous dark eyes circled Karen to
Rikki. "Of course, he *is* rather a leg-puller."

Karen smiled. "So I imagine. Do I ever take him
seriously?"

"Nearly always," his aunt replied unexpectedly.
"Rikki's extremely intuitive, expecially where women
are concerned."

"And you're a saint, Trish," Rikki grinned irrepressibly. "As a matter of fact I've just been filling in my
dear family for Karo's benefit. Pre-warned is pre-
armed, so they say."

Patricia Amber's eyes flew to Karen's. "What exactly *has* he been saying, and on your very first day?"

"Just a lightning sketch of the local legend. Nothing
too telling," Rikki quipped lightly, and jumped to his
feet, obviously bent on changing the subject. "Now

what about an aperitif before lunch, then I'll be off to the studio," he said brightly. "I've some wonderful ideas formulating."

His aunt's head veered round to Karen. "Karen, I suppose. She has the kind of bones I imagine a would-be artist would like to capture."

"Exactly," Rikki bowed, "and thank you for the faint praise. Nevertheless, I feel I can appraise my subject without diffidence. Young as she is, Karen's face is touched with a certain sadness, nostalgia perhaps. It has a most poignant effect on beauty."

Karen looked at him strangely. "Guy said almost the same thing."

Rikki winked knowingly. "I'm not surprised. Guy, let me tell you, had you possibly missed it, is highly susceptible to all forms of beauty. I've seen him handling his treasures—the *inanimate* ones, of course. He has a fine eye for beauty." The aquamarine gaze narrowed maliciously. "By the same token, all the animate ones have been tearing their hair out for years...the things I could tell you!"

"Please don't, there's a dear. You're not an *enfant terrible* any longer." Patricia Amber spoke with finality. "Now what about that drink...a martini for me, I think. What about you, Karen? Would you prefer something else, a sherry perhaps?"

"No, a martini would be lovely. Horror of horrors in this household, I don't care much for sherry."

Rikki burst into satirical cackles. "Not even the famous Amber Amontillado." He launched into full-scale advertising blurb. "Spark up your party with Amber Amontillado, and colour your world golden. Let your guests capture the soft full bouquet with the oak astringency showing through. The full 'nutty' aftertaste of Australia's finest dry sherry—Amber Amontillado."

Karen smiled. "I'm sold! I haven't, in fact, ever tried it. I'd better do so now and show the proper respect."

Rikki moved off, still chattering. "But never in a coloured glass, dear child. Always remember it. Never, never the coloured glass. I swear I've seen Guy change colour when presented with champagne in a tinted wineglass."

"Very proper too. I'm in entire agreement." His aunt smiled at him. "Perhaps I'll have one too, Rikki, and make your day."

"I say, I've timed that nicely!" They all swung round as a tall, very lean man in his seventies, with a silver shock of hair, came into the room holding Philip's hand. "One young man delivered and ready for his lunch."

Philip smiled up at his companion, then sped across the room, putting his arm around Karen. "I've had the most marvellous time, Karo. It's all terrific. You should see it—the vineyards and the cellars. The size of the casks, they're enormous! Uncle Guy has put in the most fantastic refrigeration plant because it's too hot at vintage time, and there are tractors and harvesters and all kinds of mechanical equipment—" Pip broke off for breath, though his admiration continued to effervesce. "I've learnt an awful lot off Uncle Mark, he's terribly clever. He's writing a book about the vine through the ages."

The wistfulness that touched his tone made them all laugh. Mark Amber interrupted the excited flow of chatter.

"And I couldn't have asked for a more intelligent lad to show about the place." He turned to his niece. "I think he has the makings of a true vigneron, Trish." His eyes moved back and sought Karen's. "And this, of course, is Karen." He moved swiftly across the room and took her hand, appraising her with the complete frankness of a child, or those well advanced in years. He took his time, then bent his silvery head, kissing her cheek soundly. "Welcome home, my dearest child. It's been far too long for all of us."

All at once Karen felt the tears coming. She stood

there helplessly, feeling as stiff and awkward as a
schoolgirl; as if with a gesture Mark Amber had somehow touched the well spring of her emotions.

"Gosh, you're not crying!" Philip burst out in alarm.
"Karo never cries." His widened dark eyes circled the
others with so much obvious consternation that the
moment of tension was broken.

Mark Amber put a comforting arm around Karen's
shoulders, causing the ever articulate Rikki to remark
on his easy gallantry. He reached up and touched his
silver hair. "I'm not as old as the snow on my head
would have you think, Rikki. Now shake hands with
young Philip here."

They all watched the rather awkward salute between
the child and young man, while Mark Amber continued to say, so casually and easily, all the right things. By
the time they went in to lunch, the whole party was
caught up on a tide of youthful reunion.

The great house was silent. Not a shutter banged nor
a floorboard creaked. Karen slipped out of bed and
thrust her arms into her robe—an orange winter silk. It
was one of her real extravagances, bought especially for
Belle Amber, and a wonderful foil for her black hair
and gleaming tiptilted eyes. Sleep was impossible. Her
mind was just a mad carousel flinging off people and
impressions. It had been an emotional day—her headache was proof of it. It was making itself felt by the
minute, a dull throb that threatened to stagger her eyes.
There were Veganin in the medicine cabinet in the
downstairs bathroom. She had noticed them when Pip
was washing his face and hands for dinner. Two would
certainly take care of her headache, induce a deep
sleep.

Out in the carpeted hallway she moved swiftly as a
shadow. Every inch of the house was as familiar to her
now as it had been in her childhood. She found her way
easily along the top floor with bright moonlight falling
in patches through the casement windows. In the fath-

omless dark well at the base of the stairs she moved without apprehension into an unmoving dark shadow, then her heart lunged with fright and her stifled cry was buried under a lean hand.

"The things one stumbles across in a dark house!"

At the sound of that laughing, mocking voice, Karen nipped at the hand with her small teeth, steadying her voice with an effort.

"You frightened me!"

He laughed softly, his hand moving to the curve of her shoulder.

"Frightened you, Karen? I was beginning to think that quite impossible. Characteristically you're attaching no importance whatever to my quite equal sense of shock. You're not a somnambulist, are you?"

"Of course not. I couldn't sleep..." her voice was a mixture of plaintive indignation. "I have a headache," she tacked on, feeling disorientated in the soft darkness with this wildly disturbing man. She rounded on him swiftly. "No one expected you until tomorrow, you know."

His hand encircled her bare wrist. "I come and go as I please, Karen," he laughed, and drew her along with him across the hallway and into the library.

She heard the door shut with a gentle click, then he reached out and flicked at a switch. Light flared golden on the beautifully appointed room, an entire wall of books that would satisfy the most ardent bibliophile, and contemporary furniture of simplicity and quality, club chairs upholstered in leather and heavy handwoven fabric. Karen met the dark waiting eyes, endlessly feeling as if she had stumbled into something far more than dazzling light, and she shut her own eyes briefly in sheer self-defence. He was wearing evening clothes with an elegance and splendour that could not be denied. She couldn't bear to look at him, certainly not give him the satisfaction of judging her spontaneous reactions.

His smothered laugh moved the silky dark hair at her temples. "You can't change things by shutting your eyes and wishing, Karen."

Her eyes flew open again, meeting his, amused, beneath quirking brows.

"I can try," she murmured hardily, conveying with her voice that she was in no mood to be trifled with. But she trembled as his eyes slipped over her face, touched her slender throat, moved over the subtle contours of her body.

Without moving he asked levelly, "Why do you distrust me, Karen?"

Conflict was hovering now between them with an almost compulsive fascination.

"You can't wash out the past," she said carefully, "pretend it hasn't happened."

He looked away from the accusation in her great golden eyes.

"That's very profound of you, Karen," he said sardonically, and moved over to the far end of the room; at the flick of his wrist a section of panelling opened to reveal hi-fidelity equipment, a television, and a full-scale bar. He had his broad back to her. "Tell me more. I'm always interested in the extent and depth of a young woman's observations." He drew out an exquisite crystal decanter and two matching tumblers, turning to smile slightly into her ominous eyes. "Don't look at me like that, little one. I'm not about to ply you with liquor, then sell you down the river...or worse."

She coloured at the mockery in his voice and lowered her eyes, feeling hopelessly out of her depth. The silence spun out until he drawled lazily, "You're an ornamental child, aren't you?" He walked over the smooth expanse of buff carpet and held out a watered-down whisky. "Drink that down. It will help you sleep... shift that headache." She stood unmoving and he thrust it towards her. "Do take it, child."

She took it then, tipping her head with a show of spirit.

"Please don't 'child' me, Guy. I don't care to be used for target practice."

He gave a soft mocking laugh. "My dear Karen, I'm handling you with kid gloves, if you only knew it. Up-to-date, temperamental young women and my kind of life have been mutually exclusive. You'll have to forgive me if I'm a little slow in getting the hang of you."

She hesitated, looking uncertainly at the deep golden liquid in her glass.

"Drink it, my restless butterfly. It's guaranteed to be harmless in that quantity."

Karen took a tentative sip, surprising herself by liking it, then took another sip while he glanced at his watch.

"I'd better say goodnight," she murmured hastily, feeling an intruder.

"It's morning, little one, but why worry? You said you couldn't sleep."

"But surely you need your sleep," she countered, anxious to remove herself from the circle of his compelling charm. "Though they tell me you're a human dynamo."

He smiled slightly. "I've managed on very little sleep for a long time now, Karen. But your consideration does you credit. Sit down and tell me what you've been doing."

She sank into a tan leather club chair, her gown parting over long slender legs and showing the lacy tip of her nightgown. She drew it together swiftly, biting on her lip, furious with herself for feeling so gauche.

His smile was maddening. "You shouldn't feel so ill at ease with a relative, Karen."

"Relative to your attitude to women, I don't see why not," she flared uncontrollably. "You make me at least feel like a display piece under the eye of an exacting connoisseur!"

He threw off the contents of his glass with a laugh.

"You'd pass the test any day, Karen. Which brings me to a certain matter I meant to discuss with you. You never cashed that cheque I sent you for clothes. You'll need a fairly extensive wardrobe here. We do a great deal of entertaining, but I'd hardly expect you to have earned enough in your short career to cover every exigency."

She tried to control her mounting colour. "My wardrobe is adequate," she countered repressively, feeling as absurdly prim as a milkmaid. He must have thought so too, for his mouth twitched.

"How easily you fire, little one. Are you always so prickly? You look as though you should be as soft as that silk." His eyes flickered over the orange robe. "Which, incidentally, is the only thing I've seen you in that suits you."

Karen sat up straighter. "Thank you, I must be thankful for that!"

He ignored her sarcasm. "What about the party on Sunday? Have you anything suitable for that? The women in our social circle usually dress to the eyes. Celia must spend a fortune on clothes."

"Lucky Celia," Karen said dryly. "But I really can't imagine *my* life reduced to the sole consideration of the right clothes, the right hair-do, the right make-up." She sketched a rapid gesture with her hand. "It's quite incomprehensible to me."

"It is now, my little cat. Ah well, being a true beauty you might carry the night." He was smiling faintly, thoughtfully.

Her slender shoulders moved. "I won't disgrace you at any rate, even if I don't exactly measure up to the exalted company."

"Then you refuse my offer?"

"I do." Her hand went to her temple, then pushed back the heavy fall of hair that swept her shoulder. "Do you know, I feel quite ethereal," she murmured inconsequently.

"The effect of the whisky," he smiled. "How's the headache?"

"Magically it's gone." Her admission was tinged with faint reluctance.

He had to smile. "You hate to admit any good coming from our encounters, don't you? You betray yourself with every look, every gesture." He came across to her, swiftly drawing her to her feet. She swayed slightly and he kept a steadying hand on her shoulder, running a caressing thumb over her collar bone. "Today has been too much for you. You're an emotional child. I shouldn't really fence with you, but it's proving irresistible."

"Such a change from your usual sophisticated style?" She looked up at him, unable to subdue the mischief in her eyes.

He shook her gently. "Your name should be Kate, not Karen. You'll never get a husband with that ever-ready backchat."

"But I don't *want* a husband," she managed, feeling suddenly sleepy.

"What you want won't have much to do with it, I'm afraid." He shook her again. "Come on now, Karen, call it a night. You're out on your feet."

He turned her about with gentle force, and a long skein of her hair fell over his sleeve. He curled it around his hand experimentally, then tucked it behind her ear, looking down at her lazily. "What tiny ears you have, Karen. Almost no lobe to them. I must remember never to buy you earrings."

She looked back at him with wide, startled eyes.

"You must remember never to buy me *anything*."

"I'm afraid I won't be able to keep to that, Karen. Dressing you, for one thing, would prove quite rewarding."

"I'll manage on my own!"

"Very virtuous, little one. In the days gone by you would undoubtedly have carried a banner."

"And you would have had me in chains," she countered, then laughed aloud. "This is getting us nowhere, as usual." She blinked back at him with sleepy exhaustion.

"Where exactly do you want to go?"

"To bed, of course," she retorted, mildly astonished, then fled at the glittering undercurrent in his eyes.

CHAPTER THREE

Guy and Patricia drove into town early next morning for the monthly board meeting, leaving Karen the run of the house. Philip, with a few more days of freedom before settling into his new school, was up with the sun, caught up, at ten, in the mystique of the vine. There was so much to see, so much to learn, and Uncle Mark had promised to let him ride up to the front gate on one of the bulk wine tankers.

Karen, listening to his excited chatter at breakfast time, felt quite proud of him. It was amazing what a receptive young mind could store away in such a short space of time! To their mutual satisfaction he was able to reel off the varietal names of the grapes used to make different types of wines, both red and white, and Uncle Mark, as an added incentive had promised to take him over their Lagonda Vale estate, forty miles to the north-east, and famous for its "rieslings".

In the post-breakfast quiet, Karen spent a little time tidying her room. She put her things away with a feeling of pleasure, taking time off to enjoy her surroundings. In style, her own room offered a departure from the rest of the house, for the décor was unashamedly contemporary: the tailored bedspread, the two deep armchairs, the window wall and the drapes were covered in a ravishing print of rust, gold and orange and the desk and low wall cabinets on either side of the bed, were handsome contemporary pieces that matched the dark stained shutters over windows that looked out over the pool garden.

Even the small adjoining bathroom had a distinct personality, decorated in the same striking colour scheme with an elegant eye to finish and detail. There was not the slightest doubt it had been furnished with love, specifically with Karen in mind.

Downstairs again, in the living room, she opened up the Steinway and struck a tentative chord. It reverberated in the silence, signalling her urgent desire to practise in earnest. The high ceiling and heavy carpeting would cut a lot of the piano's big tone. Besides, she wouldn't be disturbing anyone. It was all of three weeks since she last had the opportunity to play. She sat down at the keyboard and ran off a few determined arpeggios. That was the end of it!

The old deeply familiar sensation of power and pleasure rushed over her and she settled herself on to the long piano seat and began with Tausig—technical work vastly rewarding to the performer but sheer torture to anyone obliged to listen for long periods. Three-quarters of an hour flew past while she practised on, her forehead faintly pleated with concentration. These were virtuoso exercises and they required her full attention.

Rikki's voice at the doorway startled her very thoroughly.

"Just one more arpeggio and so help me I'll go out of my mind!"

Karen swung around to encounter his magnificent scowl.

"I'm sorry, Rikki. Did I disturb you?"

"Of course you did, moronic girl. Why else would I be here?" Just as suddenly he relented, gathering his persuasive powers. "I suppose all technical work is a bind, but seriously, Karo, what about sitting for me this afternoon?"

"I'd like that, Rikki. What time?"

"About two-ish." His eyes narrowed. "You know, Karo, I'm getting cardiac complications just looking at you. You have the sort of face the knights of old would joust about."

"Jest about?" she quipped lightly.

He ignored her facetiousness, completely serious in his appraisal. "I'm not sure how I'll go about this. Your face is the most intriguing mixture of hauteur and mischief."

"Good lord!" Karen laughed in earnest.

"Forgive me for being super-literal, dear girl, it's the artist in me," Rikki drawled sarcastically.

"And it's irresistible." Karen's eyes gleamed through their dark lashes. Rikki did take himself seriously!

"If any other girl but you said that, I should bolt!"

"Then why don't you? I'm going to finish my practice."

Rikki took this piece of information badly. He struck his brow. "God give me strength!"

Karen sat for a moment swinging her legs, then she drifted into an exquisite Liszt Consolation. That at least should soothe Rikki's nerves.

It did! His gilded head appeared momentarily around the door. "Now why didn't you tell me you played like an angel?"

Chopin Études followed the Liszt, then Falla, Ravel and Debussy. It was the greatest pleasure to Karen, doubly so after the few silent weeks without her piano.

Mark Amber, coming into the house in search of her, made for the living room with an expression of delighted surprise. He was in the room several moments before Karen became aware of his presence. She spun around quickly.

"Back so soon, Uncle Mark?"

"I'd have come back sooner, had I known there was going to be a recital. Pip and I wanted you to join us, but now I think I'll just stay here." He moved over to an armchair, his silvery shock of hair coming to rest against the high back. "Now why can't all women play the piano? It's such a wonderful accomplishment and yet it's so sadly out of fashion. In my day every young lady was expected to have some degree of proficiency, but I can't say I remember anyone playing half so beautifully as you, Karen."

She smiled at the genuine ring of sincerity in his voice.

"I suspect you're a charmer, Uncle Mark."

"Well, I do have a favourite piece," he smiled, not displeased by her compliment. "Schumann's *Devotion*. Do you know it? I heard Horowitz play it many years ago as an encore at one of his New York concerts, and I've never forgotten it."

Karen's left hand found the chord of A flat. "I'm no Horowitz, Uncle Mark, but if you close your eyes tightly it won't be so noticeable."

He smiled and made the gesture of shutting his eyes, only to open them a few seconds later. The combined visual and auditory effect was quite entrancing to him. Young Karen was a born musician, with a special affinity for the piano, like her father before her. When the last note died away he conveyed his great pleasure by nodding his head vigorously. He had no wish to shatter the spell by speaking. Karen smiled, her fingers seeking out another lovely old melody—Liszt's *Liebestraum*. The gentle "Ah!" from behind her told her she had guessed correctly. It too was a favourite!

But the reign of contentment was to be broken! Philip's dark head came round the living room door, tilted like a robin's. "Gosh, Uncle Mark, is this where you are? I've been hard on your trail for a quarter of an hour. You're not going to sit there and listen to Karen, are you? She can play for you any time."

Mark Amber came out of his absorption, and stood up imperturbably. "I'm afraid Pip has the prior claim, Karen, but your next recital can't come soon enough. Thank you, my dear. Now what about joining us on our tour of inspection?" He walked over to help her close down the leaf of the piano, then led both young people out into the spring sunshine.

Morning was brilliantly blue and golden and a profusion of spring flowers greeted them everywhere. Flynn, the head gardener, was an authority on the rhododendron genus and the two varieties seemed to spill over everywhere: the paper-thin azaleas, masses upon masses of them, in delicately petalled profusion, breaking up long vistas of greensward, or nestling in great pink and white drifts under the arched branches of the beautiful old scribbly gums fringed by the crimson ruffled trusses of the "true" rhododendron. Unexpected little gardens appeared behind ledges of boxwood and masses of succulents flourished in a bewildering number of varieties around the pond at the foot of the embankment.

By the time they reached the vineyards, Karen felt a great surge of happiness. They moved slowly over the sloping gravelly ground, walking the dead straight rows of luxuriant vines.

"Vitis vinifera!" Philip chanted happily, running on before them.

Mark Amber smiled into Karen's amused eyes. "The sacred vine! The symbol of both pagan and Christian deities from our earliest times."

"Incredible, isn't it, the aura that surrounds it. Yet it's the sturdiest of plants! You're writing a book about it, aren't you, Uncle Mark?"

"I've *been* writing it, on and off, for the past twenty years."

"That's a long time!" Karen looked up at his clear-cut profile. He was extraordinarily vital for a man of his years.

"There's quite a lot of ground to cover, Karen, when you consider that the vine's origins are lost in the mists of antiquity. Why, some authorities put its beginnings as early as 8000 B.C. At any rate, we can be sure the vine was established in the Tigris-Euphrates valleys before 4000 B.C. You might be interested to know the very first reference to a vineyard occurs in the earliest work of literature there is—the Epic of Gilgamesh.''

"I must confess my ignorance!'' Karen smiled, and stopped to remove a pebble from her open sandal.

"A poem in the Semitic language, my dear,'' Mark Amber steadied her, "written on earthenware and thus preserved forever.'' He began to recite in a soft, rhythmic undertone:

> "Amethyst it bore as its fruit;
> Grapevine was trellised, good to behold;
> Lapis lazuli it wore as grape clusters;
> Fruit it bore magnificent to look upon.''

"Lapis lazuli! What a beautiful word!'' Karen watched him as he bent to cradle a green cluster of berries in his hand.

"By the time Homer wrote the Iliad, wine was not only the ordinary drink of the Greeks but regarded as one of the country's finest natural products. From Greece to Rome and with Caesar's conquest of Gaul to the great home of the vine—*la belle* France! I can't imagine any wine-lover being without the great vintages of Bordeaux, Burgundy or the Loire, not to mention Champagne.''

He straightened up to smile at her. "One day soon, my dear, I hope you have the great pleasure of finding yourself in Paris with sufficient money and leisure to enjoy some of the great French wines. On a day like today, when the weather is sparkling, I think I would order champagne... Veuve Cliquot, or Pol Roget perhaps... the great classic champagnes. They lend such enchantment to an occasion.'' He gave her a wicked, sidelong look. "Actually, Karen, you won't have to go quite so far as Paris, Guy laid in quite a stock up at the house. I'll get him to open a few bottles on Saturday,

though we usually boost our own products at parties."
He laughed softly.

"I'm longing to see Aunt Celia and Liane again. I
hope they'll be home in time for it."

· "Almost certainly, my dear." Mark Amber's voice
was rather dry. He leaned towards her, serious, confidential. "You might not recognise your Aunt Celia,
Karen. She's changed a great deal in the past few
years."

"May I be permitted to ask in what way?" she asked
gravely.

"It would be too difficult to define once you got past
the obvious. Richard's death was a great tragedy for all
of us, but more so for Celia. She lost her sheet anchor
when she lost Richard. He knew how to keep her in
hand, satisfy the woman in her. Some women need...
demand, even, a man's constant regard."

"Is she unhappy, then, Uncle Mark?"

His surprise at this was genuine. "No, I wouldn't say
Celia was unhappy, my dear."

Her hand moved a little helplessly. "Rikki seems a
little...lost?"

He considered the word gravely. "Perhaps, but Rikki
will make out. It's Liane I'm concerned about. She's
very much affected by her mother's attitudes. They're
so different in type, yet Liane tries so hard to emulate
her mother. Natural enough, of course. I must say Celia is a great credit to us. She's charming and witty and a
delight to look upon—far more so at close on—forty,
let me whisper it, than she ever was as a girl, proving
indisputably that youth is not necessarily the time of a
woman's greatest glamour. Her youthful prettiness has
gained a powerful new dimension, I can tell you. Yes,"
he added reflectively, "Celia is a wonderful piece of
artifice."

Karen gave a trill of rising laughter. "That sounds
rather acid, Uncle Mark. Surely it wasn't intended?"

He answered her smile, not at all shamefaced.

"Perhaps I'd better rephrase it. Celia is a work of art!"

Her smile exonerated him. "I must admit I'm looking forward to seeing her again."

His dark eyes were intent in their steadiness. "You sound positively intrigued. Who's been talking?"

"Why, no one. What could you mean?" She widened her eyes at him innocently. "It's a wonder Aunt Celia hasn't married again, isn't it?"

His glance met hers, briefly and she thought a trifle warily. "Perhaps she's waiting for a man like Richard." He took her arm. "You know, Karen, we used to have a little kitten with eyes like yours...and it was just as inquisitive."

"Do you mean to reprove me, Uncle Mark?" She smiled up at him, her head tilted.

"No, my dear, but you're too damned observant and I'm not going to say too much. Now, to get back to a safe topic. We have some new plantings further on... more Cabernet. Come and see them. We won't let Pip get too far ahead of us. He might run under the sprays."

And so Mark Amber redirected Karen's attention gently but firmly. To mention the "new" Celia Amber was to tread on very dangerous ground indeed!

It was well after lunch before Karen found her way to Rikki's studio, over the garage. She paused outside the door, then rapped smartly. Rikki's tall, slender figure loomed up at the door, one errant lock falling over his brow in the traditional Bohemian-Beatnik fashion.

"Are you from the police?" he asked truculently, taking up a position.

"Why, are you on the run?"

He surveyed her closely. "Pushing marijuana, then?"

"Not the type!" Karen peered under his arm at the superbly equipped studio. No artist's garret this!

"Well then, is it possible to hold a serious discussion with you?" Rikki persisted, still blocking the door.

"Never about art." Somehow Karen struck on the right password and Rikki relented and pressed her shoulder.

"Come in. If there's one person I hate it's a self-confessed expert." He followed her in and waved a hand towards a stack of canvases. "Take a look, childhood chum, and enjoy an uninformed laugh."

She walked towards the canvases with an expression of interest.

"I hope you don't expect tact and consideration," she flung over her shoulder, herself well versed in receiving constructive criticism.

Rikki quirked his brow at her. "Fire away without fear of displeasure!"

Karen went straight to her task, feeling Rikki's eyes watching her. He seemed nervous yet anxious to have her opinion, however unqualified. She examined canvas after canvas, then pulled one out and left it propped up against the wall. It was a very fine picture, she thought; a landscape of hills and vineyards and a sky full of scudding clouds—the sky as she had seen today! The style wasn't abstract, yet it wasn't slavishly literal either. It was glowing and imaginative and seemed to radiate that authority inherent in any work of art.

Karen forgot Rikki, forgot everything. She pulled out another, studying it and setting it down.

"I'm experimenting a bit, now," Rikki explained almost apologetically, clearing his throat.

Karen turned towards him, her topaz eyes gleaming. "I'm no expert, Rikki, but I do think I have an instinctive eye for such things." She hesitated for a moment. "What I'm trying to say is, I think you're very good indeed. I never expected anything like this. Everything you do seems to work together—colour, form, planes, all perfectly related. I love everything here, especially that landscape. It's so deeply familiar, yet you've handled it with so much freshness and verve. I can almost see the grapes ripening."

"You can?" Rikki looked back at her with a kind of bewilderment. "Sometimes I think I'm well on my way to expressing myself. Things are so different these

days, even the method of handling the paint. My
teacher used to say that I showed a great deal of promise, but Celia said that was because we are—who we
are, if you know what I mean. The Ambers and all that.
It pays to keep in with them." He swung off the subject. "I don't go in for anything detailed, you might
have noticed, Karo. I try to lead the eye gently from
plane to plane, colour mass to colour mass." He
grinned suddenly. "I hope I'm succeeding. Anyway,
don't let me get started on my hobbyhorse."

"Why ever not? As an artist you're entitled to.
Really, Rikki, I had no idea!" Karen's eyes roamed
over the light-filled studio. "This is super-equipped,
isn't it? I thought you might not be able to live up to
the part. But you're the genuine article. I'll be honoured to sit for you, Rikki. In the years to come I'll be
able to boast, Richard Amber painted my portrait before he became famous!"

She felt a rising excitement. "How come the family
haven't encouraged you? Wouldn't you like to continue your studies overseas? It would be a marvellous
experience for you. Mastering new techniques; the
stimulating companionship of your own kind...to
learn from...to talk to."

"Karo, sweetheart, you've brushed me with angel's
wings!" Rikki lifted her hand to his mouth and kissed
it. "None of the family, with the exception of Celia and
occasionally Liane, whose artistic soul is lodged in her
stomach, have seen any of these latter canvases. Up
until about six months ago I was working my way out
of a morass. You know, trying freakish experiments.
Guy, I think, sees me as a mummy's darling, sheltered
and cherished, a pampered pet, weakened by indulgence. I've done nothing to dispel the idea. Aunt Trish,
of course, never intrudes on my privacy. She makes a
point of not interfering, so I don't think she knows
what to make of it all, what with Celia and hints of a
dithering dilettante son."

"Is that what your mother really thinks?"

Rikki's voice was strained. "I don't really know, Karo. I don't think she has any great opinion of my work, and unlike you, my pet, she's well informed on the subject. That's what worries me. You must admit she's set me up well. This is an expensive setting for the boy genius."

Karen's great topaz eyes were fixed on him with mingled scepticism and fascination. Celia was sounding more complex by the minute. She couldn't reconcile this new updated version with the pretty pink and white figurine of her childhood.

Rikki looked up and intercepted her gaze.

"Hold it!" He jumped up enthusiastically. "Sit over there...in that chair. That's it. Relax. The muse has descended upon me. I'll just fill in some structural lines. I can't even visualise the finished effect. This is only a first laying in of the skeleton, as it were." He was rattling on excitedly, preparing his palette, wiping paint on his already psychedelic pants. "I promise you, you'll be satisfied with whatever result!"

The lovely gaiety touched Karen's mouth. "I'm quite sure of it, Rikki." She smiled into his eyes, now as brilliant as any aquamarines.

He searched amid the jumble of tubes of paint, rags and brushes, found what he wanted, then busied himself squeezing liberal quantities of pigments on to his palette. He glanced up at Karen, his expression preoccupied.

"Turn your left profile just a little...that's it! Now right shoulder back...back...Heavens, no!" he came toward her, frowning. "I don't want you to strike attitudes. That's better!...relax." He patted the offending shoulder.

Karen tried not to laugh. Rikki couldn't be more intent if he was a much lauded academist. She sat back feeling faintly fatigued. Rikki swept in the structural lines while Karen let her thoughts roam further afield.

Half an hour passed, the silence unbroken except for
Rikki's intermittent comments on the phases through
which the portrait could be expected to pass.

He was in deadly earnest and clearly not disposed
towards receiving humorous suggestions from her. Despite herself, Karen, who could never take herself very
seriously, was impressed as most people are in the presence of genuine dedication. They both jumped a little
at a loud knock on the door. A girl put her head around
it, with what to Karen was a vaguely heartbreaking
smile.

"I'm home!" she announced blithely. "Idiotic thing
to say, I know, but it's all I can think of."

Karen jumped up, smiling. "Liane!" She made towards the other girl's outstretched hands.

Rikki beat his brow. "No hope of getting my model
to pose for me." His tone was mournful, but there was
an undercurrent of something like elation in his voice.

"But I will, of course," Karen flung back over her
shoulder.

"The unselfish, beautiful spirit which is yours!" He
looked over at his sister. "Come in, Lee. For God's
sake don't hover." His sister pulled a face at him, not
at all put out by his aggressive style. The two girls embraced with unfeigned pleasure in their meeting. Liane,
much taller, drew back a little, a wry smile on her
mouth.

"You look lovely, Karo. And so nice! I was afraid
you'd be madly superior or something. Guy said you
were as beautiful as an orchid." She brushed a well
kept hand over her head. "I look a mess, I bet!"

"And now you're just angling for a compliment,"
Karen smiled back at her, not quite believing in Guy's
exotic description.

"She's not, God help her, but it's a nice change, I'll
admit." Rikki ran a paint-smeared hand over his pants.

Liane stood in the centre of the room, very tall, slim
and long-legged with a slouch that undoubtedly meant

she was distressed by her height. She had good features, far better than average eyes, large and darkly lustrous, but somehow she failed to measure up to her potential. Her outfit was beautiful and obviously expensive and it should have suited her, but it didn't. Just as the short bubble of dark curls formed an entirely wrong frame for her well-defined face.

Karen leaned back against a bench beside Rikki. "I can't get over it, Lee. Just a few short years, yet you've grown up in the interval."

"Grown and grown and grown! You're disappointed, I can tell." Liane gave a small grin, gazing amiably at her brother. "As far as looks go, Rikki grabbed the lot!"

"Oh, for heaven's sake, don't keep knocking yourself, girl. There are always enough people around to do that. Where's Celia?" Rikki tacked on pretty tersely.

Liane's eyes flickered. "She has a few more engagements in town and she wanted me to come on ahead. Colin will bring her down on Saturday evening."

"Colin is the fiancé," Rikki explained, and rolled his eyes at Karen.

"My very best wishes, Liane. I was forgetting—a soignée young woman *and* engaged! I can't wait to meet Colin."

Rikki groaned, but Liane took no notice of him. She gave a very white smile. Her teeth were beautiful and so was her smile. For an instant she looked very much like her Aunt Patricia, but unlike her aunt she had yet to develop a distinctive style. A different hair-do would make all the difference, Karen decided, but eyes narrowing unconsciously. Liane simply wasn't curls! It was a wonder she didn't realise it.

"Colin's a dream!" Liane was rhapsodising. "He's clever and attractive. He's in the P.R. section of the firm." Prosaic as the words were they held some magic for Liane, for her eyes were melting with love. "I really don't know what he sees in me!"

Rikki exploded, rounding on his sister with great irritation. "Turn it up, Lee! You don't know what he sees in you. Have a heart! All this half-humorous self-deprecation makes my teeth ache."

"But you're a good-looking girl, Lee," Karen broke in hastily, catching sight of Rikki's face. He appeared to be working himself into a mild frenzy. He was undoubtedly a volatile young man, but just as clearly devoted to his sister.

Liane had her eyes fixed on Karen with a look of incredulity. "You can't *mean* it!"

"Good grief, I wouldn't *say* it if I didn't *mean* it." Even Karen sounded faintly irritated, and Rikki grinned. "I see you a little differently, perhaps. I always liked your hair as you used to wear it, straight and shiny with a deep fringe."

"Like I did as a child?" Liane almost squeaked.

"Well, the style could be modified. It gave you distinction. You have the Amber features," Karen pointed out.

"And the Amber height! What an almighty handicap," Liane lamented.

"She wants to be little!" Rikki said with soft vehemence. "Can you beat it! A tiny little thing like Celia." His voice picked up suddenly. "I reckon any girl worth her salt would want to sit tall in the saddle."

Karen burst out laughing. "That's a funny way to put it!" Her eyes questioned Liane's. "Tell me about Colin."

"Not here, she won't." Rikki straightened up with an air of absolute finality.

"He means it," Liane laughed.

"I'll say I do! Can't you see the lunatic light in my eye?" Rikki advanced on his sister and just as suddenly put his arms around her, hugging her to him. "Try to get the Big View of everything, kiddo. Run along now, and talk girl talk with Karen. She'll be a friend to you, if anyone will."

"Thank you for the kind words," Karen smiled, and moved over to Liane. "Come on, Lee, leave the boy genius to it."

"Same time tomorrow?" Rikki came after them and kissed Karen under the ear.

"Same time tomorrow," she agreed, and intercepted Liane's surprised but affectionate glance.

Saturday morning started off unexpectedly. Karen and Liane were just putting the final touches to the flowers when a delivery van swept up the drive. After a cursory glance Karen took no further notice of it. Aunt Patricia was somewhere on the terrace supervising the placing of tubs of flowering azaleas. She would attend to it. A few minutes later Karen heard her name being called. She went out on to the terrace with only a brief startled glance at Liane.

"Yes, Aunt Patricia."

"For you, dear—every last box. I'll get Flynn to put them in the service lift for you."

Karen looked down at the mountain of lilac and gold striped boxes with the flamboyant signature—Regina Gold.

"For me?" she asked inanely.

"Guy's doing, dear. I had an idea he was thinking of something like this ever since he asked me if you were size twelve." Patricia Amber laughed delightedly, the shallow dimple at the corner of her mouth flicking in and out.

"But I can't possibly accept them!"

"Go on with you!" the older woman patted her arm and waved a hand at Flynn who was wheeling a barrow full of plants from the greenhouse. "Oh, Flynn, would you mind giving us a hand here?"

He put down the barrow and walked towards them smiling, a wiry little man with a passion for all things growing.

Karen smiled a greeting, then turned uncertainly towards the house. "I'll just go and check up with Guy."
Her throat felt surprisingly dry.

"He's in his study, dear," Patricia Amber called after her, and turned away smiling.

In the house Liane's "Lucky devil!" further unnerved Karen. She walked through to the study and knocked on the door.

"Come in!"

She swallowed on the obstruction in her throat, and opened the door with an air of decision. Guy had his broad back to her, as he took a file out of a cabinet.

"Come into my parlour, said the spider to the fly. Well, what is it, Karo?"

"I think you know very well."

"You *do* sound severe!" He turned then, with a smile, and faced her, handsome and relaxed in sand-coloured slacks and a matching sweater.

Her eyes rejected his stunning physical elegance. His mouth twitched. "Regina's done her stuff, is that it?"

"The clothes have arrived...yes," she murmured repressively.

"You know, Karo, you sound positively formidable, and for such a young girl! Tell me, do you want me to deduct the cost of them from your allowance?"

"Don't try to make a fool of me, Guy. You know I couldn't possibly afford a Regina Gold handkerchief, let alone an entire wardrobe."

"Why, have you looked at them?" His dark eyebrows shot up.

"No!"

"Then what are you on about? As it happens they're all genuine reductions at near bargain basement prices, a special on all X.S.S.W.s this month."

"Please don't evade the issue." She tilted her chin at him.

"What *is* the issue, exactly?" An amused glint leapt into his dark eyes.

"Simply this. I can't have you buying my clothes, Guy."

"Why ever not?" He sounded genuinely startled. "What *is* this extraordinary masque of yours, Karen? You don't really believe Heaven will provide for you, do you?" He gave her an odd sidelong smile. "Why won't you allow me to substitute?"

Her expression was young, very haughty. "It's out of the question!"

He came around the desk, with a vital swinging movement. One look at those black, slanting brows and high cheekbones and Karen retreated, coming to rest against the door. The gleam in his eyes, so full of urgency, had a near-hypnotic effect on her, and she over-reacted.

"Don't come near me, you devil!" she burst out, sounding like a scared, inexperienced schoolgirl.

He stopped in his tracks and gave a shout of laughter.

"Good God! I've never in my life been at this sort of disadvantage." He put the back of his hand between his eyes. "Tell me, do you do it on purpose, all these missish manoeuvres? I don't think I've ever encountered a more suspicious young woman. It's quite unnerving!" His eyes travelled over her face and bare throat, conveying to her wary eyes the impression that he was about to launch some bold campaign.

"I'm sorry, but that's the way it is," she announced breathlessly.

"A life and death decision." He was definitely laughing and she had the irritating suspicion that there was more colour in her face and throat than was necessary.

"I go my own way," she added for good measure.

"Strong words, Karen." He turned away from her. "But for all that, you've restored my faith in the eternal ingénue."

"How nice!" Anger brewed up in her at his bantering tone.

"Sarcasm, little one." His eyes rested on her with

cool male speculation. "You want to look, you'd love to touch, but you just wouldn't dare," he drawled lightly.

"You'd dare anything," she corrected him, in a voice she did not altogether recognise as her own. "Forgive me for taking up your time."

He closed the gap between them, towering over her.

"Karen, my angel, you've just given way to the unbelievably feminine urge to have the last word." There was a distinct, too distinct edge to his voice. "Run along now, or I just might weaken and wring your lovely neck."

She gave a small shocked exclamation.

"Run along," he repeated, quite equably.

She gave him an almost frighteningly intense look, her topaz eyes shimmering, the pupils dilated.

He looked at her quickly. "No tears of remorse, you unpredictable child?"

She was silent a moment, trying to find her voice. "Hardly," she lied. "I don't in the least regret appearing ungracious."

"Not another word, little cat," he said softly, a dangerous gleam in his eyes. "One can resist one's impulses for only so long."

"I could stay and call your bluff," she managed, refusing to be intimidated.

"In that case I have no other choice." His hand closed over her shoulder and tightened experimentally.

In a frenzy of haste Karen broke away from him and opened the door and slammed it behind her. She was treachously near to tears; the tears of anger more than anything else. These exchanges with Guy absolutely exhausted her, yet she was determined he wouldn't get his own way!

CHAPTER FOUR

KAREN prepared for the evening with rising excitement. There was some magic in the word "party" that could never be lost. Stoically, she refused to glance in the wardrobe at the rows of mouth-watering creations bearing the Melbourne couturière's label. It was a definite temptation to pull out one of them—the autumn leaf chiffon—but she braced herself to resist it. It would be an out-and-out admission of defeat. Hadn't she sworn she would manage alone?

She moved over to the dressing table, picking things up and putting them down. Her mind really wasn't on anything. If only she *owned* the chiffon she would look rather special. At least once in her life she was entitled to look rather special. Well, wasn't she? She fought a brief, losing battle with the perverse feminine streak that couldn't resist beautiful clothes. She went to the wardrobe and took out the long evening gown, then held it up against her, twirling idly, studying her reflection.

Her eyes picked up the colour of the gown in the most entrancing fashion. She might have known they would. *He* certainly must have known, thus toppling her scruples. She swayed backwards and forwards, feeling dreamy and romantic. This is the real *me*, she thought blissfully. But it was all wishful thinking! She must be strong.

With commendable self-discipline she hung the gown back in the wardrobe, reaching for her only legitimate evening gown—a white moiré taffeta. She had worn it first and last at St. Hilda's annual prizegiving. It looked like an annual prizegiving, she decided with a flash of irritation. Ah well, there was nothing really wrong with it, if you didn't move in the exclusive Amber circles.

She ran her bath, sniffing the fragrance of expensive soap and bath salts. Aunt Patricia had supplied her with a liberal stock of both, so at least she would smell the part. Dressed in the white taffeta, her dark hair brushed and brushed again into a shining bell, she looked what she was, a beautiful young girl in a simple gown, very likely her first. Which, of course, it was! She hesitated, then wound her mother's pearls around her throat in an effort to reduce the excessive simplicity. She stood back to observe the final effect, then turned down her mouth, thoroughly dissatisfied. Perhaps Aunt Patricia would give the final verdict! Not that anyone would be looking at her with so many established society beauties present.

Crossing over to the central wing, she saw Guy Amber coming up from the cellar. She spun back under the stairs, but it was too late. His arrogant brows shot up as he caught sight of her, then he came towards her purposefully.

"Great God, what are you supposed to be? A refugee from a school concert?"

She tilted her head, her eyes beginning to sparkle. "Untrue and unkind. I think I look rather sweet— simple, unpretentious and quite sweet."

His eyes gave her a critical, head-to-toe appraisal. "My dear Karen, *sweet and simple* is the one thing you're not! But the dress is definitely unpretentious. In fact, not to put too fine a point on it, it's quite dreadful."

"Thank you. I knew I could look to you for approval." She backed away from him, but he took hold of her wrist, compelling her back the way she had come.

"Perhaps you'll tell me what you're doing?" Her skirt flared out as she tried to keep up with him. "I might add you've got my arm in a vice."

Guy's hold loosened a little and he observed her shining dark head, the flawless curve of her cheek. "I'm simply giving you the chance to do yourself justice, Karen."

"To do *you* justice, don't you mean?"

"If you prefer it, though it could be the same thing!" He moved swiftly along the long corridor until they came to her room. He opened the door and gave her a gentle push through it. Karen stood there, defenceless, in the centre of the rust-coloured carpet, her eyes widening.

"Surely you don't intend to give me personal supervision?"

"How else would I know what you're up to?" He walked across to the huge walk-in wardrobe and riffled through the rows of dresses. "Whether it makes you happy or not," he announced, his voice faintly muffled, "I intend to follow this thing through. I can't have you gumming up the works with your foolish pride."

"My foolish pride?" she echoed blankly, and refused to look at him.

"This one!" He came back towards her, flicking her averted cheek. "Go try it on, if you haven't already. I'm damn sure you're woman enough to want to look beautiful."

"As long as you think the dress will accomplish it."

He ignored her sarcasm, intent on the colour that crept under her matt ivory skin.

"It will!"

She whisked away from him then and walked into the wardrobe, shutting the long mirrored door with a gesture of wiping her hands of the whole affair. Inside the room, the white moiré taffeta slipped unheeded to the floor. So it was dreadful, was it? she fumed impotently. It wasn't *that* dreadful! In fact it wasn't dreadful at all. Several of her pupils had told her they loved it! She stepped into the beautiful swirling chiffon, refusing at first to acknowledge the transformation, then stared back at the vision in the mirror, trying ineffectually, now the moment of truth was upon her, to adjust the deep V of the tiny draped bodice. She had never in her life ventured to show so much of her milky white skin. But at least it wasn't indecent! There simply wasn't enough of her!

She pushed open the wardrobe door, speaking very rapidly to cover her confusion.

"You'll have to fix the rest of the zipper, I can go only so far." She presented her smooth ivory back to him and he made the necessary adjustment with one precise movement, his hands moving to rest briefly on her narrow waist. She met his eyes in their mirrored reflection and her heart leapt in her breast to thump erratically on.

Physical attraction was a snare, a delusion. They had no real basis for friendship. In fact they were gliding over the thin ice of antagonism. She kept her voice bantering, though it cost her an effort.

"I feel rather like Lucrezia Borgia dressed for an assignment! Are you sure there isn't some business acquaintance you want fascinated? You know, use my feminine wiles on him for family advancement."

His laugh was brief, rather pointed. "Not to be unkind, Karen, you haven't got any. You're as alarmingly direct as a child!"

She bit on her underlip. "Subtle as a landslide, that's me!" Her eyes sparkled ironically. "I might surprise you by the time the night's over."

"I've not the slightest doubt about that. Now let me have a look at you." He turned her about to face him.

"I have a little of everything," she rattled on absurdly. "Two eyes, a nose…"

"You'll need a little more than that," he murmured imperturbably. "Eye make-up, perhaps. Trish will know all about that."

"You do yourself an injustice. I thought you were

doing extremely well as a ladies' maid. In any case I don't bother much with all that junk.''

"It's about time you did," he retorted bluntly.

Karen swirled half way across the room away from him, rather enjoying the lovely movement of her skirt. "An unnecessary gilding of the lily, I was brought up to believe." Her eyes touched on his dark face. "If you're trying to crush me, and you are, I might tell you, you'll never succeed. I have inner resources."

There was a glimmer of something, not appraisal now, but approval in the depths of his eyes.

"And you'll need them if you consider I'm simply indulging you at the moment."

She smiled at him, her voice adding meaning to her words.

"You're always surprising me, Guy Amber. Some might be forgiven for thinking your actions extraordinarily high-handed."

His eyes gleamed. "I'm on the verge of pointing out..." He broke off abruptly, turning towards the door. There was another light tap and Patricia Amber called softly:

"May I come in, please, Karen?"

Guy Amber laughed and walked to the door, opening it to admit his sister.

"Like an angel you always turn up when you're needed."

"And who needs me?" Dark laughing eyes came to rest on Karen's slender figure, only to widen slightly. "Why, Karen, you look like my Queen of Sheba!"

Karen smiled at this not too unexpected simile. The Queen of Sheba was one of Aunt Patricia's favourite orchids. She gave Guy a gleaming, sidelong look. "Due entirely to your brother's exquisite taste, Aunt Patricia."

He ignored her, a mannerism that was fast becoming a habit.

"I think she could do with a little more make-up for the evening, Trish. I'll leave it to you." He bent his dark head and brushed his sister's cheek. "You look very elegant, as usual, my dear."

"The eye of the beholder, perhaps, Guy."

Karen's eyes rested thoughtfully on the tall, graceful figure in glowing brocade. "But I think so too, Aunt Patricia," she burst out impulsively. "The years have touched you with the gentlest of fingers. You're as lovely now as I ever remembered you."

There was the tiniest of silences while the tears stood momentarily in the older woman's eyes. Karen's young voice faltered, ever sensitive to what went on about her. "I haven't upset you, have I?"

"Of course not!" Patricia Amber blinked rapidly. "Of course not, my dear," she repeated. "It's just sometimes...some trick..." She broke off, her eyes filled with a strange stillness.

"Well now, what about this make-up?" Guy came to stand beside his sister, lifting his eyebrows at her.

"Yes, of course! Karen won't know herself with a touch here and there." Patricia turned to her gaily, though her mouth trembled. "Your eyes are such a fabulous colour you'd do well to enhance their natural beauty." She took hold of her brother's arm and drew him to the door. "I'll be back in a moment, Karen. I have the very jewellery to pick up your gown."

After they were gone Karen stood silently for a moment, then walked to the mirror, addressing her reflection.

"So one way or the other, my poor foolish girl, you're going to the party looking *exactly* as Guy had intended!"

Philip at least was impressed. He was sitting up in his bed watching a very noisy programme on a portable TV. Karen opened his door without knocking and came to stand at the foot of the bed. Philip looked up matter-of-factly, then did a double-take. Karen watched him switch off the set, smiling her astonishment.

"Good gracious, I would never have given you credit for that! Where did you get it from, anyway?" She inclined her head towards the set.

"From Aunt Trish," he said carelessly. "Honestly, Karo, you don't look a bit like yourself. Like Cinderella in those oven ads."

"Gosh, you'll have to do a bit better than that." Karen walked over to the dressing table and had another look at herself. Cinderella in the oven ads!

"No, really, Karo. You look terrific!" Philip began to bounce up and down in excessive admiration. "I can't explain." He continued to gaze at her while his mind made a long, painful detour. "I can't really see why you're going, and I'm not!

Karen spun around, looking shocked. "Good grief, you ought to! There's quite a bit of difference between ten and nineteen, you know."

"I *do* know." Phillp narrowed his eyes knowingly. "That makes me a slip-up."

Karen wheeled and came over to him, peering at him in astonishment. "I beg your pardon?"

Philip held her eyes, colouring slightly. "I said I guess I'm a slip-up. One of the kids in the class told me. When your brother or sister is years and years older than you, that makes you a slip-up."

Karen was torn between amusement and the necessity to correct him. "Let me tell you, Pip," she announced dryly, "you were no slip-up, whatever that might be. You always got the lion's share of Mother's attention, and Father, I remember, adored you. Besides, I don't think I care for that kind of talk."

Philip was contrite. "Sorry, Karo. I knew Murph didn't know what he was talking about. Always trying to be a smart alec."

"I suppose so," Karen smiled with sweet reasonableness. "Now don't have that thing going too long, Pip."

"Ah, come on, Karo. Just this once, seeing you're going to the party."

"Not at all, Pip." Karen's voice became firm. "Nine o'clock at the latest, and only because it's Saturday night." She bent and kissed his cheek. "Nine o'clock?" She looked into his face searchingly, exacting a promise.

"Nine o'clock!" Pip repeated, his eyes serene. "Besides, Aunt Trish is coming to collect it then. She doesn't trust me either."

Karen returned his grin and went to the door. "I'll tell you all about it in the morning."

"I bet you steal the show!" Pip called after her, then settled back on the pillows, turning on the set. Stealthily, he withdrew a half-eaten bar of chocolate from under one pillow, turning back the silver paper. Karo would kill him for going to bed without cleaning his teeth!

CHAPTER FIVE

BELLE AMBER was a glitter of lights and cars were parked six deep on the drive. The great panelled doors between the living and the drawing rooms were thrown open dramatising the full fifty-foot scale of the central wing and displaying to dazzling advantage the pair of eighteenth-century Waterford chandeliers that hung from the moulded plaster ceilings.

The beautiful old house had been decorated in the most flexible of styles, allowing it to serve all the functions and moods of a family famous for their entertaining. To this end, all alterations and modifications to the original building had been carried out without sacrificing beauty, elegance or continuity of the period. The large glass areas that opened up the back of the house admitted sunlight by day and afforded floodlit views of the pool and garden by night.

Karen came quickly down the stairway, stopping for a brief sideways glance in the gilded trumeau that hung above an antique cabinet in the hallway. Her reflection induced a gentle tingling in her veins such as a good wine might evoke. She could hold her own anywhere in this gown! From the great rooms came the mingled sound of laughter, excited voices and the music of an excellent trio. There was to be dancing on the terrace, food and wine on the patio. The house was filled with flowers and the scent of them reached her in soft fragrant drifts. Karen hesitated outside the living room, experiencing the uncertainty everyone does before being launched on a roomful of strangers. Within seconds, Patricia Amber was at her side.

"Karen darling! There are so many people I want you to meet." Her hand dropped lightly on Karen's arm. "And believe me, dear, you'd brighten up any party!" The little dimple flicked beside her mouth. "Guy is on duty out on the terrace. He's fathoms deep in conversation with a very merry widow who's reputed to be on the look-out for a third husband. I do believe he wants you to play for us later on. Of course, if you don't want to, dear, you don't have to. I remember Stephen...your father...used to get tied up in knots before performing."

Karen smiled. "You never get over being nervous, Aunt Patricia, but I'd be happy to play for you whenever you like."

"Thank you, darling. Uncle Mark has never stopped singing your praises, so I don't really think you'd be able to get out of it even if you wanted to. Now, here's our first lot..." She leaned towards Karen conspiratorially. "They say parties are to women what battlefields are to men...so here goes!"

Karen laughed and allowed herself to become the centre of a bright ever-changing circle, full of vaguely familiar faces. They would be the Beautiful People, she supposed with an inward quirk of amusement. She smiled, she spoke, she answered, poised and lovely, all the time anxious to please Aunt Patricia, to have her feel proud of her. It was only when the circle thinned out a little that Rikki came to claim her. He looked very "with-it" and a far cry from the paint-spattered boy genius.

"Karo love, you look positively flamelike amongst all this weak candle power! I swear I've got that queer feeling you get when exposed to real beauty." Suddenly laughing, he whirled her out on to the terrace, the chiffon of her skirt swirling in liquid brightness. "Well, have you met all these perfectly wonderful people?"

"Just about! " Karen looked up at him, her eyes

slightly bewitched with excitement. He gave her his rare, reckless grin.

"You've got to marry me, Karo, sooner or later. I've been giving it some thought and it seems like the very best solution. We'll head off to somewhere far-flung and I'll paint you in every possible guise." He slid his arms around her waist and started out on the downbeat of the dance tune. "You should really be grateful. I come into a small fortune when I'm twenty-five."

He swung her out on to the floor, smiling at her serene indifference to his expected wealth.

"You've been drinking!" she observed matter-of-factly.

"Of course I've been drinking. I mistrust anyone who doesn't at parties." Other couples surged round them and he drew further down the length of the terrace. She relaxed in his arms with a swift, upward smile. "I like you, Rikki. I always have and I guess I always will."

"I knew I could make you respond to my cherubic charm."

Karen broke into a laugh. "You might *look* cherubic, but I happen to know you've a mercurial temperament. Don't forget I grew up with you."

"I know nothing of the kind—we've just met!" His light, teasing voice dropped a full octave. "Now there's a real Scott Fitzgerald heroine for you. She dances on tables and drinks gallons of gin."

Karen followed his gaze and saw a delectable slightly over-weight redhead in coffee cream lace.

"Sue Paton, the heiress?"

"The same one. She's been after Guy for the best part of her girlhood and she's now thirty-five. Doesn't look it, does she? Guy can't very well avoid her, they move in the same circles, but he always lines up a counter-attraction for her at parties. That's him, the rather debauched-looking character sitting on a few millions. Never leaves anything to chance, our Guy!"

The music stopped and pairs broke up and merged into laughing groups. A waiter came through the French doors with a tray of champagne, then the music, muted and dreamy, throbbed through the house again and Rikki drew her back into his arms.

Karen, looking over his shoulder, caught sight of Liane in a blue, very feminine extravaganza, threading her way across the terrace towards them.

"Here's Liane. She looks faintly upset about something." Rikki groaned and gave up. "This is not the time to say it, but couldn't you have checked out Liane's outfit? That's pure Hollywood, and the forties at that."

"Please don't say anything to that effect, Rikki. You wouldn't want to destroy her confidence!"

Rikki gritted his teeth.

"That's being well taken care of! Poor old Lee. She's just a satellite." His blue eyes unhappy and slightly cynical. "A satellite in orbit around mother moon."

Karen laid a warning hand on his arm. Liane reached them, her dark eyes wide and anxious.

"Mother's been detained. That was Colin on the phone, now. It will take them the best part of an hour to get here."

"That's the most wonderful news in the whole wide world," Rikki said brightly.

"Everything's all right, isn't it?" Karen cut in, over the top of Rikki.

"Yes, of course." Liane looked from one to the other. "I'm just a bit anxious. Colin drives so very fast when he's late for an appointment."

"Don't worry, he has such precious cargo," Rikki pointed out unfeelingly. "By the way, sweetie, you don't need all those frill and furbelows around your neck, do you? I like you uncluttered, like Trish. You've got the same line."

Liane looked down at her foaming neckline. "Don't you like it?"

"Not much. You'd have plenty of time to change. What about that coral affair Trish bought you?"

"Oh, don't be silly, Rikki, it's much too plain for tonight." Liane dismissed the idea. "Colin will love this. It's Celia's choice, after all, and you have to admit she has perfect taste."

"A positive flair for perfection, if you ask me," Rikki drawled lightly. "But for *herself*, kiddo. You've got to study your own type. Celia can't do it for you."

"Oh, don't start that again, Rikki." Liane looked to Karen for approval.

"I'm sure Colin will think you look lovely," Karen managed, even if she agreed wholeheartedly with Rikki. One couldn't very well start picking Liane to pieces. It would be extremely hurtful and quite the wrong time and wrong place for it.

"Rikki!" A tall, horsey young woman with nut-brown hair and brown eyes and a very assured manner advanced on them, putting her arm through Rikki's. "I've some perfectly wonderful friends of mine dying to meet you." She flickered a glance and a "You'll excuse us!" at the two younger girls and drew an unenthusiastic Rikki through the maze of guests.

Liane expelled her long held breath. "You've got to hand it to Rikki, he's never anyone else but himself. It's quite funny the way he can't understand he's terribly eligible, though Roz Mazlin would chase him if he had buck teeth and a squint. She makes no secret of her plans for marrying money. Bucket-loads of it, I understand." Her white teeth glinted behind her full coral mouth. "I won't be a moment, Karo. I'd better tell Aunt Trish about Mother and Colin. I do hope they make it before supper." She looked at Karen with mock solemnity. "You'll have to watch yourself tonight, Karo. I've heard some pretty extravagant comments. You look like being the newest sensation."

"If she is, then I'm here to look after her!"

Liane swung around, amused. "I'm sort of inter-

ested in hearing what *you* think, Guy, as a connoisseur
of beautiful women.''

"I feel we need a little more time," he drawled, his
dark eyes on Karen.

Liane's answering nod was dead serious. Her eyes
veered to Karen. "I know you're going to like Colin.
I'll introduce you just as soon as he arrives."

Guy watched her retreating figure. "Many waters
cannot quench love, neither can floods drown it. Colin
seems to have fallen on his feet, and Lee's much too
young for such things."

"And you're a judge of love?" Karen arched her
slender neck to gaze away from him into the garden,
pierced with shafts of rose and gold.

"Now why sound so scornful?" He gave a brief
laugh. "Come dance with me."

"I might bungle it," she said lightly.

His dark eyes were amused. "I don't mind. Tonight
I'm all loving kindness, even towards a spitting kitten.
I've done my duty towards all the dull, really important
people, and now I have you."

"I'm speechless!" She pretended abstraction and
looked over his shoulder at the whirling vortex of
couples.

"Come here!"

She went into his arms, feeling them close round
her, hearing his voice but not hearing it. This curious
effect he had on her, there must be some chemical
explanation for it, but sensation was making logic remote.

"Decorative *and* silent, as a young girl should be!"
His voice had an unmistakable thread of laughter in it.

"I can see I'll have to do better. Splendid night, isn't
it?" She looked up at him, then suddenly mindful of
something, began to flutter her eyelashes, riveting his
attention.

"What on earth is that all about?" he asked, his eyes
narrowing. "You look quite absurd."

"Fancy! And your own idea after all! I'm merely giving you the benefit of my dramatic eye make-up." She trailed off under his sardonic look, and a hint of admiration came into his eyes.

"Not bad! Not bad at all!" he laughed softly, and drew her closer. Karen willed her limbs not to tremble. With a little maturity she could handle this situation, but his dark arrogance simply shrivelled her bones even if her head remained perfectly clear. Unconsciously she moved near him like a magnet drawn on an irresistible path.

"You're trembling, Karen," he observed conversationally.

"Just a mild form of hysteria," she answered very dryly. "I'm sure you're used to it."

A flame licked up in his dark eyes. "I would have thought you were immune. In fact, you've been very vocal about it."

She couldn't suppress the mischief in her eyes. "Perhaps I've a very realistic approach to life."

"Now don't women say idiot things!" He met her wide, jewel-bright eyes. "There's no need to look at me with so much concentrated inquiry."

"That would seem to be a woman's vocation," she murmured laconically.

There was an undercurrent of mockery in the depths of his eyes. "Now I would have thought that was to be loved!"

She pushed back against his arm. "This is a pleasantly meaningless conversation, isn't it?"

"Could it be otherwise with a babe in the woods?"

"Well, you'd certainly qualify for one of the other leading parts!"

He looked at her through half-closed lids. "Now don't spare me, Karen. I can face up to my limitations."

Her voice was silky. "Surely you're not waiting for me to agree with that? By the way, there's a mermaid swimming against the drapes with a long straight fall of blonde hair who's making me feel very guilty and uncomfortable at the moment.''

"Miaow!" he smiled very slightly. "She's very good at it—the competitive type. Name the game and she'll beat you at it.''

"Well, you may be used to this kind of thing, but I can't bear to be the target of so much distilled suspicion.''

Guy hazed his cheek over her dark hair, adding insult to injury, and Karen drew away from him very pointedly.

"I don't think I care to be used as a *muleta*—the red flag, you know.''

"I did guess at its meaning," he drawled lazily. "I've spent a little time in Spain.''

She sighed briefly and relaxed in his arms.

"When this dance is over I shall be a woman of experience.''

"I prefer you as you are!''

Her eyes met his, half laughing, half provocative. "And how is that?''

"Oh, rather magical and mysterious.''

Her breath caught suddenly. "Don't do it to me, Guy," she said huskily. "For all you know I might be an idiot child.''

"Only in as much as you like your own way.''

"I'm only human, I admit, while you, of course, are a machine, and no woman is going to gum up the machinery.''

"How clever of you, my exclusive beauty.'

"If I'm boring you, please stop," she said in a voice not her own.

"You may annoy me, but never bore me, I imagine.''

Karen hoped she didn't look as keyed up as she felt. His hold tightened on her.

"Now, now, take it easy. Your eyes are shimmering

with the most feverish intensity. I told you before, I'd never hurt you."

"If only I could believe that!" she announced rather oddly in the long stillness, then yielded completely to his encircling arm.

Shortly before supper, Patricia Amber went in search of Karen, and found her in the drawing room, being lectured on the architectural quality of its detailed Corinthian columns and handsome wall panelling. Her tutor was a fair, short-sighted, very serious young man called Jeffrey Parrish, whose father held the Chair of Architecture at the University. His father, an attractive widower, also at the party, was exhibiting his aesthetic tastes by spending the best part of the evening on the love seat with Gina Holmes, the well-known fashion model.

Karen's amused eyes flickered backwards and forwards between father and son, giving the son only half her attention. Her delight in her surroundings, Jeffrey was telling her, was not only instinctive but drawn largely from unconscious experience. Appreciation, he explained was the critical weighing of all qualities, good and bad, while taste, and Jeffrey bowed to her, was the preference for good qualities and the conscious choice of them.

Karen tried to look suitably impressed.

"I think we could safely say the one and only test of appreciation is delight!" Jeffrey said emphatically. Karen, her eyes on the love seat, had to agree.

"That statement must, of course, be qualified." The young man spun quickly, prevented from elaborating by his hostess's detaining arm on his sleeve.

"I wonder if I might borrow Karen for a moment, please, Jeffrey. She's going to play for us!"

"The *piano*?" Jeffrey's fair eyebrows disappeared under his hair. "I say, I've never actually spoken to a girl who could *play* the piano. They've had lessons, of

course, but they can't actually *play*." He trailed in their
wake, one hand on his lapel, with the deference Karen
felt should possibly be accorded to Royalty.

The room quietened with disconcerting suddenness
as Aunt Patricia announced her and Karen went to the
piano, conscious of Mark Amber's encouraging nod
and the quick assessing glance of the trio's pianist. Guy
opened up the lid of the Steinway as Karen reached it
and she swallowed rather nervously.

His eyes were intent. "You're nervous! You've lost
colour!"

"Of course I'm nervous," she said barely above a
whisper.

"You wouldn't be worth a bumper if you weren't!"
His eyes held hers for a moment, his presence a good
sedative, even an antidote for her present mood of pre-
performance nerves.

"Play your usual *tour de force*," he suggested.
"There's no sense in letting them all go to sleep on
us."

Karen settled herself on the piano seat, pitching her
voice for him alone.

"You're taking an awful risk, aren't you? I could be
the merest amateur. Think of your friends!"

"Right now I'm thinking of you, and I know all
about the Conservatorium diploma!"

His dark eyes swept her face, supremely confident,
whether of her or himself or both of them Karen had
no means of telling. She gave him an entirely false,
sweet smile. "Thank you, Guy!"

"Thank *you*, little one." He moved away from the
piano and she was on her own, with the room expec-
tantly quiet about her.

A *tour de force*, Guy said. Well, there was always
Chopin's famous study, the so-called Revolutionary
Etude. It was filled with innumerable technical difficulties but cloaked for the listener with the beauty and
emotion of a spontaneous work of art.

With the opening chord, Karen settled and the music surged into the room, proud, rebellious and full of passionate nationalism. Her left hand was impeccable as it had to be, its movements broad and sweeping from long hours of practice. Her first choice was but a prelude to her second. The audience, hard core sophisticates for the most part, were entirely charmed. It was something of a novelty for a beautiful girl to be so gifted and *so* unexpected!

There was the merest break to establish the mood, then Karen went straight into her "party piece" from Conservatorium days—Liszt's Mephisto Waltz. It poured out like a torrent, as did the unqualified applause. She bowed her slender white nape in acknowledgment, conscious of having given of her best. Mark Amber ensconced in a bergère in the corner, surrounded by his own particular friends, tilted his glass to her. She smiled in his direction and took Guy's outstretched hand. Her own hands were trembling now with a sudden draining of nervous energy. His hand tightened, the thumb caressing her palm, easing the tension out of her. He had far too many tricks to him!

"For a special occasion, there's always a special treat! I have something lined up for you, little one. Are you interested?"

"Frankly I'm intrigued!" She turned away to smile into faces that smiled back at her with heightened interest.

"You play beautifully, Karen," he added gravely.

"We learn something new every day." Excitement made her flippant. His dark eyes rested on her ivory face, the colour now returning to it.

"I said you *play* beautifully, little one, but in many respects your education has been sadly neglected."

"I'm sure you'll see to it," she returned sweetly.

"But are you sure you can stick the course?"

She smiled without answering, not even knowing how to answer him.

"Where are you taking me?"

"How far would you be prepared to go, I wonder?" His manner seemed to convey some secret challenge.

"Not very far with you, Guy Amber!"

He tut-tutted gently. "That's hardly fair and very misguided. You're palpitating like a bird under my hand. Does it affect you so very much, then?"

Her eyes, wide and startled, flew to his.

"Playing the piano," he stressed dryly.

"Of course!" She looked away from him hastily, following blindly until they came to the door of the private cellar. Guy pulled the heavy door and switched on a light. It flashed its beam over a steep flight of stone steps.

"I'll go first. Keep straight behind me and go carefully in that long skirt."

Karen narrowed her eyes against the naked bulb, seeing high walls lined with solidly constructed wine racks, stacked with meticulous care. The necks of the bottles, capped with coloured aluminium or lead alloy foil protruded from the racks, on their sides to keep the corks moist and prevent them from shrinking.

There were table wines, red and white, sparkling wines, champagne, the oak casks of fortified wines, the sherries, the brandies, the port and dessert wines, the spirits and liqueurs. Each bin was dated and each bottle entered and catalogued in the cellar book.

Her attention distracted, Karen's foot, in its light evening shoe, missed the third step. Her heart lurched with the sickening realisation that she was falling.

"Guy!" she cried out like a wounded bird.

He turned swiftly, his senses alerted before actual danger. His broad shoulders braced themselves against the single rail as he took her full weight, cradling her against him and smothering her face and hair against the beautiful blackcloth of his evening jacket. They stood there motionless, for a minute, while her heart flipped, then righted itself.

She lifted her face to him, her hair spilling back over her shoulders.

"Oh, I'm sorry, Guy. I would have fallen. You did warn me. It was my sandal—the sole is so new and shiny." Her perfume seemed to be in the air, on both of them, spiking the cool atmosphere, elusive yet persistent.

He laughed in his throat. "Excuses, excuses—and you're such a devil of a weight! Well, this should take care of the sandals." He swung her up into his arms, her flame-coloured gown foaming about her. A sensation akin to sharpest, not-to-be-borne excitement took hold of her.

"Now what are you afraid of?" he taunted her. "You can't come to that much harm!"

At the base of the stairs he held her for a moment longer, looking down into her face. "To hear you play one would never think there was so little of you."

The expression in her topaz eyes changed elusively. "Don't you like thin girls?"

His dark eyes were amused, raking her mercilessly. "I wouldn't have said you were *thin*, precisely."

"In that case, you'd better put me down." She looked back at him rather helplessly.

Guy laughed and lowered her gently to the floor, his back blocking the light.

"Mark tells me you've never tasted champagne."

"No!" she said, her attention diverted, "but there's plenty to be had upstairs."

He smiled. "Not quite the same. In any case, you haven't had any all evening."

She shot him a look of inquiry. "How do you know? You've been so... busy," she murmured dryly.

"Busy or not, I can always keep an eye on you."

Karen looked away from his mouth, speaking airily. "Actually I wouldn't be game to touch even a sherry before playing. It's disastrous, no matter what anyone else may tell you."

He laughed and moved over to the circular oak table that stood between the wine racks. At the back of the table was a cabinet, holding glasses, and on top of the cabinet an ice bucket. Only then did Karen notice the bottle reclining in it, with its elegant French label and *appelation d'origine controlée.*

Guy took it down and put it on the small table. "The unique quality of champagne is that it suits any occasion. I don't think you could say the same for any other wine. My grandmother used to drink it for breakfast, though she *was* a trifle eccentric. Some of our own champagnes are excellent, but they're not yet in the same class as the great French champagnes. I want you to try the best. Your palate is unsullied." He removed the wired-down cork, expertly controlling the natural effervescence of the wine.

Karen's eyes were sparkling. "This is quite exciting!"

"I thought you'd think so."

"A typical reaction, perhaps?" she smiled up at him, the mischief and significance apparent in her eyes.

"*Not* so typical!" His voice was very dry. "I can see quite plainly that your eyes are sparkling solely in anticipation of the wine." He took out two glasses, short-stemmed tulips, a perfect combination of size, shape and thinness, and near filled them. "Don't expect to get the best from the *wine* if you use the open-mouthed coupe for champagne, Karen, though you might get the best from the occasion. This is a mixture of three parts *pinot noir* to one part *pinot blanc*, a blend by the bottle fermentation method, of course. All good champagnes are bottled fermented, as you know." He held up the glass to the light, and the liquid scintillated the colour of pale straw. "I suppose you know if the black grapes are allowed to become too ripe it's impossible to avoid some colour in the wine, that's why the grapes must be picked at exactly the right time and handled very carefully before they reach the crushers. I'll take you over Amberleigh when we go interstate."

"I'll keep you to that," she said, her eyes brilliant over the rim of the glass.

"No need. That's a promise!" He held up his own glass. "To your beautiful eyes, little one!"

Karen buried her nose in the wineglass, trying to capture the elusive bouquet.

He laughed. "If you do *that*, my child, you're very likely to sneeze! The escaping carbon dioxide gets into the nose before the bouquet impinges."

Karen tried again, taking a mouthful and savouring the exquisitely dry flavour. He watched her, half smiling, as she finished the glass and handed it back to him.

"Nothing's ever tasted so ambrosial—the sum of perfection! I'll have another, please."

There was indulgence in the curve of his mouth. She smiled at him then, a child's smile, very sweet and innocent, devoid of the veneer of sophistication. The light threw a nimbus of gold around her head, shadowed hollows on her cheeks and a bloom over her skin.

"Karen, Karen," he said softly, "you look *exactly* as you used to look...oh, ten or more years ago." A kind of amusement seemed to play in his eyes.

"And you're *exactly* as shattering as you ever were, Guy Amber!"

"You say that very emphatically, little one." He handed her glass back to her.

"Occasionally the reckless side of my nature gets the better of me." She gave a small helpless shrug of her shoulder, feeling she was being whirled into danger. "We'd better go back, hadn't we?" She sipped at her wine, waiting for an answer.

He looked back at her, faintly smiling. "There's plenty of time!" A dark glitter of magnetic current spun out between them. He drained his own glass and refilled it. Karen tried to fix her attention on negative things... the dull sheen of the table, the multi-coloured tops of aluminium foil...she moistened her top lip, tasting champagne.

"Relax, little one! You'd drive a man crazy!"

"I'd drive a man crazy!" She accented the first word strangely. Her voice sounded excited and just a little overwrought.

"Now it's your turn to be polite," he smiled at her lazily, black brows slanting.

An exhausted sweetness seemed to come over her.

"You're the very devil, Guy! I feel utterly breathless."

"And you look utterly charming and just a tiny bit irresponsible."

"It's the champagne! It seems to transcend ordinary spheres for a while." Her voice grew dreamy, reflective. "If I shut my eyes I can travel back in time to the beautiful days... the fine, unforgettable days, so tangible I can feel the brush of the air, the smell of the earth, the flood of rising sunlight washing over the vineyards, the foothills... Pip's pure profile, the baby texture of his skin... my mother. Father, so gay and handsome... Aunt Patricia... *you*!" Her eyes flew open. His dark face was very near her, his eyes oddly brilliant. "You're dangerous!" The words seemed torn from her. She retreated a few steps, her eyes fixed on his face, almost spellbound, fighting the crazy urge to get into his arms.

"Yes, you're dangerous!" she repeated in a soft intense undertone. "I don't know what this is all about, but it's got to stop!" Her hand swept the air between them, forcibly expressive.

His laugh, brief and highly amused, eased the tension.

"The champagne has gone to your head, my pet. Whatever it is I want from you, you're not capable of giving it... at the moment." He smiled at her tilted profile. "Look at me, Karen. Finish your drink and we'll go upstairs. You're only a babe!"

"I'm very glad I am," she said simply. "You're rather frightening, Guy. You give me the distinct impression that women are only for evening, to be forgotten when the sun comes up and there's work to be done."

"You should be spanked for that!"

"By whom?"

"Me! Either way you're much too young to kiss."

She put her glass down carefully and swirled away from him, moving towards the steps. He caught her up easily, keeping a steadying hand at her waist.

"And then she fled me!" he murmured mockingly in her ear.

"Thank you for the *champagne*," she said quickly, holding up her long skirt, trying to beat him up the stairs.

His hand brushed her flushed cheek as he leaned forward to open the door for her.

"I'm glad you were able to appreciate it, little one. I haven't enjoyed myself so much in years!"

Rikki, coming through from the entrance hall, stalked up to them with a comic expression of outrage. "In a democracy there ought to be an equal distribution of privilege. Who's been sampling the best bubbly?"

Guy's mouth faintly quirked. "We have been indulging in that wicked extravagance, Rikki. But your vigil of waiting is over. You may take Karen in to supper."

Rikki peered intently into Karen's face. Her cheeks bore a faint almond blossom flush. "I was scared rotten that wouldn't be the case. A big wheeler-dealer like Guy usually rides roughshod over all the competition, puts them down with a word."

Guy's voice was mild. "Let's go in, Rick. Trish will be wanting to start supper." His reappearance signalled the start of the buffet supper: the lobster, the oysters, the prawn and avocado cocktails, the caviar with cucumber, the crab ramekins, the chicken and curries with piles of steaming snowy white rice, the tossed green salads with crusty French bread, the chocolate and chestnut cheesecakes, the brandied peaches, gingered apples, flaming strawberries, the little flagged cheeses of five different countries and a wonderful selection of wines.

The lights glowed on the vari-coloured dresses of the women, the suave black and white, the maroon, midnight blue and deep amethyst jackets of the men.

"Such beautiful harmonies!" Karen's voice in Rikki's ear was soft and rapturous. "The deep sensuous pleasure of fine china and silver, beautiful crystal and immaculate napery!" Her glance swept the table. "Not to mention the food!"

Rikki was giving it his full attention. The guests crowded into the tables and impulsively Karen drew closer to him, chattering and laughing, just the two of them, young and with each other, unguarded.

"You're thinking I'm just a little bit intoxicated, now aren't you?" Karen smiled into Rikki's intense, young face.

"I'm thinking how... beautiful you are," he answered with complete candour. The throaty little laugh she gave was just as unselfconscious and charming as a chiild's.

"You improve by the minute!"

"Ditto!" Rikki smiled, and continued to pile up their plates; not even consulting Karen for her preferences. But it was delicious and Karen could feel herself begin to take wings.

"Your eyes are melting in that weird way again, Karo, It's a trick that's interfering very seriously with my breathing."

"Not your *eating*!" she pointed out dryly, watching him spear yet another prawn cutlet. "I hope you're not going to talk like a blithering idiot all evening."

"Words to live by, Miss Hartmann. Blithering idiot, indeed! I have news for you, dear girl. I'm not mad."

She laughed at him with affection. "I know."

Rikki's eyes gleamed a hectic and brilliant blue and

she had a very clear picture of the enormous attraction a few extra years would bring him. "You're enchanting," he said softly. "For me, I hope?"

She sipped at her wine, her small elegant head slightly tipped to one side. "Do you want a frank answer? Not for anyone."

Rikki grinned, a wide, disarming grin. "Was that supposed to be a squelch?"

"What a ridiculous and spiteful suggestion! In actual fact, I'm still dreaming of the perfect admirer."

His tone and look shrivelled her. "The perfect admirer—and with me around! 'I am half sick of shadows, cried the Lady of Shalott?'"

Karen laughed. "Do you often quote Tennyson?"

"Only when I drift into the doldrums. I thought you were well on the way to loving me."

"I can't help what you think." She looked away from him to smile across the table at Mark Amber, who waggled his wineglass at her. Rikki was unabashed.

"I suppose love is a bit dicey, at that. A state of mind more than anything else. Take all the great lovers... Beatrice and Dante, Romeo and Juliet, Tristan and Isolde, Fred and Maggie. You couldn't really say they knew one another. Strangers, you might say. I can't really see that great love and day-to-day living go hand in hand."

Karen almost choked and Rikki patted her kindly.

"I can see you've grasped the realities of the situation," she managed at last.

"I wish to God I had!"

Karen looked puzzled into his face. For the first time Rikki's voice was devoid of humour.

"All this and modesty too?" she asked lightly.

His expression changed. "I suppose you know what you're saying, Karo. You're practically admitting you're feeling the pull of my fascination."

"My mind is on higher things," she pointed out, her eyes roaming over the room.

"That's what I'm afraid of," Rikki muttered *sotto voce*, noting without surprise the direction in which her eyes were constantly straying. Suddenly he glanced over his shoulder. "Do you hear?" He put his wine-glass on the table, his face inscrutable. From somewhere behind them came a voice; a voice Karen was to come to know far too well. It was a soft, sweet voice with a faint trace of husky allure. Instinctively she straightened, aware of a sudden, unaccountable tension. She tried to relax again, but she was too sensitive to Rikki's mental and physical attitude, at once alert and wary.

Then she was there! Celia Amber—framed in the doorway, poised with the studied grace that irresistibly recalled to Karen's mind the entrance of a great actress, awaiting the applause which was her due. With such a face and figure and acting ability, Karen thought inconsequentially, it was a wonder Hollywood hadn't beaten a path to her door. One moment only and she had the lasting impression of exquisite slenderness, of vivid blue eyes and an aureole of silver-gilt hair.

"Guy!" the soft husky voice sang the name, for him alone. "Darling," she stretched out her hands to him, breathless, "I've been frantic...simply *frantic*! It's just been one of those end-of-the-world days! Trish!" She gazed wide-eyed at her much taller sister-in-law, as she separated herself from her guests. A well-dressed, smooth-faced young man hovered on the periphery of the group. Colin! Karen thought with instant dismay, not quite sure why she was so disappointed.

"Stone the crows!" Rikki murmured succinctly. "That kittenish girl-child!"

Karen looked at him quickly, all the time hearing the soft husky voice, the breathless little pauses that punctuated the bursts of explanations. Heads were lifting and greetings called and exchanged. Celia smiled and waved with charm and animation, so obviously home again, among her own admiring crowd. She circled the room like a swan, tiptoed to brush her daughter's cheek, then she was coming towards them.

Rikki went rigid. "Rikki dearest!" One white arm stole through her son's, whose shoulder she barely reached. Then the blue eyes were on Karen with extraordinary vividness. There was no liking there, no warmth, nor even dislike; just a hard clear assessment like a bolt of merchandise she found vaguely unbelievable.

The expression broke so quickly Karen very nearly convinced herself she had imagined it. The voice was warm, still sweet, yet to Karen's over-sensitive ears, gently accusing.

"Why...why, Karen, you're quite *pretty*. I never dreamed...you used to be such a *fey* little thing, all long legs and big eyes!"

"Lord love me!" Rikki's snort heralded an attack. "Isn't that the understatement of the year. *Pretty!* Karen's quite beautiful!"

"Do you hear him?" The blue eyes looked from Karen, who prickled uncomfortably to her son. "Beautiful, he says!" Despite the cool, elegant little laugh that went with it Karen knew quite plainly that Celia wasn't amused. A slight tartness entered her sweet voice. "You get more like the Ambers every day, my darling, but you do have a certain indestructible quality."

"To the hills!" said Rikki, but Celia ignored him. She turned her attention to Karen. "I'm so sorry I wasn't able to meet you earlier, Karen. You do understand." Her tiny fine-boned hand lifted with a gesture of complete helplessness. "That Colin! He's such a capable young man when he's himself, but really..." her voice trilled with laughter and her eyes gleamed with something like triumph... "he's not himself!"

Karen was staring unashamedly. So this was Aunt Celia? Rikki and Liane's mother? Uncle Mark was

quite right, she would never have recognised her again.
The silver-gilt hair—it had never been that colour, although it was Rikki's exactly—was fluffed high on the
crown with a fringe of soft bangs that melted into the
pearly tones of her brow. Her eyelids were moulded
closely over her deeply blue eyes, her nose short,
slightly tilted, the lower lip full, the upper a trifle short,
the skin without blemish, the contours of the face
smoother, more clear-cut than ever before. Her evening gown of chiffon and white lace was perfection, cut
low in the bodice, her figure as firm and youthful as a
young girl's. Celia Amber was incredible. She looked
only a handful of years older than her son.

Karen tried to smile naturally. Her mouth moved
and the muscles of her face went about their appointed
business. She found herself replying, saying that it
didn't matter in the least...not to worry...how wonderful it was to see her...the family...

The luminous smile persisted. Celia listened, her
proud little head slightly tilted to the taller Karen. Her
quickened breath moved the fragile lace at her breast.
She spun her head with sweet imperativeness. "Come
back, darling! Do excuse me, children. Have fun." She
swirled away from them in a sea of chiffon, a lingering
trace of expensive perfume.

It was impossible to mistake who *darling* was. Guy
Amber, his arm thrust casually through a friend's,
lifted his dark head with its definable grace of sculpture. Deep inside of her Karen screamed a passionate
protest. Darling! An unreasonable revulsion began to
oppress her like a heavy cloak.

Guy was smiling, giving his sister-in-law a charming,
slightly formal bow.

"Honestly, darling, someone up there actually ar-
ranges these setbacks for me when I'm going out!" Celia's voice floated back to the table. Karen watched Guy
move his hand in a gesture that made explanations unimportant. He looked so tall, so sophisticated, so suc-

cessful and worldly, with the arrogant simplicity of his beautiful, expensive clothes, she felt slightly ill just looking at him. Why should he have this damnable effect on her? Rikki, in his own way, was almost as eye-catching.

Celia, superb in her self-confidence, raised her white arms to Guy and then they were dancing. Celia was an exquisite carnation he wore on his jacket—impossible to believe they were not perfectly matched! Karen sighed deeply, her appetite and high spirits—gone. Around her heart she felt the clutch of something like raw jealousy, but she still had enough common sense to dispatch it quickly. She glanced once more at Rikki, only to find him just as desolate.

"Purely out of regard for my feelings, don't say anything," he warned her.

"I don't know what you're talking about!"

"I think you do, my pet. You've very quick and delicate perceptions. Besides, it's not the first time I've seen that particular calamity. If there was to be a new heaven and a new earth, Celia would have Guy on both of them. Come to that, do you suppose there's a woman here who wouldn't be mad to have Guy make love to her? He, of course, with that wonderful arrogant habit of his, never gives a damn! He's really got more sex appeal than is actually decent." Rikki's young voice held a measure of envy.

"Leave me out of it." Karen said with fiery disdain.

Rikki looked deeply into her flashing eyes. "Your type is rapidly becoming obsolete, my girl." He glanced over her shoulder and gave an audible groan. "Look out, here comes the fiancé, all goggle-eyed. On to a free meal ticket for life, he is. Still the thickets are full of wolves!"

Colin came up and was promptly introduced. At closer quarters he was still a disappointment, though with his thick brown hair, smooth tanned skin and large hazel eyes, he had more than the usual quota of good looks. His manner towards Rikki was faintly patronizing.

"Evening, Rick. When are you going to join up with us? P.R. could do with a good man."

Rikki's expression was hard to beat. "You've been out in the midday sun," he said calmly, and glanced across at Karen. "If you'll excuse me for a moment, Karo, I'll just go and twist the tiger's tail."

"What an extremely odd young man!" Colin announced in a tone of shocked righteousness, watching Rikki make a beeline towards his mother.

"Do you think so?"

Colin redirected his hazel gaze. "Well, he does seem to deal in half phrases and innuendoes. I'm never sure whether he's actually saying something to me or not."

Karen laughed and Colin perked up. He asked her to dance, holding her too firmly, and Karen's spirits plunged.

"I say, what do you think of Celia? She's fab, isn't she? Absolutely gorgeous. I don't see anyone to match her for looks and style. And her clothes—she wears them like nothing in this world. I ask you!"

Karen hoped her smile wasn't too tight. "Well, then I'll just have to say I've taken a strong and immediate liking to her."

Colin gave a small, hooting laugh. "What more could you want! Strange, that. Celia usually has all the girls pea green, but then you're rather fab yourself, aren't you?" He bent his head for a closer examination. "Yes, you are," he reiterated slowly. Karen closed her eyes. Her partner took this as an admission of pure enjoyment and drew her yet closer, his breath stirring her hair. He began to tell her of the many and spectacular business assignments to his credit, mistaking her limpid indifference for genuine admiration. On his own admission Colin was an excellent diagnostician with a natural flair for putting his finger on trouble.

Karen opened her eyes briefly. "How very alarming!'' Conversation, however one-sided, ground to a halt.

Colin was flustered, afraid he might have given the wrong impression. "I think Guy himself would be the first to admit I'm an asset to the firm.'' His expression contracted into peevishness.

Karen was prepared to admit that that might be the case, but she very much doubted Colin's ability to make Liane happy. Colin appeared to be a self-confessed egoist. She flashed Rikki a set of distress signals and he came immediately to her rescue. Liane was swept once more into her fiancé's arms, where she clearly longed to be.

"Back to the play-pen,'' Rikki murmured into Karen's ear.

All through the rest of the evening, Karen fought to keep her eyes off Celia and Guy. Guy seemed to be playing the gallant to Celia's charm with an urbanity Karen had hitherto never encountered. Yet why should she have hit on the word "playing'' unless it was Guy's manner, so sardonic, so mocking, so blatant, it must surely be suspect unless it was real!

A tumult surged through her veins, the cause of which she was loath to put a name to. Instead she fell back on her old line of defence, inwardly blaming Guy for creating intolerable situations. Once more he was the villain of a melodrama.

The party, however, was a stunning success. Karen, had she known it, was proving quite a talking point. Malicious and witty tongues found occasion to remark on her youth and distinctive beauty and its possible repercussions in such a household. Her resemblance to her dear father was commented on and the old stories began to recirculate. One thing was certain, Celia Amber now had a powerful rival in the sphere of sheer glamour and one she was unlikely to tolerate. Horror of horrors, said the wits, the rival was young!—the unforgivable crime.

Long after the last guests had departed Karen was

still wandering aimlessly about her room, unable to bring herself to the serious business of undressing. She felt over excited, off balance and curiously frustrated. At least she had played well, and some part of her took pleasure in the many sincere compliments that came her way with the farewells. She glanced down at her hands, noticing for the first time that she was not wearing the beautiful topaz dress ring Aunt Trish had lent her. Of course she had left it on the piano. She never could bear a ring on her finger when she played. She only hoped it would still be there. How forgetful and careless!

With sudden impatience she flew out of the room, down the long corridor, towards the staircase. The house was quite deserted now, with only a few lights on. There was not even an echo of the music, the laughter, that had resounded through the house only a few short hours before.

She came on down the stairs on whispering feet, her hand going to her heart as a dark velvet voice startled her.

"I might have known you'd be walking abroad like a witch after midnight!" Guy came round the base of the stairwell, looking up at her mockingly. "Perhaps you've come to tell me what you haven't told me all night. Did you like your party?"

Karen stood silently, trying to penetrate the façade of his easy, urban manner.

"Well, little Miss-in-her-teens?" His face was too smooth to be readable, but his voice was definitely sardonic.

"*My* party!" she said, looking at him strangely, but not making any movement towards him.

"I never know what you're getting at when you look at me like that. Tell me what's on your mind, child."

The light from a wall bracket enfolded and caressed her; her face and her shoulders, the slender line to her body. She stood for a moment almost defiantly, her head high and challenging.

"I can't see myself adopting so drastic a measure. At least, not with *you*!"

Dark laughter sprang into his eyes. There was a wholly appraising, masculine look on his handsome face.

"Could you be back to your imaginative fancies, I wonder?" he asked softly, his eyes narrowing.

She gave a bitter-sweet little laugh. "How astute you are, Guy, and so very sure of yourself. But I imagine keeping your emotions under control is elementary training for a business tycoon."

He took a step nearer her. "What a one you are for words! Sly as a kitten's paw. Don't tell me you've over-heard some story put about my unfriendly elements?"

"I was brought up in a good home, so I can't tell you," she said, carried away on a tide of sheer reckless-ness.

"You've no sense of self-preservation, have you, my love?"

At once she sensed the change in him and knew a peculiar joy in arousing his temper.

"And now I don't know what *you* mean," she said sweetly, "though I couldn't help noticing the interest you took in all the good-looking women at the party."

"In only *one* woman, actually, but you wouldn't know anything about that." Their voices were clashing now, like weapons in the soft quietness.

Her eyes flashed in uncontrollable resentment. One woman! "Personally I think that sort of thing can be overdone. People can put two and two together!"

"And it still doesn't make five!" He moved then, slashing and ruthless, jerking her down to him with so much force that she lost all balance and fell heavily against him. She might have been warned by the glitter in his eyes. He grasped her shoulders through the black

mesh of her hair, not caring if he hurt her. She caught
her breath and the blood pounded in her ears.

It was too late and resistance was beyond her. He
bent his dark head and found her mouth, forcing it
open with flagrant punishing mastery. Multiple piercing
sensations shot through her and a frightening loss of
identity. The world she knew fell away from her and
there was only Guy, the male scent of him, his lean
length, the strength and the mastery, the questing
mouth that was forcing the very heart from her body.

She heard herself make a queer little sound that was
half a sob and then she was free of him, but only for a
moment. She swayed giddily, her head drooping, but
he swooped and held her wrists, his grip making her
catch her breath.

"So the grand manner has begun to collapse a
little?" Then more gently, as if in an afterthought,
"Just how long did you think you could pull off all that
fiery backchat? Next time you'll remember it's a direct
invitation to disaster."

Excitement, anger, humiliation exploded in her head
with a dull reddish glare. She tried to pull away from
him, but he was holding her hands. She was on fire
now with the urgent need to retaliate somehow.

His dark eyes lingered on her full, quivering mouth.
"You want mercy, don't you, but you can't be sure I
deal in the gentler virtues. In fact, as you've told me
once too often, I don't." He forced her to hold up her
head. "If you insist in kindling a blaze, my little cat,
you can hardly complain if you get scorched yourself."

At last she had her hand free. It flew through the air,
to be caught and imprisoned again. Guy laughed at her
predicament. "Perhaps this will serve to reduce your
childish tantrums to the insignificance they deserve.
It's time you grew up, my little Karen."

She tried to turn her head away, but the effort was
futile, and then she was incapable of all further action,
a fever of excitement entering her bloodstream. Her

youth, inexperience, her headlong physical response to him, undreamed of in all her lifetime, combined against her. For the first time in life, Karen surrendered to a force too big for her to handle and fainted dead away.

When she opened her eyes she was lying on her own bed, her hand upflung as though to shield her gaze from his turbulent dark vitality. Her soft sensuous mouth quivered with emotional imbalance. She turned her face away, a tear rolling back to fall on to the gorgeous print of the bedspread.

"For God's sake don't cry!" he said tersely. "I've had enough! You're the most volatile child, so highly strung I'm not even sure you're tame. Yet those very qualities are part of your attraction." He came towards the bed, turning up her face to him. His hand brushed back her hair with a kind of subdued violence.

"Now what's happened to all that wonderful repartee? It's quite a job keeping up with your emotional vagaries."

The tiny bodice of her gown moved with her accelerated heartbeats. Something flickered in his night-black eyes. She gazed back at him speechlessly, her golden irises shimmering with a surfeit of emotion.

"Relax, child. You over-extend your emotional capital like no one I know." His glance leaped over her. "I had the certain premonition you'd be trouble the first time I saw you again in Melbourne." His voice was unbearably cynical. "But you've no need to fear any more dishonourable advances, they won't be forthcoming. I think I've accomplished all I intended—to jar you out of your dream state." He flicked away a tear with a half tender, half impatient gesture. "Get out of that dress and into bed. Nothing and no one will seem quite so bad in the morning. Even me."

He moved to the door and Karen found her voice. It sounded oddly light, even far away to her ears.

"That's the first time I've ever fainted," she said

wonderingly. "The first time I've ever been kissed...
against my will...and I *hated* it!" She impelled herself
upwards, half reclining on her elbow.

Guy cut her off brutally. "Your reactions, my contrary little cat, were quite unmistakable. I could make
love to you now and you wouldn't even fight me...
after the first minute."

Her black, silver-sheened head on its slender neck
was tilted towards him, poetic, pre-Raphaelite. His dark
masculinity was an intolerable stimulant, but she was
determined to hold his gaze. She stared back at him,
unable to control a slight trembling.

"Oh, but I *would*!" she murmured with passionate
vehemence. His eyes, black and ironic, swept over her
and with no intention of will Karen crumpled over on
the bed and softly and helplessly began to cry, the longing of Eve upon her.

Guy was silent, but only for a minute. "A cry won't
hurt you," he observed unfeelingly. "It might even be
chastening. Pleasant dreams, little spitfire," he added,
and shut the door with finality.

CHAPTER SIX

In the weeks that slipped by, one by one, since the party, Karen found herself adjusting to a multi-faceted household that still managed to present to the outsider an impression of unity. To her great relief, Philip was fully integrated, a pound or two heavier and the constant shadow of Mark Amber, to whom he was devoted.

Karen's own relationship with Mark and Patricia Amber was at once and completely—family. Though it would have grieved her to put it into words, she found in her mother's cousin and closest girlhood companion the very qualities she had looked for and found wanting in her mother. It was strange. It was ironic, but it was true! She had come predisposed to be on her guard against the Ambers, to see through their surface charm and glitter, but daily contact made aloofness an exercise in futility. Patricia Amber was, as her brother had insisted, a wonderful woman.

Guy, of course, was Guy; a man of immense charisma. He came and went, a rocket on their horizon, but once and for all the centrifugal force around whom the household revolved. That his prolonged absences often coincided with Celia's overnight stays in town Karen not for a moment put down to coincidence. She was young, but she wasn't naive. Yet the knowledge that Celia Amber saw her brother-in-law as her own special possession was as oppressive as a heavy coat in the middle of summer.

Celia was, Karen soon discovered, the complete butterfly and on this account a fascinating psychological study: for Celia Amber was devoted—to herself. Her preoccupation with her looks, her clothes, her figure, her extraordinary diet régime was perhaps understandable in a glamorous, much photographed woman, and certainly the results were quite wonderful. Celia Amber, with care, wealth and great determination, was preserving an astonishing aura of youth.

She knew everyone who was anyone and was often photographed with a great many of them. No major event on the social scene was complete without her. Her beauty, her family connections and her fabulous clothes easily secured her an entrée. She had a penthouse apartment in town where she would stay for days in a row and often bore Liane off with her. But to Karen, Celia had little to say.

When she was at Belle Amber she breakfasted each morning in bed. Karen often saw Marie, the little household help, carry a silver breakfast tray up to Celia's suite. She noticed with wry amusement the delicate lace mat, the fragile china, the pink, dew-drenched rosebud—never the full flower—jostling the grapefruit juice in the tall, frosted glass, the slivers of dry toast and the silver pot of strong black coffee. Then around about eleven, Celia descended—to the lower orders, as Rikki put it, exquisitely dressed for luncheon, or a bridge party or whatever; her hat, her dress, her accessories perfection. These were the weapons of conquest and they were the best on the market. Long after she left, her perfume subtly pervaded the atmosphere—a vivid reminder that Celia Amber wanted the best things out of life and was getting them!

When Liane was at home she was charming. She was friendly and sought Karen's company, but so much of her conversation revolved around her mother—Celia's lovely hair, her lovely clothes, her fabulous taste, the men who were in love with her, that Karen found it hard to evince interest. Liane was too firmly tied by the fabled silver cord, and Karen was always thankful when

Rikki came along to infuse a little conflict into the conversation or a new, badly needed topic of interest. Neither of Celia Amber's children could strike the happy medium with regard to their mother. To Liane she was the sum of perfection. To Rikki—a fallen angel!

Towards the end of the month Guy flew interstate for a trade convention, leaving the whole household to bear the *ennui* of his absence. At once Celia took off for town, ostensibly to face the long wearisome hours of dress fittings. With the holiday season ahead, she explained, one simply couldn't appear in the "same old rags". This statement Karen found ludicrous. Celia Amber in rags would turn the whole town out, she thought waspishly.

Karen's own routine went on as before. She got Pip off to school, completed the few household tasks she had taken over from Aunt Patricia and in the time remaining before lunch she usually practised. Often Aunt Patricia would slip into the room to listen, her dark head with its thick chignon coming to rest against a wing-backed chair. A dreamy, abstracted expression would play over her fine, sensitive face, for she was an appreciative listener. Sometimes when Karen finished playing she would surprise a curious attitude on the part of the older woman. Aunt Patricia would start as if awakening from a sleep and look intently into Karen's face as if in search of something, and a little shiver would run down Karen's spine. It seemed to her then that the expression in the luminous dark eyes was faintly tragic. But the expression never lasted for more than an instant and everything was normal and relaxed again.

Aunt Patricia was a wonderful companion. She was quiet and contemplative when one felt inclined that way, yet she loved to talk. She would tell Karen about the places she had visited: Paris, London, Rome, Madrid and Vienna, the Americas and the South Africa

that she loved: the books she had read. She liked to talk
also about the theatre—plays and ballet and music—
but the only thing she never talked about was love.
Karen found this curious and faintly intriguing.

In her forties, Patricia Amber was still a beautiful
woman and she must have been very lovely as a girl.
Better still, she had a warm and generous nature, the
true womanly qualities that endured. Yet she had never
married! Never apparently had a serious love affair and
if she had, she never spoke of it, nor had it amounted
to anything. Her parents' broken marriage would have
affected her, made her more cautious, but it didn't
really explain anything. Patricia Amber, in her own
way, was an enigma!

One particular afternoon when she felt at a loose
end, Karen went in search of Mark Amber. She found
him in the library, occupying the tan leather armchair
behind the great desk of mahogany. He looked up
vaguely, recognition flooding his eyes.

"I didn't hear you, my dear. You just drifted in like
Trish's lilacs." His lively dark eyes twinkled under his
tufted brows. He pushed away a great sheaf of papers.
"I was just getting bogged down anyway. Come over."
Karen smiled and walked over to the desk. "May I
see?"

"Of course." He spoke without hesitation, inviting
her interest.

Karen picked up a large photograph from a scattered
pile of them. It was a picturesque stone building with
shutters over the windows and a leaf-filled pond in
front of it.

"What's this beautiful place?" she asked with interest.

Mark Amber slid his glasses back on his nose.
"Show me. Ah yes, the wine cellar at Groot Constantia
near Cape Town. The vineyard was planted in the
1680s by Governor Van der Stel. I took that shot—oh,
let me see now, about five years ago."

"That's Guy, of course, in the corner. Isn't it?" What a ridiculous question, she thought, a little annoyed with herself for asking. It couldn't be anyone else with that splendid dark head.

Mark Amber gave the photograph another casual glance. "Yes, that's Guy. He didn't know he was in it. We went together—a most beautiful place. Dutch domestic architecture was at its zenith in those days. I would say the old buildings are every bit as beautiful as those we found in Europe. The Constantia valley at the back of Table Mountain is a sight to behold, probably one of the richest valleys in the world. I hope you'll see it one day."

Karen smiled and picked up another photograph. "I hope so too. And who is this distinguished old gentleman with the whiskers? One of the Ambers?" Her eyes danced into light.

Mark Amber clicked his tongue in mock reproach. "My dearest child, such ignorance for a member of the family! That distinguished gentleman is James Busby— some say the founder of our wine industry, an Englishman like my own grandfather and a real original. He was sent out as headmaster to an orphanage at Cabramatta and lost no time at all introducing viticulture to the student curriculum."

"Heavens, he *was* an original!" Karen had a graphic mental picture of the scene.

A smile crossed Mark Amber's face and was gone. "Well, the idea was to support the orphanage with the profits and incidentally to teach the orphans a trade. He succeeded quite well at both."

"Now I remember," Karen hit on some latent knowledge. "He was the first man to publish a textbook on viticulture in the southern hemisphere."

"Now you're on the track! James Busby performed an invaluable service for his adopted country, touring the French vineyards at the request of the British Government and collecting over twenty thousand cuttings

of *cépages nobles*. Today, of course, those same vines
are protected by law. Export of cuttings is illegal. But
fortunately for us, the French vignerons at that time
were generous with their vines and advice. It's only in
our own time that the French have been forced into
keeping their knowledge and their noble vines to themselves. The competition is ferocious and too much
business has already been lost to Australia and the
Cape. Yet it took less than a century for the vine to
conquer our own land and provide us with a major industry and our own family and the countless families
that work for us with our life's blood. I only wish my
dear grandfather could see our immense population of
vines. The sight would gladden his heart... the culmi-
nation of his dreams! All our wonderful vineyards...
Coonawarra, Great Western, North and Central Victoria, the Hunter Valley, our own foothills and Southern
Vales and the beautiful Barossa Valley. You've seen the
Barossa, haven't you? I know Stephen had family connections there.''

Karen smiled. ''Yes, years ago, Uncle Mark, when
Father was alive. We went up for the Barossa Vintage
Festival. I still remember the choirs and the bands, the
grape picking, the tastings, the judging. The Valley
seemed to me then unlike any other part of Australia.''

''And so it is, with little German settlements all over
the place... quite old world, continental. We have a lot
of migrant families working for us at Ambervale, and
their pruning ability is something to see. Grape pruning, as you know, is one of the arts of wine, along with
cultivation and cellar technique. Some men are born
pruners, some never learn. There has to be this special
feeling for the needs of each individual vine, you see.
Severe pruning can result in poor quality wine while
light, right pruning tends to produce high quality wine.
Our workers are renowned for their skill and sensitiv-
ity.''

"But the trade goes back far beyond our own experience, doesn't it, Uncle Mark?"

"Well, yes, for the most part. Our immigrants came from viticultural Europe, familiar with and trained to the vines of Europe. We had a head start, as you might say. Then too, the gold rush of the 1850s provided us with scores of vinearoons. Disappointed gold prospectors from all over the world turned to planting vineyards, especially in Victoria...English, Swiss, French, German. Take your own family, my dear. The Hartmann winery of your grandfather's day produced an outstanding red. I remember it well; a complex perfume, distinctive style and an excellent grip in the finish. We own a great deal to our migrants. Indeed, Baron du Pury and the Castella brothers produced the great Lilydale Yerings. Classic wines of Australia, comparable with the wines of France's golden age."

Karen's frown was regretful. "They aren't in existence any longer, are they?"

"A million pities, no. Our dairying industry has taken over at the expense of our wonderful côtes. A tragedy for the vigneron, but there you are!"

Karen looked to the mound of closely written foolscap.

"How is your own work progressing?"

"Not as fast as I could wish. Some days I just seem to dither like Dagwood. Getting old, I suppose."

"Never that." Karen looked at the silver hair that still sprang back thickly from the fine brow, and smiled. "Who does your typing?" she asked in her musical voice.

"Guy's secretary handles everything for me, my dear. Any one of the girls in the typing pool does it, I imagine."

Karen hesitated, but only for a second. "Would you like me to help you, Uncle Mark? I'm quite a good typist and I'd be happy to help out. I've so much free

time on my hands with Pip at school. Next year I must
get a job, no matter what Guy says. I'm not really a lady
of leisure, you know. It's agin my nature!" she smiled
at him, showing her small, pretty teeth.

"Are you serious, my dear?"

"Perfectly!" she assured him.

Mark Amber whipped off his glasses. "Well, really I
don't know what to say. It would be the ideal arrangement so far as I'm concerned. As it is now, I have to be
careful with my longhand, make it perfectly legible,
and that in itself is an ordeal, I can tell you. But with
you in the house! . . . and you're a typist?" He looked at
her with renewed admiration.

"Well then, it's settled."

"On one condition. I pay you a wage."

Karen lost her smile.

"Good grief, I'm on more than adequate allowance
now. Guy simply ignores all my protests as though they
don't exist."

Mark Amber smiled.

"That would be Guy, and you have a surprising way
of speaking your mind. However, a wage, dear, otherwise I wouldn't consider it. I'm not exactly down to my
last three-penny bit, you know."

"Very well, then. I must say I feel happy about it.
Like Pip, I feel I've so much to learn. It will be quite an
experience for me."

"Well now, let's be businesslike, seeing we're *in*
business. How about two hours a day, starting next
Monday? Your timetable will be quite elastic. I know
how much Trish enjoys your company and you practice
in the mornings. I've some wonderful things to show
you as well. Luke and I picked them up in our travels
when we were boys."

"I don't remember Uncle Luke," Karen said carefully, a flicker of expression crossing her face.

Mark Amber's eyes leapt into life, the deep grooves
in his cheeks pronounced.

"Lionhearted, my brother. A lion of a man, tremendously vital. There couldn't be two of him."

Karen's eyes suddenly stung. She sensed what he might be feeling and was moved.

Mark Amber contemplated a spot on the ceiling.

"Richard's death finished him off. Though it was as well Luke died, he would have made an intolerable invalid. Intolerable for him, intolerable for us all to have to watch him brought down; a vigorous man no longer whole. He adored the children, though it was always Guy who was closest to him. Richard was a little like Julia, his mother, you know."

"No one ever seems to mention Aunt Julia."

"No, dear, perhaps not. Trish and Guy feel a degree of disappointment in their mother. Perhaps they feel she let their father down. There was the divorce, of course. They never were suited, though Julia was very pretty as a girl. But with such reserve! I often wonder how they got together in the first place. Julia couldn't stand the life—a handsome, vital, increasingly successful husband, an expanding business, the demands on Luke's time, the increasing social obligations her position imposed on her. Some women would lap it up, Celia for one, but Julia just seemed to fold up under it."

"She remarried, didn't she?"

"Yes, an American. Writer fellow. They live in the States, California. Trish and Guy usually call on her once or twice a year. I believe she's quite happy." His expression was turned inwards, impassive, remote.

"Misalliances," Karen said sadly.

"Yes, dear. One grows, the other stays still or grows in another direction. I often think Trish and Guy have been affected to a certain extent. Women have been hurling themselves at Guy's head, to my knowledge, since he's been in his teens, and Trish was always a beautiful girl, yet neither of them are married. Much too cautious, I'd say! I've even tried to chat Guy up

about it, after all he has a responsibility as head of the
family, but he just laughs it off. He tells me he'll know
her when he sees her and damn it all, he's thirty-five!
You'd think he'd have seen her by now."

"Perhaps he *has*!" Karen said very dryly, then recol-
lected herself. She had not meant to say that. The
words presented themselves, unbidden.

Instant comprehension flared in the still bright eyes.

"No, my dear, that would never do. Now why is it
you induce me to talk? Unless it's those great golden
eyes." He changed the subject abruptly. "Now what
say I run you in to pick up Pip this afternoon? It's
much too hot for him to walk from the bus. You don't
drive, do you, my dear, though I think perhaps you're
about to. Guy was only saying about sending a car out
for you."

"A car?" Karen looked her bewilderment. "He
didn't say anything at all to me."

"Well now, that's his way. Guy's been making a lot
of decisions since he's been little more than a boy. Add
that to a naturally autocratic disposition and there you
are! Guy's a lot like Luke, and that's saying something!"

Karen said nothing at all. What was there to say, anyway? A naturally autocratic disposition! She couldn't
agree more!

CHAPTER SEVEN

THE car was delivered the same afternoon Guy returned from Interstate; a four-cylinder Torana with a metallic bronze paint finish and a plush vinyl interior to match. Karen was torn between a feeling of excitement and pure outrage. Every minute of the day her independence was being usurped. She could just feel her defences crumbling bit by bit. No one seemed to appreciate her dilemma. Aunt Trish merely patted her arm with a fond "How nice," Pip pronounced himself thrilled and promptly buried his nose, like a puppy, in the wonderful-smelling upholstery and Uncle Mark offered to give her driving lessons. Only Celia and Liane, who were rarely at home with the endless round of social commitments, were not available for comment. Rikki, blinded perhaps by his expected fortune, couldn't hit on the right note either.

Standing in the drive admiring the car, despite herself Karen announced quite bitterly: "This is the ultimate humiliation! I feel like a garlanded calf. I'm quite sure Guy would put a ring through my nose if he felt like it, and what's more he'd expect me to wear it."

"Now what are you on about?" Rikki's blond head emerged from an examination of the woodgrain dash. "You're quite a card, Karo. You'll need a car—run Pip about and all that! What's a car here or there to Guy? He's got three himself. You have to admire how he handles our affairs. You've just got to see things in perspective, kiddo. You're not on your own now. You have a family and thank your lucky stars you can dig deep in the old coffers. Now hop in and we'll go for a burn."

Karen hopped in, still grumbling. After a few minutes it occurred to her that "burn" was the operative word. Rikki drove in short furious bursts more suited to a Grand Prix, she thought edgily. Certainly he had control of the car, but Karen began to feel a certain proprietorial interest in its paintwork. After all, it was brand new!

Outside the tall wrought iron gates at the end of the drive Rikki reversed the car and pulled over on the grass.

"Change places, kiddo."

"My first lesson?"

"Nothing less. Come on now, don't look so morose. Driving is a piece of cake, nothing to it. Even young Pip could do it—with his eyes closed, by the look of him."

Karen hesitated. "I don't think I can. Not today, Rikki. I feel like I've got banana legs. I just could hit something."

Rikki patted her shoulder. "Never fear, my little pal. I'll keep my fingers crossed for you till they ache."

"Well, I'll try it, but this time without the wisecracks."

Rikki continued to be facetious, showing a fine contempt for the elementary principles of driver training. A quick run down on the dash, the gears and the pedals, and Karen was expected to take off.

"Through the gates?" she asked, swallowing visibly.

"I don't see why not. They're as big as a mountain."

She put the car in gear with no trouble at all, but unfamiliar with clutch control, made the car buck like a brumby colt, though mercifully it cleared the tall pillars.

"God save us all!" Rikki uncovered his eyes. "You can put your foot down now, dear. Second gear, that's it. You've got it! There's been that much improvement, at any rate."

Karen put her foot down. "Go and soak your head! What next, master mind?"

"I'll think of something," Rikki promised. "When you're up to twenty, change to third gear. You do *steer* nicely, dear," he pointed out kindly as she narrowly missed quite a large rock to the side of the drive.

Karen threw him a long, unfriendly look. "Take a week's notice, starting last week. I don't wish to appear ungrateful or unappreciative, but you're a lousy driving instructor. Shouldn't all this be explained to me from a stationary position? I mean I've had pupils myself, you know!" The car, following the direction of her eyes, travelled towards the embankment.

"God, not there!" Rikki sat bolt upright with a jerk and straightened the wheel. "It's a fair old jump from there." Carefully he eased himself back into his seat. "Not cottoning on to this too quickly, are you, love? Still, you *look* gorgeous. That yellow dress—it's wonderful! You keep coming at me like a Van Gogh sunflower. Now pull up over there and start off again. Get the feel of the clutch, if you can. It can't be too different from pedalling a piano."

"It's quite different, I assure you!" So complete was Karen's concentration, she missed first gear and the car shot into reverse. On the edge of her panic she could hear Rikki yelling: "The brake, girl, the brake! Hit the brake. For God's sake, I haven't even shown you reverse!"

Sick and shaken by the speed of the car, Karen finally got her foot off the accelerator. She brought the car to a halt well off the drive and heading for the trees.

Rikki was looking at her with honest perplexity. "'Struth, sweet, you worry the gears like a terrier worries an old shoe! Just what were you going for?"

Karen's sense of humour reasserted itself. "First, believe it or not." Her legs felt awfully wobbly. "I've had enough for today, Rikki. I haven't got the hang of it, and if you'll forgive my saying so you're a shocking teacher. All this drive as you go, and sunflowers coming at you... the trees were coming at us, more like it!"

Rikki leant over and switched off the ignition, pulling on the handbrake. "You could be right, love. I'm more at one with the flowering world and the nesting birds. Besides, I'd like to make love to you."

He was not laughing now but serious, with the "little boy", slightly wilful expression, she remembered.

"You've got a lovely mouth, Karo," he said dreamily, "and the mouth reveals the personality, so they say."

Karen smiled. "Thanks for something! I've almost no morale left. Now, any better ideas?"

Rikki's eyes shone with a sudden light. "Give me time, kiddo." He leant over and pulled her towards him. "Kiss me, you glorious dimwit."

"No!"

"Yes. I've been hanging on the vine long enough." His voice was insistent. The sun turned the silver-gilt hair to a glory and Karen glanced at him appreciatively through half-closed lids.

"You're very easy on the eye, Rikki."

He smiled at her lazily. "I admire your taste."

"Even so, I'm afraid I'll have to ask you to be platonic."

"God, nothing that drastic!" Rikki's eyes were fastened longingly on her full, moulded mouth. It tilted suddenly.

"Oh, all right!" She leaned forwards and ran her mouth across his cheek, a caress as delicate as a butterfly's wing. Rikki's hands tightened on her, long-fingered and very strong.

"You provoking little devil! How dare you insult my manhood? Just remember you're only a very commonplace set of chemicals."

There was a slight scuffle broken up by the unmistakable sound of a car horn. It was the Jaguar, coming up the drive—and fast. Their heads spun as one.

Guy swung the big car up behind them and got out, moving over the sloping ground with long, easy strides. He cleared his throat delicately, his dark eyes alive with all the dynamic energy that was so vitally a part of him.

"Am I intruding on some sort of crisis?" he inquired smoothly, flicking a sardonic, half amused eye over their young, upflung faces. "What's this? Deserts of silence?"

"That's blown it sky-high!" Rikki fell back against the seat, his eyes closed in disgust.

Guy's mouth twitched. "And how are you, little one? In the middle of a lesson?"

"End of one," Rikki supplied laconically. "If I'm to die I prefer to do it by my own hand."

Karen turned on him, her eyes huge with protest. "I never realised you could be such a traitor!"

"Joke, dear," Rikki reassured her, then sat up quickly. "I have it, suddenly and completely! Guy will teach you. He's the ideal man in a crisis. Fearless... unflappable... This kind of thing is against all my principles. Where there's danger Richard is always first to quit the field. I might look a tough nut, but I'm jelly inside."

Karen's high-spirited face was beginning to flash fire. "Your wit isn't affecting me at all today, Rikki."

He merely grinned, his eyes on Guy. "Getting a bee in her bonnet, is she?"

Guy smiled and looked at Karen. "My time is very short!"

"That's what I thought myself," she said huffily.

He seemed to reconsider. "Now let's see. I can think of a dozen different solutions... all equally impossible."

Karen shot him a dazzling topaz glance. "This is getting us nowhere." She began to move her head fretfully from side to side in nervous dissatisfaction. "I never wanted a car in the first place. I don't even want to learn how to drive."

"Karo, love!" All at once Rikki sounded contrite, stabbed by the slight break in her voice. Guy merely laughed and opened the car door and pulled her out to him.

"Don't you know when you're being teased, my lamb? It's an old Amber habit. You're not bad at it yourself."

She looked up at him with a mixture of emotions, feeling herself at a disadvantage. His hand closed over her collarbone with its now familiar caressing movement of the thumb. She expelled a long breath and tossed her black hair over her shoulder in uneasy fascination.

"You bring out the worst in me, Guy, and that's a fact!"

"Did you think I was unaware of it?"

Rikki looked from one to the other, his eyes narrowing against the sun. "Exit Sir Galahad on his way to the Holy Land."

Guy gave a brief laugh. "I take it you're going to stable the car. Thanks, Rick. We'll defer lessons until tomorrow when I have more time."

"The urgency's not that extreme," Karen bit out, barely able to contain herself at such patronage.

Guy glanced at her haughty young face reprovingly. "Don't you want to thank me in that wonderfully individual manner of yours?"

"I think she does," Rikki volunteered. "Right-oh, people. I think I'll have a drink before the boat sails." He swung the car back on to the drive, making short work of clearing the bend in the drive. Karen looked after him with new-found admiration. Surely if Rikki could do it, so could she!

"That's what I call magnificent panache," she murmured wistfully. "I don't think I can be mechanically minded."

Guy looked philosophical and took her arm to put her into his car. "It's not as hard as it looks, though a couple of minor points do occur to me. One is—kissing on the job! It's apt to weaken a beginner's concentration."

"Kissing?" Karen's slanting brows shot up incredulously. Did he ever miss anything?

"That's what I said. Doesn't it strike you as a trifle unusual for the first lesson?" He looked into her flushed face then held the point of her chin. "With no effort from you, my pet, you could knock Rikki for six, and that would never do. I don't believe in early alliances."

Karen gave an audible gasp. "You're a dead ringer for Cesare Borgia! I don't think I've ever encountered such proud authority."

His voice slowed to a drawl. "Try to hold your enthusiasm in check, my pet. I merely passed a remark. You and Rick are my responsibility. Neither of you is twenty-one yet. Besides, no good could come of anything there, my girl."

She tossed her wilful dark head. "Why don't you add—mark my words!"

"Mark my words!" Guy obliged weightily, and suddenly laughed, his teeth very white in his tanned face.

Just as suddenly Karen's resentment crumpled like so much tissue paper. That smile was unfairly devastating, creasing his lean cheeks, whirling her into danger.

"Now why is it you always make me feel there's a war on and I'm right in the middle of it?"

His eyes were on the pure curve of her throat. "Maybe because you're such a *female* female. You want to be dominated, but you insist on fighting it every inch of the way."

"Do I?" she smiled at him. "I think I'm frightened."

"Well, it's damned well time. Now tell me, how do you like the car? I didn't think you'd want anything bigger, not at this stage, anyway." He brushed his knuckle against her cheekbone. "Turn your head this

way and say thank you. With practice it may come a
little easier.''

"It will have to, won't it?" Her mouth curved and
her eyes tilted deepening with colour. Guy's face
altered and she drew in her breath sharply, filled with
the wildest notion that he meant to kiss her. She
couldn't bear it. Not in broad daylight when she was so
defenceless. Instinctively she arched away from him,
without the slightest weapon.

Guy regarded her manoeuvres coolly. "I never make
the same mistake twice, my pet."

Karen ran the tip of her tongue over her top lip. Her
efforts to appear casual fell hopelessly flat.

"I'm sure no one can ever remember your making
the *first* one."

He laughed. "God, you've got a kick like a contrary
mule!"

She could smile at him now, the bad moment over.
"Now how is that possible?"

Lazily Guy moved his hand from the back of the seat
to her white nape. "If we ever do have a confrontation,
little one, I promise you Vesuvius will seem a mere
bagatelle compared to it."

She kept her head up, her eyes clear and direct.
"That's the *dear* thing about you, Guy. You're so tolerant!"

He shook her then, none too lightly, and her head
lolled like a flower on its slender stalk. "If it will please
you," she mocked him, "from now on I'll tremble
when you frown."

His brilliant dark gaze was ironic. "How prettily you
lie! Sometimes you act as much nine as nineteen."

She sighed. "If that's the case, I give up."

"That's all right. You just give up." He released her
with a quick grin. "Besides, it's already been ordained
that I should influence your life."

"Don't say another word!" Karen warned him. "I
won't listen!" A subtle excitement began to stir in her.

His eyes glittered tauntingly in his handsome dark face.

"Don't be so melodramatic, my orchid. You'll listen if I want you to."

Karen turned her head away, a restraint upon her, unspoken but very real. It was dangerous to get too close to Guy, yet perversely she was hopelessly drawn to a man who could only hurt her, a man worlds removed from her in experience and sophistication. She would have to steel herself against his masterful ways.

Guy leaned forward and switched on the ignition and Karen allowed herself one glance at his dark profile. She was trembling a little at his nearness. He turned his head swiftly, pinning her gaze, and the look in his night-dark eyes told her quite plainly that he was fully aware of her predicament.

Karen sat back and followed the line of the poplars with her eyes. More than anything she wanted to be alone. She was disturbed and alerted now to anything that might lie beneath the surface. To yearn for the impossible was little short of insanity!

CHAPTER EIGHT

IT was Aunt Patricia who suggested that Karen and Liane spend a day in town before Pip started his holidays. Perhaps lunch and a show, she mentioned over breakfast, and thus innocently set off a chain of events that were to draw into line the inevitable antagonists—Karen and Celia.

It all started off harmlessly enough. The day was crisp and beautiful with an air of complete normality; the open enjoyment and laughing during the drive to the city, their giggling search for a parking space big enough for Karen to back the car in with any degree of safety, all lent strength to Karen's feeling that this was going to be a good day.

Lunch was a hilarious affair, partially due to the not one but two unaccustomed cocktails that preceded it, with Liane laughing helplessly at Karen's more outrageous *bons mots*. Afterwards it was Liane who suggested they take in a main feature film of the glossy variety—not one Karen would have picked on herself, but she went along happily, infected by the younger girl's high spirits.

In the near cold dimness of the theatre Karen decided that only one thing saved the film from being consigned to the garbage can—the presence of the anti-heroine, a tall, good-looking brunette, who bore a marked physical resemblance to Liane—or rather, to a Liane dressed to type. Karen was thoroughly intrigued. She sat to attention and prodded Liane in the ribs.

"That's you!"

Liane looked blank. "Who?"

"That dishy type up there."

Liane looked back at the screen, but the "Ssh!" from behind them silenced all further conversation. Karen's fertile brain was evolving a plan. She sat there isolated in her dream world, churning it over. A complete change of hairstyle was the focal point of the plan. It would make the world of difference to Liane's appearance. With Liane's celluloid double up there on the screen she could hardly fail to miss that. But how did one go about instant transformation? Liane's short bubble cut didn't lend itself to adaptation. It would be ages before it would grow out to a length.

A wig, of course! It was the obvious and simple solution. Everyone was wearing one. The more Karen thought about it the better the idea seemed. The interval couldn't come soon enough! She sat on, bored stiff with all the unintentional parody and the radiantly amoral female lead.

Even in the post-theatre dazzle of sunshine Karen's enthusiasm was unabated. Liane, only eighteen, for all her look of ripe young maturity, was easily talked into the experiment. In the exclusive wig boutique she drank in her reflection like a lost soul at a waterhole.

"Hello, Cleopatra!" Karen said mischievously, her piquant eyes alight with admiration.

"Is this really me?"

Karen grinned. "Didn't I tell you a fringe would suit you? It really is a super wig, and the colour match is perfect. You can't tell the difference from your own hair. Luckily you're tall enough to wear that style beautifully."

"But a wig!" Liane was twirling this way and that, not quite crediting the transformation.

"Oh, go on! All the glamour girls have a whole wardrobe of wigs and hair-pieces. Don't tell me Gina Holmes didn't have one on at the party."

"She must have," Liane said thoughtfully. "She was a blonde at the afternoon parade. I do look rather nice, don't I?"

"You know darned well you do. Remarkably chic, like a cover on *Vogue* magazine. You've got good bones, like Aunt Trish."

"I'm not beautiful like Trish," Liane said simply.

"You will be." Karen spoke with such finality that Liane took heart from it. "Now, what about some new clothes to go with the new image?"

Liane smiled. "Why not?"

"Why not indeed? You're not hampered by a depressing bank balance."

In the stores Liane bought magnificently. In that respect at least, she was the image of her mother. Karen, who was used to going from store to store comparing merchandise and prices, was both amused and awed. Liane swept through departments with "charge it" and "put it on my account", and saleswomen, with an eye to commission, charged her, deserting their less profitable customers. It was "Good afternoon, Miss Amber. How are you, Miss Amber? We have some wonderful new styles, Miss Amber...just come in...too too lovely...just you, in fact."

They weren't in the least like Liane, Karen thought, and the flattery was outrageous. Her eyes sparkled and she looked across at Liane, expecting to encounter a matching twinkle, but Liane seemed completely unaware of it. This was the same fulsome attention she had received all her life.

They had a wonderful time! Liane gave Karen *carte blanche* in choosing the various outfits, perhaps as a reward for hitting on the idea of the wig. In the clothes that suited her, with her shoulders held back and her head high, Liane revealed a svelte figure and a lovely long length of thigh. By the time they were through, both girls were flushed and excited and the admiring glances they received over coffee had the effect on

Liane of rain on a desert flower. She blossomed astonishingly, her cheeks full of unwonted colour.

Their high spirits lasted all the way back to Belle Amber and Karen felt a special thrill in being able to bring
about such a change. More remarkable than anything
was the transformation in Liane's posture. She was
walking with free, swinging movements, tossing her
black, glossy mane. Her dark eyes under the thick
straight fringe held a new self-awareness and there was
a look of competence and forthrightness about her.
Karen regarded her with warmth and affection. The
family were in for a few surprises!

As it happened, the girls were the ones to be surprised. Laughing and chattering just inside the entrance
hall, they were greeted by Aunt Trish coming through
to meet them. Her eyes registered her instant approval
of the metamorphosis. She opened her mouth to comment, but was arrested by the sound of small high-
arched feet, tapping their way down the staircase. They
all looked up simultaneously.

Celia was coming on down the stairs, creamed and
perfumed and dressed to perfection, smoothing her
gloves over her fragile wrists. At the first sight of the
two girls she stood transfixed, then gave a curious,
high-pitched squeal. Instantly Rikki appeared in the
hallway.

"What was that?"

His aunt answered him. "Nothing, dear."

"God, I thought it was a train heading for a level
crossing!"

Celia paid no attention to her son. Her eyes were all
for her daughter.

"My dearest child!" the sweet voice held the crack of
a whip. "You look positively eye-catching...*gaudy*...
and what is that *thing* you have on your head?"

Rikki reeled in his tracks. "Oh, the selfless shining
love of a mother! A heart as big as the world!" He gave
his sister a long earnest glance. "You look terrific, kid.

One hell of a good-looking girl, not a carpet to be trampled on. Your idea, Karo?"

Celia's blue eyes slanted disparagingly over the older girl. Karen felt the chill off them right to where she was standing, yet Celia maintained a rather terrifying sweetness. "How *kind* of you to take such an interest, Karen. But I do think you might have consulted me before you went rushing off. After all, I know what is best for my little girl."

Rikki threw up his hands. "This is the bloody end, as Shakespeare would say. Stick with it, kid. If you look gaudy then I'm Queen of the May." He prepared to depart. "Well, be seein' you, girls. This is no place for man or beast." He hit a hand to his chest, gazing at his sister. "My heart goes out to you in your brave fight!"

Liane looked ludicrously surprised. Used as she was to Rikki's extravagant turn of phrase, his words usually failed to register. Besides, he was always having a shot at Mother! The colour swept into her face.

"What do you think, Aunt Trish?"

"What strange modesty is this?" Patricia Amber smiled. "I think you look very stylish indeed. You can always grow your hair out. I agree with Karen and Rikki."

"But of course you do!" There was distinct malice in Celia's voice beneath the layers of sugar coating. She looked from one to the other like an exquisite Siamese kitten about to sink its little claws at the psychological moment. "I certainly don't underrate your opinion, Trish," she said sweetly, "but I do think Liane looks that teeniest bit... *theatrical*. It would appeal to Rikki, being what he is." The sweet voice thinned with sarcasm. "Really, that boy gets odder every day!"

"Odd behaviour doesn't necessarily mean one is odd in the head," Karen burst out impetuously, her clear topaz eyes momentarily too big for the delicate oval of her face.

Celia's glance annihilated her. Karen was too tiny a

pebble to cause a ripple in Celia's supreme self-confidence. Liane's face, however, was a flurry of tangled doubts which gradually resolved themselves.

"I'll go and straighten myself out," she announced listlessly, and walked up the stairs without giving her mother another glance. At the top she stared down at them for a moment, a wilted lily, with her habitual slouch.

Karen stood silently trying to hold on to her temper. She felt vaguely out of sorts with Liane. Surely Liane could have shown more spirit than that? By no stretch of the imagination could she be described as gaudy or theatrical, yet she had accepted her mother's judgment as dogma, virtually irreversible.

"Well now," Celia turned to the two silent women, her voice silky, "I'm so grateful to you, Karen. I realise now that you have a kind heart. But you *are* very young, my dear, and your taste is unformed. That's a style I don't care for Liane to copy."

"What, to look like her aunt?" Karen burst out irrepressibly, her quick temper coming to the boil.

Celia's eyes were the clear blue green of a glacier, but not half so warm. "Don't interrupt me, my dear, and don't question what I say. You're not as clever as you think you are. Also, you've got rather a malicious sense of humour. Liane didn't look in the least like Trish. *That* would have been an entirely different matter." She turned to her sister-in-law, a half smile hovering on her soft pink mouth, now that Karen was firmly reprimanded. "I must fly, Trish. Really I hadn't dreamed it was that late. I'll have to rush like mad. I'm dining with Paul Rand this evening and what with one thing and another I just know I'll look a wreck, and Paul would hate *that*!" She turned to flash an empty smile at both of them, once more on balance, in control of the situation. In her own mind at least, her malevolence was only a memory to be wielded upon occasions like a baton.

With elaborate deliberation she inspected her flaw-less profile in the trumeau. "That I should have a daughter with no pretension to beauty!" she murmured complacently.

The statement took Karen's breath away. "But I don't agree," she said after a minute. "Liane has enormous potential," she pointed out gallantly, "and what's more, she'll mature well!"

But Karen was tilting at windmills. Celia's glance met hers with gleaming malevolence. "Not really!" She held her voice to lightness implying that Karen's opinion was less than unimportant. "That height!" she murmured. "Liane was five feet nine when she was fifteen. Imagine!"

Patricia Amber made a convulsive protesting movement of her hand, her dark eyes wide with distress.

"She's suffered unduly because you're so tiny."

In every way, Karen thought with fierce resentment. Celia was quite peculiar. Secure in her world of frivol-ity, she never stopped to count the ultimate cost of her empty successes. Wasn't obsessive behaviour sympto-matic of something? But what was Celia's trouble? Why was she filling her days with endless distractions? Karen stood there milling her thoughts over.

Celia turned at last from the mirror. "Heavens, Karen, you do look fierce! Glowering would probably be the most apt term." She gave a pretty laugh. "Now be good!"

Her heels clicked, the car door slammed, then she was gone.

The two women drifted into the living room and sank down into the yielding softness of the divan. Patri-cia Amber's fine dark eyes were clouded and her sensi-tive face mirrored her mood.

"How do you stand it?" Karen spoke her thoughts aloud.

"Over the years, I've become used to it." For once Patricia was thrown off guard and the words came tumbling out. "I've come off second best to Celia for God knows how long. If I paid too much attention to her I'd find her malice clear and her every word suspect, but I've learnt to keep quiet to hold on to my loved ones. Rikki and Liane are all that is left of Richard. I love them dearly, though I could wish Liane would show a little of your spirit. If I'd antagonised Celia in the past as I've often wanted to I might have had to forfeit their company as I forfeited yours and Pip's for so long. One must tread warily with difficult natures. Occasionally I experience a great wave of indignation when I'd like to hit back as hard as I can, but my hands are tied. I simply don't know where I am. It takes another woman to fully appreciate Celia. She certainly knows her way around the men, but she has no time for her own sex. It wouldn't do for me to create friction and restraint. An armed truce is better than open conflict, I keep telling myself, but one of these days, even I'm not going to listen." Her eyes sought Karen's, pleading for understanding. "I suppose you've noticed Celia is devoted to Guy. The sun, the moon and the stars shine out of him. He's been very good to her, of course. She is, after all, our brother's widow, but Guy has lived all his life not letting his left hand know what his right hand is doing. It's his nature and his training, I suppose. I could never force him into the position where he feels he must choose between us. One thing is certain, if Celia ever becomes mistress of Belle Amber my days are numbered. Celia doesn't share her possessions. Belle Amber would be lost to me; the beloved home where we were all born. I could accept it from any other woman, but not from Celia. There's no heart to her. You've seen her with the children. She loved them when they were little, but her whole capacity for love is selfish in the last resort."

"Dear, oh dear, oh dear!" Karen was sitting mournfully looking down at her clasped hands. Stark as that summary was, she knew it was the truth.

At the sight of her young, unhappy face, warmth flowed back into Patricia's eyes. "There now, I've said too much and upset you. You're such a sensitive child, Karen, and your own life hasn't been a particularly happy one. Don't ever let anyone tell you money is everything." She smiled. "Now what say we get dressed and go out for dinner? We should be able to persuade Rikki and Lee to come with us. I don't think they're doing anything in particular."

Liane did not accompany them and in the morning she emerged from her room pale and tense with faint purple smudges under her eyes. The high gloss was completely worn off and her expensive smartness forsaken. Never had her long-legged angularity been more apparent.

The three of them sat down to the breakfast table: Karen, Liane and Rikki. Liane was staring vacantly in front of her, beating a mindless tattoo against the rim of her untouched glass of apricot juice. Without a word Karen went to the side buffet with its built-in warming plates and helped them all to eggs and bacon. The morning sun was bright in the yellow and white solarium, but the atmosphere was distinctly gloomy.

Rikki ate silently, accepting his cup of coffee from Karen in true masculine fashion, with never a word of thanks, and glancing from time to time at his sister. It took longer than Karen expected for him to whip into words.

"Well, is the reverie over?"

"What?" Liane looked up, quite startled.

"You are in a trance, dear girl. The Return of the Zombie, isn't it?"

"Knock it off, chum." Lee gave her brother a faint smile.

Rikki's face was quite sober. "Why do you do it to yourself, girl?"

"Honestly, Rikki," Liane came right out of her torpor, "some days I can't make head or tail of you! You really are an oddball." She looked down at her clenched hands, none too well adjusted herself.

Rikki tried again. "It's for your sake, kiddo, I'm persisting. You're very dear to me, if we must be slushy, and you did look terrific yesterday. You must know it. Ask Karo, ask Trish. Ask anyone but Mother," he groaned in a fury of impotence. "Now why isn't Guy here when we need him, damn his splendid hide?"

"You heard what *Mother* said!" Liane winced again at the memory.

"To hell with her!" Rikki shouted. "Motherhood isn't always a refining influence, you know."

"You should be ashamed...*ashamed*!" Liane began to flare up defensively. "To speak of Mother in that fashion, and with Karen present!" Her large dark eyes glimmered with tears.

Karen was inexpressibly moved and her heart began to ache in sympathy.

"Oh, the hypocrisy of it all!" Rikki groaned, and took a great gulp of scalding coffee, then put it down with an oath. "Don't you ever take any notice of anyone but darling Celia?" he bellowed, as much in pain as anything else.

"No!" Liane was tearful but unequivocal.

"You poor twisted girl," Rikki shook his head in resignation. "It's going to go hard for you, Lee." He transferred his glance to Karen. "I can't make it out. She used to get quite good grades at school, even if it was an idiot establishment for over-privileged girls."

"Oh, please!" Liane jumped to her feet, the tears falling on to her pale cheeks. Her chair went over with a crash and Karen jumped to her feet, one hand going out to the other girl. "Oh, Liane, please don't upset yourself!"

"Leave me. Leave me!" Liane tore from the room, stumbling over everything as she went.

"Do as she says," Rikki said tersely. "Leave her. She'll just have to work it out for herself. God, I feel sad," he mourned soulfully. "Sad enough to commit suicide."

Even at that moment Karen could laugh at him.

"You'll never commit suicide, Rikki—though you just could drive someone else to it," she added unkindly.

Rikki's look was reproachful. "Well, I've tried. God knows I've tried—to help, that is. But it's going to take something really big to bring Lee to her senses." His eyes glowed hotly as something occurred to him. "What about that silly twit Colin? Wouldn't you think he'd give Lee some confidence—but all he can do is rave on about Celia—isn't she *gorgeous*, fab!—" He gave a very good imitation of Colin's rather affected style. "God knows what we'll all do when Celia's a grandmother. Go underground, I suppose, or hide the poor dear babe."

Karen was growing increasingly morose. "I don't like him!"

"Who?"

"Colin!" She looked up, surprised. "I can't imagine what Liane sees in him, the conceited oaf!"

Rikki blinked. "Now that we're being frank, dear, neither can I. But Celia can, and there you are. Colin is, in his way, as malleable as Lee. There'll be no problems there. Celia can queen bee it over both households."

"I don't like him," Karen repeated herself.

"My sentiments exactly." Rikki brightened. "What say we cook up a ploy?"

Karen came back to her senses. Rikki's ploys would be predictably combustible. "Liane wouldn't thank you for it," she said with special emphasis.

Rikki desisted under her eye. "Hunger is a terrible sickness, as Pinocchio said, and I guess we're all hungry for something or someone."

Karen could only agree. But wasn't one impossible situation enough?

The next few days were grey and wet and unexpectedly cold, keeping everyone indoors, but the weekend brought stability, a hot sun and the faintest zephyr of breeze. In the light-filled studio Rikki glanced across at Karen, suddenly gay.

"That's it for today, sweetie."

"May I see?"

"Definitely not. This is all very hush-hush at the moment. Your moment will come." Rikki stood back from the easel to examine his handiwork. "Let not the spell be broken!"

"You're pleased, then?"

He merely looked at her and smiled. "I am, love. I think I've captured the essential you, that little intangible air of sadness... but it's frankly sensuous too."

"Well, well, how interesting!" The dreamy look left Karen's face. "Surely you haven't painted me as a voluptuous woman?"

"But you are, love," Rikki answered quite seriously. "You're coolly voluptuous and terribly sexy in the nicest possible way."

Karen made a wry little grimace. "Ugh!"

Rikki looked over at her with great penetration. "What gives with all you 'nice' puritanical women? You're all dying to be sexy, yet you all nearly faint with fright if you're accused of making the grade." He stood back and looked at the portrait. "I'm really terribly pleased with it, pet. All that lovely flawless flesh!"

Karen's face was a study. "Heavens, that talk will shift me if anything will. Flawless flesh! You talk more like the real thing every day."

"Then I take everything back, bar one thing."

"What?" Karen looked over at him suspiciously.

"You are sexy, you sweet enigmatical girl." His glance swept over her. "You know, Karo, I can't in all honesty say you'll be my last love, but you're definitely my *first*!"

"How nice of you to warn me!" Her eyes gleamed

maliciously. He grinned and patted her shoulder. A
good deal of their conversation followed this pattern.
Impersonal—personal—always ending on a bantering
note. Sometimes their talks were very serious and
touched with the special melancholy that arises from
youth and a rather unhappy childhood. Karen could
easily read what was in Rikki's mind and she accepted
the fact that Rikki, in his own way, was a little in love
with her. Just as easily she accepted that Rikki would
always be a little in love with a woman who fired his
artistic imagination.

As for herself ever since it happened Karen carried
about with her at once and for ever the memory of
Guy's kiss and its profound effect on her. At regular
intervals she relived it vividly. Always at the back of
her mind and at the back of everything was the simple
ever-present fact of her feeling for Guy. She tried to
conceal it from herself and everyone else and believed
that she succeeded. Except for Rikki. That would be
futile. Her heart knew and she was certain Rikki
knew...but he did not disapprove!

Rikki's voice roused her from her reverie: "What
say we go for a drive this afternoon, sweetie? Seeing
you *can* drive—God knows how Guy managed it," he
added the essence of good will and humour.

"A systematic approach," Karen said dryly. "You
said yourself that Guy leaves nothing to chance. In actual fact he's an excellent teacher—witness one Karen
Hartmann. We'll have to take Pip," she added matter-
of-factly.

"You're joking!" Rikki's expression was ludicrous.
"You can't bring the kid along. I have designs on you,
don't you know? Honourable, of course."

Her smile was a masterpiece of acknowledgement
and dismissal.

"I'm sorry, Rikki, but I like to give Uncle Mark a
break at the weekend. Pip tires him out, so we'll take
Pip. He'll be no trouble." She patted his hand consol-

ingly. "Come and tell him now. He should be doing his homework on the sun-porch."

Pip wasn't on the sun-porch, but his homework was spread out all over the table.

"Australia is the home of *psittaciformes*?" Rikki asked with open disbelief.

"Parrots," Pip volunteered, coming back into the room, hearing voices. "Australia has the most beautiful and prolific bird life in the world. It's my end-of-term essay. The rosellas in the garden gave me the idea. I've had a lot of fun watching them, though you have to be careful, otherwise they scoot off like greased lightning. There's the father, you see..."

"There always is," Rikki put in sarcastically. Pip ignored him and looked at his sister. "The father always stays behind the trunk and the mother (she's much prettier) forages around on the ground gathering grass seeds and anything she can find for the babies. Their feathers are beautiful, when the sun shines on them... all iridescent."

"Put in a bit about galahs," Rikki said quite kindly, gathering interest in the project. "The pink cockatoos on Grandfather Forester's property are something to see. They wheel overhead in their hundreds. It's quite a common sight in the Outback, but I never could get over it. The displays are magnificent... pink and silver swirling against a cobalt sky. Along the watercourses little mulga parrots gather. Just shut your eyes, Pip, and picture a beautiful desert river winding between bizarre rose-red cliffs. All is peace and silence... then suddenly down sweeps the bird life, flashing fire to land amongst the mulga. The lorikeets wander from region to region with the flowering trees. They swarm over the stunted mallees on the sand-plains and in midsummer when the honey starts flowing from the forest giants they literally screech to high heaven from the crown of the Karris."

"Wait, you're going too fast for me! Down sweeps

the bird life..." Pip hadn't his eyes closed at all, but was writing frantically.

"This is *your* composition," Rikki pointed out, his every word a censure.

"Gee, I'm glad you showed up," Pip replied. "I've only got a paragraph left now. On extinction...the changing...?" he looked at his sister.

Karen smiled and spelt it for him. "E-n-v-i-r-o-n-m-e-n-t."

Rikki looked pained. "Don't talk extinction to me, much less environment." As he sat there, Rikki, seemingly without moving his pencil was covering the page with wheeling, diving, nesting birds.

"Gee, you're clever!" Pip said admiringly.

"I am that!" Rikki agreed.

"You don't suppose...?"

"What's that?" Rikki shot him a piercing glance.

"You don't suppose you could border my essay with bird life? Like you're doing now?" Pip was unabashed. "I'd tell everyone it was *you*."

"That would hardly be necessary," Rikki pointed out unkindly. "These are quite exceptional drawings."

"I can draw too!" Pip announced, for the first time aggrieved.

"Right-oh." Rikki shoved the pencil at him. "Let's see you."

Pip bent his head, clamping his tongue between his teeth in concentration. He worked swiftly and Rikki looked surprised.

"A creditable effort. Here, let me show you the beak—yours is all blazes. How do you suppose a parrot can cut through extremely hard objects? The beak, of course. Watch this, the beak is all-important." Pip moved closer. "Now don't get on top of me," Rikki warned. "I can't stand anyone breathing down my neck. It gives me the screaming heebie-jeebies. Sit down, there's a good lad!"

Karen left them to it, smiling a little. Rikki was temperamentally unsuited to imparting his knowledge with any degree of calm or civility, but already at ten, Pip had an awareness of the artistic temperament, its strengths and its limitations. When she looked back, Pip was sitting to attention, his silky dark head a respectful distance from his mentor's.

He looked up suddenly and caught his sister's eye, and his own closed on a huge wink. Karen smiled. Impressed he might have been, but overawed he was not! She felt proud of him.

"By the way, Pip," she said smilingly, "we're going for a drive this afternoon. Be a good boy."

Rikki looked up and scowled horribly. "Are you going to scoot?"

She waggled her fingers at them. " 'Bye now!"

With the advent of the holidays, Rikki's studio now had another frequent visitor—Pip. Rikki, with unusual magnanimity and considerable pressure from Karen, had consented to allow Pip to sit quietly at a drawing board working at whatever he liked while Karen had her sitting. On these occasions a rare, companionable silence pervaded the studio. Indeed, so far as Karen was concerned it was the ideal arrangement, for then she had her small energetic brother under her nose.

The portrait was progressing smoothly, reaching its final stages. Karen alone had been permitted a glance. She was not asked her opinion, but privately thought she couldn't be that beautiful! The countless times she had looked back at her own face, yet Rikki saw her so differently. Surely her eyes weren't that remarkable, the tilt to her eyebrows so exotic, balanced by the lovely curve Rikki had painted to her mouth. The canvas was light-charged, shimmering with clean colour, and it seemed to Karen to show tremendous promise. Rikki had experienced no difficulty at all in choosing the gown for her to sit in—the autumn leaf chiffon. One could almost reach out and grasp its gossamer softness.

The portrait showed her sitting in a gilt chair, three-quarter length, her body inclined in a fascinating attitude. Her two hands were extended, seemingly in a momentarily arrested gesture, her head on its long slender neck rising out of the creamy contours of her shoulders. It was a difficult pose, suspended animation, but Rikki demanded and got the best out of her. No matter how tiring Karen found it all, she still considered it an honour to sit for a star on the ascendant and suffered accordingly. Rikki found it nothing out of the way!

Nowadays, far from having too much time on her hands, Karen found she had very little indeed. Her work for Uncle Mark she let run over into all hours, fascinated by one man's dedication and the extraordinary saga of the sacred plant—the grapevine, with its history much longer than man's. In her thirst for even a smattering of Uncle Mark's great knowledge she often fell asleep over stories of the Bacchae in Greece, the vine's spectacular expansion through Europe, and its final world conquest in her own country. Gratified and astounded by her enthusiasm, Mark Amber had presented her with a beautiful blue *amphora* from Naples decorated with *amorini* at play among the vines. Karen loved it, but wasn't sure where to put it because she knew it was very valuable and she couldn't bear the thought of its being broken. At last she bought a small gilt wall bracket and placed it high above her head. She often lay in her bed gazing up at it, loving it, and worrying about it. But of course it never did get broken.

CHAPTER NINE

THE days to Christmas ran out like sand, bringing all the things that spell Christmas to everyone, everywhere. At that time of the year, Guy was extremely busy and often stayed overnight at his town apartment, but the cards and parcels and gifts continued to stream in, delivered to the house in vanloads from friends and business connections all over the world. Even Uncle Mark was forced to concede that his work would have to be abandoned until well into the New Year.

All this time Celia and Liane flitted hither and yon. There were endless pre-Christmas functions and parties demanding their presence and they attended almost every one; the mother as fair and beautiful as a Botticelli angel, the daughter thinner, a little indifferent to what went on about her, both of them keeping messengers busy delivering enormous beribboned boxes from the leading couturiers.

As Christmas Day approached, there was only Karen and Pip to help Aunt Patricia decorate the tree. Aunt Patricia, too, received the usual windfall of invitations, but she nearly always found an excuse for avoiding each one. She couldn't have been more different from her glamorous, frivolous sister-in-law.

The Christmas tree rose to the ceiling in the living room, glittering, resplendent, hung with fragile coloured baubles that tinkled in the breeze. As they worked they sang Christmas carols and funny old songs, with Karen hitting out a few bars on the piano, laughing and joking, and once when Pip rested his dark head comfortably on Aunt Patricia's shoulder she burst into tears. Karen and Pip gazed back at her in deepest consternation, though she smiled through her tears and shrugged it all off with, "This always happens to me at Christmas. Now don't take any notice!" The moment passed and they plunged once more into merriment.

Rikki only appeared once on the scene with a sprig of mistletoe declaring with a theatrical leer that "someone is bound to fall into my trap!" But as the gaiety of the others seemed to intensify, a funny thing happened to Karen. She found herself becoming strangely dejected, depressed and unhappy. Perhaps it was because this was her first Christmas without her mother; her strange, difficult mother who had died. Though she had never understood her mother Karen missed her, and a shaft of grief for what might have been pierced her heart.

Her depression deepened, slowly, irresistibly, until one evening she had to lock herself in her room to cry her heart out. Christmas wasn't a happy time, she told herself fiercely, trying unsuccessfully to stop this paroxysm. Christmas was sad. Very sad. She fell back on the pillow again, wishing and wishing the whole festive season was over.

The tap at her door startled her. As a purely involuntary act she switched off her tears and assumed a misleadingly cheerful expression. It was probably Aunt Trish and the sight of tears would only bewilder her. Karen ran a hand over her hair, smoothed her skirt down and bit hard on her lips, colouring them the red of wild cherries.

Guy was at the door, the palest fawn of his shirt throwing his tan into stunning relief. Their eyes met and Karen obeyed a totally reckless impulse and held up her face to him.

His mouth tilted slightly and he bent his dark head and kissed the curve of her cheek. "You've been crying, darling!" His beautiful voice and the careless endearment turned her heart over. They stood close together and Karen, looking up with a kind of surprised curiosity, divined in those dark eyes a fondness for her.

Guy broke the strange silence. "Why were you crying, my little orphan?"

His perception didn't startle her. She had become used to it.

"I was sad, I suppose," she gave a wry little smile and inexplicably her mood brightened. "I'm so glad you're home again, Guy."

"You're what?" One black eyebrow shot up sardonically.

"It's no good, Guy," she said sweetly. "I refuse to cross swords with you. I've that much of the Christmas spirit."

He smiled at the odd defensiveness of her tone and she was conscious of the same old excitement. She had come to accept now, with a chronic fatalism, Guy's power to excite and disturb her. His presence focused and intensified her deepest, most complex feelings for him.

The wild illogicality of love! Her life simply wasn't her own any more, but hopelessly entangled with Guy's. His brilliant dark eyes never moved from her face. He stood, strangely silent and insistent. Under this unblinking appraisal, Karen's thoughts became wild and chaotic, the force of her emotions deepening the colour of her eyes, the most piquant feature of her beauty.

"Sadness becomes you," Guy murmured obliquely, his eyes lingering on her face and shoulders. His words overlay something he would not or could not say. His real thoughts seemed to be hidden from her, disguised by a teasing ambiguity.

Karen was jolted into speaking her thoughts aloud.

"You're the most fearfully complicated man I know!"

"Am I?"

All at once she knew this was something different.

She knew it from the wild, frightened beating of her heart and the hot blood that rushed to the extremities of her body. But most of all she knew it from Guy's face.

"Guy!" she managed to get out. "Please, Guy!"

He took not the slightest notice of her, if he even heard her. He drew her against his hard, taut body and began kissing the breath out of her. He wasn't teasing any more. He was in deadly earnest.

"Please stop!" she whispered against his mouth, but he never seemed to hear her. Suddenly all the strength left her and she let herself be crushed up against him. Her mouth opened convulsively and she clung to him...clung to him...her long, shuddering sigh trembling on the night air.

"Guy!...Guy!...Guy...!"

Celia, on her way to her own suite, heard this strange little moan, but could see nothing. At first her face was ludicrously perplexed, then it froze into a fearful, unlovely mask.

She leaned against the wall, one hand going to her side, like a woman in agony. The first surge of shock passed and she was steadied by actuality. So it had happened! The unspeakable...the inevitable...Fate reached out to everyone, everywhere...even to her! But Guy was hers or no one's, and by God, she would fight for him. She continued on to her room, unnoticed.

Karen felt the first wild presentiment of disaster. She pulled away from Guy with a kind of silent ferocity, fearful now of this intolerable excitement, the loss of self, he engendered in her.

"I've said you're dangerous, Guy, and you are! Cruel and brilliant, like a ton of square-cut diamonds." She lashed out at him, fighting for self-preservation, seeking any weapon, no matter how unfair.

His expression hardened. His eyes had that queer glittery look of rising anger.

"You've just got to claw at me, haven't you, Karen?"

She retreated a step from those brilliant dark eyes.

"Yes, I have! And you know why."

He grasped her under both elbows, pulling her to him and shaking her like a rag doll.

"*I* know why, but *you* know nothing, you crazy little cat. I don't know why I bother with you."

His anger only fanned the bright blaze in her.

"Oh, you arrogant...arrogant...*devil*!" Her hot words were dredged up from the best forgotten past; an echo of humiliation, her mother's strange bitterness.

Without a word Guy turned on his heel and left her, his face a teak carving.

Karen looked after him, struggling against the urge to run after him, to throw herself into his arms where she longed to be; to beg him to forgive her...to try to understand her...Her pride and her uncertainty kept her there. Her hand moved to her bruised, pulsing mouth and the tears started to well again.

She moved back into her room and slammed the door, then burst into a frenzy of weeping.

Celia, in her room, was not indulging in the unconstructive extravagance of weeping. She was long past the age to risk suffering the consequences. She was sitting by her window, an exquisite porcelain figure, but she was already planning...vengeance!

There was no Christmas spirit after that, for underneath the superficial gaiety and signs of good will ran a current of tension. With the exception of Pip, who was enjoying himself immensely, with far too many expensive presents, the tension was beginning to be felt by everyone in the house.

Celia, with all the little oblique ways only detectable to another woman, was making it her business to make Karen feel like an outsider, with no legitimate claim to the family...no real place among them. Eva, after all, had been only a second cousin, and that made Karen practically—nothing!

Karen pretended not to notice. There were always so many people calling at Belle Amber; other branches of the family, old friends and visitors, politicians and celebrities, that she found it easy to avoid over-contact with someone whom she felt in her bones was her mortal enemy.

Celia, her eyes unnaturally bright, never failed to take stock of Karen's whereabouts, though with a certain relief she noticed that the girl stayed close to Rikki and made up a foursome with Liane and Colin. Guy was clearly avoiding the girl, and for a moment Celia felt she could have been mistaken, but her razor-sharp senses were too alerted for there to be any mistake!

After that, as if driven by some strange compulsion, Celia kept Karen under constant surveillance. The deep-driven flaw in her character was surfacing under pressure.

New Year's Eve naturally called for a lavish entertainment. Karen went along to Liane's room shortly before seven that evening. If only she could talk Liane into wearing the wig again! With so many people present, there was bound to be comment, all of it favourable, she felt sure. She would incur Celia's wrath, of course, but she wasn't really frightened. Or was she? A shiver ran down her spine and she knocked overloud on Liane's door, waiting for the cheerful "Come in!"

Liane was standing in the centre of the room rubbing cream into her elbows. Her negligée was a midsummer night's dream!

"Hello, Karo. What are you wearing?"

"That's *my* question!" Karen sank down on a silk-upholstered love seat.

"*You* tell *me*," Liane said surprisingly, now taking to brushing her short curly hair.

"You actually want me to pick the gown for you?"

"Go ahead!" Liane smiled a curious little smile. Karen got up at once and went to the built-in wardrobe, ruffling through the left-hand side of it which held all the ornate evening dresses.

Liane watched, very erect, with a prim air of anticipation. Karen realised she was taking a very long time about it with such a bewildering array to choose from, but there wasn't really anything she cared for. Perfect for someone, but not for Liane. Then, right at the back, she saw it—perfectly plain, but the superb master cut was unmistakable, even on the hanger. Karen reached for it and ran her hand over the beautiful deep coral brocade. She held it out to Liane, who took it with a snort of amusement.

"Aunt Trish bought this. You and Rikki seem to agree on everything."

"It's beautiful, Lee!" Karen's clear topaz eyes held a determined persuasiveness. "Slip it on and let me see."

Liane obeyed, quite cheerful, even gay about it. It looked even better on, Karen decided, and drew a sigh of mingled pleasure and relief. "You've got a lovely figure, Lee. All you have to remember is to keep your shoulders back. With a little practice you won't even have to remember to do that."

"Yes, ma'am!" Liane laughed, and saluted. "You sound like a forthright old lady."

Karen smiled, not denying it. She had heard her own tone. "I do hope I live to be a forthright old lady. I see nothing wrong in it. Guy told me I'd probably floor everyone with a look or a few words."

Liane was smiling back at her and Karen tacked on deliberately: "Now how about..."

Liane held up a warning finger. "Don't say it, my girl!"

"But you'd look sensational."

Liane wasn't yielding. "Enough is enough! That's my motto."

"I hope you remember it," Karen said cryptically. "Well, see you later, Miss Amber."

Liane smiled absently. With Karen gone, she turned back to the mirror. She *did* have a nice figure. Funny how a particular style showed it up. She smoothed her hands over the lovely long line of her hips in blissful satisfaction.

In her own room, Karen dressed for the evening with no such sense of pleasure or anticipation. She wore a beautiful sari-type gown Aunt Patricia had made up for her as a Christmas present. The material was a gorgeous Indian silk, embroidered in gold, that Aunt Trish had picked up in her travels. To complement it, Karen twisted her black hair into the unfamiliar style of a heavy chignon. Her mother's peridot earrings, her only jewellery, swung from her ears and she looked beautiful and quite exotic with her strange tilted eyes.

The young men were rather dazed by her, but she realised this slowly. In the rare moment she stood with Guy and Liane, Liane laughingly commented on this strange phenomenon. She herself was very much in demand. Guy's eyes on Karen were as deep as the night and twice as unfathomable. Karen thought he wasn't going to answer at all, but at last he said tersely: "Beauty is not without a certain awesome fascination. Karen wouldn't be everyone's cup of tea, I imagine."

Liane bit off a laugh and looked to Guy to explain, but he moved away on the pretext that there were more guests arriving. Liane was, in fact, having the time of her life; except for that fearful Dave Barron, an old friend of Rikki's, she explained, and he had this most infuriating manner! Following Liane's eyes, Karen saw a tall, powerfully built young man with a clever-ugly face and who just could be infuriating. Despite this she said clearly: "I like him."

"You do?" Liane gave an exclamation of incredulity. "But he's impossible. You don't know him. Ever since he won that Rhodes Scholarship! The way he goes on. He's even accused me of being intellectually stunted.'' She patted Karen's arm, then sauntered off in search of Colin.

Less than a minute later she was waylaid by the same Dave Barron, who announced to a first nonplussed then wildly amused young woman: "Rikki tells me you're determined to dance with me!" Liane went into his arms, laughing in spite of herself. At least he was a veritable giant and she could get the most delicious crick in her neck just looking up at him. Marvellous, that! Liane smiled her transforming smile and to her surprise Dave Barron responded, drawing her closer.

Later in the evening when Karen was asked to play, she saw Celia drift out on to the terrace with Colin. Not for Celia to sit through another woman's monopolising everyone's attention. Karen's eyes moved rather bleakly back over the room and she saw Guy was looking at her. He nodded his head imperceptibly and she began to play.

It wasn't cheerful music. In fact it was Chopin at his most tormented, but that was her mood and there was very little she could do about it. Afterwards her hands fell away from the piano with a strange exhaustion. Her audience, rather moved, demanded more, but she smiled and took Uncle Mark's hand. He bore her off to be introduced to a particular friend, fully prepared, he said, to jostle young Rikki out of taking her in to supper.

Of course she was not to escape Colin. There were more of his exploits just waiting to be told, including the brilliance of his latest television commercial for the firm. Karen had to concede that it *was* good! Colin broke off his monologue to say sharply: "Just look at that big oaf with Liane."

Karen didn't turn her head. "I don't think that would describe him. I understand he's a Rhodes scholar."

"Pfutt!" Colin made an exclamation of disgust. "An

egghead! Dime a dozen, all of them, and no good for anything else!''

"Oh well, if you say so, Colin!"

Colin redirected his gaze sharply, but the perfect oval face of his companion was quite bland.

"I don't think Liane likes him," she murmured consolingly, but Liane's merry peal of laughter broke out and spoiled the effect of the statement. Colin hunched his shoulders.

Though she had no liking for him, Karen thought it best to mention to Liane that her fiancé was getting restive, so later on in the evening the two girls went in search of him. Soft colour bloomed in Liane's cheeks, her eyes were gay; she looked happy. They moved out into the crowded terrace, then decided on an impulse to re-enter the house through the library. It was easier that way.

The sky was studded with stars, but there was no moon to welcome in the New Year. Liane was the first to see them. They were standing a little way out into the garden, almost directly outside the dimly lit library. Celia was caught in a beam of dull gold, smiling faintly, her silver-gilt head tilted, far back, her arms slid, oh so gently, possessively, around Colin's neck. Colin's brown head was bent to her, the muscles at the back of his neck knotted, his back tense, unable to withstand her.

Karen's heart quivered with shock. She grasped for Liane's icy hand, but Liane was gone. She moved with incredible speed; a speed that Karen could neither match nor credit. She herself stood rooted to the ground, risking discovery. A total apathy towards life was working its way through her, making her stand limp like a rag doll. Celia and Colin! Was there no man immune to her?

Colin spun, alerted, and saw her. Shame, self-contempt, defiance, flashed across his good-looking face. Celia's voice was little more than a hiss: "So—the little sneak-thief!"

Karen didn't answer, feeling submerged by a wave of sheer exhaustion. It threatened to rise up and engulf her on the spot. She stood fighting it off, until a hard protective shell closed about her.

"I wouldn't have chosen to see you for the world," she said in a completely dead tone.

"You'll not tell Liane?" Colin looked over at her, completely vanquished. Karen felt a sudden hostility for him that showed in her face. He saw it, mumbled something and even withdrew his arm from Celia.

"You may as well go," Celia said scornfully. "I can't stand you, if you must know. You're your father all over again. Besides, you've seen nothing out of the ordinary. Colin is a man as other men are."

"Don't ask me to believe that," Karen flashed back contemptuously. Celia stared back at her, loathing in her vivid blue eyes.

"*Any* man is my man if I want it that way!" Her silvery head was flung up imperiously. Karen would have laughed if Celia hadn't been in such deadly earnest. She took an involuntary step backwards.

"You're disgusting!" she said quietly. "A desire for conquest should have some decent limits." She was aware of her clenched hands, the blood roaring in her ears, then she fled before the naked violence in the other woman's eyes.

The New Year pealed in as Karen ran in search of Liane. She found her in her room, lying face down on the bed. Her white, tearless face reflected more completely than anything else her utter annihilation. Karen went to stand beside her and spoke her name. How could she comfort her? With what words?

"Liane!" The girl slipped out of her grasp and went to stand at the window. "Happy New Year," she said tragically.

"Liane dear," Karen's own voice was strained, "you know the strangest things happen at New Year parties. People get thrown a little off balance, do things they would never normally dream of doing."

Liane laughed bitterly.

"Please, Liane," Karen persisted, "everyone downstairs is going a little mad at the moment. It's just an old custom."

Liane actually laughed if the sound was not quite so heartbreaking. "So that's what we saw! Or rather what we didn't quite see. An old custom! Just as well we missed the rest of it. I don't think I'd recover in a whole lifetime."

"Couldn't you be taking this a little too seriously?" Karen found herself saying, wondering at the same time why she was being so inane, but Lee's white face was frightening her.

"Would *you* be caught kissing someone else's fiancé?" Liane asked with bitter derision.

"Oh, heavens, Lee!" Karen tried to be objective, feeling more like crying. "It could happen. One mad moment...None of us is perfect. If I loved him..." she raved on distractedly.

"And you think Mother loves Colin?" Liane turned on her vehemently.

"I can't imagine how anyone loves him," Karen was stung into truth.

"*I* loved him," Liane pointed out quietly. "Not now. But Mother loves no one. I could forgive her a little if her heart was involved. But Mother loves no one. Her preoccupation with herself is appalling." She repeated herself with dreadful clarity, for the first time in her life facing up to the hard cold fact.

Karen's eyes slipped compassionately over the white, drained face. "You're not coming down again?"

"No. I haven't got that kind of guts. Make up some story for me, Karo. But keep Mother away from me."

Karen hesitated at the door. "She...neither of them...realised you were there."

Liane's head shot up. "You never told them?"

"No!"

"Thank you, Karen," Liane said tiredly, and shut her eyes on the world.

CHAPTER TEN

INEVITABLY the morning followed the night before, and no one with the exception of Guy got up before lunch. One day was pretty much like another to Guy and he always had business to attend to. He retired to his study and didn't emerge. The New Year dinner was scheduled for the evening and no one felt much inclined towards eating before then.

Uncle Mark had a tray in his room and the rest of them drifted in, one by one, to the solarium for coffee and perhaps a sandwich. Amazingly Celia had condescended to join them, and only Karen knew it was not condescension on Celia's part but her warning antennae.

They all seemed to wait for Liane. She slipped into the room quietly, except for her pronounced pallor—stunning! She wore a tailored black linen pants suit, buttoned and buckled in gold, with taupe stripes on the jacket, and a taupe and black silk scarf held her glossy mane. It was Liane at her best, Karen decided, with her lovely lean hips and long, long legs. Celia could never get away with trousers, she was built too close to the ground. Karen sat back smiling.

Rikki, however, let out a long-drawn whistle and even Pip, young as he was, looked his admiration. Karen's instincts told her to sit perfectly still and not say anything. Everyone waited for the bomb to go off, but Celia said nothing! She stirred a sugar substitute into her coffee and said brightly: "We were waiting for you, my darling. I was thinking we might make up a

party for this evening and go somewhere exciting. I'll
speak to Guy...when I see him," she trilled. "Why
not ring Colin?"

Liane accepted a chicken sandwich from her aunt,
then lifted her head blankly. "Who's Colin?" Her aunt
maintained an air of desperate composure. Something
was wrong, she had felt it. Rikki and Pip were agog,
their faces betraying shocked surprise and delight. No
one liked Colin.

Celia shot Karen a swift baleful look promising retribution. Karen was shocked by the sudden hardness beneath the sweetly feminine contours of her face. But
Celia had admirable control. She only smiled at her
daughter.

"All right, dearest," she drawled. "A joke, is it? A
lovers' tiff?" The persistent notion occurred to Karen
that this was going to develop into an unlovely scene.
She turned to her interested young brother.

"If you're finished, Pip, you can go to your room.
We might go for a run this afternoon."

Pip looked slightly put out, much loath to leave just
when things were developing, but he was used to obey-
ing his sister. He got up without another word.

Celia flashed Karen a look of bright malevolence.
"Quite the little mother, aren't you? You're over-
attached to that child." Her eyes slewed to her daughter. "Well, what do you say, dearest, or don't you feel
up to it?" Her laugh tinkled merrily. "Of course, you'll
have to leave that God-awful wig behind."

A pulse beat heavily at the base of Liane's throat.
She started to speak, groping for the almost forgotten
words, but they emerged with pulverising impact.

"In law, what plea so tainted and corrupt but being
seasoned with a gracious voice obscures the show of
evil?"

Celia looked genuinely stricken, her face paling into
transparency. Even Rikki appeared to be struck dumb.

Karen sought Aunt Patricia's eyes. Tension was mounting. There was no telling how far Liane's reaction would take her.

Celia spoke barely above a whisper. "How could you say such a thing to me, your mother, who loves you?" The soft husky voice broke pathetically.

Liane stood up suddenly, a shocking grimness about her mouth. "Pray God no one else loves me in quite the same say!"

Celia let out her breath in a whirring moan. Her eyes flicked venomously towards Karen.

"No, *Celia*," Liane said with great deliberation. "You're barking up the wrong tree. The heart knows its own bitterness. Now if you'll excuse me I do have a few phone calls to make, though it will only take a minute to dispose of Colin." She moved with swift grace out of the room, her head up, her shoulders back, gallant like a young knight.

Celia left them without a word. She was not following her daughter. Patricia Amber stared down into the black dregs in her cup. "What a damnable mess!"

"You do put things very mildly, Trish, old girl," Rikki found his tongue at last.

"It seemed appropriate enough," his aunt replied mildly.

Rikki laughed. "You've got a positive genius for reducing everything to normality, Trish. But then you've been doing it for years, haven't you...standing between Celia and us. God, for a minute there I thought I'd have to referee a slanging match. Lee looked as if she was about to up and at 'em!"

"She could hardly attack her mother," his aunt pointed out sadly.

"Oh, I don't know. Think of the times *Lee's* been attacked. You don't always win with a misplaced sense of decency."

Rikki's aquamarine eyes veered to Karen. "There's a story here, sweetie. What is it?"

Karen exchanged a look with the other woman. "Not *my* story, Rikki. This isn't my affair."

"Isn't it now, precious?" Rikki's eyes glinted. "Your coming has changed a lot of things in this house."

His aunt intervened gently, "I think it's about time you demonstrated your ability to suppress your curiosity, Rikki. Whatever Karen knows she's obviously not going to tell you, and for a very good reason, I know."

"Hallellujah!" Rikki jumped to his feet. "This has been a deep spiritual experience for me, girls. You'll have to excuse me. I've got a little unfinished business myself."

Neither of the two women were sorry to see him go. They had plenty to talk about!

Whether intentionally or not, Rikki was to complete Celia's débâcle and contribute to his own sorrows. Much later that evening when everyone was toying with coffee and liqueurs but really thinking about Liane's broken engagement and her extraordinary decision to accept Dave Barron's dinner invitation for that evening, Rikki came to the drawing room door, his bright eyes elated.

"Kindly step this way, everyone, if you care to be impressed."

Guy looked up with his first smile of that evening.

"Well, I for one would welcome it. Lead the way."

As soon as Guy made a move they all followed with varying degrees of mystification—all except Karen. She knew what Rikki had in mind.

The portrait stood on its easel in the centre of the library, placed for correct lighting. The most profound silence fell over the room, to be broken by Aunt Trish, who said wonderingly: "Unbelievable!" Her eyes added the words, "And quite beautiful!"

Mark Amber took short quick steps neared the canvas. "My boy, my boy! I never suspected."

"I know," Rikki grinned.

"The first spark, which precedes the breaking out of the great flame." The quiet voice was almost reverent. "It has a true musical feeling, my boy. This is indeed our little Karen."

Only Celia and Guy stood back, strangely silent. Karen, as the subject of the painting, was not expected to comment. Rikki was breaking into quick, uncontrollable smiles, looking from one to the other. His world suddenly seemed bright and beautiful.

Celia's frown was thoughtful. "It's a highly commendable effort, dearest. Especially in view of your age." Her tongue moistened her dry lips. "Your subject is over-idealised, perhaps, but that's understandable. But the pose is exaggerated, my darling. It quite upsets the balance."

Rikki began crowing madly, hopping all over the room holding up one foot. "A blow beneath the belt! Proof, proof, I've arrived!"

Celia's eyes flickered spears of resentment. After an age, Karen thought, Guy spoke: "You can put your own price on it."

Rikki just could not conceal his immense gratification. His ardent young face filled with colour. "What more could an artist want...? To be crowned with success during his lifetime. Put my own price on it, whacko!" His eyes sparkled impishly. "Perhaps I won't sell to you."

"You'll have to!" Guy said nonchalantly, and moved over to the canvas. "The eyes are remarkable...the most remarkable feature in a remarkable face. I've never seen eyes remotely like them except for Stephen." He moved slightly, studying the portrait from another angle. "I congratulate you, Rikki. At this rate, you'll surpass the lot of us."

Celia's small gulp of laughter was deprecatory. "Oh, Guy darling, don't be too kind to my poor boy."

"It isn't kind to give someone a false impression of their capabilities," Guy replied mildly. "I think Rikki has great talent, Celia, though why in the name of God he has chosen to hide it all this time I'll never know." He seemed about to say more, then thought better of it.

Karen found herself preparing to face Celia. Every nerve in her body tensed at the knowledge that she must be on her guard. They were all examining the portrait now, admiring it, its loveliness and outstanding technical ability.

"It's gorgeous!" Patricia Amber said happily, her spirits rising rapidly. "Where shall we hang it?"

"Wait until it wins a prize first," Rikki admonished her. "In just over a fortnight!" He leaned over and kissed Karen's cheek. "You blessed damozel! Praise the day Guy brought you back to us." He looked over at Guy, an urchin grin on his face. "How would five hundred dollars strike you?"

Guy raised his head and looked fleetingly at Karen through half-closed lids. "Never undersell yourself, Rikki."

"'Struth!" Rikki looked as if he would burst into tears! "How about a thousand?"

"I'll write you a cheque," Guy said matter-of-factly.

Karen for one scarcely heard him. Her whole attention was concentrated on Celia, the bright unblinking gaze, that was moving steadily over the portrait. Her heart lunged with a new, secret fear.

On the face of it Liane took her broken engagement extremely well. If she cried herself to sleep some nights there was no one to bear witness to it. Colin's name was never mentioned, for Guy, with the superb ease of chairman of the board of directors, had him transferred to the Sydney office, a piece of information Liane digested with a vast indifference.

To Karen's mind, out of her private heartache, Liane had emerged with a shining new image. Over-long in the nest, she had spread her wings with disconcerting

thoroughness. These days Liane Amber was a striking
and original young woman, willing and able to think for
herself. One evening she announced to the family that
she intended working for an arts degree at the University. As Rikki had said, she had been considered a very
good student at school. So far as those who loved her
were concerned, Liane could have rocketed off to the
moon if it would have helped her over a bad patch, but
Celia found her daughter's ambition vastly amusing.

"Why, dearest," she said mischievously, "next you'll
be joining the women's liberation front and carrying
banners."

"My current beau likes intellectual women," Liane
said with deliberate carelessness. Her current beau did
indeed encourage her to sharpen her wits on him, but
he liked quite a few other things besides. Liane looked
over to smile at Karen, who shared her confidences,
but she gazed past her mother as though she never existed. But Celia couldn't let things lie. She threw back
her gleaming pale head and hooted delightfully.

"An *intellectual* woman, what next?" she mocked
prettily, her deeply blue eyes skimming her daughter.
"Oh well, I suppose..." It was amazing the meanings
Celia seemed able to get into harmless words. She
laughed again, her eyes impish. "If a woman has what
is really important, she doesn't need anything else. But
if she's missed out on that all-important something it
might be as well for her to cultivate some of her other
resources."

"Her voice was ever soft, gentle and low," Rikki
murmured, apparently apropos of nothing. "Do tell us,
Celia, what *is* that all-important something?"

Celia's eyes glimmered with secret laughter. One
bare white shoulder shrugged nonchalantly. "Why, sex
appeal, dearest. I wonder you ask. It's what a man
wants."

Rikki took his mother very seriously. "True allure,
or sex appeal as you call it, is often a *hidden* dimension,

and it doesn't necessarily go hand in hand with physical perfection. If it does, the more powerful the impact, if it doesn't, the impact is still there." His glance veered to Karen. "With a pair of beautiful eyes, it's the expression at the back of the eyes, the reflection of the inner psyche that makes them so deeply alluring... invested with the timeless fascination of Eve. Where there is only self-reflection, even great beauty palls."

"Gracious!" Celia's small proud head tilted. "I'm grateful I belong in the first category, my darling." Her aimless, drifting eyes returned to her daughter. But Celia's hold on her daughter was broken. Out in the hallway the telephone shrilled and Liane excused herself with an eager light in her luminous dark eyes. "That will be David," she announced, rather breathless for a girl who once professed to find that particular young man "frightful". Celia's eyes watched her daughter's straight back, seeming unable to accept this newly attained confidence.

Without looking up, Karen could guess at the intent frown that had come between the vivid blue eyes. She had come to realise that there was no adequate explanation for Celia's being the way she was. Being the centre of attention had become a compulsion with her.

The evening dragged on, shadowy and insubstantial. Nothing in this beautiful house was as it seemed. Behind Celia's porcelain face and sweet manner lay a scheming, frivolous mind. Karen paid very little attention to what went on about her, reflecting miserably that Guy was avoiding her.

When Uncle Mark asked her to play she went to the piano with a sense of relief. Aunt Patricia settled herself in her favourite chair to listen, conscious that Karen was disturbed and unhappy. Out of the corner of her eye Karen was watching Guy bend his sculptured dark head to Celia. She was whispering something to him, her lovely face glowing with laughter. Then after a while even Celia was forced into listening because Guy tipped his dark head back and closed his eyes, a faint curious expression on his face.

Karen drifted from one composer to the other... indifferent now to Celia's watching, waiting eyes. There was nothing to worry about...nothing to worry about...nothing to worry about! Yet why was she fighting this incomprehensible feeling?

The next ten minutes gave her the answer. Rikki came to stand in the doorway, incredibly tears in his eyes! His aunt was the first to find her voice, alerted to danger.

"Whatever's wrong, Rikki?"

"What's wrong? What's wrong? I'll show you what's bloody well wrong!" He jerked away, muttering what sounded like basic Anglo-Saxon, but wasn't, then faced them holding a large canvas. Karen's heart stopped beating. She knew what it was. Of course she knew what it was. It seemed she had always known. Rikki turned the canvas towards them and the silence of the grave fell over the room. They all sat motionless, held in thrall. The portrait was ruined, reduced to a dreadful caricature by a childish or wantonly malicious hand! Squiggles of pure pigment were squeezed haphazardly over the sheer topaz of the gown and the face was almost obliterated by the favourite manoeuvre of drawing in a pair of owlish dark glasses. Long curls were added to hang over the shoulders and as a jarring touch of colour—ultramarine beads!

If there was anything remotely funny about the changes no one saw it. The expressions were uniform and menace towards the perpetrator was gathering like mists on a mountain top. Rikki sank down on a chair, struggling with his own private devil of bitterness and frustration. His white, drained face revealed the trenchantness of the blow.

Karen got to her feet with a curiously delayed motion, breaking the tableau. She sat down on the arm of Rikki's chair and stroked his hand.

"Rikki! Rikki!" Under her hand Rikki's long fingers twitched in an agony. She sat beyond thinking for a while.

"Where's Philip?" Celia flung up her head, something almost avid in her expression. The expression, so angrily confident, struck at Karen like a blow. She winced at its impact, her eyes flashing. Patricia Amber looked quickly at her, willing her to be silent. She realised now that Celia *hated* the girl. Karen tried to remain calm but the words sprang up unbidden:

"What's Pip got to do with it?" she said tersely, her burden of worry and bewilderment showing on her face. Celia's eyes glittered. One could almost hear the ice cracking. "We'll very soon know, my dear. Isn't it bad enough without having *you* to contend with?" She spoke curtly, all pretence at civility gone.

"*I'll* get Pip," Patricia Amber said quietly, "though I doubt if it's necessary," she added without emphasis.

"Oh, what a black and dirty night!" Rikki burst out, then reverted to stone. His aunt left the room swiftly, thinking that Celia's stratagem was plain. Her courage almost deserted her!

In the living room Karen felt the mood building up in her. Her nervous system was already reacting to Celia's rapid-fire question and its implication. She turned over the tormenting question in her mind, a strange uneasiness possessing her spirit. Children, even the best of them, sometimes did the most unaccountable things, without realising the effects of their actions. But Pip was so intelligent, so careful of property! His own, as well as anyone else's. She sat ensnared in the pointless goading of her thoughts. Mark Amber lay back in his chair, looking over his steepled fingers. His face was saddened. He would have staked his life on young Pip. Such an intelligent lad! The old, wise eyes studied his nephew.

Guy looked inscrutable as ever, a guard on his thoughts. Nothing was revealed. It was the board meet-

ing face Mark Amber was used to, when Guy let the
other party make all the first moves.

To Karen, only a few feet away, Guy seemed frighteningly remote. If Pip was responsible, and who else
could be, they would have to leave Belle Amber. It
would be an intolerable situation.

Patricia was back within minutes holding Pip's hand.
He wore a dressing gown over his pyjamas. His dark
head was faintly tousled, quickly brushed over on top.
His alert young face, conditioned by a childhood of siz-
ing up adult situations, held a maturity far beyond his
years. He crossed to his sister, his dark eyes filled with
an unchildlike wariness.

"What's up, Karo?"

She found the soft curl that formed around his ear,
brushing it back, without finding words. This was her
little brother no matter what he had done.

Rikki threw himself up and away, his temper on the
ascendant.

"Leave it to me, Karen," Guy said quietly.

"No, please, Guy!" The force of her protest vaguely
shocked her.

"I think you will," he inserted deftly. Controlled as
his voice was it flicked at her like a whiplash. It brought
her back to control and she subsided.

"Come here, Pip," Guy said evenly. The child went
to him at once and Guy took him by the shoulders and
turned him towards the light. "I'm going to ask you a
question for which there is only one possible answer—
the truth. You know that, don't you, Pip?"

The small body tensed under his hands, but Pip's
eyes were as direct as his sister's.

"Yes, sir!"

Guy came down to Pip's level. "You know Rikki's
portrait of Karen, the one he's entering in the competition?"

"Of course!" Pip's head swivelled to Karen, but Guy
laid a finger on his chin and turned his head back to
him.

"Have you touched it in any way, Pip? Added a few improvements, perhaps?"

Pip flushed scarlet, then quickly paled again. "I most certainly have not! I'm not stupid, Uncle Guy, and it certainly doesn't need improving!" For an instant he looked like a small replica of his sister. The expression more than anything else, Guy thought with one part of his mind, for their looks were totally dissimilar.

"You've seen it, then," he prompted the child gently. From behind him came a gasp of horror. Celia put her hand to her throat as if to alleviate the strangling ache there. Philip glanced towards her chair, sensing some devious and stealthy purpose.

"Yes, I went up to the studio to see if Rikki was there. I wanted him to help me with something. I draw too, you know. I knocked on the door, but there was no answer, I kept it up because sometimes Rikki ignores you, but he'll let you in if you persist long enough. Anyway, I opened the door for a quick peek and I saw the portrait. It was up on the easel. I just said to myself, 'Gee, you look lovely, Karo,' then I came away. I knew Rikki would show it to me when he was ready."

"And you never touched anything?"

"No, Uncle Guy." There was a flash of spirit in Pip's eyes. "I don't tell lies, Uncle Guy. Ask Karen."

"That's all right!" Guy got to his feet, towering over the child. "You can go to bed now, Pip."

"Aren't you going to tell me what's happened? I won't be able to sleep otherwise." The child's eyes on him were grave and searching.

"Yes, I am, Pip. Turn the painting around, please, Karen." She found the strength to do so. The nightmare feeling was receding. Surely Guy's voice held conviction, a wonderful faith in her young brother. Pip's face mirrored a whole world of dismay.

"Oh, Karo, what's happened to it? Just look at those stupid glasses and the beads! Surely you didn't think I'd do it?"

"Of course not, pet." She got up and hugged him to

her, ashamed of her bad moments. Guy put a hand on Pip's shoulder.

"Off to bed now, son. I'll straighten things out here."

Pip had scarcely left the room when Celia lashed out in a fury, her voice out of restraint.

"Surely you're not going to place any faith in that child's integrity, Guy? A ten-year-old who freely admits he was the last person to be in the studio!"

Under the dark gaze her voice lost its passion. Guy's eyebrows shot up with hauteur. "I don't think he did admit to that, Celia. Besides, I've had some experience in reading faces, and the child is innocent. You saw yourself how he reacted. He loves his sister. The idea of defacing her portrait was abhorrent to him. He's far too intelligent, anyway. I'm rather ashamed of doubting him."

Celia threw discretion to the winds. "Well, there's no more to be said. I never thought I would see *you* aid and abet the child, Guy. I'm only sorry I'm not in a position to deal with this myself. It's my son who has suffered!" She suddenly swooped towards Rikki, even at that moment avoiding too close contact.

"Oh, Mother, for God's sake!" Rikki reacted strangely, looking for all the world as though he was fighting a battle he did not care to win.

"The boy's cunning enough, I grant you," Celia said tightly. "You could see he was on the alert as soon as he came into the room."

"Children aren't fools, Celia. I fear you've overlooked that." There was a sombre, relentless cast to Guy's features. The level, quietly pitched voice was devastating. Guy turned to Rikki, and missed Celia's shocked, aggrieved expression. "What have you to say, Rick?"

"I'd sooner endure a red-hot poker than put a name to it," Rikki cried frantically.

There was a speculative look to Guy's eyes.

"You know, Rick, there's always a way round a problem if only one can come up with it." He spoke matter-of-factly as though offering an alternative route to a destination. "A man is as strong as his own determination, his will to succeed."

Rikki stood mute for a minute, his face bleak. "Oh, don't, Guy. I'll go clean off my trolley if I think about it. It's too late. Far, far too late!"

Celia watched the two of them, a waiting stillness in the attitude of her fragile body. A strange emanation of wariness hung about her like a cloud. The origins of intuition are strange! Karen lost colour perceptibly and light flooded the shadows that lurked at the back of her mind. The varying elements blended and shaped themselves into a pattern.

She slumped in her chair, dumbfounded. But didn't defeats demand victories with a jealous nature? Yet what purpose could Celia have in snatching away Rikki's chance at success? But at that moment Celia's reasons didn't matter. Only Rikki mattered, and he was staring at his uncle as though he could feed on that radiant energy that Guy seemed only too willing to lend to him.

Mark Amber struggled out of his chair, drawing the painful scene to a close. "If you'll excuse me, everyone, I'll go up to my room. I suddenly feel old." Without a word Patricia Amber went to him and slipped a hand under his arm. Her eyes as they met Karen's were dark pools of desolation. Her face seemed thinner, drawn. She reached and touched Karen's hand as if for reassurance. A force was on the move that threatened to split up the household; a force she knew she was powerless to meet.

Not so Guy! He stood in the centre of the room and began to quote from Thomas Wolfe, the words and his beautiful voice riveting their attention:

"If a man has a talent and cannot use it, he has failed. If he has a talent and uses only half of it he has partly failed. If he has a talent and learns somehow to use the whole of it he has gloriously succeeded and won a satisfaction few men ever know."

They all stood silently, almost facing each other, and Rikki was looking with piercing intensity into Guy's face. Not one of them was unaffected. Guy's expression was tranquil, but his dark eyes were lit with many small flames. There was something especially challenging and personal in his next words:

"You have a great talent, Rikki. That Richard would have lived to see it! And you have something your father possessed in abundance—a wonderful resilience of soul. I know you'll come up with something."

Rikki's brilliant aquamarine eyes shimmered with the fiercely repressed tears of a young man.

"Uncle Guy," he said shakily, "if I never say it again in my lifetime, I love and admire you." With that he hurled himself out of the room.

Celia laughed. It was an odd laugh, high-pitched and a little wild. To Karen's ears it was not inappropriate!

CHAPTER ELEVEN

SUMMER drifted by and nothing happened to visibly ruffle the surface harmony. The Havilland Prize came and went without an entry from Richard Amber. Though Rikki had confided to Karen he was still very much "a going concern" the two-thousand-dollar prize was awarded to a twenty-six-year-old artist from the neighbouring state of Western Australia. Rikki had worked feverishly on blocking and repainting the portrait of Karen, but as he confessed with a white and bitter face, the "face of the vandal" came between him and his work.

To this, Karen thought it better to make no answer. Some things had to remain forever unspoken. A few weeks later, when she read of the approaching Statton-Logan Gift, the rich national award for the most original oil painting, Rikki did not appear to have any interest. The competition was open, he explained, unlike the Havilland Prize, and that meant the finest artists in the country would be competing for the prize. "I'm good, but not *that* good!" he dismissed it with a shrug. If Guy had implied that Rikki hadn't begun to tap his resources Rikki had forgotten about it. Karen said no more, but she was inexpressibly saddened.

Pip returned to school as brown as a berry from long hours under a hot sun, and Karen drove him there and picked him up afterwards, at least until the weather got cooler. In any case, Pip announced to an indulgent Aunt Patricia, by then he could do with a bonzer new bike, like the one Jeff Sweeney got for Christmas.

Celia's behaviour towards Karen was a masterpiece of

insolence, but if Karen detected the scorn and the mockery she made no sign of it, treatment which Celia found very disconcerting. With an awareness of Karen's quick temper she had thought to provoke the girl into unbecoming behaviour in front of the family, but Karen was learning. One thing at least, she thought with irony, it was never dull with Celia in the house, and she could still, with some part of her, admire the way Celia used her natural graces with such precise and calculated effect, even to placing cushions for Uncle Mark after dinner. But her own sex was a race apart!

Of Guy, Karen found herself making a continual mental circuit. She was bewildered and more than a little frightened of the strength of her love for him. Love!—the word just slipped into her mind. She had never before given a name to it. It had always been "feeling" or "attraction", anything but what it was... love! He had only to walk into a room for her heart to turn over; she had only to answer the telephone and unexpectedly hear his beautiful voice to know the full extent of her bondage.

But now they were rarely alone together. Guy saw to that. With his experience of women he was more than aware of her "schoolgirl crush" on him, she thought with a *frisson* of humiliation. By now he would be bitterly regretting the indiscretion of kissing her. Only very young girls took such things seriously. If Guy had married every woman he had kissed, she reflected unhappily, even the vineyards wouldn't accommodate the resultant harem at one sitting.

Liane, at least, was profiting from *her* experience. She was dating Dave Barron quite frequently now, and often Karen and Rikki made up a foursome for dinner or a party or Liane's beloved ballet. They were all of an age, if not similar interests (Dave hated ballet), but they did have similar high spirits. The shared outings went wonderfully well.

One thing alone would have endeared Dave to Karen

and Rikki—his ability to bring out the best in Liane, to encourage her to develop her capabilities, to infuse her with new confidence. Dave had only met Celia the once and the meeting had not been successful. Intuitively Dave recognised Celia's hidden "vice" and his manner towards her had been that of a well-brought-up young man in the presence of a venerable dowager. Celia had deeply resented it, but the rest of the family breathed a sigh of relief. Colin had never been popular. "Given enough rope, I just knew he would hang himself," Rikki would comment, trying to draw Karen's confidence, but she never would tell him. Even had she Liane's permission, she couldn't bring herself to further blacken Rikki's image of his mother.

As the time of the vintage drew near a subtle anxiety pervaded the atmosphere. There was always the possibility of a late summer thunderstorm bringing the dreaded hail to ruin the crop. So far everything had gone so well—too well perhaps, to a superstitious vigneron. The berries hung plump on the vine with a soft purplish bloom on them, filled out with the occasional summer shower, and the summer sunlight had been hot but not so hot as to affect quality. It should be a great year, but as Uncle Mark pointed out pessimistically, top wines had been made in quite poor years and now and again, *but not at Belle Amber*, inferior wines had been made in very good years. Fascinating as the fermentation process might be, it was by no means the most important. At Belle Amber the growth of the grape was treated as all-important.

Towards the end of February, sample bunches of grapes were brought in from different parts of the vineyard, for grapes on one vine could be noticeably different from those on another. The berries were crushed and the sugar content measured, then a big conference went on between the family and their technical manager. Now was the time for the vigneron to turn into a chemist. Now was the time for him to display the excel-

lence of his judgment, for on the measurement of the
sugar and acid content was based his decision to pick. If
the grapes were too high in sugar it would be at the
expense of the acids and if the grapes were too low in
sugar content the vigneron could not get sufficient alcohol into his wine.

So every day they waited. It was for Guy to give the
final decision, for the gift was born in him and developed to an outstanding degree. He had a recognised
palate and a very clear view of the style the home vineyard had developed. The Belle Amber reds were renowned for their superb berry bouquet and their soft
and elegant roundness of flavour. There was a deep
soft depth of colour to the wine and an outstanding
balance of acidity and tannin finish. The vineyard
showed two styles, both excellent, but the straight Cabernet had that extra something that lifted a wine into
greatness.

So every day they waited. The grapes had to be *exactly* ripe for picking. It was an anxious time, but not
for Karen and Pip. They found it wonderfully exciting.
This was their first vintage since their return to Belle
Amber and nothing could dim its magic.

Each morning it got harder and harder for Karen to
get Pip off to school. He even went so far as to stage a
very sick "turn" with all the symptoms of peritonitis
until Guy promised he would be given plenty of warning of the day of the picking. Pip could stay home from
school on that day, and not only that, he could help
bring in the crop. There was always room for a small
boy on a harvester.

It seemed to Karen, on her endless excursions
around the vineyard and cellar, that everyone on the
estate was engaged in a welter of conference and comment on this occasion of marvellous complexity—the
vintage. Only the foothills, from the first mother-
of-pearl wash of the morning to the pink and gold glory
of sunset, were the *silent* watchers.

CHAPTER TWELVE

THE day began with a rosy dawn and soon the sun woke her. Karen kicked the sheets aside with a feeling of luxury and abandon, then reached for her lemon batiste peignoir and thrust her arms into it. It was a beautiful morning, one of those mornings almost anything could happen. A great pinky gold sea-horse was trailing his curly tail across the sky and she went to the window and pushed back the shutters the better to see it. She stood poised, her dark head tilted to the sky, polished like a blackbird's wing. She looked ready for flight, young and transient, her tilted eyes oddly beautiful. This was the day, she just knew it!

"Dare I intrude on this pretty scene?"

Karen looked down, startled, to where the feathery Japanese maples were bowing on a wave of silver. Guy was looking up at her, one hand holding a branch back, his black eyes brilliant with mockery. "I did come to wake you in the traditional manner, a shower of pebbles at the window, but I see you've beaten me to it. You look like the dawn bird—do you know it?"

The face she showed to him was full of animation, so different from her aloofness of late. The scented earth was stirring, alive with anticipation and high above them a silver dart of a bird was warbling in ecstasy. She released her breath on a long, sweet sigh.

"What is it?" she whispered.

Guy smiled, deliberately tantalising. "Get dressed and come on down, or I could at a pinch come up." He looked quite serious and Karen took one look at the trailing branches of a creeper and said quickly,

"I'll come running!"

His smile was lazy. "That's what I like to hear. Five minutes, no more. Those creepers would hold me."

She smiled and withdrew her dark head, moving swiftly. She brushed her teeth, splashed icy water over her face; the eyes that looked back at her from the wall mirror were sparkling with all the joy of the morning. She ran a comb through her hair, decided she dared not risk taking time off to apply a little make-up and paid little attention to her choice of a frock—a filamel print in an oriental pattern.

Guy was waiting for her. He tilted her face to him, his dark eyes amused and admiring.

"Oh, to be nineteen and not fear the morning! You look like a Balinese dancing girl. Even the curve of your hair is elegant."

She was unable to suppress the sombre excitement that sprang to her eyes. There could be no escape from Guy. It was so beautiful out there with him, so silent and secret, she could only marvel at its completeness. The scent of the garden came into her lungs and tell-tale colour mounted beneath her ivory skin.

His own eyes held a question. "I hope you don't look at all men as you're looking at me?"

A pulse drummed away in her throat. "I've never *seen* anyone who looks like you," she answered quickly, and evaded him, running on down the path to where the tall poplars soared to the shimmering heavens.

She had to give herself time to control the overwhelming feelings that the sight of him and the touch of him aroused in her. She ran on ahead, feeling the cooling, calming breeze in her face. It whipped her dress around her slender young body and caught at her long black hair, trailing it after her.

Guy caught her up easily and grasped a long coil of her hair. Her lovely mouth quivered and her eyes were starry, dancing with comprehension.

"Why are you forever running away from me?" he asked, his black brows slanting.

"You don't really want to know that, do you?" She looked up at him and blinked rapidly. He didn't answer, but stood there smiling, then he took her hand, ignoring her first, convulsive withdrawal. Lean strong fingers twined through her own and then they were walking, and it seemed a tremendous thing that they should be together, suspended between the sky, filled with scudding white clouds, and the earth with its luxuriant vines.

But she would not meet his eyes, though she knew she had waited for this to happen, through all the days of her life. Her shining dark head was bent and she walked in silence beside this man she knew in her heart was her completion; for without him she would die.

The whole beautiful scene opened out for her in all its dimensions of depth and colour and brilliance so that it almost seemed to her as if she had never truly seen it before. The foothills were bathed in a translucent light and everything was so fresh and strange and beautiful. She could feel the young, eager blood racing in her and Guy stopped on a sunny plateau and turned her about his hands, holding her shoulders, pointing down the slopes. She rested against him, sheafed in the sound of his dark velvet voice.

"I have set my green and clustered vines to robe it round. Far now behind me lies the golden ground..."

"Of Belle Amber," she finished softly, feeling a great rush of love for this place. "Lydian and Phrygian couldn't have been more beautiful!"

He smiled. "You've been doing your homework, my lamb."

She turned and faced him. "One never knows when one might be required to quote the *Bacchae* at six-thirty in the morning."

His dark eyes changed expression and he looked out

over her head. She tried to recapture his interest, conscious of his sudden withdrawal.

"When the Queen of Sheba came visiting Solomon she brought with her the fruit of the vine."

He laughed out loud, his white teeth flashing. "That would have been the very least of it, I should think!"

She shaded her eyes against the delicate brilliance of the early morning sunlight.

"Don't women start everything now," Guy continued conversationally, "even to the wine cult? It's a very old legend that one of the ladies in the harem of King Jemisheed of Persia was distracted by the pain of headache and drank some of the fermented juice of grapes left in a pot, hoping it was poison. The wine overpowered her and she fell asleep. She awakened refreshed with all trace of her headache gone. Needless to say King Jemisheed and all the court took to this wonderful new pastime."

Karen smiled and Guy turned away and twisted a ripe purple cluster of Sauvignon berries from its vine, holding it out to her.

"Now is your moment to enjoy one of nature's greatest gifts, little one. Crush the berries in your mouth and savour the flavour. The fresh skin of the ripe berry will yield all the character of developing wine. Sometimes it even takes years for a red to regain the floral character of the ripe grape. Try it for yourself."

Karen took the small cluster from him, eager for the experiment. The juice pricked her taste buds and ran down her throat with its special astringent flavour. She swallowed the skin and pips in her first *ampelographical* experience. Guy was watching her, half amused, half indulgent, his dark eyes never leaving her face. Laughingly she tossed the stems away and brushed her fingers against her skirt, the juice still glistening on her mouth, full and enticing.

She looked up at Guy, still laughing, and stopped.

The same sensation was stirring in her now as then...the same never-to-be-borne excitement. She closed her eyes and swayed towards him and Guy took her mouth and tasted—wine. When at last she could speak, her voice was pulsing unsteadily.

"Why do you do it?" All her youth and uncertainty was in her eyes.

He seemed to regard her very gravely for a minute then suddenly shrugged and smiled:

"You've typed me so completely as a villain, my love, I guess I'm just keeping in style. Don't villains always have their way with a woman, and you *are* very beautiful." Her topaz eyes sparkled and her mouth half opened, but Guy laid a warning finger across it.

"No backchat, my angel! That tongue of yours will land you in serious trouble. Besides, your mouth is redolent of violets. Today we start picking!"

Belle Amber was pulsing with life and swarms of itinerant workers moved over the estate, stripping the laden vines. Harvesters brought the grapes in from the vineyards to the winery where they were shovelled into the crushers with a loud *bang bang*. The crushers broke the skins, separating the stalks, and sending the juice into the great thousand-gallon fermenting vats. Fermentation usually took five to six days and there was no one on the whole estate immune to the fascination of seeing the vigorous, bubbling liquid, no more than escaping carbon dioxide.

When fermentation was complete, the new wine would be taken to the wine-press, to separate the liquid must from the *marc*—the skins, pips and stalks. From the press the wine would be run into casks of French Nevers oak, then pumped from its first cask into another, leaving behind the lees that would settle at the bottom. This process would be completed several times before the wine was ready to be bottled—at Belle Amber, usually around its second birthday.

The reds, fermented with their skins, took colour, strength and flavour from them, unlike the whites of Amberleigh, which parted from their skins before fermentation, were more delicate and required much more careful handling. Last year's vintage had produced the two styles: the Shiraz Cabernet, a luscious full-bodied ruby red, and the straight Sauvignon Cabernet, dryer, more delicate, with its exquisite floral bouquet. This year the family and the whole staff were hoping for even better!

That first day was exhausting and the nape of her neck was sunburnt. Karen had no trouble at all getting Pip off to bed. He was out on his feet after a day of unaccustomed toil and excitement. Just to complete things Uncle Mark had slipped a few dollars into an envelope which Karen typed Pip's name on and went off to sleep with his very first wages under his pillow. In no time at all, he told Karen, complacently, he would have that new bike with "all the extras".

The house was very quiet that evening. Guy had a late afternoon business appointment and wasn't expected back until late that night. Incredibly, Liane and Rikki had summoned up enough energy to go on to a party which Karen found she could not for the life of her manage. She was deliciously tired out, not at all an unpleasant sensation, but parties were definitely out!

Not long after the two of them left, Karen wandered into the living room and sat down at the piano—nothing energetic tonight, but the sweet nostalgia of Noel Coward. Aunt Trish would be down soon. She was resting a while after dinner, having done every bit as much work as any of the hired help on the estate. Soon Karen became engrossed in working out a new arrangement of the old favourite—"I'll See You Again". She experimented with chords, filling in the time. It was so quiet and peaceful, and *so* prophetic!

A voice from the doorway startled her very completely.

"Girl at a piano! How delightful. Don't you ever get tired of that thing?"

Karen looked over to where Celia, in a swirling pattern of blue and lilac chiffon, stood in the doorway. She was trailing a long matching stole and she looked lovely and quite dangerous.

"Oh, hello! I didn't know you were home." Karen forced herself to be courteous.

Celia, aware of it, gave a brittle laugh and advanced into the room. "I always take off at the vintage. It's so damned boring with tiresome people swarming all over the place. So wearing having to smile at them. Your home isn't your home any more." She waved a small jewelled hand in widening circles in the air and it came to Karen's mind that Celia was very slightly drunk—a most unusual state of affairs, for Celia rarely touched alcohol in any form. She believed it disastrous for the skin and the figure.

Karen shut the lid of the piano, conscious of Celia's active dislike.

"Don't go," Celia said persuasively. "I want to have a little chat with you." She arranged herself artfully in a bergère and tipped her fair head back. "How long have you been here, my dear?"

"Six months," Karen said quietly. There was a kind of sickening familiarity about the scene, as though it had all happened before.

"And the *damage* you've done," Celia said quite pleasantly, not allowing her true feelings to flash out of her eyes.

"I don't understand you."

Now the bitterness in Celia's heart showed in her face.

"I don't mean the way you've alienated my children, my dear. No, don't deny it! They go their own way these days with no thought for their mother. Liane will have me a laughing stock yet with all that gear she goes in for. I'm talking about someone far more important." She sat there almost impassively, a porcelain figure, with a heart like ice. It was foreshadowed in her glittering eyes. "Just let me look at you, my dear. Yes, I can see what he sees in you. Young face, young body, all the beautiful clothes he's bought you. Tell me, my dear, what did you give him in return?" She laughed, delicately, crudely.

Karen recoiled in disgust. "You must be drunk! I can't listen to you."

"You'll listen!" The sweet voice became strident. "Sit down!" The harshness died out of her voice. "When I was your age I never thought I'd be thirty. Then one day I was thirty. I didn't feel any different. I didn't look any different. But I *was* different. I was thirty—beginning to lose my desirability, all that is important to a woman like me. Now I'm forty with the ghastly years ahead. God help me, forty! Celia Amber, they say, isn't she a marvel, and long for me to crumble." She swung on Karen with frightening vehemence. "Just how long do you think I can maintain this face...this figure? The strain is killing me!"

It was necessary to say something...anything. Karen was even caught up into a reluctant sympathy for her.

"Please don't upset yourself, Celia."

There was a bitter, dangerous light in Celia's eyes. "Mrs. Amber to you, dear. Once Mrs. Amber always Mrs. Amber."

She got up and found a cigarette from the Chinese box letting the smoke trail like incense to the ceiling. She swayed a little and sat down quickly, her face whitening. "I've had a ghastly, ruinous evening."

Karen made a desperate attempt to avert a scene.

"It's sad, I know, but time is against every woman. We're all in the same boat. One day I hope to renew myself through my children...my grandchildren. When I was a little girl my father used to say to me: the greatest unhappiness in life, my darling, comes from reaching for the moon. I've never forgotten it."

Celia's wild crack of laughter was totally unexpected.

"Stephen! My God, that's rich! Reach for the moon? I should say so! He did it for long enough." One look at Karen's shocked look of incomprehension and Celia found her way to a little revenge. She was eager now to placate her *humiliated* ego.

"Don't look so shocked, my dear. Stephen, your father, we're talking about. A terribly sexy man, Stephen, you're a lot like him, worse luck, and Stephen was a good man too, except for one trivial detail; he was on with Trish for years. Dear sainted Trish, the perfect sister-in-law. And Eva never knew! Can you beat it? Imperious, jealous, possessive Eva, *never knew*. A first-class affair right under that stuffy nose of hers and she never knew. It was too good to resist."

Karen reeled with a sudden wave of nausea. Everything became clear to her, reflected in Celia's burning eyes, the delicate colourless face. Now she could see behind her father's fatal flight, the dark mystery in the depths of Aunt Patricia's eyes, her mother's bitterness towards the Ambers! But Eva *did know* and someone had told her.

"It was you, wasn't it?" she said sombrely, her own judge and jury, and Celia was convicted.

Celia didn't even bother to deny it but smiled steadiy in a most peculiar way.

"You know, my dear, I don't feel the least bit of animosity towards you now. You look so comically tragic. And why not? You've grown very fond of Trish, haven't you? But you can't stay now. You'll have to leave this house, won't you? You couldn't possibly stay on in the same house as your mother's usurper...your father's lover...condoning her."

"There's always been something *sinister* about you, Celia, but I never guessed at the full extent of your viciousness. You leave me no way out. You must leave this house." Patricia Amber stood watching them with one hand to her throbbing temple, white to the lips.

Celia laughed—not a pretty laugh. "I'm sure I don't

know what you're talking about, Trish. Leave this house? It's Guy's house, remember, and I'm sure he would have something to say about that. Even if you were game enough to try and push me out. You've always had it in for me, haven't you, dear. Don't think I wasn't aware of it behind the stiff upper lip and the gracious civility." She rested her silver-gilt head, looking suddenly drained.

"You're ill. Why don't you go to your room?" her sister-in-law said with forced calm.

Karen gazed mutely across the room at this woman who had meant so much to her father. Then a strange thing happened to her. She found she didn't care. Her father had loved this woman. That was his affair. Besides, she loved her herself. They could never have been deliberately cruel to her mother. Her head was pounding and the voices were getting fainter and fainter.

Patricia crossed to her side, her voice sharp with anxiety: "Karen!"

"I'm all right." Karen sat down quickly.

Celia looked at them and laughed. "She's all right, Trish. Don't worry about her. You're a thwarted mother and no mistake." She pursed her soft mouth. "So you deny it?"

"I'm simply not discussing it. Not with you, Celia." Patricia spoke tiredly.

"That's no answer at all!"

The other woman seemed to hesitate for a minute, then her eyes found Karen's. "I'm grieved you should hear it this way. I would have told you myself if I thought the old stories would come up again. Yes, Karen, I loved your father, very deeply. It was the strongest, deepest emotion I've ever felt. There was no one before Stephen and it's been my lot that I've never cared for anyone after him. We met just a week before the wedding. How ironic that I should come back from Europe to be your mother's bridesmaid! Our love just happened and it grew and grew, the deep joy in one another's company. We loved, but we were never lovers—I swear this is true. Eva was my cousin, she trusted me implicitly. There were you children. The situation was impossible. We agreed, Stephen and Guy and I, that I should join my mother in California for an indefinite period. That night of the party I know *now* what happened. Eva became inflamed with jealousy. She was stung into saying things that could never be forgotten by any of us. Your father took her home, quickly, quietly."

Her voice broke as she stared down the corridor of the years. "There was the accident, and it *was* an accident, I'm certain of that. Stephen would never, never have deserted you children. He loved you far too much for that." She turned back to Celia. "But you didn't tell it that way, did you, Celia? Not to Eva. Not to her daughter. What was it, Celia? Some dark, uncontrollable force, a desire to wound anybody, everybody who was living. Richard had just been killed. You were so frantic."

Celia looked strange. "Do you know, I think I will go to my room. You always did bore me, Trish. Extraordinary how the daughter condones your offence. Like father, like daughter, so they say." She swayed past them, but as she got near Karen she suddenly spat the words out: "Don't let's go after the same thing, darling!"

Karen shivered visibly—not at the words but the underlying threat of violence.

"You're mad!" she said clearly. "No ordinary woman will satisfy Guy, I know that, and you're no ordinary woman—but he deserves a real woman with a heart and mind, not a painted, frivolous doll with an ugly streak a mile wide."

Celia gave a dreadful cry, which was what it was—a war-cry! She reached for a small bronze sculpture of mother and child and hurled it with superhuman ferocity but a woman's poor aim. It missed its intended victim and crashed into an exquisite Mei Lei vase, shattering it irreparably.

Patricia advanced on her, her tall form menacing.

"Get out!"

Celia trailed her stole, her aberration forgotten. "Don't threaten me, Trish. You're wasting your time. There's only one person I take any notice of, and we all know who *that* is. As for this insufferable little bitch, I'll speak to Guy as soon as he gets home. No one has ever dared to speak to me as she's done. She'll live to regret it!"

They waited until Celia had left the room, then automatically the two women fell to picking up the shattered pieces of the once priceless antique. Patricia looked across at Karen, shocked at her extreme pallor.

"My dear, please don't do any more. This has been too much for you. You're as white as a ghost!"

Karen shrugged off her shock and her white face. "I'm not very bright, am I, Aunt Trish? I never knew!"

The older woman made a gesture of complete and utter distress. "Oh, Karen, my child, how *could* you know? I could count on one hand the number of people who did know. Ours was no flamboyant affair, flying in the face of society. My love for your father was deep and enduring, but not to be. Much as we wished it different, the price of happiness came too high."

"Yes, I think I see, but *she*'s quite dreadful, isn't she?" Karen spoke the words baldly. She got to her feet and held out her hand to the older woman. Patricia took the long, slender fingers and gave them a reassuring shake.

"Yes, Celia is dreadful, and perhaps it's our own fault. All of us in some way have conspired to cloak her sins. She's not aware of them and we won't even confess them to one another. Have any of us openly accused her of what she did to Rikki... Liane? No, we're all too distressed and embarrassed by her treachery, her lack of love and pride in her own children. But this time she's gone too far!" A blinding migraine was beginning to stagger her eyes, disturbing her vision. She moaned softly. "I'll have to slip up to my room for a while, dear. I haven't had a migraine in God knows how long. Come up with me now. Watch a little television if you can. We'll just have to hide out until Guy comes home. He's never failed me, but there's no winning with Celia. She hasn't even heard of the rules, let alone how to abide by them."

They walked together up the stairway. In her room, Patricia swallowed two largish white tablets and lay down on her bed. Her face in repose was oddly sad. This time Celia had gone too far. She meant to hurt Karen, and that she would never allow! The girl was very dear to her, not only because she was Stephen's daughter and so very like him, but because of her own generous, spirited nature. Celia had made too many people suffer. Patricia closed her eyes.

Hours later, when Guy returned home, it was Celia who got to him first. Seeing the lights of the car sweep up the drive, Karen slipped out of her room, along the corridor, and paused for a moment to look over the top of the balustrade.

Guy was there, standing just inside the front door, the dark splendour on him, his head glossy under the light of the big chandelier. She was reminded forcibly of the first time she had seen him again in Melbourne. Celia stood poised a few feet away from him, furled in a negligée as beautiful and foaming as the sea itself, an exquisite blue-green... an indescribable colour.

"Guy!" she said in her sweet, husky voice. "I've been waiting for you. For so long! I'm so upset you see."

His dark eyes were alert, his face concerned. "What is it, my dear?"

Celia floated towards him right into his arms, clinging to the lapels of his jacket with pearl-tipped fingers.

"I have to speak to you, Guy. Oh, my dear, I'm so
unhappy!" Her silvery head fell forward to rest against
the frosted linen of his shirt.

"Celia!" For a dismal moment Karen had the notion
Guy meant to kiss her, but he merely put his arm about
her frail shoulders. "Come into the library, my dear.
We can talk there."

She seemed to melt into him, heartbreakingly small
and fragile beside his tall, powerful frame.

A death knell sounded on Karen's hopes. Its rever-
berations made themselves felt right down to her toes.
And now it had become real, her own private nightmare. Was there no escape from human dilemma?
How does she do it? The words surfaced from the
depths of her abysmal disillusionment. *I'll have to go
now,* she thought with a kind of dull placidity. The
more she considered her situation the more insoluble it
seemed. The library door was still shut. Over the house
reigned a hushed silence.

Karen wrenched herself out of her trance-like stupor
and flew on down the stairs. It was amazing to her how
swiftly and steadily she moved. Had she realised it, the
tears were coursing down her tragic young face. But she
was caught up in an all-consuming hopelessness...a
monumental despair...unnoticing.

Her car stood in the drive. She let herself into it, and
her despair disappeared. She felt only resignation and a
dull acceptance of defeat. And so Celia defeated everybody as she had done for years. They would have to
leave Belle Amber, she and Pip—no doubt with a
struggle. Guy would have powerful objections, but she
would learn to be a good actress. She would have to
accept life in its stark, unromantic inevitability as the
women of her family had done to a large degree.

The car slid past the great wrought iron gates. In only
a few days—the end of everything! Her mind turned to

oddments and through all the confusion, loud and clear, came the memory of Guy's kiss. In the silent portals of her heart she cried aloud: "Guy, Guy, please help me!"

The wind swished through the window as the car gathered speed for the downhill run. With a curious detachment she recognised that she didn't care. Not in the least. Shock carried its own anodyne. She grew sober and contemplative. Not far from here on a fatal night, her father had died. Where had it been? God, that was a bad bend, and she wasn't used to night driving.

Aunt Patricia had said it had been an accident. Had it been an accident? Instinctively she changed down to hold the car on the steep grade. Pip wouldn't thank her for having an accident. What would her small brother do without her? They were a team. Yes, of course it had been an accident, or her mother had grabbed the wheel. With her knowledge of both parents she could picture the scene. The tears sprang into her eyes, blurring her vision. She blinked furiously. Wondering what on earth she was doing, out on the road, driving to nowhere...to no one. She really had no one to turn to.

After a minute she became conscious of lights in her rear vision. There was a car gaining on her. She put her foot down, demanding more speed, but the car in pursuit was by far the more powerful vehicle. It zoomed past her as the road widened with a flash of its long silver bonnet, then pulled up ahead, blocking the road.

This is impossible! Karen thought in an agony, and pulled off the road. She clenched her fists, waiting for that tall figure to loom up into the circle of light. Her unhappiness suddenly broke all barriers, and she buried her face in her hands.

"Karen!" It was Guy's voice as she had never heard it before with anyone. He swung the door of the car open and got in, pulling her to him. At his touch she seemed to go wild, crying and moaning and turning her

head away. His hand closed over the tilted curve of her
breast, and after the first shock of contact, she held it
fiercely to her, letting him feel for himself the tumultuous beating of her heart.

"That's what you do to me," she cried distractedly,
past all pretending. "Every time you come near me.
Can't you feel it? Go on, feel it, the crazy throb of my
heart! Oh, God help me!"

His dark eyes flamed into sensual brilliance. He
pulled her across his knees with a tender brutality and
that same heart was drumming outside of her, for Guy
was kissing her, caressing her, deeply, possessively, as
only a man can the beloved woman. A wild elation
filled her, transmuting her into one living emotion. Her
body became pliant, incredibly soft and seductive, and
all through the knowledge that this man really loved
her. It couldn't be otherwise. Not this fierce rapture,
the exultation, the pulsing, the charging light of the
universe!

She clung to him, crying a little at this soaring release, until, exhausted with sweetness, she turned her
burning mouth into his throat. Her heavy silken hair
fell across his cheek with the clean fragrance of a
child's. "Oh, Guy!"

His hand went out and tilted her face to him. "Look
at me, Karen. Never deny now that you love me."

"How could I?" she said simply. "I always have,
ever since I can remember."

Guy took a deep steadying breath. "As soon as I can
arrange it, we'll be married. I must have you part of
me. I want to be able to put out my hand in the night
and hear your quiet breathing. I want to be able to hear
that breathing changing!" His hand caressed her cheek
and she shivered in a kind of ecstasy, realising with a
little shock that Guy's own hand was trembling.

"You'll have only one master, my little Karen. I love
you—too much, my yielding flower." He bent his
mouth and found hers, hearing her speak the one

name that hovered like a phantom on the edge of her dream world.

"And Celia?"

He drew away from her and looked out to where a late moon, large and pale, rose above the vineyards. "Celia is Celia," he said slowly. "Beyond my explanations and really, my love, outside my sphere of interest. Had Richard lived, she might have been different. He kept her in hand. These past few years she's developed a certain feeling for me, I know that. Perhaps I remind her of Richard or the what-might-have-been. She was very much in love with him and that was the beginning of her tragedy. I've tried to be kind. Some women are strong enough to get through life alone. Others only live through a man. But the woman Celia is, I'd rather not speak of. All that is important is, she has never had one indiscreet glance from me. Celia has never been anything more than my brother's widow. On that alone we've put up with a great deal from her, though Trish has never complained. Sometimes I wish she had." His hand caressed the delicate hollow at the base of her throat. "We won't be seeing much of her anyway. She knows now that I mean to marry you."

Karen lifted her head to look at him. "You told her?"

"No, my love. Women like Celia don't need telling." His voice was tinged with a kind of wry amusement. "She'll present no problem, never fear. I guard my own."

He drew her back into his arms, urgently, nuzzling her white neck. "Don't let's talk about Celia."

Six weeks later Rikki was awarded the Statton-Logan Gift for the finest original oil painting of that year. His entry was a portrait, or more accurately an "impression", of his mother. Neither Celia nor any of her friends liked it. It was terribly modernistic and not even recognisably Celia, for it took no account of her exquisite porcelain fragility.

But Karen, when she saw it, recognised it for what it was: a brilliant psychological study. Celia's portrait, unlike Karen's, was never destined to hang at Belle Amber, for by that time, Guy and Karen were married.